I0583620

ENGINE 8-12

SCOTT OFFERMANN

Black Rose Writing | Texas

©2020 by Scott Offermann
All rights reserved. No part of this book may be reproduced, stored in a retrieval system or transmitted in any form or by any means without the prior written permission of the publishers, except by a reviewer who may quote brief passages in a review to be printed in a newspaper, magazine or journal.

The author grants the final approval for this literary material.

First printing

This is a work of fiction. Names, characters, businesses, places, events, and incidents are either the products of the author's imagination or used in a fictitious manner. Any resemblance to actual persons, living or dead, or actual events is purely coincidental.

ISBN: 978-1-68433-568-8
PUBLISHED BY BLACK ROSE WRITING
www.blackrosewriting.com

Printed in the United States of America
Suggested Retail Price (SRP) $20.95

Engine 8-12 is printed in Chaparral Pro

*As a planet-friendly publisher, Black Rose Writing does its best to eliminate unnecessary waste to reduce paper usage and energy costs, while never compromising the reading experience. As a result, the final word count vs. page count may not meet common expectations.

This book is dedicated to the First Responders and their families
To the Fallen: You will never be forgotten
To the Foundered: May you find the peace you desire
To the Families of the First Responder: Thank you for your sacrifice

I want to thank my wife and children for supporting me while I worked on this book. A special acknowledgment to the editors who have helped make this novel better.

ENGINE 8-12

Darcy was sitting by herself in the hospital café trying to read her tablet. Since the start of her evening shift she had been anxious about something. The Cardiac Care Unit, where she worked, only had two patients, so she decided to take a break to try to clear her head.

Trish Cooper, the Emergency Room Charge Nurse, let her tray drop as her body fell into the chair in frustration.

Startled, Darcy asked, "Rough night?"

"Yeah. Everyone is pissed off because someone coded in the waiting room."

"What happened?"

"Some old guy drove himself to the hospital and told the intake clerk that he had indigestion and his arm hurt. She said he was nice. He told her, 'It's nothing ma'am, but at my age any excuse for some excitement is worth checking out.' He sat down to fill out his paperwork, then about forty-five minutes later he collapsed in the waiting room. One of the other people waiting yelled in panic, which got the attention of the intake coordinator."

"That's it?"

"Pretty much. An orderly and a nurse retrieved him from the floor and rushed him into the ER. We worked on him for forty-five minutes before the doctor declared him dead. No one was with him and the intake clerks never got around to completing his intake paper to create the electronic chart. The man dropped the clipboard in the waiting room. When the chart finally caught up with the patient two hours after being declared, there was no next of kin listed."

"That stinks. Hospital will investigate and dig into everything that happened. Anything to worry about?"

"Nah. We weren't even that busy, and no one critical. Guy just slipped through the intake triage."

"Don't worry about it then. It will just be routine and over in a few weeks."

"Now I have to try to figure out who to notify based on the half filled out paperwork and empty wallet of one Mr. Larry Butler." She tossed her fork down on the tray of the dull hospital food.

From listlessly staring into her own food, Darcy's eyes flew up to meet Trish's eyes. "What was his name?"

"Butler, Larry Butler. Why?"

"How old?"

"Seventy-five," she said slowly. "I think."

"Is he still in the ER, or has he been taken to the morgue?"

"Moved him because no next of kin. You know him?"

"Maybe." Shoving her food tray away, she quickly got up and headed to the door.

Trish jumped up and followed her. "Hey if you know him that would be awesome. Then I could close out the chart," she said hopefully.

Darcy nodded at her as she pushed her way out of the café and headed to the morgue.

Quickly walking into the morgue, she asked to see the body.

Without a question the attendant pulled the body from the refrigerator and unceremoniously flipped the sheet back, uncovering his face.

Darcy stared into the old, weathered face, a tear unexpectedly escaping from the corner of her eye.

"Hey, you OK?"

Looking at the dead man on the stainless-steel table, fighting back a flood of tears and trying to maintain control, she nodded her head, afraid to speak.

"You know him?"

"Yeah."

"Do you know who to call?"

Inhaling deeply, she got control of her emotions. "Yeah. I'll make the calls. Someone will be here in the morning to pick him up."

"Thanks, I'll let them know." A little cheerfulness entered his voice. "Hey, you want me to stay here with you for a few?" he offered.

"No. I need to get back to the floor." She tenderly pulled the sheet over the old man's face and gently pushed the rolling table back into the refrigerator, letting the latch click quietly. Like she was trying close the door without waking a sleeping baby.

Leaving the morgue Darcy was headed back to the floor to finish her shift. Pulling her smartphone from her pocket, she typed a quick text— "Call me at work"—and pressed send.

Getting back to the Cardiac Care Unit she checked in with the other nurse on duty and sat down behind the desk waiting. One of the monitors abruptly changed from a steady beeping tone to a series of high and low beeps. Checking on the patient, she recognized that he had turned over in his sleep. The tones would settle in a few minutes.

She heard the phone ringing at the station and quickly reached over, grabbing the phone. "Fallston CCU, Darcy speaking."

"Hey it's Rob, what's up?"

"Larry Butler died tonight."

There was silence

"Rob?" pausing for a moment she tried again "Robby?"

"What happened?" he finally said.

"Heart attack." She did not bother telling him all the details. That would come later.

"I'll make some calls." He paused. "We need to find a few of them."

The drive home was routine, traveling down the 101 trying to get to his exit. The radio was playing—some sort of AM talk show discussing the ongoing social and political dribble plaguing our cities. Talk radio now dominated his daily commutes, not because he was a social radical or had any undying desire to change the world—they just gave the traffic every ten minutes.

"The idiots are out in force today," he muttered to himself as he switched on the left turn signal trying to merge from the 101 South onto the 60 East. The driver of the Honda two car lengths behind him sped up the second the turn signal went on so they could try to get in front of the merging car. Not needing to switch lanes, he matched the speed of the car, just hovering next to the quarter panel, waiting to see if the driver wanted to make the next exit. A slightly malevolent smile crept across his face as the woman driving the Honda began to panic, realizing that his car was blocking the exit she wanted. After three seconds of panic, she slowed down to make it over to her exit.

He continued on his way, casually watching the idiots in the other lanes speeding up to cut other drivers off as they merged onto the freeway. *This is why I dislike people,* he thought to himself.

Parking his car and going into the house, the scene was exactly what he expected. His wife of seventeen years was working in the kitchen while their two kids were hanging out in the living room doing homework and surfing the net, waiting for dinner.

"How was your day?" Debbie asked with a quick kiss.

Tossing his briefcase onto his desk he replied, "It was a good day. Cleared my email box down to about forty emails. Don't have anything pressing, so we can relax tonight."

The phone rang and a teenage voice called out from the living room, "Someone is calling from Maryland!" Now that the telephone was connected to the cable TV, caller ID appeared on the TV set.

Debbie, whose family lived in Maryland, answered the phone from the kitchen with a cheerfully sing-song "Yello." As he came around the corner into the kitchen, the expression on her face instantly told him that it was not her mom on the phone. Debbie, who hated talking to strangers and telemarketers with a passion, had clearly been duped into answering an unwanted call. "Yep, hang on." She playfully poked her tongue out as she shoved the phone at him.

"Hello."

"Is this Steve Quinn?"

"Yes, it is."

"This is Robert McMaster."

With an internal groan realizing that he had been caught by some sort of telemarketing scheme, he sarcastically replied, "Well Robert McMaster, how can I help you?"

"Stevey, it's Robby. From the Fire Station..."

This was a voice that had been forgotten long ago. Leaning over the counter, he grasped the edge as the blood drained from his face and an icy feeling crawled over his skin. He barely managed to get his voice working enough to say, "Yeah, Robby, I remember."

"Steve, it's Larry, Chief Butler. He died this morning. We're having the funeral in a few days." Subtlety was not needed. Something as mundane as death did not really warrant diplomacy or a soft delivery. "It's been a while since we connected and I didn't know if you cared or not, but I thought you might want to know."

"Thanks Robby. I'm glad you called me. What number can I reach you at?"

"Call my cell at 443-555-1212. That will be the best way."

"Got it. Let me check my schedule and I'll let you know if I can get out there."

"Steve, good to hear your voice. I often wonder what ever happened to you. I hope you can get out here."

"Thanks." Managing to maintain his composure, he said, "I'll call you and we can catch up."

As he hung up the phone, Debbie was staring with those eyes only your soul mate can have, knowing that something had happened that had shaken her husband.

Steve's mind was reeling, and the emotions were rapidly piling up inside. The helplessness of not knowing whether he should scream, cry, or just walk away. Emotions that had long ago been buried deep within were starting to break down the walls he had spent years building within his mind, bringing with them all the shitty places he had been so long ago. The fear of facing his demons once again.

He started to get his brain under control, running though the old training drilled into him. When you are lost and panicking, start with the basics. *Where am I?* Kitchen. *Who else is there?* Debbie, kids in the other room. *What is the situation?* I just heard from a ghost. Someone who had been forgotten and buried with time. Someone that I thought I would not hear from ever again. Memories I struggled to bury a lifetime ago. He sat down at the table. "I think I spoiled dinner for today," was all he could say.

"What's that about?" Debbie began. "Who is Robby?"

Staring at the table, Steve simply said, "Shit" in a quiet and reserved voice.

"Ok, you're scaring me." Her voice began to shake as she spoke. "What the hell is going on?"

His eyes snapped onto Debbie's face, seeing the fear in her eyes. For a brief second he realized that the fear she was foreshadowing was nothing compared to what was about to happen. The demons hidden for years would be brought into the light. What they were going to go through would test their marriage to the core. "Larry died."

"Who was that on the phone?" she demanded

"That was Robby."

She was now starting to get pissed off. "Who is Robby?"

"Robby was with the fire department. He called to tell me that Larry died," he responded in a flat tone.

Debbie, beginning to calm down now, started asking those questions that he knew were coming. He was dreading them.

"What fire department?"

"I told you that before we met, I was a firefighter."

"Yeah, but that was a long time ago."

"Well, I never really told you everything about it."

"I never gave it much thought to be honest; it was long before we even met."

Standing up and quietly moving to the liquor cabinet, he reached into the far back for a bottle of Glenlivet. She watched as he took the dust-covered bottle out of the cabinet and set it on the table.

"You have always ragged me about this damn bottle that I dragged around with us." For the past thirty years there was always a bottle of scotch. This bottle. Never opened, never lost. "I guess it's time to tell you everything." He poured himself a double, neat.

Chapter 1

The beat-up old Duster roared up the hill to the fire station off Trimble Road, radio blaring through the open windows. Cresting the top of the driveway, Station Two rose into view. It was a one-story rectangular brick building, with a single fuel pump outside used to fill the fire engines with the vital diesel fuel.

The Duster quickly crossed the tarmac, the deep thrum of the engine echoing off the building and the surrounding hills that led to the thick woods. As the car rolled to a stop, the radio stopped playing. The door opened with the push of a foot and out rolled the first of the crew. Wearing jeans and a t-shirt with a duffel bag thrown over his shoulder, he crossed the parking lot. Walking with a purpose he pulled a white card from his front pocket. Passing the bay doors, he approached the entrance and casually slapped the card on the black square. The door unlocked with a loud click. Without a sound he walked into the fire house and disappeared into the darkness. The door closed ominously with a loud clap.

Turning quickly right he opened the door to the bunk room. It was a rectangular room with two sets of bunk beds that allowed for the engine crew to sleep when necessary. The room had an entrance off the engine bays and another directly into the lounge. Without stopping, he tossed his duffel bag onto the top bunk of the first set of bunk beds. Everyone knew that the bunks were unofficially assigned by the position on the engine. First bunk bottom was the lieutenant's, first bunk top was the passenger jump seat, second bunk bottom the driver's, while the top is the driver side jump seat. This unspoken rule was to allow the crew to react as quickly as possible to each of the positions on the engine when a call wakes them in the night. Continuing through the lounge, he passed the old beat-up couches and walked into the engine bay, to the back of the first engine. Fingers lightly sweeping down the side of the engine, he felt the red metal, caressing the engine, secretly hoping to get a small rush as he walked alongside it. Coming around the rear of the engine, along the wall to the right was the tool room. There was an old pool table behind the engine. The second engine sat next to the first and directly behind that engine were racks of turn-out gear used by the firefighters.

Stopping in front of the turn-out gear he paused, breathing in the smell. Old smoke from wood, oils, and plastics from countless fires over many years lingered on the gear. The smell brought memories of fires, accidents and calls that he had been on. It sparked a small rush, preparing him for the possibilities of tonight. "*Maybe we'll see some action tonight,*" he thought to himself.

Lost in his own thoughts, he was startled by the bay doors rumbling to life as someone pushed the buttons that opened the doors, flooding the engine bays with light and fresh air diluting the smell of smoke as it swirled into the bay.

Turning to make his way back to the front of the station, a man twenty years his senior came around the engine. "Why didn't you open the bay doors?"

"Just got here. Was stowing my gear."

"Nice days you should always open the doors first thing. The old girls like fresh air," Larry said, gazing across the engine with a sigh of lost youth.

"You pullin' duty from here tonight Chief?"

Larry Butler was the First Assistant Chief of the fire department. He was a white helmet. Always said that he never wanted to be the chief: too much paperwork, too many politics. Larry also oversaw the operations of Station Two, where this crew pulled duty. He was a third-generation firefighter. His father and grandfather had both been in the fire department. Both now deceased, he would be the last. Divorced and past having children, his only legacy was being a father figure to the young recruits he had over the years. Providing advice and support to those that listened. Watching the boys grow into men, the men into fathers.

"Naw. I'm going up to Station One. Besides, if the rest of you are here tonight, I'm pretty sure I don't want to know what's going on."

"Hey, we haven't gotten suspended in—what—three or four months? We're on our best behavior, sir," Steve said with a sarcastic salute.

Steve was the Rescue Specialist and Emergency Medical Technician of the crew. He was also the swimmer. A member of the high school swim team and certified scuba diver, in his time away from the fire station he was also a sailing instructor. The others considered him well-read and well-traveled. He was one of the few who had moved to this small suburban town from elsewhere. He was a first-generation firefighter, the son of some kind of white-collar, college educated parents, both professionals that sat behind a desk.

The rumble of a small diesel pickup truck announced the arrival of the next crew member. The two men walked to the front of the engines to watch Robby's truck roll into the parking spot. He casually stepped out and began walking over, tipping up his chin in greeting as he crossed the tarmac. "Hey," was all the greeting he gave.

Robby was a second-generation firefighter and the station's Senior Engineer, overseeing equipment maintenance at Station Two. His dad was also in the fire department and the company's engineer. While a gifted driver and mechanic, Robby's passion was singing, performing in garage bands whenever he could.

"'Sup?" Steve said

"Not too much. Hey Larry, Dad says he took a look at the transmission of Ambo 8-92 and he adjusted it. Someone is probably doing neutral drops."

"Yeah that figures. I'll check the roster, but I'm pretty sure I know who was driving when the transmission failed," Larry said with a shrewd look.

Out of the woods came another of the crew, gamboling down the hill and onto the parking lot. Walking quickly across the lot with his duffle bag in tow, Royce headed to the group gathering in front of the engine. Surveying the small group, he asked, "Anyone heard from Ted today?"

Royce was the nozzleman of the group. He always led the attack in a fire. Not having much desire for the medical side, preferring that someone else take care of the sick and bleeding, he studied and took courses in specialty fires, incident command, high rise fires, aircraft fires and whatever he could find that would increase his knowledge and skill. He was a first-generation firefighter, and he understood fires. He understood how they burned, instinctively knowing how the fire would develop. He tried to talk to the state fire marshals every time one came to a fire. An added benefit was that he lived in the house adjacent to the fire station: a twenty-five-yard walk through the woods and he was there.

The crew was waiting for Ted, the final member needed to complete the engine's compliment for the shift.

"I saw him earlier," Robby responded. "He said he was going to stop by Rene's and then come on over to the station."

"Great!" Royce quipped. "If he is going to his girlfriend's before coming to the station, he's going to be late."

Ted had been dating Rene and it was pretty serious. The two had known each other for several years and had heated up about nine months ago. The entire group figured that there would be a wedding in the next couple of years.

"Speaking of girls, who was the blond I saw you with the other day?" Royce asked Robby.

"That's Julie. I met her a few weeks ago cashiering at the Giant. I talked her up a few times while I was there, so I asked her out." Being six foot four, a firefighter and a singer, Robby was the Casanova of the fire house. He could smooth talk any girl and had a new one every few weeks.

"Not too shabby Robby. She's one of the better ones you've bagged," Royce responded with a lurid glint in his eyes. Royce had on-and-off girlfriends and was always interested in what the other guys were up to. "What about you Steve? Anything in the wind?"

"Nothing worth mentioning." Steve wasn't very interested in dating. He'd had a long-term girlfriend that ended badly about six months before. Quickly changing the subject, he directed the group's attention to the AMC Eagle rolling up the drive. "Ted's here."

Ted parked with the other cars and walked across to the open bay door where the others were talking. "Hey guys."

"Hey," they all said in unison.

"Well, trouble has assembled and I'm going to make myself scarce so I don't have to yell at you boys for doing something you shouldn't," Larry said mockingly to the crew. "I'm heading over to Station One to check on things over there." As he started to walk away, he threatened, "I might stop back later tonight, check on you hoodlums and make sure you haven't done anything you shouldn't." Larry knew that on the night shift boredom led to antics unbecoming of a firefighter. He had recognized a while ago that this crew was his best and brightest—he would take them into any situation without a moment's hesitation. Not being here was often the best way to protect his prized crew.

"See ya later," the crew responded as the chief climbed into his brown Chevy pickup and drove off.

"Well guys, what do ya think? Will we be busy tonight, or will we sit still?" Ted asked the others.

"I hope we get a good one tonight," Royce piped in. "I ain't seen a good call in weeks."

"I'm thinking we're going to get something good tonight," Robby chimed in.

"Maybe a good multi-car on I-95," Steve added.

"Heard about any parties this weekend? The high school kids are always good for some action," Ted inquired of Steve and Royce.

"I haven't heard of any," Royce answered.

"I just heard that the usual crowd was heading up to Winters Run Road for a bonfire. Nothing out of the ordinary," Steve added.

"Well, whatever comes tonight we should get ready. Standing here talking about it won't do us any good," Ted suggested.

With that, the four headed into the station to begin the night shift.

Chapter 2

The crew began getting ready for their shift, transforming from civilians to fearless heroes, saviors, and protectors of the weak and injured. It began with the simple act of changing from their street clothes to the blue pants and shirt of their uniforms. This was their superhero costume, changing each into a person of authority, who could take command of any situation, civilians following their directions without question. Just the act of putting on the uniform triggered a high that brought out their inner superhero. Unstoppable individually, the uniform made them a defined member of the crew, and the crew was invincible.

They each moved with the skill, precision, and confidence of experience, preparing for the unknown in the night ahead. The routine was drilled into their brains, each having done this hundreds of times. The ritual began with them grabbing their turn-out gear from the rack and placing it carefully at their position on the engine.

As the four firefighters went about the routine there was little talk between them. Nothing needed to be said since each one knew what had to be done, and what would be required. They each knew and trusted the three others, often with their lives. The bond of trust between firefighters is unbreakable. Regardless of whether they like you or hate you, none will allow another firefighter to be harmed or injured. It is the foundation of the trust required to put your life on the line in order to save others.

Engine 8-12 was a 1975 Seagrave. Painted fire engine red with chrome bumpers. The door hinges and latch and the pump panel were also highlighted in chrome. It had a Federal siren and big air horns. It was not a wimpy electronic siren that made different noises. It was powered by compressed air.

Once you pushed the pedal on the floor it would slowly wind up and peak at over 120 decibels. When you released the pedal, it would slowly wind down its wail. This was the siren of a classic fire engine. The new engine, Engine 8-11, sounded like an ambulance coming down the road with electric sirens and electric air horns.

Directly behind the driver's cab were two jump seats, with the engine sitting between them. Wrapped in diamond-plated metal, this engine was hot as hell during the summer and toasty warm in the winter. Stepping up and into the jump seat, it was about seven feet long with an air pack against the back of the cab and a folding jump seat at the steps. A chain was clipped across the opening to keep someone from falling off. Axes were mounted on the sides of the engine compartment, and there were four rechargeable lanterns on the top. If you positioned yourself just right, two firemen could lie flat on top of the engine compartment and grab some sleep.

Just behind the jump seats and engine compartment was the pump panel. This is where the engineer could control the flow of water. Covered with chrome dials, levers, and switches, this was the most difficult part of the fire equipment to operate. Level with the top half of the pump panel were three separate 1.5-inch hoses ready to be pulled out. They were 150 feet, 200 feet and 250 feet long. At a fire you pulled the shortest one needed. This was important, because the hose was damn heavy when filled with water, and when you were done, you had to put the hose back. The shorter the hose, the less work to put back into service.

On the top of the pump panel between the engine and the hoses sat the deck gun. This was a water cannon that could spray water hundreds of feet. It was permanently mounted to the engine because it sprayed water at high pressure. With the ability to throw water over two hundred feet, if it wasn't mounted to the engine the water pressure would send whoever was using it flying. Deck guns were disappearing from new equipment, relegated to being mounted on ladder trucks to spray down on fires.

Behind the pump panel were the gear cabinets that held miscellaneous equipment needed for almost every situation. Above the cabinets were ladders of various styles and sizes. The ladders sandwiched the hose bed. This was where 1000 feet of three-inch fire hose was stored to bring water from a fire hydrant to the engine for large fires. The engine was designed to be a work horse of equipment and interconnected systems. Holding five hundred gallons of water, it was built to take water from the fire hydrant, or it could use a connection in the front to suck water out of a lake or river. The engine was also a generator and had air compressors to operate specialty equipment.

As the engineer Robby drove the fire engine and provided water, lights and whatever other support was required, his turn-out pants and boots were positioned at the driver's door, while his coat was placed in the cab behind the driver's seat. He preferred to drive without his turn-out coat on so he could move more easily as he wheeled the sixteen-ton engine down the back roads. His helmet sat on the dash, balancing on the steering wheel, so he could put it on just before pulling out of the bay. He was the link between the real world and the hell of a fire. He controlled the amount and the pressure of the water, and when required could use the water pressure to signal the fire crew inside. If he wanted, he could make the pressure so high that the fire hose could not be held, or he could reduce the flow to that of a garden hose.

Starting the engine, he checked the gauges and the fuel level. Checking in the mirrors for the location of the others, he blasted the air horn, trying scare them. After he checked the engine, he moved to the pump panel, checking the operation and the supplies that he would be relying on. Then climbing to the top of the engine he checked the water level of the 500-gallon tank.

Ted placed his turn-out pants next to the passenger door of the engine. His blue helmet was placed on the dash ready to be put on as he entered the cab. His turn-out coat was hung on the door handle so that he could grab it quickly. Ted was the lieutenant and would be in charge while at any incident, commanding the crew. After he had checked the supplies in the cab – the maps, paperwork, clipboards, and the supplies he might need for the night – he climbed out of the engine and wandered into the office to complete the shift paperwork.

Royce was checking the hoses and nozzles to make sure they were there and appeared to be undamaged. He crawled into the jump seat and turned the SCOT pack on. This was the self-contained breathing apparatus. It allows the firefighter to have clean air to breath inside of a burning building. As the airlines pressurized, a familiar hiss and a ding of the bell was heard as the air reached the regulator controlling the flow of air to the mask. The bell was built into the regulator as an indicator of how much air was in the tank. When the pack was worn, the chrome box sat right in the middle of your chest, over your heart. This allowed the face mask to be connected and disconnected and a switch to change between constant pressure air supply and an on-demand air supply. The pack was designed to keep you alive inside a fire. If the seal was broken and smoke started to get into the face mask, or when highly toxic contaminates were in the air, you would switch to positive pressure. When the tank's air pressure fell below a certain level, the bell would sound, telling the firefighters the air was running low and that they needed to get out. When you heard a bell sounding you would grab the regulator sitting directly over your heart. The ringing of the bell could be felt through thick gloves. When the bell rang, it replaced your heartbeat. As the air was used up, the clanging of the bell became softer, and harder to feel. When it stopped ringing, you were dead.

Royce snatched the pack out of its metal clips with an annoyed grunt. Slinging it over one shoulder he stepped off the truck and walked to the back of the engine. Tossing the pack onto the pool table, he disconnected the bottle from the pack. Taking the bottle, he walked down to the support unit that was parked between Engine 8-11 and the retired ladder truck, a 1952 Ward LaFrance with a 100-foot aerial ladder and several dozen support ladders, all made out of wood. The support unit was simply referred to as the Pie Truck because it looked like the truck used to deliver the fresh bakery goods to the grocery store. This unit provided a place to make coffee and transport people and equipment needed to support a long duration fire call. But primarily it held the cascade system for refilling air bottles.

Royce disappeared into the back of the Pie Truck. Several loud clanking noises could be heard as he filled the air tank. Within ten minutes, he emerged again, carrying the same air bottle. "Ted," hollered Royce, "whoever used this last only left 1800 pounds in it!" He reconnected the air bottle to the SCOT pack on the pool table. "Jesus, I hate it when someone is in a hurry and doesn't put the equipment back into service."

The cascade system was made of six large tanks, each one pressurized to 3000 pounds. When a bottle needed to be refilled, you connected it to the fill hose of the cascade system and opened the valve to the first large bottle. The pressure would equalize. If the pressure in the small bottle was below 2800 to 3000 pounds of pressure, you closed the valve on the first large tank and opened the valve on the next bottle until the tank was refilled. The large tanks of the cascade system were refilled about once a year.

Royce shoved the air pack back into its spring steel holder with a dull thunk and began inspecting the rest of the equipment: taking out flashlights and turning them on, checking the axes, removing wrenches from where they were clipped in to make sure they could be taken out when needed. He moved across the engine with efficiency as he inspected every piece of equipment they might need.

Steve dropped his turn-out gear directly behind Ted's on the passenger side jump seat. Reaching into the pockets of his turn-out coat, he checked that everything that he needed was there. Heavy leather gloves in each pocket, a folding spanner wrench for attaching and detaching fire hose, and a spring-loaded center punch for breaking car windows. His yellow helmet had two stickers identifying him as an Emergency Medical Technician and as a HURST Rescue specialist.

The HURST Rescue tool was more commonly known as the Jaws of Life. It was a hydraulic tool used to cut cars into pieces when needed. The Jaws of Life had been purchased by the fire department only nine months earlier and Steve was one of ten that had completed training. Fifteen had been selected to go to the training, and of those two did not complete the course and three did not pass the final exam. Even though he was the youngest certified, he was considered the best at operating the tool, mostly because he understood the mechanics of the cars and how they would change when you cut them into pieces.

Steve was on the passenger side, with the cabinet doors open and a large first aid kit open on the floor. He had already gone through the HURST tools and was satisfied that they were all in working order and the pieces were on the engine. Checking the medical kit, he assessed the oxygen tanks to make sure there was enough oxygen to get through the shift and provide any first aid required until the ambulance arrived. For car accidents, cardiac arrests and injuries where time was a critical factor, the fire engine would be dispatched along with an ambulance to ensure that emergency help arrived as fast as possible. The ambulance could be further away because it was returning from the hospital or was at another call and the next closest ambulance would be dispatched. A key piece of equipment was the ambu bag. This was the football shaped bag with a face mask that was used to inject air into the lungs of a person who was not breathing. It could be hooked up to the oxygen tank to provide more oxygen if needed. The best part was that you did not have to lock lips with someone who was not breathing. When you are forced to do mouth to mouth resuscitation, there is a good chance the victim will vomit – usually when your mouth is wide open over theirs. When this happened, you would just roll off the patient and "add to the pile." Hopefully, someone else would take over, or when you're done you just start mouth to mouth again.

Each one of the crew knew that one missing or broken piece of equipment could cause lost time, ultimately causing someone to die. They completed their part of the inspection by reporting the status and findings to Ted. As the officer in charge it was his responsibility to ensure that the unit was prepared and reporting any issues found, such as an empty air bottle, in the officers meeting. When all four had reported that the unit was ready to go Ted reached across the desk and pressed the button on the base station microphone. "Engine 8-12 to Dispatch," he said into it.

"Dispatch. Go ahead 8-12."

"Engine 8-12 is in service."

"Engine 8-12 in service 16:06."

"Well, now we wait," Robby said to no one in particular as he wandered from the office into the lounge. Grabbing the TV remote from the top of the set he pointed the remote over his shoulder and flicked on the TV. As he sat down in the chair, he began surfing channels looking for something interesting.

Royce flopped in the chair next to Robby with one leg over the armrest. "Find anything?"

Steve dumped into the couch and started flipping through a thick stack of brochures.

"What's that?" Robby asked.

"Looking at the course work for rescue diver. It's taught up in New York State and it is supposed to certify you as a rescue diver in two weeks."

"Why bother?" Ted asked. "You already dive for us."

Steve was one of two certified SCUBA Divers in the fire department and the only one who owned all his gear. Since the department didn't have an official water rescue division, they did not provide any equipment. It was easy to be the rescue diver when you were the only one who could do it. In the summer he would keep his dive gear with him to respond to water rescues. Most rescue diving consisted of body recoveries at the local swimming holes or hooking tow cables to cars in the water.

"Who knows, maybe I'll move to some tropical island and get a job as a firefighter," he said with a sarcastic smile. "If I'm certified, then they'll hire me before you."

"Good idea," Royce chimed in. "Then I'll have a free place to stay when I take a vacation."

"No problem. I'll send you my address in Montana," Steve quickly retorted.

"Montana's not an island?" Royce said, more as a question than a retort.

"Now you're getting the point genius. My beer will remain safe in an undisclosed tropical location."

"Hey Ted, you ever find out what happened with that house fire over on Meadowood?" Robby asked.

"Not much more than we already knew. Fire marshal says that there was an accelerant, but the owner told him he had bought acetone for some work he was doing around the house. Says it must have busted open or something."

"The pattern looked like it was a puddle of liquid. Never seen a can of acetone melt and spread across the floor like that. Had to have been poured out on the floor. It would have vaporized and flashed if the can melted," Royce responded.

The crew continued to make small talk while they waited. This was a ritual of nervous banter waiting for a call. Between the good-natured jesting and discussion of past calls the unidentified tension in the room became more subdued. The anticipation of a call can become electric in the air as each person secretly waits for disaster to happen, secretly wishing to be the hero today.

Finally, Royce asked, "Anyone else getting hungry?"

"Yeah," Steve answered. "What do you want to eat?"

"I'm hungry for just about anything," Ted added. "Let's go to one of the places that will feed us for free. I didn't bring any cash."

"How about John's Sandwich Shop over at the Joppa Town shopping center?" Royce offered.

"We could also go to Stewarts on I-40. We haven't been there in a while and it's easy to get the engine in and out," Robby added.

"The girls are cuter than John," Ted offered.

"I'm driving!" Royce yelled as he jumped from the seat and ran to the fire engine.

As the rest of the crew started moving into the engine bay, the sound of 8-12 thundering to life stopped the conversation.

Robby shot up and quickly made it across the squad room, disappearing into the engine bay.

Ted and Steve followed behind. Steve cut to the right, walking calmly around the back of the engine. Ted stopped and grabbed the red telephone on the wall and pushed the single black button that dialed Dispatch. Both took their time, in no hurry. This allowed time for Robby to remove Royce from the driver's seat.

Sauntering towards the engine Robby moved with little concern. Reaching the cab, he reached into the open driver's door and grabbed Royce by the front of his shirt, pulling him playfully out of the cab. "Not on my watch," he threatened.

As Robby was helping Royce exit the driver's seat he said with jest, "Hey now. I just got her ready for you. I hear sometimes you're a slow starter."

"No little boy. I have no problems getting things fired up. I just take my time."

"Does that mean that it takes you a while to blow up your date?"

In the middle of the exchange the speakers within the fire station sounded with the alert for an incoming message. They froze, waiting for it, adrenaline building inside, waiting to surge. "Box 804, Company 8, Ambulance 8-92, respond to 234 Stingray Court. Time 16:17."

"It's close. At least in our territory," Royce said to no one in particular.

"Night's still young," Ted shouted over the top of the cab as he was climbing in. "We'll get one. Dispatcher told me it's some kid that took a fall on a skateboard and broke himself."

Steve had climbed into the passenger jump seat and was pulling on his turn-out coat as Robby pulled the engine out of the bay.

Royce was standing by the bay door putting his coat on as the engine glided out of the building onto the tarmac.

The loudspeaker erupted. "8-92 responding."

The engine rumbled onto the asphalt in front of the station, slowly rolling toward the driveway. It didn't slow as Royce pushed the button mounted on the wall, closing the overhead door and quickly running to the engine. He climbed into the jump seat while it continued to roll forward.

"8-92 responding 16:19."

"Dinner sounds much more exciting than some whining kid and bat crazy mother all bitchy because 'I never wanted junior to have that damn thing'," Steve interjected in a mocking tone as Royce climbed onto the engine.

"You got that right, Steve," Royce yelled over the roar of engine.

Ted grabbed the radio mic. "8-12 in service on the air."

Robby was watching in the side mirror and as Royce's foot hit the jump seat step, Robby revved the engine. When the engine reached the top of the drive Robby let off the gas, allowing the weight of the engine to pull it quickly down the drive, slowing just enough to check traffic and roll onto the road.

"8-12, 16:22."

Chapter 3

The two crewmen stood facing forward on the jump seat opposite the SCOT pack. Turn-out pants and coat on but open, helmets strapped to their heads. It was policy that all gear is worn while on the engine. The two of them push this often, not wearing helmets or turn-out coats when the mood struck them. Both had been reprimanded and suspended for not wearing their full gear when riding the engine. It didn't help that the chief saw them as they were hanging off the engine at a traffic light talking to four girls in the car alongside. Of course, they weren't wearing helmets or coats while they were jumping on and off the engine stopped at a traffic light to talk to them.

A five-minute ride later Engine 8-12 was pulling into Stewarts Root Beer stand. This had been here since the 1960s and was forgotten by most of the young kids in the area. It was never very busy. The owner was a lifelong resident and always made it clear that no firefighter or police officer would pay for a meal. As many businesses do, firefighters and police were given discounts, meals, cleaning of uniforms and the like as a way of saying thanks and showing support to those willing to sacrifice.

There was only one other car at the restaurant as the engine pulled into the drive and circled around the building, parking off to the side, close to the road so they wouldn't get blocked in. The crew climbed down to go and place their order. Wearing their uniforms, they walked with confidence as though they were the most important people around. They were not arrogant, just confident in their authority and power they held. As they approached the picnic tables in front of the hamburger stand, a forty-something woman appeared with a friendly, "Hey guys. Stopping by for some dinner?"

"You betcha Beth," Ted answered for the crew. "What's good today?"

"Well boys, the special today is hamburger. If you want to try something different you can have a cheeseburger. What do ya'll want today?"

"I'll do a cheeseburger," said Steve

"Me too," said Robby.

"Just a hamburger for me," said Royce.

"I'll do that also," added Ted.

"OK two cheeseburgers, two hamburgers, four soda pops, four fries," Beth happily repeated back.

"Hey, can I get some onion rings?" Royce decided.

The speaker on the engine came to life. "8-92 on location."

"Sure thing hon." Beth smiled and was off to put the order in.

"8-92 on location, 16:49."

The crew of 8-12 sat at the table making small talk and watching the commuter traffic on Route 40 heading to some unknown destination with a fictitious schedule in their mind. Another car rolled in and pulled into a parking spot on the other side of the drive-in to order food.

"You guys hear 'bout the call Aberdeen got?" Robby started.

The others shook their heads. "What one?" Royce asked.

"Up at the proving grounds a few days ago. Heard that one of the Army guys was coming in the main gate too fast and probably drunk," Robby answered.

"Bad crash?" Steve asked.

"You know they have all those tanks in the center median of the entrance roads?"

"Sure. Got yelled at 'cause I parked my car and climbed on a big ass tank. MPs were there fast," Royce responded.

"Heard the driver moved a medium tank when his car slammed into it."

"Holy crap!" Ted jumped in. "How fast was he going?"

"No idea. No skid marks. He didn't even hit the brakes. Just slammed into the tank," Robby said. "Trooper Paul told me he guessed it was over a hundred miles an hour when he hit."

"That's not a fire call. That's a body recovery. Must have used a can opener to get him out," Steve added. "Any idea why? Was he just drunk, or did he kill himself?" Steve asked no one in particular. He wanted to understand why people did stupid things, trying to understand what motivated people to act the way they did.

Beth brought two trays of food to the table and the crew dug in.

"8-92 en route to Fallston General."

"Yeah, they think it was probably both. Went over to Susan's and got drunk, then bounced his car off a tank." Susan's was the local strip club outside of Aberdeen Proving Grounds and a favorite of young service men.

While they were hanging out making more small talk Beth came by and asked, "Hey, do you know what happed with the car accident last Wednesday over at the Philadelphia Road intersection?"

"8-92 en route, 17:12."

Almost in unison the four responded, "Nope." None of them had been on the call that day. It was such a minor accident that there wasn't any gossip or conversation about it.

"Haven't heard anything about it. Someone you know?" Robby asked.

"Amb'lance 8-92 arrived at Fallston General."

"Don't know. The car looked like my asshole ex's. Was wondering if you knew who was involved."

"Didn't know you were married Beth," Ted said.

"Yeah, married my high school sweetheart. Got knocked up so it was the right thing to do."

"Went bad?" Steve asked.

"We was poor, both worked. He worked days as a mechanic, and I worked nights waiting tables. I thought we was doing OK until one night the restaurant was slow, so they sent me home."

"Uh oh. Sounds like you got a surprise."

"Yep. When I got home found him in bed with some bitch. Kids asleep in the next bedroom."

The four of them just shook their heads in sympathy.

"Well, that was a while ago, but it would still make me feel better if the asshole busted up his car."

"I'll check around and see what I can figure out," Robby offered. "You gonna be here tomorrow?"

"8-92 at Fallston General Hospital, 17:48."

In a sing-song voice Beth said, "Always am. Hope you boys enjoyed the chow. It's on the house. Be safe out there alright."

"Thanks hon," they all replied in unison.

"That would suck," Royce said.

"If I caught Rene in bed with someone, I would probably kill them," Ted offered.

"Yeah, when I broke up with my last girlfriend, I was pretty pissed when she was 'going steady' with someone else inside of a week," Steve said.

"Shit. I didn't know she hooked up that quickly," Robby said with surprise.

"I still think the bitch was dating him for a while before she dumped me."

"Hey, we could go over to her house and blow the air horn and sirens at two a.m.," Royce suggested with a deviant smile.

"She's not worth the effort at this point," Steve defended. "She dumped me because I spent too much time at the fire station." He shrugged indifferently. "I decided that if she thinks she can do better, have at it. Besides, she has already broken up with him and is on the second or third already."

With that they cleaned off the table, tossing the trash in the container. Ted took the trays back to the service window used by the car hops. As the others slowly headed towards the engine; tones sounded over the engine's PA speakers: "Box 8-95, Company 8, Engine 8-12, Ambulance 8-92, 1050 PI with rescue, I-95 northbound, approximate mile marker 70.7, between Bradshaw Road overpass and Raphael Road overpass. Reporting multiple cars involved. Time 17:56."

This is what they wanted, what they craved. This was the addiction. What is a horrific event for most people is a narcotic to firefighters. The rush starts with the sounds of the tones and does not stop until you are back at the station. Through a call the waves of adrenaline that barrage your body, placing you in a state of ecstasy that cannot be matched. The more extreme, the more dangerous, the bigger the incident, the bigger the rush. After you feel it for the first time, you are addicted. Hooked worse than any junky. There is nothing more powerful, more addictive. Nothing that is craved more. It is the dirty secret of firefighters. They want it. They cannot or will not admit to wanting it. But oh, how they crave, desire, wish for the rush. The fire call is the only way to get a fix. Someone badly hurt, a building burning down, someone dying to get the fix. Some people cannot handle the guilt. The desire for the call, the need for the fix only satisfied with destruction, injury and death is too much for some. It can tear you apart inside if you let it. Most of the time you don't even know it's shredding your insides. Worst of all, those around you have no idea that your soul is under constant attack.

As the tones echoed inside their heads, each was reveling in the rush. Beginning to imagine a horrible accident. Not caring that someone was dead or injured. Only caring that they would get their fix.

As the dispatcher blurted out the details of the call over 8-12's speakers, they began to feel the rush building, each with their own personal twist. The surge of adrenaline triggering them into a superhuman state. Running to the engine and jumping into their places, Robby flicked on the emergency lights. Red and white light starting to rotate. The Mars light in the front of the engine, bobbing up and down, side to side, commanding the cars to clear a path for the red monster. Ted pressed the pedal and the Federal siren began to scream into the evening air, yelling a warning to the traffic around.

With the excitement of a five-year-old at Christmas, Ted grabbed the radio mic and shouted, "Engine 8-12 responding!"

Robby gave a long pull on the air horn, adding to the scream of the siren, the sound shattering the evening commute. His heart was calm. His senses heightened. The sixteen-ton machine rolled down the road. Behind the wheel of 8-12, he was becoming one with the machine. One with the road. Eyes seeing everything. The world was in slow motion as he guided the engine around the stopped cars. Robby was the center of the universe. The engine disrupting the routine drive home. Occupants craning their necks to get a glimpse of the screaming red machine flying down the road toward who knows where. The power was his to make the people of the community stop in their tracks and wait for this beast to move through their lives.

The speaker came to life. "8-12 responding 17:57," barely audible over the scream of the siren, the blasting air horn and the roar of the engine.

The rush increased.

The drivers of the other cars feel the surge as well. They are in awe as the engine passes by. Unknown feelings of anxiety are evoked as the blaring sirens, flashing lights and the feeling of urgency spread. The rush encompasses them. They wonder if it is going to their family, their friends. Thinking briefly about who might be gone. Then the secret thought of *Will I see an accident?* creeping into their mind. No one wants to be in an accident, but everyone wants to see it. This gives them a rush. That's why everyone always stares at accidents.

Controlling the engine flying above the road, doing what is needed to get to the scene as fast as possible, this was what got Robby juiced. This was what released the natural high. Like the addict hiding in abandoned buildings, this was his drug of choice: driving the fire engine. He was in ecstasy as he swerved the thundering monster down the road. The more complicated, the more dangerous the drive, the bigger the rush.

Ted's addiction was command. This was what he craved. Control. Power. Authority. Testing his decisions against people's lives. He would decide what was done, what equipment would be needed, where the other fire apparatus would be staged. This was his juice: taking control of the chaos. Giving hope to the injured. His decisions could determine who would live and who would die. The adrenaline surging through his body, heightening his senses. His mind reaching ahead, picturing the location of the accident. He knew that there was no exit for eight miles. Cars would be stuck on the highway. They may be blocking the road so that they could glimpse the chaos for themselves. Ted decided to let Robby determine the limit of 8-12 as he piloted the engine thought traffic.

Royce was also feeling the rush. He knew that he would take a secondary role in this call. He was the firefighter. He would assist in whatever was required. Still, the excitement of the call gave him the fix he craved. Not as intense as a fire, but he would take it all the same. *Maybe the car will be on fire,* he thought. The possibility increasing his rush.

These thoughts often crept into the minds of this crew. Wanting more. Craving a bigger rush than the last time. Not caring about those innocent people who were involved, only getting a bigger and better rush.

Steve was engulfed by it. Adrenalin surging through his body with unimaginable ecstasy. He was the center of this call. That is why he got on the engine at the start of every shift. He would be the one to rescue whoever was trapped in the car. His actions would save someone's life. Knowing that he was the only thing standing between life and death, the only one between the victim seeing their family again. It was his skill and his actions that would determine the fate of those in the crash. The rush was strong. Someone may be trapped in the car. This would require the Jaws of Life to cut them out. Steve would be the one to operate the tool. Imagining the feel of them in his hands, the crunch of the metal, the popping of the glass as he peeled the mangled steel from around the helpless victim. The surge increased again at the thought of having to use the Jaws. Running through his mind, he began to prepare for the scene. Trying to remember if there was a concrete divider, or a wide grass area dividing the highway in the area. The accident was on the northbound side of I-95. The engine was approaching from the southbound side. Robby would park the engine on the opposite side of the highway in the left-hand median. The crew would need to move the equipment to the accident. They may have to use the portable generator to operate the jaws.

Steve prepared himself by first putting on a pair of latex gloves and then a second pair. AIDS was becoming a major issue and concern. Some firefighters never wore gloves and just took their chance, covered in blood after a bad call. Steve always wore gloves and never did mouth to mouth. He always carried an ambu bag and a resuscitation mask with several pair of gloves. The old timers harassed him for wearing two sets of gloves, but the top pair ripped most of the time. There was constant debate about not needing gloves or protection, when to use it and who to be cautious of.

Robby was focusing on the road, weaving the engine in and out of the traffic, sometimes going down the shoulder in order to pass the cars, the siren screaming the entire way. Ted was sitting in the passenger's seat pulling on the cord hanging from the ceiling every few minutes, blasting the air horn, startling inattentive drivers into the present. Neither one was saying a word to each other.

Royce and Steve stood in the jump seats facing forward, looking over the cab. The fully clothed firefighters gently swayed with the movement of the engine as it swerved in and out of traffic.

The entire crew appeared calm and relaxed, hypnotized with the movement of the engine. Inside, they were each engulfed in a personal high.

Chapter 4

As the engine approached the accident, Royce and Steve were looking over the top trying to scope out the situation as the accident came into view about one half mile north of Raphael Road on the other side of the median. The first indication was the sudden wall of traffic stopped on the highway.

Pulling up to the scene the crew could see three cars that appeared to be involved. They were in the third and fourth lane of the highway. The cars were accordioned together, creating what looked like one long car. It was easy to see someone was not paying attention when the car in front of them stopped abruptly, causing a chain reaction. The first car in the line also had damage to the front end, but no car was sitting in front of it. There was no smoke or steam coming from any of the cars.

Seeing the accident created an increased rush. A new flood of chemicals shot into the four firefighters, intensifying the already strong high.

Robby pulled the engine into the median, while Ted picked up the mic and said, "Engine 8-12 on location. Investigating."

The crew moved with expert precision, knowing what they would manage, focusing on their own independent mission that would ensure the success of this rescue. They did not need to talk. They knew from experience and needed no direction.

The radio speaker blared back, "8-12 on location 18:12." The radio was the only connection between the solitary engine and any help needed. Listening to the radio told them what units were available, who was responding, and you could speak directly to the other fire engines or ambulances. Every firefighter is unconsciously tuned to the radio.

Steve and Royce were the first off the engine. Each one opened the compartment directly behind the jump seat. Steve grabbed the medical kit while Royce grabbed a fire extinguisher and a pair of large bolt cutters in case he needed to cut any battery cables.

Robby and Ted emerged out of the cab immediately after.

Ted quickly came around the front to walk with Royce towards the scene.

Robby, securing the engine, climbed down and grabbed a handful of flares, putting then into his coat pockets.

Steve walked around the back of the engine emerging on the driver's side. Crossing the median, he spotted Royce and Ted moving slightly ahead of him.

At the two approached the scene, Royce walked directly to the damaged cars with a look of solid determination and defined purpose in his eyes, leaving him unmolested by the mulling crowd. His first priority was to make sure the rest of the crew was safe and that the cars would cause no additional threats. Quickly surveying the cars for signs of possible ignition, leaking fuel, and potential hazards, he saw none. The three cars were in a line. The middle car had the doors shut and three people standing around the driver's door. Royce went to the first car in the line. The driver's door was open. He slid into the driver's seat and checked that the car was in park. The parking brake was not set, so he pushed the peddle with his right foot, setting it hard. He then removed the keys from the ignition and dropped them on the center of the dash. He then reached under the dash and released the hood, took a quick look around the car and got out.

Closing the driver's door, he went to the front of the car. Surveying the car, he noticed the damage to the front bumper. It was obvious that this car had hit another car as well, and he looked around to try to find it. Not immediately seeing another car, he turned his focus back to the hood, reaching under it and releasing the safety latch, pulling the hood open. The rush hit again. Not knowing what would happen when the hood flew open triggered the flow. Quickly assessing the engine, he determined that the battery was OK, and the damage was not enough to pose any additional threat. Leaving the hood open he walked to the next car. Once the cars were secure and the rest of the crew was safe, he would help the others.

Robby headed into the traffic considering how he would get the cars moving to clear the area so that the crew would be safe working the scene. If he could get the slow lane moving, he could get the traffic flowing. When people get stuck in traffic jams, they get stupid. The put firefighters and police in danger. As he approached the northbound lanes, he popped the top off the red flare and struck the exposed ignition pad. The flare burst into a hot red glow. Holding the flare in his hand he walked into the fast lane, blocking off the car and signaling to the driver to stop. Placing the flare on the ground in the center of the lane, he stopped the drivers with a look in the eyes and a hand motion to stop. He struck the second flare and moved into the next lane, repeating the process.

When he got to the second lane, he tossed more flares, blocking the lane with a line of flares, he created a safe work zone, provided the drivers would pay attention and follow the directions given.

When he got to the slow lane, he instructed the car to drive with a wave of the flare in his hand. Standing between the slow lane and the second lane he moved upstream of the traffic about five car lengths to allow room for the other traffic lanes to move when he allowed them. He created a step pattern of traffic that allowed the cars to move to the right without blocking the other lanes.

After about one minute of letting cars through, Robby stopped the first lane of traffic and let the second lane move. He did this for all four lanes and repeated the process, allowing the cars to move with some coordination, relieving some of the traffic congestion. Maintaining a vigil, Robby made sure that the drivers stuck on the highway would not interfere with the work of the others. He felt the rush.

Ted arrived at the scene with Royce and was a little ahead of Steve. He needed to manage the crowd until the state police arrived to allow the others to do their jobs. He would control the gathering crowd, asking people not involved or a witness to leave the scene. For that he needed to take control of the incident immediately.

As they approached the scene, there were three people standing outside of the middle car hovering around someone in the driver's seat. They did not see anyone else lying on the ground or visible in the other cars and continued to the middle car.

Approaching the small crowd Ted loudly announced, "Hello, we're with Fire and Rescue. Can someone tell me what happened?" This was done more to get the attention of the people gathered around than to get any real information. This also identified the person in command so that Steve could continue to the patient unobstructed.

The first witness yelled, "Oh my god! He is trapped! The door won't open – he can't get out!" The panic in his voice was almost comical. Steve, hearing the man's alarm, figured that this must be the driver of the car that hit him from behind.

Finishing up with the first car, Royce came to the middle car on the passenger's side. This one had someone in the driver's seat. Ted and Steve were talking with a few people at the driver's door. Knowing that they would deal with the victim, he continued. Taking a quick look under the car he did not see any fluids dripping. There was nothing that appeared to be creating a hazard. Checking the doors, he found that they couldn't be opened. Steve would deal with the doors. He moved to the final car, repeating the process of securing the vehicle.

The cars said everything about the accident. From the position of the cars and the skid marks it was easy to see that the middle car was hit from the back and then slammed into the car in front of it. From the damage it looked like the car was going thirty to forty miles per hour when it hit the back end. No skid marks from the last car. Running through his mind Steve began to identify the potential injuries. The first concern was neck and spine injury, possible concussion, broken bones etc. Secondly, if the driver was not wearing a seat belt, there could be trauma to the sternum. This can cause breathing problems that range from pain, shortness of breath, to not breathing at all. Additionally, the trauma can cause injury to the heart, resulting in cardiac arrest at the worst.

As Steve got to the middle car, he could see the driver moving slightly. He could see him lifting and dropping his right hand. His chest moving as he was moaning. The car door was closed, the window was rolled up. A quick pull on the door handle confirmed the door was locked. Looking at the gaps between the drivers and passenger doors and the front quarter panel confirmed that there was not enough damage to keep the doors from opening. He reached back to the driver side rear door and gave it a quick pull, confirming it was locked. With the driver unconscious the doors would need to be opened another way.

Ted was behind Steve and trying to get the people under control and moved out of the way. "How bad Steve? Do we need the jaws?"

The rush hit Steve like a punch in the gut. The mere thought of having to execute a full-scale rescue using the Jaws of Life sent him into a state of ecstasy. Taking control of the rush and allowing common sense to dictate the next actions, he responded, "Not yet. Let's try unlocking the door." Quickly looking around he spotted Royce on the passenger's side. "Royce."

"Yeah."

"Check the passenger door to see if they're locked."

Grabbing the front and then rear door handle Royce confirmed that the doors were locked. "Doors look good, no bending and the gap still looks even between the door and the jamb. I think they're locked."

"Alright, let's take out the rear passenger window. We can't get in to cover the driver so try to be delicate when you break it," Steve instructed.

Swinging the bolt cutters like a baseball bat, Royce responded. "I'll use the punch so I don't send glass flying everywhere."

Pulling the glass punch from his turn-out coat pocket, Royce lowered the visor on his helmet, and positioned the punch in the bottom center of the rear passenger's window. Turning his head away he yelled, "Clear!" warning the others he was about to break the glass. Ted and Steve flipped the visors of their helmets down and looked away as Royce yelled, "Fire in the hole!" With a quick motion the spring-loaded glass punch made a small pop like an air gun being shot, causing the window to shatter.

The punch takes a small metal spike using the force of pushing it in activates a spring mechanism that causes the spike to punch the glass with more strength than a person can. With the force and the small, centered point, the glass shatters easily.

With the window shattered, Royce used the bolt cutters to clear the broken glass and then put his glove-covered hand into the car, fishing around to unlock the door.

This car did not have automatic locks, so Royce pulled the locking mechanism and opened the door. He then got in the back seat and quickly slid across to unlock the opposite door.

Ted had positioned himself at the rear driver door. When the lock clicked, he opened the door quickly, reaching in and unlocking the front door. This was done to prevent any unwanted bumping of the driver. If Royce had reached around him to unlock the door, there was a very real potential of hitting the driver's head with his arm, causing it to move. This needed to be avoided in case there were any spinal injuries.

Steve opened the driver's door and knelt beside the driver. "Hi, my name is Steve and I'm with Fire and Rescue. Can you tell me your name?"

The driver replied with a moan and began to turn his head from side to side.

"Royce," Steve began, "stabilize his head while I get a collar on him." Reaching around for the medical kit, Steve opened it and found the cervical collar he was looking for at the bottom. The medical kit looked like a very large tackle box. When it was opened there were three trays that stair-stepped out on each side, holding various pieces of first aid equipment and bandages.

Ted had gone back at the engine to update Dispatch. "8-12 to Dispatch."

"Go ahead 8-12."

"Updating working accident. One injury requiring transport."

"10-4 Engine 8-12, Ambulance 892 is en route to your location. Time 18:19."

Back inside the car Steve was trying to talk to the patient. "Sir. Try to stay with me. I'm going to put on a cervical collar to prevent any further injury to your neck. Just relax."

"I'm putting the back piece into position," Steve softly slid the back half of the collar behind the driver's neck. "You may feel it sliding into place," he said to the driver.

"Sir, this is going to feel a little strange. I need to put the front half of the collar on." "It may feel like I'm going to choke you, but I'm not going to hurt you. Just relax." Leaving his right hand in position holding the back half of the collar in place, he took the front half and positioned over the front of his neck.

Royce moved his fingers one at a time, holding the patient's head still and allowing the collar to be slipped into place and to keep out of the way of Steve.

With the two pieces of the collar in place, Steve grabbed the Velcro straps and secured it.

"OK Royce, you can let go." After releasing the driver's head, Royce gave his hands a quick shake to relieve the muscle strain.

"OK sir, I've got your neck stable. I need to check for other injuries."

The driver was still moaning a little, but he managed to say, "What's going on?"

"Well hello there. I'm with Fire and Rescue. It seems that you got yourself into a little accident," Steve said as he unbuckled the seat belt and removed it from around the patient's waist and arm.

"What. What happened? I don't remember!"

"It's OK. That happens with accidents. What's your name?"

"Mike."

"Damn glad to meet you Mike. I'm an Emergency Medical Technician and I'll be taking care of you until the ambulance arrives."

Looking into the back seat at Royce, Steve said, "Let's get the KED and prep him for extraction."

Royce simply nodded. He slid out of the back seat and headed toward the engine to grab the KED.

While the others were dealing with the victim, Robby had been successful in directing traffic to relieve some congestion. Several state police cruisers had arrived on the scene. One of the officers was helping Robby direct traffic and the other officers were starting to talk to the drivers and witnesses.

Ted was working with the officers while Royce and Steve attended to the patient. When something was needed inside one of the damaged cars, such as the registration, he went to retrieve it. It was standard practice that once the fire department arrived no one entered the car except for a firefighter. This accomplished two things. First, there was no opportunity for someone to get accidently injured in the damaged car. Second, it did not allow any of the drivers or passengers any opportunity to remove something from the car – drugs, weapons, anything that they did not want found.

Royce retuned with a green duffel bag and dropped it by Steve then slid back into the back seat behind the driver. He had helped with the KED a few times and knew what he needed to do.

The KED, or Kendrick Extrication Device, is a flexible half back brace used specifically to remove people from a car in a sitting position. The device consists of a series of one-inch aluminum strips that run from the hip to the top of the head. The bars are designed so that the longest is behind the head with cut-outs for the arms. A flexible vinyl cover allows the device to be wrapped around the patient and secured by several straps. Then leg straps are placed under each thigh and tightened to prevent the head and spine from moving while the patient is being extricated. When the device is applied correctly you can remove a person from a car in the sitting position, lay them on a backboard and then lower the legs with almost no movement to the spine. The KED was introduced in 1978 and it was designed to replace the half backboard with more stabilization and less risk of spine movement during extrication. It was still considered new, and several of the old timers refused to use it at all – almost like it was witchcraft or magic that should be shunned.

Steve unfolded the KED and got it into position. With Royce holding the patient's neck he prepared to immobilize him. "Mike," Steve commanded, "I'm going to put you into a spinal restraint. This is to stabilize your neck and spine while we get you out of the car and into the ambulance."

As he was getting into position, he explained, "We are going to lean you forward enough to slide the device behind your back. Now you're going to feel me put something behind your back. Just relax and we'll have you taken care of in two shakes."

Steve gave a quick nod to Royce. He responded with a single nod.

"OK Mike, here we go." With that the two moved him forward about 4 inches, allowing enough room to slide the KED behind his back.

Explaining how and why the device was being put on came as second nature. Part of training is to practice, practice, practice. Part of the practice is to be the patient as well. This provides the opportunity to experience what a patient is going through. To relieve some of the monotony when they aren't on calls, the crew creates scenarios for practice. As part of the practice they liked blindfolding each other. When the "patient" is blindfolded it's not so bad, you just take time and explain. When the rescuer is blindfolded, it is harder to help. The EMTs and paramedics liked to see who could immobilize the patients the fastest when blindfolded.

With the KED positioned in the middle of Mike's back, they slowly lowered him back against the car seat. "Good job Mike. Next I need to get your arms ready. I'm going to reach around you. Do you have anything in your pockets like a wallet?"

The patient groaned a little and said, "Yeah. My wallet."

Steve moved his face in front of Mike to get a clear look into his eyes. "Ok, I'm going to take it out of your pocket." Reaching around Mike he began searching for the wallet. Finding it quickly, he removed it from Mike's right-hand back pocket and placed it on the dashboard.

"All right Mike, I'm going to get your arms in position. I'm going to lift them up a little to wrap this device around you. When we're done your arms will be on the outside, so you won't feel all tied up."

Somewhere in the background Steve and Royce heard the speaker on the engine scream out, "Ambulance 8-92 on location."

Another voice responded, "8-92 on location 18:24."

Steve gently picked up the right arm. Royce wrapped the KED around Mike's torso and held it in place until Steve took it with his free hand. Lowering the arm, the device was held against his body while the two repeated the process with the other arm.

Outside of the car, Ted went to meet the ambulance, briefing the medic on the situation and the equipment needed.

"Hang in there Mike, we're almost done. Now I'm going to tighten the straps around you to keep you still." With that Royce handed the straps to Steve, who buckled the three clips in the front, then placed the Velcro straps around his head and chin, securing Mike in the KED.

Steve looked into the patient's eyes and asked, "How ya doing?" He shined the light from a small penlight into Mike's eyes, checking his pupils. If there was a concussion or brain injury, the pupils would not respond properly to the light.

"I'm Ok, I think. I don't need all this stuff."

"Probably not, but we need to practice every once and a while and no one else volunteered today."

"Funny guy," Mike mumbled.

"Alright, now it's time for you to do some work Mike," Steve said. Reaching down Steve placed his hand inside both of Mike's. "Mike, can you squeeze my hands?"

Mike lightly squeezed Steve's hands. "That's good Mike. Do you hurt anywhere?"

"No. I'm Ok," he said as he tried to lift his arm and get out of the car.

"Just sit tight Mike. I know this is weird, but we need to be sure that you aren't hurt. Just relax."

"I need to get home," Mike said.

"Don't worry, someone will call and let them know what's happening. We still have one more thing to do before we take you out of the car. I need to put on the leg straps. This will be the last part. What I'm going to do is put a strap around each leg. You'll feel me put the straps under your legs and pull them up to your crotch. This will hold your legs in place while we get you out of the car and onto the ambulance stretcher."

Steve slid the two leg straps under Mike's knees and worked them up towards his crotch, snapping the straps into the clips on the body of the KED snugging them down. This would hold his legs in a bent position when he was taken out of the car.

Suddenly someone came up to the car and stuck her head in the driver's door. "Hey Steve, what you got?"

Steve immediately recognized the voice behind him. "Hey Darcy. Single patient rear end and front-end collision. Patient was wearing a seat belt. Applied cervical collar and KED. Pupils are equal and reactive, appears to have full motor skills. No vitals yet."

"OK. What's next?" Darcy asked.

"Let's take him out and get him on the stretcher for you to work him up."

Looking out the door at who was standing around, Steve saw Darcy in the driver's side passenger door, and John, the ambo driver, looking over her shoulder into the driver's side door. He instructed, "Royce, take the right side, Darcy take the back and John grab the right side from Royce when he comes out. I'll take the left side."

The four people moved into position, preparing to remove the patient from the car. The stretcher had been brought from the ambulance by John and Darcy when they arrived at the scene, having been briefed by Ted.

"OK Mike. We're going to move you out of the car. When we move you, you're going to be in a sitting position until we get you on the stretcher. When we get you on the stretcher, we'll lay your legs flat. Just relax and let us do all of the work." Grabbing the wallet from the dash, he handed it to the patient, adding, "I want you to hang onto your wallet with both hands crossed across your lap."

Once in position the four of them began to remove the patient from the car. Royce slid into the passenger's seat, ready to move him. Steve was standing at the driver's door while John was standing by the passenger's door with Darcy right behind him, out of the way and ready for the extrication to begin.

"Everyone ready?" Steve asked.

All three responded, "Yes."

"OK on three. One, two, three."

In perfect unison Royce and Steve lifted the patient off the seat in a perfect sitting position.

With Steve outside of the driver's door, the two strained keeping the patient level.

Royce struggled slightly using his adrenaline filled muscles to lift in an unnatural and difficult position, with his left knee on the passenger's seat, right leg on the floorboard of the driver's side, straddling the gear shift. With his arms extended, he lifted the patent with extreme care and exacting precision. If they lifted him too high, his head would hit the ceiling. But before he hit his head, his immobilized legs would hit the steering wheel. Twist the wrong way, his head would hit the door jamb. Too low and his butt would drag on the seat. Both could cause more damage.

As Royce extended his arms towards the door, Steve began to step away from the car. John reached his left arm down to take some of the weight from Royce. As the patient emerged from the car, Royce crawled across the center console from the passenger's seat while John worked his way around to the right side taking the full weight, relieving Royce. As John moved from the back to the side, Darcy eased in and took his place, supporting and guiding. With the patient cleared from the car Steve and John stood up and allowed him to rock backwards.

"How ya doing Mike?" Steve asked.

"OK, I guess."

"Hang in we're almost done. By the way, that's John there on your right. He's going to be driving the ambulance today."

John gave a glance towards Mike and greeted him briefly.

Steve continued, "We're moving you to the stretcher now and then we will release your legs and get you lying down flat for the ride."

Moving five steps from the car to the stretcher the small group positioned themselves to transfer the patient.

John and Steve started at the head of the stretcher. Standing on either side, they began to move Mike to the end of the stretcher. This was where Darcy automatically took control of the patient. The hand-off was almost imperceptible to anyone other than the firefighters. "Stop there," she commanded. "Lay him back."

As his head tilted back and he became horizontal, Mike could see Darcy's face coming into view directly above his. Looked down and with a smile she said, "Hi, I'm Darcy. I'll be your paramedic until we get you to the hospital."

Mike gave a weak smile back to her. Being completely restrained he was helpless to do anything but listen.

"Down a little," Darcy insisted. "There! Set him down and let's release his legs."

With the instruction given, both John and Steve set Mike on the backboard of the stretcher with his legs still in a seated position, like an astronaut waiting for blast off. Next, they reached down and released the straps, allowing his legs to be lowered on to the backboard.

Darcy and John then took over the management of the patient. Mike began to secure him on the backboard to prevent any movement during transport while Darcy began getting vitals.

A state trooper come over and asked Darcy, "Can I ask the driver a few questions?"

Chapter 5

Relinquishing care of the victim to the ambulance crew, Steve's work was done. Looking for Ted, he spotted him behind the last car, talking with a trooper and the other two drivers. Steve quickly surveyed the rest of the scene to see where he was needed. Seeing that everything was under control he focused on the medical kit and began packing it up and taking it back to the engine, readying it for the next call. He made a mental note that a large cervical collar had been used and needed to be replaced.

Royce had come over to where Steve was packing up. "Well, that's over except to for the ride home."

"At least we got out of the station."

"Wish the car was on fire or someone was really trapped."

Royce and Steve watched the ambo crew roll the stretcher across the median, seeing the patient get loaded into the ambulance. Darcy disappearing into the back. John shut the doors and then climbed into the driver's seat of 8-92.

"Can't always be the superhero," Steve joked.

"Hope we get lucky and get another one."

With the gear packed up Steve grabbed the medical kit and he and Royce began strutting across the accident scene, grabbing secretive glances into the passing cars to see who was watching, noticing the venerating looks from the drivers. The crew secretly held the belief that every little boy wanted to be a firefighter and every woman wanted one. Swirling in those thoughts, their confidence elevated, imagining themselves as the modern combination of Hercules and Adonis.

Seeing the two packing up Ted realized that everything was wrapped up. "We're under control here. We'll hang out for a while to keep directing traffic. The tow truck should be here in a few minutes."

"Amb'lance 8-92 en route to Franklin Square."

The high was beginning to wear off. The patients had been removed; the cars were being taken away. This was the time during a call when the clean-up was done, and they were waiting for some sign that signaled the end of the call. This was usually the cars being taken away and the scene cleared.

"8-92 en route, 18:57."

While waiting for the tow truck the crew gathered in a group with the two state police officers, the other drivers and one person who was "a witness" to the accident.

"How's the driver?" Paul, the first trooper asked.

"Shaken, I don't think there is any serious injury. Everything looked good when we took him out," replied Steve to the group. "Hey, did you ever find the fourth car?"

"No. Witness said that it took off after being hit. Since the car didn't hit anyone, we won't be spending a lot of time tracking that driver down," Jim, the other trooper, responded.

"Guess he didn't want to hang around and talk to anyone," Steve quipped.

"Why would someone leave an accident that's not their fault?" the witness asked.

"Could be many reasons. Perhaps there was no insurance or registration. Or they could have a warrant for their arrest. Might be that they were running drugs up the Ninety-Five corridor," Trooper Jim said to no one in particular.

Royce and Steve rolled their eyes at each other. These people were all over the place. They wanted to be connected with the glory of the rescue, the accident or the fire, but they did not have the skills or the ambition to properly address the situation. Or any apparent skills, for that matter. These "witnesses" were the first to fold when needed. Pass out when there is blood. Panic when calm was required. The ability to control these responses are some of the attributes that make firefighters different. Firefighters have the ability to control their emotions, recognize and provide what is needed during an emergency and to remain calm and focused when other's panic. These "witnesses" are treated as a nuisance and often evoke a feeling of disgust. Most of the time the crews tried to ignore them.

Not being particularly interested in the conversation happening, both Steve and Royce went over to help Robby with the traffic control.

With the three firefighters working together, the traffic continued to clear while the crew waited.

After a short time, they saw a tow truck coming down the northbound side trying to get to the accident. The driver would have to go past the scene and do a U-turn at the first available spot, about three quarters of a mile up the road, and then come back through the traffic.

"Amb'lance 8-92 arrived Franklin Square."

Seeing the flow of traffic Robby directed the others to get the fast lane and shoulder clear so that the tow truck could get to them quickly.

"8-92 at Franklin Square, 19:15."

In short order the tow truck had pushed one car off to the shoulder and had secured the others. One was on the flat bed and the other being towed behind. The third car would be picked up later that evening by another tow truck or after this one had delivered its load.

During the process one of the driver's wives had arrived to pick him up. The other one rode in the cab of the tow truck to the impound yard.

This event marked the end of the call. The fire department was no longer needed. The crew climbed on the fire engine and headed back to the station.

"Engine 8-12 in service. Returning to station," Ted said causally into the mic.

"8-12 in service 19:32."

Chapter 6

The ride back to the station was quiet. Robby had wheeled the engine onto the highway still heading south. Pulling off at the White Marsh exit and headed to Route 40 to avoid the backup they just left on I-95.

When they returned to Station Two, the engine pulled into the area in front of the bay doors preparing for a U-turn, allowing the engine to back into the station. When the engine slowed, Steve jumped off and used his key card to enter. As he disappeared into the darkness the bay door opened.

Ted notified Dispatch that they had returned to the station. "8-12 Dispatch."

"Go ahead 8-12."

"8-12 off the air standing by."

Rather than backing into the bay, Robby pulled the engine forward and then backed alongside the fuel pump.

The crew appeared to scatter. Ted disappeared into the office area, Steve wandered into the fire station and Robby was refueling the engine.

"8-12, off the air 19:56."

As Robby fueled the engine, Royce and Steve re-emerged from the station. Both had removed their turn-out gear. Steve was carrying a replacement cervical collar and Royce had a handful of flares, each of them replacing the used equipment and making 8-12 fully prepared for the next call.

After fueling the engine, Robby backed it into the bay. Royce and Steve positioned themselves behind the engine as spotters, guiding the engine into the station.

With the engine ready for the next call, the crew went to relax in the break room.

The recent rush fading, the craving for the next was strong.

Some mindless show was on the TV as the crew lounged around.

"That was a pretty simple call," Royce started.

Thus began an evening of recounting past calls. Re-living the last call. Discussing what each one did. What they could have done differently. What the others were doing during the call. By piecing together everyone's actions, the crew could get the entire picture of the call.

"Yeah, the guy was lucky that he was wearing a seat belt and the cars weren't going too fast," Ted added.

"What happened to the dumb ass who wasn't paying attention?" Robby asked.

"Oh, the guy got a ticket. Trooper also is giving a ticket to the guy who went to the hospital for following too close," Ted advised.

"Hey, you remember that accident over on Philadelphia and Joppa road?" Royce asked.

Steve replied, "The one where the kid missed the turn and kissed the tree?"

"I heard the kid's out of shock trauma but is going to be in a halo for the next six months," Ted answered. A halo is a metal bracket attached to your head and body to prevent your neck from moving while you heal.

"That was a good call," Steve suggested. "Had to cut him out of that mangled Chevy. He never regained consciousness."

"Had to land the medevac in the parking lot of the liquor store," Robby added.

"Shame that Nova was trashed. It was a cool car," Royce added.

"The best call is still the Great Mercedes Rescue," Ted tossed in.

Laughter erupted in the lounge as the four of them laughed at the memory. "I thought his dad was going to have an aneurism on the spot!" Ted added.

"Hey, I still stand by my story that to safely extricate the asshole I used all means at my disposal to guard against further damage," Steve defended. "I did not deserve that suspension."

"You weren't suspended because of the car. You got suspended because you insulted and pissed off the driver's dad, who is some big ass attorney," Ted corrected.

"It was a ninety thousand-dollar Mercedes. The car was worth more than the kid driving," Robby piped in. "Why did you cut it in half?"

"Officially? Save the bastard son, safest possible method to minimize injury to the patient. That's the story and I'm sticking to it!" Steve retorted.

"Bullshit," Royce responded. "I wasn't on the call but heard the story. Come on, fess up."

"OK. So, you know the kid smashed into a parked car. When I got there, I could smell the alcohol. His girlfriend was also drunk as hell. Stupid little prick and his girl weren't wearing seat belts when they hit the other car. His girl bounced her face off the windshield and put a scar-generating slice across her face," Steve explained.

"So?" Royce said. "That's nothing to make you cut the car up?"

"It started with the drunk bastard who was driving," Steve clarified. "When I was checking out him and his girlfriend the little prick tells me that if his girlfriend is hurt, he is going to sue 'my ass off'."

"What a shit!" Royce added.

Steve continued, "I asked him his name and he told me I didn't need to worry about it, he was going to call his father to deal with 'you people' and to just do my job."

"This is why I drive the engine," Robby said. "I would have wanted to smother the little bastard."

"That's not what sent me over the edge. The car was mangled. The engine was in his lap, he must have been going sixty miles an hour when he slammed the car," Steve added. "Then tells me not to scratch his daddy's car."

"People get stupid when there drunk. How old?" Ted asked.

"Like eighteen," Steve clarified.

"Don't think Daddy will get him out this. How bad was the girl?" Robby asked.

"Bad facial lacerations. Contusions, whiplash, broken ankle. Will leave a bad scar on her face," Steve answered.

"So, what about cutting the car in half?" Royce demanded.

"It wasn't all the way in half. Just mostly," Steve sheepishly answered.

"Whatever. What happened?" Royce encouraged.

"Car was pretty bashed, couldn't even open the doors. Used the jaws to get both of them out. The ambo was there, and I managed the extraction. I popped the doors and peeled the roof back. After I peeled the roof, I was checking the car deciding what to do next," Steve explained.

"Why?" Royce asked.

"I needed to figure out if I had to bend the steering column off him or if there was enough room to take him out. The other option was to cut the steering wheel off and leave the column in place," Steve explained.

"Did you bend the steering column?" Royce questioned.

"Um..."

"Go ahead and tell him. This is great," Robby encouraged.

"Before I could finish checking everything the little punk tells me that he's going to make me pay for fucking up his car," Steve said, becoming animated.

"No way!" Royce exclaimed.

"I heard him say it right to Steve," Ted said.

"And you still got him out of the car?" Robby snidely replied.

"Unfortunately, he didn't have any life threating injuries. If I left him, he just would have moaned and bitched for hours. But I got so pissed off that I used a new extrication procedure," Steve said.

"What do you mean?" Royce questioned.

"Well, to remove him we laid him down and took him out through the back," Steve responded as if to clarify.

"What the hell are you talking about? There's not enough room in the back seat," Royce demanded.

Robby and Ted were laughing and said, "He made the room."

"I cut the car in half," Steve stated.

"That's fucking beautiful" Royce shouted.

"Since I had the toys out, and he pissed me off, it was pretty easy. I just cut the floor of the back seat. When I got to the drive shaft, I popped the U-joint. The jaws are awesome. Snip snip and the car is in half. Cut the seat back posts and out he came." Steve emphasized by making scissor motions with his hand.

"That's what got you suspended?" Royce asked.

"No, it was his dad," Ted inserted.

"What?" Royce asked.

Steve continued, "They needed an extra hand on the meat wagon, so I hopped in. When we were at the hospital his old man showed up. Guess the state police got in touch with him. Things did not go well."

"Yeah, I heard about it that night. But I never heard your side," Ted said.

"Simple: the guy walks in, ER doc lets him see his dumb ass son, drunk and being stupid. Yelling and threatening the ER staff. He asks what happened to the car," Steve continued with indignation. "Not 'How's my son?' No 'Will he be OK?' Just, 'What about my car?' They told him that they did not know. Apparently, he did not like that answer."

"What was his problem?" Royce wanted to know.

"He started screaming about how he wanted to know who cut his car up. That the person responsible bla bla bla..." Pausing to take a drink, Steve continued, "That's when I lost it. I told him that I was the firefighter who managed the extraction and operated the rescue tools. And said 'How can I help you?' in a rather condescending tone.

"He jumped right into the yelling about it was a ninety-thousand-dollar car and it better not be damaged. He was an attorney and he would make whoever was responsible pay."

"I hate idiots."

"Yep. Well that's when I started into him. Told him that first, if he was so upset about the car, he clearly couldn't afford owning it. Then I told him that he should go and sue the person driving the car drunk. Oh, that's right. That would be your son. Guess you get to pay for it after all. Oh, and by the way do you have any idea how your son is doing in the hospital?" Steve finished.

"That's great!" Royce commented.

"Well, that's when he started pointing his finger at me and threatening to sue me personally for 'destroying his car.' That's when I lost my cool and really laid into the prick. The first thing I told him was that he should get his money back from the hack school that gave him a law degree since he did not learn the law."

"Maryland law, can't sue a firefighter for doing his duty." Ted said.

"That pissed him off enough for him to stop yelling and for me to keep going. I hope you have a good attorney since your drunk son was driving your car with an under aged girl, who, since you haven't bothered to ask, will have a scar on her face for the rest of her life," Steve told them.

"No way! What did he do?" Royce questioned.

"Not much. He was standing there with his mouth flapping like a fish out of water," Steve continued. "I wrapped it up by thanking him for threatening me in front of all of those witnesses. Told him that my attorney cost more than his and juries love to see attorneys sued. Then I said, 'If you'll excuse me I have to make sure the passenger has my contact information.' Then I left his dumb ass standing in the middle of the ER."

"That's perfect. I always wanted to go after an asshole like that," Robby commented.

"Unfortunately, that's not where it ended," Steve added. "You can tell them the rest Ted."

"Yeah. The ambo crew called the chief and let him know what happened, just in case. The next day the guy shows up at the fire station demanding to talk to the chief," Ted went on.

"Jeeze, what a tool," Royce mumbled.

"Well Chief Doherty came down to the station and dealt with the guy. Don't know what was said exactly, but he's not trying to sue the department anymore. But he did let him know that the firefighter in question would be disciplined." Ted finished by clarifying, "That bought Steve a two-week suspension."

"Is that where you were?" Royce asked Steve.

"Yep. Called me and told me I was suspended."

"That sucks," Robby commented.

"Oh well it was worth it to put that asshole in his place. I hope the girl's parents sue the crap out of him," Steve replied.

"We've all bought a suspension for some stupid reason. Until your first suspension you're still a probee," Robby jibed the room.

"As a lieutenant I cannot support actions that will result in suspension, but I agree. I think we've all been suspended in the past," Ted chimed in.

"Shit you're a nobody until the chief starts telling stories about you to the new recruits," Robby laughed.

This type of banter goes on every shift with every crew. Slowly the conversation drifts to past calls. Accidents. Fires. Funny events. They are all discussed. It is a way to relive these past events. Relive the high that was felt. Like the serial killer returning to the scene of the crime, the firefighters remember those calls that they have been on. They also talk about calls that they were not on. Ones that they would have liked to have been on. They also discuss what others were doing during the call. One crew in the house, one on the roof. Imagining themselves on the scene lets them experience the rush.

The rush is not discussed. It is not acknowledged; it remains a secret held inside each person. The fear of admitting that you get enjoyment out of others' loss and death is buried deep in your mind. The shifting from the all caring hero to someone who does these things not to help others but to get a rush for themselves.

Chapter 7

The crew was in a post-adrenaline high, their craving satisfied for now. In the calm of the brain resulting from the junkies getting a fix, they were secretly jubilant that they had any kind of a call tonight. There are many days, weeks and sometimes months that you pull your shift and never turn wheels. After a while without a call, you crave a fix. Even a false alarm or simple dumpster fire gives a fix. Tonight, they got lucky. They had a good multi-car collision. But they were all secretly wishing that the car had been on fire, or a full rescue had been needed. Wishing the call was more complicated, took more time, needing more skills. Bigger rush, bigger fix.

Knowing that this could be the last call in the next few weeks the team began to settle into an evening of waiting for the shift to end. Two calls in one night with no storm or high school parties was unlikely.

"Anyone want to shoot pool?" Royce challenged.

"You're on," Robby shot back. "I'll rack."

"Cool, I'll break," Royce said with a smile.

While Robby pulled the triangle from under the table Royce was tossing the balls from the pockets onto the table. Robby was snatching them up and dropping them into positions in the triangle.

While Robby rearranged the balls in the right order for a game of eight ball, Royce took a pool cue from the wall and rolled it across the table to test for straightness.

Finding a reasonably strait cue, Royce positioned himself at the end of the table.

After taking the triangle off the balls, Robby pulled a ring full of keys off a clip on his belt. He unlocked a door and disappeared into the tool room.

Seconds later, while Royce was still lining up his shot, he re-emerged caring a black leather cue case.

The sight caused Royce to lose his focus. "Crap, I didn't know you had that hidden in there," he said with a sinking voice.

Steve was sitting on the railing that separated the basement stairwell from the engine bay. Watching the exchange between Royce and Robby he said, "I was going to challenge the winner, but I guess I can just say I'll play Robby."

Royce finally took his shot, breaking the rack and sending the balls scattering around the table. None of the balls fell into a pocket.

Ted was sitting on the tail board of 8-12. "When was the last time you were at the pool hall?" he asked Robby.

Taking only moments to shoot Robby announced, "Five in the corner." With a clack of the balls the five found its mark and dropped into the pocket. "Six weeks or so. The regulars were getting pissed that I was winning."

"Any problems?" Steve asked.

Robby pointed with the queue, "Seven side." Without breaking his stride, he continued, "Nope, I wasn't shooting for money. A few tried to insist on a bet, but I knew I'd kick their asses and refused. Told them I was only there for practice." Robby, while not a hustler, was the best player in the company. Whenever there was a pool match, he was the winner.

"Amb'lance 8-92 to Dispatch."

Lining up a three-rail shot, Robby slid the cue across the fingers of his left hand as the others watched intently.

"8-92."

The cue ball worked its way around the seven ball and bounced off the first rail, ricocheting off the second rail and cutting across the corner packet. Bouncing, it started losing momentum as it rolled down the length of the table, seeking to connect with the two ball near the far corner.

"8-92 in service, returning to station."

Connecting, but with too little force, the two ball never completed the roll to the corner pocket.

"8-92, 20:32."

"I get to shoot again?" Royce joked.

"Well, I have to miss every once in a while, or no one would ever play me," Robby teased as he leaned against the stair-rail.

The crew continued to shoot pool, each taking a turn playing the last winner. After three games Robby decided he had enough pool for the night and let the others continue playing.

The pool game was interrupted by a noise. "Was that a car door?" Robby asked as he strained to listen for more sound.

It didn't happen often but there had been a few times when someone had driven an injured person to the station rather than to the hospital. The four of them moved quickly. Scurrying to the open bay door, they came around the engine to find the ambulance parked and Darcy reaching into the back of 8-92.

"What you guys doing here?" Royce asked.

"Brought back your KED," Darcy answered.

"Usually, we don't get that back for a few days," Ted observed.

Dave had come around the back of the ambulance. "Yeah, the doc had him out of the KED before we got packed, so figured we would grab it and bring it back."

"Figured if we didn't grab it tonight it would end up on 8-14 before the weekend was over," Darcy added.

"Thanks," Steve said taking the KED. "I'll clean it up and get it back in service."

"How's the guy you took to the ER?" Royce asked, leaning his back against the front of 8-12.

John was resting against the side of 8-92 and said, "He's fine. By the time we got to the hospital he was conscious and talking. Don't think there were any injuries other than bruising."

"The ER dock took him off the backboard and out of the KED before he even started to examine him," Darcy clarified.

"Not even any X-Rays or a quick check before pulling him out?" Ted asked in amazement. "Was the doc new?"

"Nah. He's been there for a few years. He's pretty good so I guess he figured that there weren't any injuries," Darcy defended.

"Remember when that on doc cut off the MAS trousers?" Steve asked. "Did they ever sue him?"

"No. He was in rotation and the supervising physician was indisposed." Darcy smirked. "First time the poor guy ever saw a pair."

"What happened?" Royce asked.

"Took in a trauma patient. We put the MAS trousers on him. When he got to the ER it was chaotic. They were loaded up with a waiting room full of people," Darcy explained. "When we brought him in, we tossed him onto a table and started telling the team the vitals. The rotation doc came up on the bed all cocky and full of himself. Without a second thought he simply said, 'Let's see what we have under here,' then grabbed a pair of bandage scissors and cut the trousers off."

MAS trousers are military anti-shock trousers. There are essentially a pair of inflatable pants that compresses the legs. The idea is to move the blood from the legs to the upper body in the event of significant blood loss. The trousers move several pints of blood back into the upper body to provide oxygen to the vital organs. They are intended to be depressurized slowly, allowing the body to compensate for the increased blood flow. If they are removed quickly it is like losing a lot of blood instantly. The patient crashes and goes into cardiac arrest, almost instantly.

Robby's eyes bulged out of his head, followed with a "Holy Crap! Did the guy just crash right there on the table?"

"Yep. Flatlined before he got them off. The doc just stood there as the guy bled out. Had no idea what was going on."

"No one stopped him?"

"No time. One second we were talking with the nurses. You know how it is, the docs don't know anything, just rely on the nurses to tell them what to do. Never expected him to just jump into action and do something." Darcy sighed. "By the time we yelled out, it was too late."

"Jesus. We spend all that effort in the field to get the patients to the hospital and the fucking doctor kills them," Steve spat out.

"Win some and lose some," Ted responded.

"We need to get back to Station One," John interrupted.

Darcy added, "Guess you're right. Duty calls."

The two climbed into the ambo, headed around the tarmac and disappeared down the hill of the driveway. The engine crew was casually standing outside the engine bay watching the ambo disappearing over the hill.

"OK. Why the hell did Darcy bring the KED back?" Robby questioned with a sideways glance at Steve.

Darcy was the older sister or cool aunt of the fire house. She was about ten years older that the youngest members of the crew and provided guidance, support and council when required. As one of the senior paramedics, this crew considered her one of the best. She was also a firefighter and could pull duty on either the ambo or the engine, making her valuable.

She was one of the first active women in the department and getting to the position had been hard. Many of the 'Old Timers' did not believe that women should be a fireman and some still refused to get on an engine with her.

This crew did not have any issue with Darcy. Any member of 8-12 would happily go into a fire with her and given the choice she was at the top of the list. Not only was she technically good at fighting fire, she had nothing to prove to anybody. She took no chances, she knew when to walk away, and when to run.

With a huge smile Royce answered, "'cause she likes us more than you."

"Bullshit," Robby joked back. "The ambo crew does not return gear to Station Two. What makes you special?"

"Did you remember her birthday a couple of months ago?" Steve asked in a degrading tone.

"Birthday?" Ted questioned. "How the hell do you know when Darcy's birthday is?"

"Easy, if you actually listen to people," Steve responded. "One day Royce and I were hanging out and she swung by the station. She was heading up to her job at Fallston and was bitching that she had to work the night shift on her birthday."

"Yeah, about 11:30 Steve and I were bored," Royce continued. "So we drove up to the hospital and surprised her."

"That's it? You drove up there and said, 'Happy birthday'?" Ted asked.

"Well, we took her some flowers for her birthday," Royce clarified.

"You sneaky bastards," Robby said in awe. "I bet she loves you now."

"That's why she is being nice," Ted summarized with a sly grin.

"No one else bothered." Royce smirked. "We're her bestest friends now."

"I can't tell if you're up to something or just being nice," Ted threw out.

"Did you ever think it was both?" Steve queried.

"I need to keep a better eye on you two," Ted informed them. "I think you're sneakier than I give you credit for."

Steve made his face look innocent with eyes open wide. "We're pure as the driven snow."

"Innocent as babies," Royce added.

"Ambo 8-92 in service, off the air."

"8-92 off the air in service, 20:47."

"Seems like the excitement of the evening is ending," Robby announced. "Let's go check out what's on cable tonight."

"Hope it's an action movie," Royce offered as the crew made their way into by station. "Not going to watch a chick flick with a bunch of guys."

Chapter 8

The glow of a digital clock lit the bunkroom, the only sounds those of the sleeping crew.

The loud ringing of the red phone on the wall shattered the quiet.

Jumping from his bunk Ted grabbed the phone on the third ring. "Company 8 House 2." Trying to shake the sleep from his head, he focused on the distant voice giving information. A surg began to fuel Ted, jolting him from grogginess to fully awake in a fraction of a second.

The ringing catapulted Steve and Royce from the top bunks, each leaping to the ground still wrapped in the sheets. The unexpected noise injected adrenaline into their bodies, increasing as they recognized what was making the noise.

Robby was sitting up on the edge of his bunk, trying to figure out why he was awake and why the others were moving. In a deep daze he began to go through the motions of getting dressed, not knowing why.

Landing on the floor they untangled the sheets and started pulling on their clothes. With practiced motion and the precision of a ballet, socks, pants, shirt were pulled on in sequence. Trying to buckle and zip their pants with shirt tails flying behind them they quickly walked, just short of the speed of jogging, through the bunkroom door, the sound of Ted's reply echoing in their ears as they disappeared into the engine bay.

Ted simply said, "Were responding" into the red handset. The surg flooding his body, moving back on the edge of the bunk, he sat to dress. Without looking up or interrupting pulling on his clothes he simply said, "House fire."

In the engine bay, Steve punched the button opening the overhead door as he ran around the back of the engine on the way to his jump seat. As he ran around the engine, he instinctively scanned the engine for any issues, loose tools, or missing gear.

Robby, fully awake with Ted's announcement, accelerated with a rush, he finished dressing as he headed through the bunk room door. The low rumble of the bay door opening enhanced the rush.

Ted was a fraction of a second behind Robby, the bunk room door only closing halfway before he pushed it open, bursting into the bay. "HOUSE FIRE!!"

Steve and Royce were pulling on their turn-out gear that sat on the floor by the engine. Climbing into the jump seats Ted's announcement hit them like a bolt of lightning. This was what they dreamed of. This is what they craved. Nothing – NOTHING – is more intoxicating than a house fire. All fires cause an incredible rush. This is the addiction, one that is hard to equal. The thought of meeting the devil himself. Fighting the demon. Kicking its ass! The adrenaline coursing through their bodies as they imagined a working house fire was outstanding.

The speakers on the wall, in the jump seat and in the cab exploded into the night. "Beep boop, beep boop, dododododa. Box 8-08, Company 8, Joppa-Magnolia Engine 8-12, Baltimore County Company 4, Kingsville, Mutual Aid. Dwelling fire 725 Charmouth Court. Engine 8-12 responding. Time 00:43."

The dispatcher was announcing the information as the engine was rolling out of the engine bay.

Royce was waiting by the bay door as the engine slowly pulled out. As the engine cleared the opening, he punched the button closing the door. Running alongside the slowly moving engine, he jumped onto the sidestep to climb into the jump seat. As he cleared the ground jumping, the engine accelerated.

Robby, watching in the side mirror, accelerated as Royce's trailing foot left the ground with his final step onto the engine.

Steve and Royce reached over the engine compartment giving a high five and yelling, "Hell yeah!" then dove into the jump seats to get geared up.

The engine came down the hill from the fire station, growling against its own weight as it pushed itself down the hill, red and white lights reflecting off the surrounding houses, Mars light bouncing up and down. Turning right onto Trimble Road, 8-12 started the run to the fire.

Robby masterfully guided 8-12 down this twisty back road. Set with steep hills and blind curves, this road had produced its share of accidents, some fatal. It was challenging to drive at the best of times. In the middle of the night, a Friday night, this road could quickly become deadly.

Robby was reveling in the rush, momentarily satisfied with his current fix. Indulging in the joy of a second fix in the same night. It didn't matter if the house was on fire or not, running this engine towards a house fire produced enough of a high that he was barely maintaining control over his mind and body. So close to just shutting down in ecstasy, he balanced on the edge of overdose. Skillfully maintaining, increasing, and decreasing speed to get to the fire scene as quickly as possible, reading the signs of the road, he looked for car headlights reflecting off the trees, mailboxes' and miscellaneous reflectors scattered about the road. Searching for signs of someone else using this street so he could use both sides of the road, crossing the yellow line, eating up the asphalt to get the highest speed possible, he commanded the road. A brief memory flashed across his mind, remembering the times he sped down this road in his car. The rush he felt then was non-existent compared to the rush he now felt.

Ted was manning the siren and horns. Trying to focus on the road, ready to sound the signal if a car should appear. He was engulfed in the rush. He was confident in the skills of his crew. He never considered the speed they were traveling. Never doubted the control of the driver. Never reaching for phantom brakes. Never gasped in surprise at a twist or turn. He gently swayed with the motion of the speeding engine, knowing that they would safely reach the scene in record time.

His confidence was steadfast towards the two in the jump seats as well. He knew that when they arrived, they would spring into action without hesitation and attack the fire with tactical precision. Always textbook perfect in their response. He was safe in the intoxication provided by the rush.

Ted had been in command of a few working fires. Dumpster, brush, car fires. On three occasions he was in command of a house fire and one building fire. None had been working fires, only investigations. He alone on the crew knew that Dispatch had received three calls about this fire, from three different people. This one was almost certainly a working fire. He secretly hoped that it wouldn't go out on its own or be put out by some damn do-gooder. A momentary flash of guilt welled inside as he realized that he was wishing for someone to lose their house. Maybe their life. A shudder ran through his body and he was overcome with a surge caused by the simple thought of "rescue" flashing into his head. With the rush, he pushed the flash of guilt into the dungeon of his mind. This would be a first. The pinnacle of the high. He had been in a few dozen house fires. Some were rolling, some not so much. The thought of commanding the scene of a full working dwelling fire with rescue produced a rush that was almost uncontrollable. Tonight, he would be the master of this scene. *Keep control*, he thought to himself. A self-satisfied smile crept onto his lips as the engine glided around a tight curve. There was no guilt about his secret thoughts of someone losing their house, getting injured, dying, just to satisfy his addiction. This was a secret kept to himself. The addiction overpowered any feelings of guilt.

In the jump seat Royce and Steve prepared for the fire. In complete unison they went through the graceful dance, the rhythm of the engine creating the beat that they moved to as they began the ritual dance, the actions transforming them from a mere mortal to an invincible hero. Reaching toward the bottom of the SCOT pack they turned the valve, releasing the pressurized air. At almost the exact same time each pack let out a ping as the regulator pressurized. The rush was all-consuming. Facing the air pack, they reached for the right shoulder strap with their right hand then spun into the seat, sliding their shoulders into the strap. Then leaning far to the right, sliding into the left strap. Grabbing the chest strap, they connect the two sides. Pulling on the shoulder straps, snugging the pack, attaching to it, becoming one with their air supply. Standing up in unison, a twang of the steel bracket released the pack from the clip. The rush flooding their bodies. Taking one and a half steps, the two turned and face each other as they came out from under the jump seat overhang and stood.

Riding down Trimble Road Royce and Steve reached over the engine compartment, grabbing each other's right hand, pulling themselves closer to each other. "IT'S GONNA BE A WORKER!" Royce shouted.

"HELL YEAH!"

The adrenaline coursing through their bodies was electric, being delivered at an intensity making it impossible for them to be still. It was the feel of an electrical current going over their skin. The hair on their necks and arms standing up. With fifty pounds of turn-out gear they were jumping on the balls of their feet, one hand on the top of the cab, the other hanging onto the rail mounted on the engine cover. This was the feeling that they craved.

The speakers on the engine broke the symphony of the engine's roar. "Ladder 8-52 responding."

"8-52 responding, 00:45."

"We'll be the first," Royce hollered. "When we pull into the cul-de-sac the house will be on your side. I'll let you know what hose to pull."

The entire crew knew this route. They knew the neighborhood. They had driven the roads. They had lived here for years. Robby and Royce had lived in this town for their entire lives.

The engine careened down the two-lane road, its own weight pulling it down and creating resistance going up as it encountered the hills. The throaty rumble of the engine changing with the terrain. Robby trying not to let the gravity of the hill pull her into an uncontrollable speed. Using the engine to reduce the downhill speed, letting his foot hover in the air between the gas and the brake pedal, waiting to decide which one to jam his foot onto. As he neared the bottom of the hill, the entire crew felt the engine leap forward as he slammed his foot on the gas pedal, using the last 50 feet of the hill to slingshot them back up the other side.

As the engine used the gravity to its advantage, Robby thought, "This is the way they made it home from the moon," wondering if a spaceship would give this kind of a rush. Analyzing the thought as he continued to search the road for oncoming cars he quietly chuckled to himself, "Don't like flying, I'm going to stick to the dirt."

"Engine 8-13 responding."

The road was eerily empty for a midnight on a Friday night. They had not passed a single car since leaving the fire station. *Wonder where the kids are?* Ted thought. They usually liked to race up and down the road. When they weren't racing, they were at the park. Shifting his thoughts from the road, he began staging the fire scene from memory. Charmouth Court was a cul-de-sac off Haverhill Road. Last left before Joppa Farm Road. Five houses, all two-story split levels. Hydrant on Haverhill across from the court. Second engine in could pick it up if they needed. He continued staring out of the front windshield hand on the pull cord for the air horn, waiting. He was pumped. He remembered going into burning buildings. His rush increased at the thought. He would be in command. At least until a senior office showed up.

He was the newest lieutenant, so it was almost certain that a higher-ranking officer would be on the scene soon. Unless it wasn't a working fire.

His rush momentarily dipped. Houses were seldom really flaming. Mostly a smoke smell, maybe a small kitchen fire. In the middle of the night it was probably an electrical short or the heater blowing smoke. It probably wouldn't be very exciting, but he was still in command of a house fire. His rush increased.

"8-13 responding 00:47."

8-12 moved to the oncoming lane, swinging across the entire road as it made the right onto Haverhill Road. Never tapping the brakes, Robby kept the engine moving fast. *Hope no one pulls out of their driveway. I'll never be able to stop*, he thought. Realizing that the engine was just fifteen hundred feet to the turn into Charmouth Court, his rush plateaued knowing that this was at the end of the ride. He got his fix finding relief for the time being. If the house wasn't on fire his job would be done and the rush would fade away.

Five hundred feet from the corner, all four were trying to see through the trees and houses, wanting to know if the house was on fire. The rush was holding strong. Scanning the skies to see if there was any glow from flames, the crew was eagerly waiting for the engine to come around the corner. Wanting the house to be on fire. Knowing that you should not want such things to happen created conflict within each man. The rush was more important.

Robby throttled back on the engine and pushed on the peddle creating a loud "kwosh" as the air activated the brakes, slowing the red glowing beast just enough to make the turn into the cul-de-sac.

With the world moving in adrenaline-fueled slow motion, the first houses on the small street came into view. Too many lights were on in the first house. The door was open. The second house was the same. Too many lights. Too many people. They should be asleep this late at night. Something was very wrong in this small suburban neighborhood.

The third house had people standing in the yard frantically flapping their arms at the engine, panic taking its grip on them. Seeing the panic in the crowd the crew knew this was an exceptional fire.

Humor crept into Ted's smile, thinking to himself, *Wow, it's a good thing they're out here. We would never find the house.*

Chapter 9

The house coming into full view, the people scattered across the surrounding lawns vanished into the background. Nothing else mattered as the firefighter's attention fixated on the house.

The glow was all the four needed to see. One window was alive with fire. The flickering of the flames cast shadows and changing light patterns against the glass. Pieces of the drapes smoldering against the smoke-stained glass. Shadows dancing across the ceiling, the contents of the room being consumed by the flame.

Royce's knees buckled, causing him to drop four inches before he recovered.

Steve's body froze. His mind ceased to see anything else. A snapshot of the house frozen into his mind.

Robby, maintaining control, immediately began surveying the area, checking the location of the spectators, the cars, seeing everything at once.

Ted, eyes fixed on the house, picked up the mic from the dash, pressed the lever on the side and said, "Engine 8-12 on location. Working fire."

The firefighters knew this house layout well. It was a two-story split level that littered the subdivision. Every one of them had been in a similar house countless times over the years, being firefighters and living in the town.

Walk in the front door and you are standing on a landing with stairs going up or down. Go down and you walk into a family room that runs from the front of the house at basement level to the back going out a sliding glass door into the yard. Turn right and you find a bathroom to the left and a bedroom to the right. Straight ahead is the door to the two-car garage.

Go up at the landing and you walk across the hall into the kitchen. Turn left at the top of the stairs and you go into the living room toward the front and the dining room at the back. Turn right at the top of the stairs and halfway down the hall you come to a bathroom on the left and a bedroom on the right looking out over the front yard. Move down to the end and there is the master bedroom on the left facing the back of the house, a linen closet at the end of the hall and the door to another bedroom above the garage, overlooking the driveway.

It was the front bedroom at the end of the hall overlooking the driveway and above the garage that captivated the engine crew's attention.

The adrenaline exploded. The smell of smoke, sweat, destruction, death in the air mixed with thoughts of fear, heroism, rescue, victory, and bragging rights. An emotional overload rushing into you with abandon. Feelings that others cannot understand and will never experience. The feeling of facing the end. Taking control. Defeating the monster. Being victorious. Doing what the others won't do. What they can't do.

The engine roared into the cul-de-sac, appearing as the vessel of angels for those standing about. The helpless seeing the engine as a sign of hope or security.

"Engine 8-12 on location. Working fire. 00:48."

Robby had already determined what needed to be done. As he drove into the circle, he pulled the engine to the right, and then circled to the left. This would put the pump panel away from the burning house, the suction connection facing the location of the fire hydrant at the end of the cul-de-sac across the street. The road would be shut down, but he did not care about that right now. This position would also protect him from anything that could happen in the burning house. He pulled past the driveway, just to the left edge of the house. The hoses lined up almost perfectly with the front door. This would leave room for the ladder truck and the other equipment en route.

The initial staging of the scene fueled the rush. Uncontrollable waves ripped through their bodies, sending them into an unparalleled state of ecstasy. Reacting to the intoxicating effect, their bodies senses were heightened, strength increased, they became invincible. They were each consumed within their own high.

The quiet neighborhood was transformed to an alien environment by the arrival of Engine 8-12. The red and white circling lights cast a mesmerizing glow across the surrounding houses, the lights reflecting each time they struck the glass of the windows. The red hue changed the coloring of the gathering people, morphing them from humans to strange red creatures.

As the engine circled into position the crew was launching into action. Royce and Steve had already unfastened the safety chains from the jump seats. Royce yelled across the engine compartment for Steve to pull the 150 foot attack hose.

Steve jumped off the engine and grabbed the middle attack line. This would give enough fire hose to reach inside of the house, but no more. With a single yank, he pulled it off the engine into a pile on the ground.

With a loud "kwosh" of the airbrakes bleeding off, Robby set the engine for the work ahead. Flying out of the cab he immediately opened the lower compartment directly behind the jump seat, grabbing the wheel chock and in one smooth motion shoving it under the back wheel of 8-12, not bothering to acknowledge Royce as he disappeared around the back of the engine.

Royce was off and moving quickly around the engine. As he disappeared, he yelled, "One fifty" over his shoulder to Robby.

Ted emerged from the cab as Steve was pulling the hose. Scanning the small crowd, he saw two women clutched together, one screaming.

The hose hit the ground with a dull thud mixed with metal striking metal, the couplings clashing against each other as it dropped to the ground. Steve's adrenalin-fueled body had propelled the 250 pounds of hose almost ten feet past where he stood.

As Royce came around the back of the engine Ted was making his way toward the people gathered to get the details on the situation. Locking eyes with Royce, he asked, "Interior attack?"

"Exterior. Going to hit the window and blow it out. Looks hot. After we open it up we'll go inside and knock it out."

"Good call." Ted nodded in agreement. "I'll go and deal with the civilians." As he headed around the back of the engine Ted began to focus on the crowd and sort out the situation.

Royce and Steve began untangling the hose, trying to drag it close to the burning house before it filled with water.

As the crew prepared to fight the fire a woman could be seen yelling and crying hysterically. Another woman was standing between her and the burning house, holding her back. A man rushed from the crowd toward the man in the blue helmet. Before Ted could speak the man yelled, "Her kid's still inside," repeatedly flapping his arm towards the house. The look of helplessness in his eyes. He did not know what to do. How to help. All he could do was to holler the information at the firefighters, helpless in the alien surroundings. He was terrified.

Seeing the commotion, the crew sensed something was wrong.

Dismissing the man Ted simply said, "Right," then moved to the screaming woman. Gently pushing the other woman aside, he moved directly in front of her. He lowered his body so he was at eye level, trying to get her to focus on him. "Ma'am! Ma'am."

The woman stared vacantly toward the house. Overwhelmed with panic she did not see the lieutenant standing directly in front of her. "In the house..." was all she could utter, tears flowing from her eyes down her face.

Ted grabbed the woman's shoulder and gave it a firm shake. *Shit I'm gonna have to slap her like in the movies*, he thought. "Where is the baby's room!" he yelled directly in her face.

Someone is grabbing my shoulder. Shaking me. These realizations began to bring her back from whatever dark place her mind was taking her. The smell of smoke assaulted her nostrils. She knew that smell. Why did she know the smell? The house. The house that was burning. That was the smell of the smoke in the house. Something shaking her...no, the demon shaking her. He was here to take her back into the flames. Horror rocketed through her body. Fear overcame her as she yelled, sending pellets of spittle into the face of demon in front of her.

Ted maintained his composure. He had seen this before. Some people cannot handle this. They close down. Curl into a ball. Try to crawl into a corner and hide from the thing they cannot understand or control, of the things that terrify them. She was on the verge of becoming completely useless to Ted. He had only seconds to get the information he needed. Quickly tilting his head forward, he bounced the brim of his helmet into the woman forehead to get her attention. "Where is the baby's room?!" he yelled into the terrified woman's face.

"My baby! In the house. The front room! SHE'S IN THE FRONT BEDROOM! MY GOD, SHES BURNING ALIVE."

Ted and Royce locked eyes. With a nod of the head, he gave the order, "Go into the house!"

In a fraction of a second the entire crew understood the shift in strategy. This was now an interior attack and a search and rescue. The idea of a safe exterior attack was instantly abandoned. The textbook says to attack the fire from the outside. Break open windows, ventilate the roof, then go inside and finish the job. Going inside was dangerous. The potential of damaged structure and flashover. This happens when the oxygen falls below the amount needed to burn. Open a door or window and the oxygen level rises rapidly, causing the hot combustibles to explode, and they ignite.

The entire crew moved fast. They knew that if a senior officer took over the scene, they crew would be stopped from going in. It was better to let the child die than risk a firefighter being injured.

Screw that, these two wanted to face the devil. Saving the child became the reason to go into the burning house. This was the excuse. There was no consideration for safety. They would go into the inferno. The rush would be intense. Their minds saw everything at once. The woman screaming, the other woman holding her, the man flailing his arms toward the burning house, slowly screaming, "The baby...the baby." The teenage neighbor coming out of the house, frozen in air as he jumped over the bushes in front of the door to his house. The fire in the house. They could see the heat. The flames appeared in slow motion.

The adrenaline elevated to a level never achieved. The high it provided was, until then, the stuff of myth and legend. A working fire. A child trapped inside, these four, each in their own way, would be the only link between life and death for the unknown infant. The overwhelming effect of the natural drug coursing through their bodies sent each of them into a private state of ecstasy. Simultaneously they experienced a physical reaction that was unparalleled. The world around them froze while they continued moving through it. They seemed to be moving at the speed of light, others around them stuck in slow motion. Their strength increased to superhuman levels. They could lift the fire engine if they chose to.

With the decision to go in the house, the surged pushed to a new level. The two firefighters knew that they were the only ones who could have the slightest possibility of finding the child. It was only the fact that the two of them were dragging several hundred pounds of fire hose, water and equipment that kept others from seeing them physically shudder with the overwhelming rush.

Ted looked into the woman's eyes. "We're going to get her. The crew is going in now." He knew that the veiled promise he made was only a body recovery.

"She'll be Ok. You'll get her?"

Ted froze for just a moment. "The baby is dead. She was dead when you ran out of the house without her. The only one who could have saved her was you. You failed. You are a coward thinking only of yourself. You let your child die. We'll find the dead lifeless body. It'll be blackened with soot. Wet from the water. Once outside we'll do mouth to mouth and get her into an ambulance. An act. Pretending to save her. Making you, your neighbors, everyone feel better. Giving you the chance to say. 'They did everything they could. If only they'd gotten here sooner.' We'll give you the lie to help you make it through the pain. It should have been you that stayed inside the fire not the child you selfish bitch!" is what Ted wanted to say. What came out was, "We will do everything we can." With a stone face he turned and went to the engine.

As Robby climbed out of the driver's door, he heard Royce yelling, "One fifty" as he disappeared around the back of the engine. After chocking the wheel, he stood in front of the pump panel, moving the levers and switches that transformed the darkness into the center of the universe. Manipulating the levers and turning the chrome plated knobs the rumble of the engine dipped as the pump engaged. Stepping onto the jump seat step he looked over the engine and surveyed the scene. The hose was on the ground and the two firefighters were straightening it, preparing it to fill with water. Ted was talking with the screaming woman. The fire was glowing in the window. Twenty seconds and the hose would be ready to fill, he calculated.

Seeing the commotion from the civilians, Ted talking with the lady. The activity from the other two, he knew they were going inside. From his vantage point he looked at the slope of the driveway. The steps leading up to the house. The length from the engine to the house. Twenty-five feet from the engine to the front door straight across the yard. Driveway sloping up. His head level with the third step from the top. At six foot two inches and standing, eighteen inches above the street he calculated that the step was about eight feet above the street. Add another three feet for the remaining three steps and the rise from the street to the front of the house was approximately ten feet. Once inside the door Royce and Steve would go up, where the fire was, split level, add five feet to the top of the stairs. Fifteen feet of rise.

Instantly in his mind he was calculating the distance, lift, and friction loss of the water flowing through the hose. He was responsible for getting the right amount of water from the five-hundred-gallon tank of the engine, up the hill and into the house to the end of the hose. The only thing to keep the men inside the house alive would be the engine pumping the water to the hose, like the heart pumping blood.

Firefighting is not just aimlessly throwing water onto something that is burning. It is a calculated event that disrupts the process of fire. A fire needs three things: fuel, heat and oxygen. Remove one of those items and the fire is interrupted. The water removes the heat and reduces the oxygen. This is done when the water flashes into steam, absorbing the heat. As it expands it pushes the air away. In a situation where one of the three required elements are not present and then replaced rapidly, boom.

From the glow in the window, the markings of the smoke on the outside of the house, the stillness of the air, Robby instinctively knew that he would need more water than what the engine carried. Twisting the knobs on the pump panel, he engaged the pump and with a groan it was sucking the water from the tank and sending it down the hose. He could feel the pump react to the hose, filling and straightening out. Each time a kink was encountered, the pump speed slowing as it strained to push water through the bent hose then increasing as the kink straightened. He could feel the life in the engine as he manipulated the flow of the water.

Ted watched the two men straightening the hose, pulling it closer to the front door, preparing to go into the burning house. He had a momentary flash of envy. Knowing that this fire should be knocked down from the outside first, but it did not matter. Saving the child was the excuse to go into the inferno. To go into this fire would be spectacular. Watching the two prepare to go into the house, he remembered that he was now the lieutenant. He moved to the driver's door of the engine and reached in to grab the radio mic.

Robby interrupted his thoughts. "Ted have the next engine lay a line!"

Pulling the mic out of the cab to where he could move around to manage the fire scene, he keyed the mic and began giving commands. "8-12 to Dispatch, updating situation. Working fire with a rescue. Child reported inside. Engine 8-14 lay a line to 8-12. Have ambulance respond for standby. Ladder 8-52 stage at front of house for aerial attack. All other units' stage on Haverhill Road. Send crews to 8-12 for instructions."

"8-14 copy."

"Ambulance 8-92 responding."

"Dispatch to all units responding to Box 8-08, go to channel two upon arrival. 8-12 is now command. Ambo 8-92 responding 00:59."

A series of "Ten-fours" sounded through the radio speakers. Dispatch did not bother responding to each unit. They would change the channel when they arrived, and he would remind them if needed.

"Engine 8-11 responding."

"Engine 8-15 responding."

Chapter 10

The speaker erupted with another series of tones. "Box 808, working dwelling fire 725 Charmouth Court. Company 4, Baltimore County Mutual aid. Engine 8-11, Engine 8-15 responding 00:54."

"Ladder 8-52 on location. Switching to channel two!"

"8-52 on location 00:54."

Robby looked over his shoulder and saw the lights from the truck reflecting in the windows of the surrounding houses as the ladder truck made the turn into the cul-de-sac. Ted moved quickly to direct the arriving equipment by standing in the center of the court.

As 8-52 pulled into the cul-de-sac, Ted waved his arms and pointed to where he wanted the truck. Nodding to Ted, the driver already knew where to put the truck. Swinging the truck hard to the left, then spinning the wheel quickly, he swung it to the right. Turning the ladder truck 160 degrees in the tight cul-de-sac, it faced almost back out the way it had just come from, positioned so that the driver could back the rear of the ladder truck just to the side of the driveway. As the truck slowed, the driver quickly began reversing without stopping. In the instant the truck was changing directions, the two jump seat doors opened in unison, one on each side, firefighters ejecting onto the scene, each quickly moving to guide the truck as it backed into position. The loud beeping of the backup alarm echoed against the surrounding houses while the two men clad in turn-out gear added to the chaotic scene.

The ladder truck moved into position with the back corner of the truck was almost even with the side of the house. This would allow the stabilizers to be deployed and the ladder to be extended the full 100 feet.

Royce and Steve, preparing to go into the burning house, finished positioning the hose, face masks hanging from the silver regulator over their hearts, swinging back and forth as they finished straightening the hose. They had dragged it in a wide arc from the engine, across the driveway and up the front steps of the burning house, allowing them to manhandle the heavy hose as they pulled it through the house.

With it in position the two stood at the base of the steps, one on each side of the hose. In unison the two finished the ritual of getting ready. Helmet off and between the legs. Mask over the head, head bent back, the mask sliding down the face until the top of the mask touched the nose, then pressing against the face, sliding back up, pushing hair out of the way to ensure a tight seal. Right hand holding the mask, fingers wrapped around the black corrugated hose, the left face strap tightened. Switching hands, the right strap is tightened. With the mask on, the end of the corrugated hose is placed into their palms. Each one inhaling to verify that there is a good seal, the mask pressed against their faces. Helmets back on, they were ready to go into the inferno.

Nodding to each other, they connected the end of the face mask hose to the regulator and took a breath. A breathing sound like Darth Vader signifying readiness.

Royce reached down and grabbed the nozzle. Steve moved directly behind him, wrapping his right arm around the hose, pinching it against his body with his arm. In position, the two began to go up the last step. With one last glance around the fire scene they saw Ladder 8-52 backing up to the front of the house. The two disappeared into the darkness. They went through the door, now unable to communicate with the outside until they came back out heightened the ever increasing high. This was the fire call they dreamed about. A house burning down. A helpless person trapped inside. The thought of rescuing someone was intoxicating.

Inside, Royce led them up the steps to the second floor of the house.

As they reached the top of the stairs, Royce turned the team to the right, facing down the hallway. An eerie light occupied the house. A flickering red glow with a mixture of incandescent light from the fixtures left on as the occupants fled. The sound of their breathing mixed in with the beeping of the smoke detectors.

The process of working the way down the twenty-five-foot hallway was cumbersome. Pausing at the top of the stairs the two worked together to pull another thirty feet of ridged hose into the house, pushing it to the left opposite of the fire. Doing this would give then enough to get into the burning room. Pulling the water erected hose in a straight line was much easier than trying to pull it around a corner.

With the hose in position Royce turned and put his helmet against Steve's, taping their foreheads like two lovers pressing together in an intimate conversation. "Skip the first bedroom, go right to the fire, we can circle back when we knock it down," he yelled through his mask. This was a practice the two of them developed over their time fighting fires together. It was only used when there was a decision to deviate from normal procedures and insured that there was no misunderstanding. Normally during a search and rescue they would check the first room quickly then move on, always turning right to make sure they didn't get lost.

"Right behind," Steve yelled back through his mask, crouching down on their hands and knees, ready to move down the hallway.

The two men moved down the dark, smoke-filled hall, pulling the hose as they went. They could feel the heat. The smoke was rolling down the narrow corridor, filling the house. The layer of smoke hung from the ceiling, stratifying. It created a ghostly barrier, a foot above their heads.

As they moved, Steve rose from a crouched position just enough to get his head into the layer of smoke above. As his head disappeared into the smoke, he could feel the heat rising around his head, warming the small patches of exposed skin. This caused the high to increase, intensifying the rush.

"What the fuck?!" Royce yelled feeling Steve rising behind him.

"They're going to vent. Won't see this again soon," Steve responded with giddy laughter.

With this Royce joined him in raising his head into the smoke. Heads and shoulders disappearing into the dark smoke. The thick smoke engulfed them. Blinded them. Cutting them off from the world. In the darkness of the smoke, the only sound was the loud whoosh of the air being drawn from the SCOT pack followed by the quieter sound of their partner breathing with the ever-present sound of the smoke detector, continually warning of danger.

Chapter 11

"Engine 8-14 on location, pick'in up hydrant."

8-14 went flying past the cul-de-sac and continued toward Joppa Farm Road. Mel, the driver, and Jeff the officer, were looking for the closest fire hydrant. Making a right onto Joppa Farm Road, Mel slowed as the engine approached the hydrant allowing one of the firefighters to jump off. Watching the firefighter in the passenger jump seat spring from the engine, he accelerated quickly making a U-turn in the middle of the empty road. Circling back, the engine came to a quick stop at the fire hydrant.

"8-14 on location 01:01. 8-14 go to channel two."

Fred, the senior firefighter, waited by the hydrant as the engine circled around and came to a stop with the back of the engine lined up with the hydrant. He sprang the spanner wrench free from the clip on the back step and shoved it into his turn-out coat pocket. Then he grabbed the hydrant wrench next to it. He climbed onto the diamond plate step and grabbed the three-inch hose lying in the back of the engine and pulled out one section. Dragging the hose over to the hydrant, he wrapped the hose around the fire hydrant, sat on the ground, and placed both feet against the hose, pinching it against the hydrant and yelling "Line secure" as he waved with one hand. His heart was pounding, barely able to breath, the rush blasting his body. *I could tear the hydrant out of the ground if I push too hard*, he thought to himself. The feeling of being a superhuman engulfed him.

8-14 turned into the cul-de-sac, hose flying out of the bed with a metallic "clink" as the couplings slammed into the ground. Pulling along the right side of 8-52, 8-14 circled around the street. It stopped just forward of 8-12. As it slowed the firefighter in the driver side jump seat came off the engine and ran around the back. Pulling off another section of hose he quickly disconnected the coupling, leaving the remaining hose in the bed. He pressed the silver button on the back step twice, signaling the driver he was done. 8-14 pulled forward and away from 8-12. The firefighter stood with the end of the hose in his hand, staring at the burning house.

The firefighter was new. He had only been with the company about four months. His excitement was palpable. It was obvious that this was the first time that he had laid a line at a working fire. It was his first time at a working fire. He stood frozen, unable to move. Unable to make his mind work.

Robby searched his memory for his name. "Firefighter!" he barked at the scared and confused firefighter standing there.

The newbie, eyes wide with excitement, was lost in the rush. He could only stare at the house on fire. He did not notice the people. He did not see the engine. He stared at the window of the burning house. Lost in the rush. Desiring to run into the burning building. Scared to move. Frozen with indecision. He was captivated by the big fire. Entrapped by the rush. Desiring the feeling. Too scared to move, not remembering what to do. he stood frozen. This was his first rush. It was overpowering. He could not control it. The rush consumed him.

Robby, still trying to get his attention yelled, "Hey, bring the hose over here!" he commanded.

While Engine 8-14 was pulling the supply line toward the fire scene, the firefighter at the hydrant moved into action. Using the hydrant wrench, he loosened the cap and then, busting with energy from the surge, spun the cap off with enough force that it flew off the threads. The chain attaching it to the hydrant snapped taunt, creating a metallic twang as it was flung by the momentum. His mind focused on the steps that had been drilled into his head during basic training, moving through the tasks with precision and speed. He knelt onto one knee, the cap swung at the end of the chain, striking him in the forearm. Without noticing the pain, he continued with his work. Quickly running his gloved hand inside the opening, checking for any debris, he then stood and placed the wrench on the top of the hydrant. Turning it one turn, water began to flow out of the hydrant. Satisfied that no debris would clog the hose or the pumper, he closed the valve and connected the hose. After the hose was connected, he stood and looked toward 8-12, waiting anxiously for the signal. He took a moment to feel the rush within. In his mind he knew that it was his actions that would save everyone. The water he would send to the scene would be the reason that the fire would be out. The rush increased with the thought.

Standing next to the hydrant, he searched the area, his eyes straining to see the scene located around the corner, the rush staying constant within him. He was so close. He could see himself charging into the building. Attacking the fire. The dry heat suddenly becoming a smothering steam bath as the water from the hose flashed into steam, taking the heat from the fire. He would be the one to put out the fire and save the house. This is what he wanted, the rush he craved. Secretly fantasizing about being the hero of the day.

Ted and Mark, the lieutenant from 8-52, were gathered to coordinate the crews.

Jeff, the officer in charge of 8-14, came over to the two and asked, "What's up Ted?" with a nod of the head.

"Got two inside attacking. Mark, get 8-52 set for an aerial attack. When the roof is opened, we may have to drown it. Get your crew on the roof with the K-12 and ventilate." Pointing at the other blue helmet, he continued, "Jeff, have Mel, with Robby to get the supply line set up. As soon as your crew gets clear have them report back to command for orders." Spinning on his heels and heading back to Robby signaled the other two that it was time to act.

Jeff signaled Mel with a wave of his hand for him to go over to Robby at 8-12.

Mel understood instantly. He took a few minutes to go back to the 8-14 to secure the engine. He left the radio on Channel One to allow the crews to keep up with other fire calls.

Mark flagged the two crew members from 8-52 and laid out the task assigned to them. The two crew members launched with a purpose. While one was getting a ladder from 8-52 the second one retrieved the K-12 saw from the compartment. The idea was to take as little equipment out of service as possible. Everything would be taken from 8-12 and 8-52, leaving the other engines ready to be placed back in service if needed.

The K-12 is a gas-powered circular saw used to cut almost anything. It is exceptional on cutting openings in any kind of roof as well as the ability to cut steel bars and car metal.

The ladder crew was busy setting the truck, carefully placing the steel pads under the outriggers to prevent the heavy truck from sinking into the asphalt.

This would allow the 100-foot ladder to extend to any position over the house, allowing water to be showered onto the fire.

Robby was still trying to get the newbie's attention focused on the fire engine and bring the supply hose over. Getting frustrated, Robby pulled a glove off his hand and threw it at the zombielike firefighter's head. As the glove was flying through the air Robby remembered the firefighter's name. "KIRK!"

Somewhere in the distance Kirk heard his name being called. As he was starting to come out of his daze, something hit him in the side of the face. "What the hell?" he said as he was coming back into full awareness.

"Kirk! Bring the damn hose over here NOW!"

Becoming focused, Kirk moved into action, running over and shoved the hose at him.

Grabbing the hose Robby quickly attached it to the pump panel. Turning halfway around he flipped the hose to straighten it.

Mel was just approaching 8-12 when Bobby said, "Give it a blast for me."

With a quick nod, Mel climbed into the cab of 8-12 and grabbed the cord for the air horn. Pulling on the cord he sounded a loud blast, counted to two, released, counted to two, and pulled the cord a second time, letting the horn shatter the night for another two count.

Headlights flashed across the houses as the speakers on the engines erupted. "Chief 8-2 on location."

Inside, the two were making their way to the end of the hall, feeling along the wall, trying to identify their location by feel and memory. Looking for the doorframe and the indentation of the doorway breaking the flow of the smooth wall that their right hands ran along. This doorway was in the middle of the hallway. The door that they were looking for should be at the end of the hallway.

The sound of the horn launched Fred into action. This was the signal he had been waiting for. Opening the valve on the top of the fire hydrant, releasing the water. The hose wiggled and popped as it filed.

The expanding hose disappearing around the corner and into the darkness, Fred began to jog along the length, following it to check for kinks as he made his way back to the engine.

In the back of the house the crew of 8-52 had set the ladder and was climbing onto the roof, working their way over the peak to the opposite side, above of the burning room.

Robby had the pump ready. He was waiting for Royce to open the nozzle and allow the pressurized water out, feeling the vibration of the pump as it strained, waiting to release the water.

Inside the burning house Royce, reaching the door at the end of the hall, gently pushed on the base of the door. It was closed. He needed to reach up and turn the knob to push open the door. This is one of the most dangerous situations during a working fire. If the conditions inside the room are right, when the door is opened oxygen will rush into the room and causing an explosion. One big enough to kill.

The two men inside crouched low. Knowing the danger and the possibility of an explosion, they pressed themselves low to the floor to allow the blast to go over their head. Royce reached up and grabbed the door, now ready to push the door open.

On the roof the K-12 roared to life as the crew prepared to cut a hole. This would allow heat, smoke, and steam to escape from the house.

The saw cut through the roof like butter. The two were careful to stay back from the area being cut. Creating a fall hazard for themselves was not in the plan.

Inside Royce pushed. The door flew open. The two readied for the blast that would follow.

Nothing.

Royce crawled through the door. Looking quickly to take in as much as possible. The orange glow through the thick smoke in the room. The glow was everywhere. It was all around.

Steve, right behind, watching the shaded orange dancing in the darkness.

The rush consumed the two. Royce hesitated for just a moment to bathe in the feeling. They were both holding their breath.

Royce opened the nozzle and whipped the hose around the room, spraying water into the heat. Water flashing to steam. Absorbing the heat. Taking away a part of the fire. One gallon of water creates seventeen hundred cubic feet of steam. The room is approximately one thousand cubic feet. The gallons of water coming from the nozzle displacing the oxygen in the room and removing the heat caused the glow of the fire to disappear in the darkness.

Robby felt the hose come to life as the water flowed. The sound of the pump changing as water was pumped though the hose.

Steve slapped Royce on the shoulder and yelled, "Searching," and disappeared into the darkness.

The adrenaline fueled him as he moved away from the safety of the hose, moving sightless into the room. Starting to the right, along the wall, he searched the room. Right hand against the wall, slowly moving forward, sweeping the floor and in front of him with his left arm. Stretching as far across the room as he could without letting go of the wall with his right hand.

His right arm bumped into something. Two posts coming up from the floor, a top. It felt like a desk. Sweeping underneath, he felt the wall, the other side. Just past the desk he bumped into something else. Low to the ground his shoulder bumped into something firm. Running his hands over the surface he figured out that it is a chair. Probably sitting in the corner of the room. Sweeping his hand under the chair he searched. Nothing.

Outside, Fred arrived at 8-12. Jeff instructed the crew from 8-14 to get a supply line from 8-12 to 8-52. This would provide water for the deluge nozzle on the end of the ladder. Grabbing a supply line from the bed of 8-12 the two began dragging the hose across the cul-de-sac.

Bill, the driver of 8-52, had finished setting the outriggers of the ladder truck and unlatched the ladder bed, and was slowly raising the ladder straight above the truck and turning it toward the house. He would then turn the ladder to swing over the house, extending from the back of the truck.

Fred, followed by an unsure Kirk, dragged the hose to Bill, who was preparing to connect it to the ladder truck.

In a fire, children are scared. They hide. They run from the firefighters. Steve knew that a fireman, in full turn-out gear, is a monster. Fear of the fire, the monster and the unknown lead children to hide in cabinets, under beds, in closets. They try to hide from the monsters.

Reaching into the seat of the chair Steve felt what could be a blanket covering something. Pulling the wet blanket onto the floor and reaching back into the chair, feeling, hoping it was empty. His gloved hand landed on something on the chair, hidden under the blanket. As he wrapped his fingers around the unmoving discovery, he knew in his heart it was an arm.

The crew on the roof was making the second cut. Smoke and steam starting to pour from the incision made by the saw.

Chief Butler parked his truck and was pulling on his turn-out coat as he passed Robby and Mel at Engine 8-12.

Pulling the lifeless body from the chair, Steve pulled it close to his facemask trying to confirm his worst fears. His heart beating fast, knowing what he would see, not wanting it to be the dead child. As the limp body came into view Steve saw a hole where the face of the child should be. Melted plastic instead of the face of a child. It was a life-sized doll that had been aimlessly tossed onto the chair.

Steve yelled into his mask, "A doll!"

There was a noticeable silence in the room as if everything froze. Steve could see clouds of steam and smoke frozen in space. The room seemed to become a vacuum. There was a bright glow coming from the other side of the room.

The split second of quiet and stillness ended with an earth-shattering BOOM!

Everything went black.

Chapter 12

A fireball erupted from the bedroom where the two firefighters focused the attack. The explosion was deafening. The noise drowned out the engines, radios, the yelling between the different crews. Several people dropped to the ground as if reacting to an attack. The two men on the roof were gone. The crew setting the hose on the ladder truck were crouched next to 8-52. Robby and Mel were safely protected by Engine 8-12. Chief Butler was staring at the house from behind the back of 8-12.

Ted, Jeff, and Mark were caught in the open between 8-12 and 8-52. As the explosion erupted, they turned their backs to the house and squatted down as glass and debris came flying out the window above the garage.

The three slowly rose from a squat into a low crouch as they turned to look at the house. The normally rock-solid team, which knew what to do in any situation, was shaken. Focus and direction lost. They just crouched in the cul-de-sac staring at the house, quickly glancing at each other, not knowing what to do. This kind of explosion usually meant injuries. It was bad.

The rush completely changed. It no longer came from the joy and excitement of facing danger; it had now changed to fear of survival. This was a rush not felt by the crews before. The blast reinforcing the reality that people could die. They could die. The invincible firemen were only mortals. Instead of the rush giving superhuman strength, it only reinforced the feeling to run.

Chief Butler, attempting to regain the command of the scene, started barking orders in a staccato voice. "Is everyone OK?"

The officers, now standing, were looking around, searching for the crews. Seeing Robby and Mel standing by 8-12, Ted tried to get eye contact with one of them.

Robby and Mel looked at each other, making sure they were both OK. Looking to where the officers were clustered, he found Ted and gave him a nod, indicating that they were OK.

The three firefighters by 8-52 waved at the officers, indicating they were OK as they tried to return to what they were doing.

Chief Butler began talking as he urged the officers toward the safety of Engine 8-12. "Mel, get with Dispatch. I want all roads closed and get some police here for crowd control. Shut down Haverhill in both directions. Push these folks back to Haverhill across the street. Until we figure out what blew, distance is safety. Where do we have people?"

In an unsteady voice Ted answered, "Crew on roof, crew inside."

"Mark, go check the back of the house, report to 8-12. Robby, keep the pressure up. Let me know if the flow changes. Who's still inside?"

"Steve and Royce."

"Any contact?"

Robby replied, "No. Waters not flowing."

"Get them out! I want a positive head count and injury report."

Mark disappeared around the side of the house, searching for his crew.

Robby changed the pressure on the fire hose, dipping it from 145 pounds of pressure to 90, then quickly raising it back up and then repeating it two more times. Three pressure drops. That was the sign to get the hell out. It was used only in emergencies and impending disasters. Roof collapse, loss of containment, injury. When you were inside and got the signal, there was no second thought. No hesitation. Only one reaction. RUN!!

Robby focused intensely on the pump panel. Allowing nothing else into his mind. By focusing on the chrome panel and gauges he blocked the emotion of having two of his best friends at the center of an explosion. He only saw the pump panel. He naturally quarantined his emotions, locking them away before the dark and debilitating thoughts could enter his mind.

Mark had circled around the front of 8-12 and ran to the house. Running in a low crouch he chose the path to keep himself as far away from the burning side as possible, around the side opposite the fire to reach the back of the house. Clearing the back, he quickly scanned for anything on the lawn. Specifically, injured firemen blown off the roof. Not seeing any, he moved into the center of the yard until he could see the roof. Straining his eyes against the shifting light he searched the roof for the crew. Searching for what seemed an eternity he located two men splayed across the roof a few feet from the peak on the back side of the house. "Jason, Jack, are you OK?"

They had either crawled or been blown over the peak and were lying against the asphalt shingles on the back side of the house. From the positions of the bodies John was guessing they had been blown back down the roof. Unmoving. Unconscious? Maybe dead?

No response. His mouth was dry. No one was moving. Everything disappeared from his world except the two men clinging to each other on the roof.

Shit, shit, shit was all he could think. His mind froze as he stared at the lifeless bodies lying out of his reach. Unable to perform basic checks he was relegated to diagnosing the injuries from fifty feet away. "Goddamn it, answer me!" he yelled.

No response. Unable to take his eyes off the two bodies, he was frozen. Unable to react. Unable to think. In that instant he saw the men unconscious, injured, maybe dead, he was reduced to an observer. Useless. His emotions were starting to overwhelm him. Panic was creeping into his mind. The adrenaline surging through him only yelled, "RUN!" in his mind. In seconds he would lose all control. He needed to get control. His mind grasping for something to do. An action to take. Something to break the paralysis of his mind and body as he stared at the two men.

Trying to decide the next action – run to get a ladder, yell again, or just have a breakdown – he began to focus of his welling anger, with a surge of tears forming in his eyes, more for his own pity than the loss of his friends. *They have to be OK* kept flashed through his mind. "If they are dead, I don't know what I'll do," he pleaded to himself.

He knew he needed to regain control. Shifting his brain from his injured crew, his friends, he began to focus on the situation. Two people injured after an explosion. They were no longer his friends. They were victims. He removed the personal feelings from his mind. They were faceless, civilian blobs, requiring him to do the impossible and rescue them. Burying the emotions of fear, failure, loss, and inadequacy deep into the special place in his mind that he kept those disabling feelings; he began to regain control. The demons in his mind that were crippling him had been locked somewhere deep inside. Locked into his dungeon, to be dealt with later or never at all. He was now regaining control.

He started to assess the situation. Two men injured after an explosion. Unmoving on the roof. He needed to get to them. "Ladder. Need to get on the roof," he began to methodically think through the situation.

As he struggled to keep control of the emotional demons locked within, his anger welled, momentarily starting to lose control, using all his will to fight back tears. Looking at the bodies, he saw one foot move.

The lifeless bodies on the roof came to life. Slowly at first. Cautiously shifting a foot. Moving a hand away from the head it was protecting. Head moving side to side, checking for danger. Finally sitting up and looking at the surroundings.

"Damn it, are you guys OK!" Mark yelled again.

"Think so," Jason replied. "Knocked the crap out of us."

"Move to the other end of the roof. I'm gonna reset the ladder for you to get down." It was seven seconds from the time he rounded the corner of the house until the two on the roof began to move. It felt like hours. The relief that Mark felt was not in the men being OK. It was that he was saved from facing the demons locked in his brain fighting to break out. The rush was welling inside of him again as the idea of him rescuing the trapped crew from the roof released a surge. The high he was craving returned to his body. The addiction once again being satisfied. The adrenaline gives the strength to push the demons in his mind's dungeon. Locked away, for now.

Ted had moved around between the engine and the house, his foot firmly planted on the hose that Royce and Steve had taken with them. Hoping and praying to feel the hose reacting to movement 150 feet away. The sign that they were coming out.

Chief Butler continued, "Bill, let's get the ladder set and spraying. We are moving from direct attack to surround and drown."

Turning to Ted he said, "Get another line going. Hit the front of the house, in the window, house next door, garage."

Ted yelled commands to Fred and Kirk to get set up. The crew once more moving with a purpose. Kirk was frozen, overwhelmed with the situation.

Jeff pushed him aside and yelled "go help with the ladder truck" as he went to help Fred.

Inside the burning house fire had splattered around the small room. Steve began to move slowly, small pieces of the house falling off him. Trying to get oriented he sat up and put his hand on his face. Mask still there. Breathe in.

He felt the air fill his lungs. He closed his eyes for a second to savor the taste of the bottled air in his mouth. His lungs. Something was different. He felt the breathing, but he couldn't hear his own breathing. The Darth Vader sound of air being drawn from the tank was gone.

He looked around the room. Trying to remember what happened. Where was he? The fire? The girl inside? He and Royce went inside to find her. He found the doll.

The explosion!

Royce! Where the hell was Royce? Moving quickly, he felt around the dark room finding a wall. Taking a split second to get oriented he began moving to the left, the fingers of his left hand floating along the wall. His right searching into the room, sweeping back and forth as he crawled along, intently searching. He found the desk, now lying on its side, and kept moving. After what felt like crawling for miles, his knee found what he was looking for. Placing his hand over on the top, he followed the hose to his right, hopefully into the room. Letting go of the solid wall providing the anchor in the chaos, he disappeared into the center of the room, hoping that Royce was at the end, or at least somewhere near.

Running through his training in his mind helped him focus and find a mental anchor. Search a room. Enter move to right. Always turn right. No matter where you go in the pitch-black building you always go in one direction. Keep going to the right and you will always complete the circle and go around the room, never duplicating the search.

Only once did this method fail. One of the senior firefighters, Bill, had been assigned a search detail in a possible house fire. He was searching a room and began by turning to the right. He found a door. Entering the doorway, he turned right. In a few feet he hit a corner and turned left. A few more feet and hit another corner. He turned left at the corner again. Crawling along the floor a few more feet and he hit another corner. Turning left and moving forward he knew that he would be coming to the same doorway that he came in. It was obviously a closet that he was crawling around. In a few more feet, he found another corner. Turning left he began to think he had miscounted turns. He should have found a door after the fourth ninety-degree turn.

Outside the room the other part of the crew had found the source of the smoke. It was a florescent light ballast that had smoked. It was an insignificant fire and they were finishing up when they heard Bill screaming from down the hall.

When the others followed the screaming to Bill, they found him trapped in the bedroom closet. When he entered the closet, the door closed behind him. There was no trim around the door and with his gloves on he couldn't feel the door in the wall. After making two laps around the closet he started yelling, on the verge of panic, until someone found him.

The great Bill Rescue was still retold whenever possible. And everyone still laughed their asses off. *I hope they will be laughing at Royce and I when this is over*, Steve thought.

The small room that was an adventure just a few minutes ago had now become the worst nightmare. Alone, in the dark, only the hose in his hand to anchor him to the exit, he kept moving into the room. The other member of the crew was lost, maybe dead. Unknown damage to the house. Moving through dark, knowing he could go straight into a hole in the floor and fall, breaking his back as he landed on the family's car below.

The loneliness was unbearable. He yelled into his mask, "Royce!" He couldn't hear himself screaming. How would he find his partner? Sealed off from sight and sound, alone in the darkness. Determined to find his partner, his friend, or to die trying.

The ringing in his ears started slowly building. Moving his hand along the round hose he found the nozzle. Relieved that he had followed it in the right direction, he picked up the hose, tucking it under his right arm, gripping the hose between his ribs and his crooked arm, wincing in surprise at the pain in his side. *Must have bruised my ribs*. Rocking back and sitting on his legs, bracing himself for the push of the hose, he opened the nozzle and sprayed around the room, knocking down the fire. Steam clouding his limited view even more. The flow of the nozzle grabbed some of the smoke, clearing the air around the floor enough so he could see a few feet. Remembering how he learned to breathe off the nozzle in basic training, he recognized the Venturi effect caused by the flow of water as it affected the air and smoke in the room.

Desperately sweeping his eyes around and reaching with his left arm, he continued to feel for Royce lying on the floor. Scanning the room with his eyes, then sweeping the floor with his left hand, then his right. Crawling forward two steps on his hands and knees, he repeated the search. Through the steam, smoke, darkness, and debris he saw the still shape of Royce lying half on his side, face down a few feet in front of him.

"Royce, Royce." Reaching his partner, he knew he would not be responsive. "Shit, Shit, Shit!" His rescue training took over.

On his knees he scooted up to Royce's back. Leaning over he began working up the victim. With the heavy coat, he couldn't tell if he was bleeding. Couldn't hear if he was breathing. First thing was to roll him onto his back. Moving into position he carefully reached his gloved left hand around the face. He set up the right hand on his chest, slowly rolled him over, trying to keep the head in alignment with the spine in case there were any neck injuries.

As Royce rolled, his body flopped without any reaction. Steve knew that he was unconscious. Quickly running his hands over Royce, he tried to determine the extent of his injuries.

Robby felt the hose open and flow inside the house. At least someone there was alive. Hopefully they were not hurt. The water flowed for about ten seconds and then stopped again.

With a flash of relief, he yelled, "GOT FLOW!"

"OK let's get the ambo staged. Even if they're not hurt, I want them checked out. Get another crew here to take the attack," Chief Butler barked at Robby.

Robby reached for the mic hanging on the pump panel and issued commands, "8-12 to 8-92, come to command for possible injuries. Dispatch, have next engine in send full crew to command."

The surge of excitement flooded the entire scene with the announcement of activity in the house. The moments of indecision and shock were gone. The fear of loss momentarily restrained, the high began flowing back into their bodies, fueling each of them, giving back the rush that had been briefly taken away.

The two men on the roof left the K-12 and were working their way down the ladder. Their arms and legs were shaking as they slowly climbed down from the roof. The rush caused by a mixture of survival, excitement, and fear was pushing their bodies to the extreme.

No one ever talks about it, but an overdose of adrenaline can cause the human body to go into shock. To shut down.

Inside Steve was continuing the assessment of his unconscious partner. Starting at his head he ran his glove-covered hands gently down trying to determine any injuries. His gloved fingers ran over the top of his helmet. Finding the safety shield pulled up on the helmet, his fingers continued to where the air mask and brim came together, covering his face. Moving his fingers down the face mask, he realized that he would not feel anything of value against the plastic shield protecting his partner's face, until his fingers fell into a hole in the plastic and brushed against the flesh of his face. The protective plastic was gone, exposing him to the smoke filling the room.

Moving his gloved fingers carefully over the area where the face mask should be, Steve felt from side to side. His fingers found the edge of the mask, the leather of his glove snagging on the jagged edge. Moving his fingers up down and to the other side, he began to build the picture in his mind. The left upper side of the mask was gone. His gloves were slick with some sort of liquid.

"8-92 on location."

"8-92 on location 01:09."

"8-92, Bring the wagon up to 8-12." Robby's voice erupted over the speakers.

More people had gathered from the surrounding houses. Two state trooper cars were at the intersection of the cul-de-sac and the main street. Officers trying to herd the people to the side of the street away from the fire scene. One county sheriff's car was parked at the intersection of Joppa Farm and Haverhill Road, blocking any traffic from coming in.

The ambulance moved its way past the trooper's car and into the cul-de-sac, trying to avoid the fire hose and ladder truck. The burning house grabbed the attention of the ambo crew as they rolled toward the house. Both were also trained and experienced firefighters. Seeing the fire, the rush engulfed them. Forgetting for a moment that they were the medical crew, they both fantasized about fighting the fire themselves. Thinking of the rush as they entered the burning house. The feel of the moist heat crawling across their flesh as the water from the hose turned to steam. Thinking of the feel of the flames and heat on their faces.

Chief Butler was waving at the ambo signaling them to pull up next to 8-12. His movements showed just a touch of panic as he flung his arms indicating where he wanted them to stage.

John pulled Ambo 8-92 next to 8-12, leaving plenty of room to maneuver manpower and equipment.

Darcy had the door open and her right foot hanging out as the ambo slid into place. She was out of the cab before the ambo had come to a stop. "What's up?"

Without looking at her, Chief Butler said, "Explosion, two still inside, two on roof. Waiting for status on the roof team."

"Who?" Darcy demanded.

Three firefighters emerged from behind the house. Mel was the first to spot them. He gave a sharp whistle to get the attention of the chief, pointing his chin in the direction of the crew indicating to Chief Butler to look in that direction.

Both Darcy and the chief glanced at the crew, seeing that they were all walking.

Looking back into Chief Butler's eyes, Darcy demanded again, "Who is inside?" The fear welling inside her. She knew who was on the engine. The two that were missing.

Larry knew that the news would slam her hard. These two were her favorites. No one knew why, but she protected them like a mother bear. "It's Royce and Steve."

"Any movement?"

"Yeah, hose flowed for about ten seconds then shut off."

Inside, Steve quickly continued to triage. Running his hands down Royce's torso, legs and arms almost like searching him. He was looking for any major injuries. After the initial body check, he realized that any more triage would be useless. He couldn't tell if Royce was breathing or not. He couldn't do CPR inside the house. He needed to get Royce out of there.

The steam and smoke had cleared enough to get his bearings on the room and their location. Through the haze he found the door. Making the decision to get the fuck out, he prepared to move Royce.

"When they come out, I want them checked out," Chief Butler was instructing Darcy. "If they're even bruised, get them out of here."

Nodding at the chief she began giving instructions, "John, stretcher, O2, and med kit. I'm gonna check on Jason and Jack." Waving to the three men working their way across the lawn, she shouted, "Back step of 8-12."

Happily sitting down on the step, Jack's hands were visibly shaking at the close call he had just experienced.

"How you guys doing?" Darcy asked, and she looked the three of them over.

The two that were on the roof mumbled that they were OK as Darcy began working on them. Taking the penlight from her pocket she shined it in Jack's eyes first, then moved to Jason.

Inside Steve positioned himself straddling Royce, feet at his waist. Reaching down he grabbed the front of his turn-out coat. Preparing himself he rocked forward and back once, twice, an on the third time he put all his weight and muscles into pulling Royce off the floor. In one smooth action he pulled him from lying on the floor to almost standing and then Steve ducked his body to place his right shoulder into Royce's abdomen, letting his torso and head fall across his back. Wrapping Royce's legs with both arms he stood. Stopping before he was standing straight up, staying slightly bent at the waist, he instinctively compensated for the added weight, steadying himself to keep the new combined center of gravity above his legs. Royce secured; Steve was ready to make the run out of the building with his injured partner. No way to tell them he was coming out. He would just have to keep going.

On the back of 8-12 Darcy was examining the firefighters. Kneeling in front of Jack she asked, "Any pain?"

Shaking his head, he mumbled, "Uh-uh."

Taking both hands in hers, she instructed, "Squeeze."

He gave a slight squeeze to the paramedic's hands.

"Squeeze like you're a man. My three-year-old niece squeezes harder than that." She was doing more than just checking his motor skills for any signs of injury. She was seeing how his mental state was. Going into shock was a major concern. From the close call on the roof and the adrenaline. He was close.

With Royce over his shoulder, Steve began the walk down out of the room and down the hallway. He imagined himself bursting out of the door to the house, an unconscious firefighter over his shoulder. Emerging onto the steps of the house. The people watching seeing him bringing out the wounded. The other firefighters looking on with admiration as Steve and Steve alone saved the injured comrade. This would be the talk of the fire house for years to come. The high was pushing him to the edge of control.

Carefully stepping over debris in the room he began the long walk down the dark hallway.

Fred and Jeff were preparing to attack the house from the outside. While the ambo was arriving, they pulled the hundred-foot attack line from 8-12 and were in the process of straightening the hose.

8-52 was preparing to raise the ladder and attack. Robby and Mel pulled a three-inch supply line from 8-12 and attached it between the two pump panels. Mel had drug Kirk along and taken over the ladder truck. They were preparing to attack with the aerial and spray water on the outside of the house.

Robby was carefully monitoring the crews and hoses. As the two crews had the hoses ready to go, he was charging the lines with water.

Steve quickly cleared the bedroom doorway and started to move down the hall, following the hose with a foot on either side. He would be able to move quickly. The only thing to trip over was the fire hose leading out of the house and with it between his legs, he knew just where it was. Coming to the top of the stairs he knew that this would be the most dangerous place. Balancing an extra 190 pounds of dead weight, on top of the extra weight he was carrying, going down the stairs would be difficult. In the room and hallway all he had to do to regain balance was lean against a wall. The stairs did not provide this safety. If he started to fall, he would roll down the stairs with Royce on top of him.

Balancing at the top of the stairs Steve grabbed the handrail on the wall with his left hand and leaned toward it. He took the first step down. Wobbling a bit but readjusting his body to compensate, he moved down the next five steps. Reaching the landing he stopped for a moment to regain his footing, check the positioning of Royce on his shoulder and reflect on the grand entrance he was about to make. His status as a hero assured with the rescue of the firefighter. He would also be able to torment Royce for years about getting him out of the house.

Darcy had turned her attention to Jason and was running through the assessment.

Fred and Jeff were getting ready to spray water on the outside of the house in hopes of getting the fire under control.

Robby was managing the water flow to three hoses, waiting for them to start the flow.

Ladder 8-52 was set up and had raised the ladder off of the bed of the truck. Bill was rotating it around to extend over the house. The hose from 8-

12 had been connected and was standing by to supply water to the deluge nozzle attached to the ladder. Kirk and Mel were waiting at the step of the truck, ready to scramble up the ladder the second it was positioned.

Steve kicked the half-closed door of the house open from the inside and triumphantly stepped onto the concrete landing. Pausing for half a second, trying to look around through the mask covered with smoke and soot. Carrying Royce down the steps of the house, trying to decide where to take him, he saw a movement through the haze. The world silent in his ears.

The front door of the house exploded outward as the firefighters emerged from the inferno. One being carried by the other. It was impossible to tell who was being carried. The closest firefighters leapt toward the two coming down the steps.

Jeff and Fred dropped the hose they were preparing to use and rushed to the two.

Darcy began running up the drive to get to them as fast as she could, leaving the three sitting on the back of the engine.

John was pushing the ambulance stretcher toward the driveway, hitting the curb to the driveway as the others reached the two firefighters.

Fred and Jeff each went to a side. Fred yelled, "Flip him over and we'll take him."

Overcome with exhaustion and the overdose of adrenaline, Steve lost his footing and twisted his right foot on the final step. He collapsed to one knee as the two came and grabbed him. Starting to fall forward, he felt Royce being taken off his shoulder.

When Royce was off his shoulder, Steve fell onto his hands, holding himself on all fours.

Lifting the injured firefighter from the shoulder Jeff and Fred lay him on the ground.

Ted had made his way to the steps, pushing Jeff away to look into the face of Royce. Greeted only by a dead stare and a face covered in blood. He froze. Death he had seen many times. Even people he knew. He had never looked into the face of a dead firefighter.

Darcy pulled Ted out of the way to begin examining Royce. With one look she realized that there was nothing that she or anyone would be able to do.

Steve had sat up, moving his weight to kneeling on his knees. In one swipe he removed his facemask and helmet. The helmet falling silently to the ground. He moved to where Royce was laying.

Before he got to him, he realized that he was dead.

Royce's face mask was broken open. There was something sticking out of his face just to the left of the center of his right eye between the bridge of the nose and what was left of his eye. Blood covered his face. His eyes were open and staring into the sky.

Steve leaned to the side and vomited.

Seeing what was going on Jeff grabbed Fred and ran to the hose that was left lying on the driveway.

John arrived with the stretcher, placing his hand on Darcy's shoulder. Letting her know he was there.

She reached up and put her hand on his. The two stared into the dead face of the fallen firefighter.

With muscle memory reaction, she removed her trauma shears and cut the SCOT pack straps and the corrugated hose to the face mask. "Get him on the stretcher and into the ambo."

Looking up she saw Steve. Tears were streaking clean lines through the dirt and grime on his face. "Steve. Steve. Come on, let's get to the ambo."

8-52 had the ladder raised and swung over the roof. Jason was at the top of the ladder and opened the nozzle, flooding the hole in the roof.

Steve did not hear. He could not stop the tears. He knew he had not been able to save his partner.

Darcy got up and grabbed Steve under the chin, lifting his face from Royce's into hers. "Steve, let's go. You need to get into the ambo."

Steve stared at Darcy. Watched her lips move. All he could hear was a ringing in his ears and some muffled noises. He knew she was saying something.

Tightening her grip on his chin she tried to get him into action. "Steve. Now."

"I can't hear you," he yelled

She stood up. Steve's chin still grasped in her hand. Royce in between them. She nodded to him and pointed to the ambulance waiting behind 8-12.

Darcy stepped over Royce to guide Steve. John and Mel grabbed Royce and put him on the waiting stretcher, leaving the SCOT pack lying on the ground.

Steve took a step and began to collapse from the pain in his right ankle. Darcy quickly moved under his shoulder, supporting him with her body.

The two slowly limped to the ambo.

Royce was already in the back lying lifeless on the stretcher. Darcy climbed in the side door and into the medic seat while Mel and John helped Steve climb the steps. He collapsed onto the bench opposite the stretcher.

Ted appeared in the back of the ambulance holding Steve's helmet. "Steve, give me the SCOT."

Steve just kept staring at Royce lying lifeless on the stretcher.

Darcy reached across and grabbed the straps on Steve's chest, giving a firm tug.

Without thinking about it he automatically released the straps and let the pack drop to the floor of the ambo. Ted had moved to the side door and quickly slid the pack out.

When Ted had closed the side door, Mel pushed the two back doors closed and quickly smacked the door three times, indicating that the ambo was clear to move.

The ambo began to drive away with the red lights flickering off the surrounding houses.

"8-92 en route to Fallston General."

Chief Butler did not come and look at the two firefighters that were taken away. Telling himself that the crew could handle it. He knew it was bad. He was terrified that he would lose control. Right now, he needed to keep command of the fire scene and get the job done.

He took a moment to look around. Found the mother whose child was inside. Looking at her, she seemed happy. Relieved. She was hugging someone who was probably her mother by the way she looked. *If she hasn't figured it out, I'll have to tell her that her daughter was not found. We will find her body in the mess after the fire is out*, he thought to himself. Then he turned his attention back to the fire.

"8-92 en route 01:17."

Chapter 13

The crew from 8-15 had arrived at the scene and reported to the chief. Both firefighters were in full turn-out gear and SCOT packs.

"You two, go into the house and pick up the hose. Now that it's knocked down and vented, we can hit it from inside," the chief commanded.

The two men went to the house, stopped on the front steps and began pulling the fire hose out of the house. Once the nozzle was firmly in their grasp they disappeared, enjoying the rush.

Adrenaline coursing through their body removed fear as they entered the house. They never stopped to consider why the hose was left. They just did their job, unaware that the two men had been taken away in an ambulance.

The fire was quickly extinguished. The crews gathered at the back of 8-12 to drop air packs and grab pike poles and shovels to clear debris. They would open walls and go into the attic to make sure the fire was completely out.

After Chief Butler got the crews situated and gave instructions, he began to focus on the next unwanted task. Like it or not, he would have to go talk to the mother. He would have to give her the new that her daughter was dead, lost in the debris of the house.

As he approached the small crowd of neighbors the woman's back was facing him. Clearing his throat loudly, he said, "Ma'am, I'm Chief Butler."

She turned to see who was speaking to her.

There is never an easy way to tell someone bad news and you never know how they will take it. "I'm sorry ma'am but we did not find your daughter," he said as he looked directly into her eyes. He braced for the onslaught of emotions she would hurl at him.

The woman just looked back at him with her eyes puffy from crying.

"We're in there now searching." He took a breath in. "I'll let you know when we find her." He waited for the anger to erupt.

A big smile came across her face. "Oh, she's not in the house," she replied. "I forgot she spent the night at my mothers."

It was like someone had slammed Chief Butler with a two by four. "Excuse me?"

"She wasn't there. I forgot that she left," the mother was explaining. "We were painting her room today and it smelled, so she went to her grandmother's house for the night. I was the only one in the house," she happily explained. "Mom came over when she heard all the sirens to see what was going on."

Chief Butler simply said, "I see," as he turned and walked away from her, fury building within.

Not knowing what to do or how to handle the information, he focused on the fire scene. Pushing the injured firefighters out of his mind for now.

No one discussed where Royce and Steve were. A large portion of the crew were unaware that two firefighters had been injured. Those who knew focused on their tasks. Not thinking about the injured crew members.

Trying to control his anger over the mother Chief Butler had decided to go into the house to check on the situation. *No*, he thought to himself. *That's a lie. It's to get the hell away from the crowd.* Going into the burnt-out building would get him away from the people, the situation, his anger.

Walking up the drive he yelled over to the few people standing around the engines, "Grab some pikes and tools. Let's open the walls up and check for hot spots."

The lieutenant from 8-14 asked, "Do we need to lay out a grid for search and rescue?"

Each of the firefighters was secretly feeling the rush as they thought about going into the house. The ability to open walls and spray water gives a rush to those left on the scene. Even though the fire was out, the ability to imagine fighting the fire. Looking for a lost child. Only you find the hiding child alive, crying for their mother.

Chief Butler responded, "Check for hot spots. There is no search. The kid was spending the night with her grandmother." He paused for a moment. "Open every wall, every ceiling. Rip the shit out of the house."

The fire scene went smoothly for the rest of the night. The men from the various engines ripped through the house with pike poles and axes to pull down drywall, exposing the interior of the walls, opening the garage door and checking the space below the bedroom for any hot spots or fire hidden in the walls.

The crews laughed and joked with each other. Recounted the fire. Talked about where they were when the explosion shook the fire scene. Each of those present re-living the scene to get another fix. Those who showed up late fantasized about what it would have been like had they been there. The desire of the rush pushing all other emotions away. There was no mention of the two injured firefighters.

To those watching from the outside, the process seems mysterious and involved. The reality is that it was undirected destruction. While there is no deliberate damage being done, the crews are not worried about breaking anything or the mess that they are leaving. A little water here and there is of no consequence to the crews in the dark house.

During the night the electric company showed up and pulled the electric meter from the house, removing the electricity until all of the damage could be assessed.

The fire scene was quickly broken down and the trucks were put back into service. Truck 8-52 lowered its ladder onto the truck bed, darkening the spotlights that had been illuminating the scene.

Grabbing the fresh crew from the last engine to arrive, they replaced the attack hose and switched out the spent air bottles with spares from the engine.

Hoses repacked; the engines stood by. Flashing lights out. The firefighters recounting the night with each other. Using the energy of the night to fuel their thirst for the rush.

Chief Butler cut 8-12 loose around two o'clock, allowing Ted and Robby the chance to go check on their crew.

"8-12 to Dispatch."

"Go ahead 8-12."

"8-12 out of services returning to station."

"8-12 returning out of service 02:14."

Ted was running through his mind what needed to be done when they got to the station. Top off the fuel, top off the water, replace the SCOT packs with spares. The ones used tonight placed out of service. As soon as the engine was ready to go, they could head to the hospital to check on their other crew members. Ted had an idea about the shape the two were in but had not thought about it since they had been put into the ambulance.

Robby did not see them coming out of the fire and had no idea what shape they were in. He imagined that there was some smoke inhalation and a few bumps and bruises. Hell, they were firefighters. They didn't get hurt. He secretly relished the idea of having all the nurses' attention, being the injured firefighter in the hospital. The awe and envy of the other firefighters.

"How bad are they?" Robby asked.

"Steve was walking. Royce was bad. Half his mask was gone and there was a lot of blood covering his face."

"We going to the hospital after we drop off the engine?"

"That's the plan."

"Will they let us see them? We're not family."

"Yes, they will. I am the lieutenant and need to know how my crew is doing," Ted said. The reality of one of his crew members being seriously hurt was creeping into his mind. "Just let them try to stop me."

"I'll drive," Robby said.

The fire marshal arrived about two hours after the fire was out. The last crews finally packed up and left about six o'clock in the morning.

Chief Butler left around Four AM, after talking with the fire marshal and handing the scene over to the senior lieutenant from Engine 8-15. He was going over to the hospital to check on his crew.

Chief Butler had talked to the state trooper on the scene before he left and arranged for them to go pick up the two injured firefighters' parents. He had set it up so that they would pick up the parents and bring them to the hospital. He would just call the barracks when he was ready, and they would send the troopers. That would give him time to get there and to figure out what shape his crew was in and to prepare what he was going to tell the parents. He knew that bad news was going to be delivered to the families tonight.

The rush was something still felt on every call, but it's not limited just to fire calls. He was feeling the rush now as he drove towards the hospital. He began to think about the two men that were taken from the fire scene. He didn't get a look at them, but he knew Royce was in bad shape. He wasn't sure about Steve, but at least he walked out of the house. Secretly he was juiced about having to deal with injured firefighters. He had never had one taken away in an ambulance before.

He tried to remain calm and collected as he sped toward the hospital.

Chapter 14

Chief Butler arrived at the hospital, walked into the emergency room and asked the admissions clerk where to find Steve and Royce.

"Just one moment sir," was all she could whisper as she rushed into the back area.

Larry just stood there surprised at the quick exit. *Hell, all I need is a room number*, he thought to himself.

"Excuse me sir," a uniformed nurse said to him.

"Yes."

"Were you inquiring about Royce Edwards?"

"Yes, I was. Can you tell me where he is?"

"Are you family?"

"I'm the chief of the fire department miss," Larry stated. "Please tell me where my man is."

Not questioning him any further she said, "Come with me sir," and quickly directed him though the emergency room, past a seemingly vacant patient area to a small room. Opening the door for Larry to enter she said, "Wait here please. The doctor will be here as soon as possible."

Larry went into the small room, managing to mumble, "Thank you" as he passed the nurse.

Alone in the room he desperately tried to find something to keep him from thinking about the inevitable.

The door opened and a man in a white doctor's coat walked in unceremoniously. "I'm Doctor Jackman. I understand you're here about Royce Edwards?"

"Yes. I'm Chief Butler."

"Um, sit?" he said, pointing to the chair.

Shaking his head Larry said, "Doc, just tell me what's going on. Where is Edwards and Quinn? I would like to see them now."

"Chief. I'm sorry but Royce Edwards was pronounced dead on arrival."

Drawing in a breath to fight back emotions, he asked, "What about Quinn?"

"He's stable." The doctor was flipping through the chart in his hand. "Contusions and bruising, cracked ribs, sprained ankle. The worst injury is his hearing loss."

"He's deaf?"

"We don't know for sure. He has diminished hearing due to the explosion. We're hopeful that he will regain most if not all of his hearing."

"He'll hear again. Other than that, he's OK?"

"We won't know about the hearing until we do some more tests," the doctor clarified. "The rest of his injuries are minor."

"Ok. Now what?"

"Nothing. We wait. We watch. Firefighter Edwards is in the morgue. We brought in the medical examiner to do a quick autopsy. He should be finishing up and we'll release the body."

Larry had always prided himself on his ability to take control of the situation. To think under pressure. To react when others could not. This is what made a good firefighter and a good officer. Now he was frozen. Unable to decide what he should do next. On the edges of his mind lurked the rush. Fighting his own desires, he secretly wanted the rush to flow throughout his body. Even after all of the years, all of the fires, all of the injuries. it was a welcome friend to him. He knew he still craved the rush, even a small one. This time he fought the silent guilt. He knew that the rush was because he had lost a firefighter. Something he never wanted to do or even thought about. The thrill of having to face this situation, and take control, was causing an unexpected rush. He was seeing himself as the stoic chief who was providing support and advice to the young firefighters in his charge. Helping them through this loss. The family of the survivors exalting him for bringing their loved ones home safe. The family of the dead firefighter leaning on him for support and strength as they would lay their son and brother to rest in the cemetery with a thousand firemen joining in their grief. Himself delivering a eulogy that would strengthen the souls of men. The rush was building.

He was struggling with the guilt of his addiction being satiated because one of his firefighters was injured and one was dead. The conflict was becoming unbearable. How could he, the chief, the mentor – shit, he was their firefighter father – be getting a fix in the death and pain of his boys?

He was being pulled apart as he battled the guilt against the joy of the rush. He should feel bad for the loss, but all he wanted was to feel the rush flood his body. Taking him back to the magic place that he felt as he would run into a burning building. The way he felt as he brought someone back from the edge of death. As he aged, he knew that getting the rush would be achieved differently. The death of his firefighter could be the new peak.

He dealt with it the only way he could. Standing here exposed to the world, knowing that he must maintain himself in front of the doctor and those others he would have to talk with throughout the day, he pushed the identity of those fallen and injured from his mind. Using skills honed over years. He dehumanized those now lying in the hospital. He viewed them as a tool from the fire engine, like the broken axe that needed to be dealt with and replaced. Not unlike the way the serial killer will look at a victim as an inanimate object, removing the humanity to allow them to torture and kill their victims.

It is a dangerous balancing act used to protect the mind. Dehumanize too much and you lose all perspective of the people involved. Focus too much on the people and you are overcome with emotions, risking that your mind is not able to handle the totality of the situation. Causing it to snap and deal with it any way it can. Becoming a monster. Becoming disassociated from humans, just shutting down. He was struggling to keep his mind balanced.

Mentally preparing himself for the next question, Larry said, "Tell me about Firefighter Edwards."

"How much detail?" Dr. Jackman asked, recognizing that too little would leave a void and too much would overwhelm the man. He wasn't sure what the chief could handle.

"Everything."

With a long inhalation he looked at the first page of the chart. "Patient was transported to ER by ambulance. During the transport paramedic reported performing CPR. Upon arrival patient was observed with significant trauma to the right upper quarter of the face caused by a piece of metal being impaled in the forehead just above the eye."

Larry was imagining the damage to Royce's face as the doctor described the injuries.

"The patient was declared at 01:57."

Larry began to lower himself to sit on the couch, not knowing if he could remain standing after realizing with absolute certainty that Royce was dead.

Dr. Jackman quickly grabbed Larry's arm and turned his body so that he actually sat on the couch. Had the doctor not done this he would have missed and ended up on the floor.

"He's dead?"

"Chief, based on the injuries sustained I believe he died instantly. There was nothing anyone could have done to save him."

"Where is he now?"

"Morgue. After the medical examiner is done then we can clean up the body and release it."

"I see. Where's Steve?"

"The other patient was taken to a room. He was sedated and is resting. The other two firefighters are in with him."

"The others from the crew?"

"Yea. The lieutenant and driver came in a couple of hours ago. I didn't know they were firefighters until then."

"Do they know Royce is dead?"

"Yeah."

"OK. I'll go up and see them," Larry began. "Oh, I guess I'll need to notify the parents. Is there someplace I can make some calls?"

"The room is yours. Phone in the corner. Dial nine to get an outside line." Turning to leave he paused. "If you need anything just have me paged Chief." Pausing as he left the room, he said, "Sorry for your loss."

With his brow wrinkled thinking about what he needed to do next, he nodded at the doc as he left the room.

After staring at the phone for a few minutes, he snatched it off the hook and dialed a number he knew by heart. The phone rang at the other end. He waited for someone to answer.

A tired voice answered the phone, "Company 8 House 1."

"Hey, its Chief Butler. Is Chief Doherty around?"

"Hang on, he's in the office." The phone made noises as it was shuffled at the other end. "Chief," a distant yell came over the receiver. "Chief Butler on the phone."

"Yeah Larry, its Jim. What's the status?"

"It's bad."

"Hang on," Jim said and moved the handset away from his mouth. "Hang up the phone, I've got it."

A second later both men heard the third receiver hang up and disconnect.

"OK Larry, it's just us. What's going on?"

"I talked to the doc. Royce is dead and Steve is injured."

"Shit, how bad is Steve?"

"He'll live. Bruised ribs, sprained ankle, and hearing loss from the explosion."

"Is he deaf?"

"Don't know. Doc thinks some or most of his hearing will recover."

"OK. Anything else?"

"Ted and Robby are up with Steve. He's sedated. I'll go up in a while and check on them."

"Good. Now Royce."

"He was DOA. Took a piece of metal in the forehead. Doc says he died instantly."

Jim sighed heavily. "Shit. Now what?"

"How the hell am I supposed to know?" Larry shot back. "I guess we need to call the parents."

"Yeah. Do you want me to call them?"

"I already talked to the state police. Just call the barracks and they'll send cruisers to the houses and bring them to the hospital."

"Good idea. We can talk to them in person." Jim started to get control of the situation. "I'll call the troopers and get the parents notified. Go and check on the others. I'll head down to the hospital after I talk to the troopers."

"OK Jim. This is going to be a shitty day."

"You got that brother. I'm going to make a couple of calls and then head to the hospital. See you in a while."

"Check you later," Larry said as he hung up the phone.

Pausing for a moment after he hung up the phone Larry prepared himself to go and see the firefighters waiting upstairs. He knew it was going to be a long day. Eventually he would have to face the families of the firefighters, and he was not looking forward to that.

The first order of business on today's parade of shitty tasks was to see Ted and Robby. He headed up to Steve's room knowing he would find them there.

Chapter 15

The two firefighters sat in the dark room lost in their own thoughts. When the door opened; light sliced into the darkened room.

Chief Butler stuck his head in the door, looked at Steve sleeping in the bed for a few moments then turned to the two sitting in the chairs.

They both nodded at him and started to get up as the chief swept his head to one side indicating for them to come into the hallway.

Larry moved down the hallway to the nurse's station as the two followed, quietly closing the door to the hospital room.

He stopped at the station and let the others catch up with him. "How you guys holding up?"

Robby shrugged his shoulders without a word.

"Hanging in," Ted replied.

"Let's go down to the cafeteria and get some coffee." He started to head to the elevator. "We can talk down there."

The three walked in silence to the cafeteria. Robby found a table while Larry got a cup of hot black coffee and Ted found a soda fountain.

Sitting at a small table in the back of the cafeteria the three were waiting for someone else to start the conversation.

After a few moments Larry began, "We're in for a long day. How you two holding up?"

"OK I guess," Ted started. "Considering why we're here."

"Yep. I talked to the doc. He told me about Royce"

Robby nodded as he stared at his interlaced fingers on the table. "Got the nurses to let us hang out in Steve's room."

"Yeah, he didn't want to at first 'cause we're not 'family'. Robby badged him," Ted said with a snicker, remembering the look of shock on the doctor's face when the annoyed six-foot four man shoved a shiny badge in his face.

"He should have just let us see him without me having to push the issue," Robby stated. "He didn't even know that Royce was a firefighter until we told him."

Larry looked confused.

"Yeah, by the time the doc got to him all his clothes were cut off."

"Same with Steve," Robby added. "They cut off his turn-out pants and his boots."

"How do you know?" Larry asked.

"They were tossed in the corner of the ER when we got here," Robby explained. "Royce's coat was here but Steve's turn-out coat is missing."

"Could still be in the ambo," Ted interjected. "He was walking wounded."

"What happened?" Robby asked, getting tired of the small talk.

"Don't know. Fire marshal's investigating," Larry began. "Found out the room was being painted by the mother and daughter. Found paint, spray paint and paint thinner that had been left in the room."

"Was anything left?" Robby asked

"No. Well, nothing recognizable." Larry said. "I'm sure that the fire marshal will confirm when he's done."

"What about the girl. Did we find the body?" Ted asked.

Larry took in a heavy breath through his nose, fighting the anger inside. "Yeah we found her. She was staying at her grandmother's house a couple of blocks away."

"What?" both Ted and Robby said at the same time.

Shaking his head Larry continued, "After we knocked the fire down, I went to talk to the mother. That's when she told me that the room smelled so bad from painting that her daughter spent the night at the grandmother's house."

"She couldn't remember that BEFORE we went into the house?" Ted spat out.

"Apparently not. She didn't even remember until her mother came over to the scene," Larry said.

"Huh?" Robby grunted as a question.

"The grandmother heard all the sirens and trucks, came over to see what the commotion was. When she saw that it was her daughter's house, she was freaking out," Larry was explaining. "When she found her daughter in the crowd, all crying and upset because her daughter was in the burning house." Larry was disgusted. "That's when she reminded her that the granddaughter was at her house asleep and safe."

"Motherfucker," Ted blurted out. "Royce died for fucking nothing!"

Robby sat silently as he considered the information.

"I can't believe that," Larry said. "He did his job. He died doing what he loved to do."

"We're not supposed to die," Ted continued.

"No," Larry whispered. "No we're not."

"Look, we all knew what we signed up for," Robby said. "We all knew the danger of what we do. Hell, that's the fun of it."

Larry and Ted each let a sly grin creep across their lips through the anger.

"No one forced us to go into the house," he continued. "Steve and Royce went in and they were excited to do it. Shit, even I wanted to go in."

Larry and Ted were nodding their heads in agreement.

"We talk about this. We face death and dying every call. When it's your time to go it's your time," Robby said. "There's nothing you can do about it."

"We could have done an exterior attack," Ted countered. "That's what we were going to do until the mom told us the girl was in the house. If it hadn't been for that Royce would still be alive and Steve wouldn't be lying in a hospital bed," he said, the anger emphasizing his words.

"Then he would have fallen through the roof. Been run over by a car or fallen from his top bunk and broken his neck," Larry said. "Robby's right. It was his time."

"Would we have done anything different had we known?" Robby asked to no one in particular.

"I don't think we could have stopped them if we tried," Ted said. "The second that the woman said there was a child inside, nothing could have stopped them from going in. Shit, when I saw them going through the front door, I was jealous. I wanted to go in."

"I was pumped just watching them," Robby said. "I wanted to go in too. I never gave it any other thought."

The three sat in silence, each reflecting on their own inner thoughts. Trying to wrangle with their feelings. Each recognizing that they were addicted. Just the conversation was bringing a surge of adrenaline into them, flooding their bodies with the fix they craved.

The loss of their friend challenging their own beliefs. Up until today the fire department was fun. They were invincible, transformed into superheroes when they put on the turn-out coats and helmets. They never worried about being hurt; they never worried about themselves dying.

There had been other firefighters killed in the line of duty, but they never knew any of them personally. There had been a few taken to the hospital for various injuries over the years, but no one gave it much thought. No one close had ever died fighting fires.

While they were talking Chief Doherty arrived. The three didn't notice him until he was pulling out a chair to sit down. "Hey guys," he said.

"Hey Chief," they replied.

"We don't have much time, so I'll make it a quick briefing," Chief Doherty started. "Troopers have been sent to both Royce's and Steve's house to get their parents. When they get here, I'll talk to them first."

"Wait Jim," Larry interrupted. "I was the senior officer; I think I should be the one to tell them."

"No, I need you to be there after the initial shock. I've given this a lot of thought. They can scream and curse me, but in the end, they will need to talk to you," Chief Doherty counseled. "I'll be the evil person with the news, and they can hate me."

"What about me?" Ted asked.

"Same. Look, after the shock wears off, they may want to talk to you guys. You were the last to see their son before he..." Chief Doherty stopped. "Before the accident."

They were all silent for a moment, thinking about the situation.

Looking at Robby and Ted he continued, "You two be scarce when they get here. Depending on how it goes, you might talk to them later."

Robby and Ted nodded.

"Larry just be around in case I need you," Jim continued. "I also need to go and coordinate all of the hospital and funeral arrangements. I don't know if this is going to get ugly with the parents or not, but we need to be prepared."

"Are you getting Steve's mom too?" Ted asked.

"Yes. The troopers will pick up Royce's first then bring in Steve's parents. Why?" Jim asked.

Robby chuckled. "You've never met his mom?"

Jim shook his head.

"Good luck with that. I'll be hiding somewhere," Robby stated.

"She can't be that bad, can she?" Larry asked.

"She's a piece of work that one. I have no interest in seeing her. Good luck both of you," Ted added.

"Thanks for the heads up, I guess," Jim said. "I'm going to go and wait for the parents to arrive." He stood up and left the table.

"We're going to hang out in Steve's room," Ted said. "Can you send word before his mother comes up so we can go and hide?"

Chapter 16

The families of the two firefighters were brought to the hospital. State troopers woke them in the early morning hour, banging on the doors of their houses, asking them to come with them to the hospital. The troopers had no more information to give them and simply responded that they did not know why they were being asked to come to the hospital.

Royce's parents had arrived first. As the police cruiser pulled through the emergency entrance and went directly to where the ambulances normally parked, Royce's parents were scared and confused. When they saw a man in uniform waiting at the ambo entrance, they knew it was bad.

Chief Doherty was standing outside the emergency room entrance waiting for the trooper to pull up with Royce's parents. He had prepared for the onslaught of emotions coming from the parents: anger, hurt, sadness, abandonment. Chief Doherty new all of the firefighters by name, but he did not know Royce or Steve well. Here he waited to talk to the parents of his firefighters, to tell them that their son was dead.

Jim watched as the police cruiser silently pulled up and swung around. The trooper stepped out of the cruiser and looked over the top, locked eyes with him for a long moment. The two men knew each other from the many accidents that they had worked together. Each opened the rear door of the cruiser, allowing the nervous occupants to exit.

"Mr. and Mrs. Edwards, I'm Chief Jeffery Doherty of Joppa-Magnolia Fire Company."

"Why are we here?" Mr. Edwards asked as his wife came alongside and took his hand.

He had known for hours that he would have to have this conversation. He was dreading having to say the words out loud. "I'm going to take you to a waiting room so that we can talk."

"Why?" Mr. Edwards asked. He knew that someone was hurt badly or dead. Which of his three children was lying somewhere in the hospital?

"We should talk in private," the chief replied.

His wife was shaking. She squeezed his hand as they were led through the corridors of the hospital.

Chief Doherty came to a small doorway labeled "Meditation Room A", one of several for talking with family members. Holding the door open and invited the couple in with a sweep of his arm.

Once inside the room Chief Doherty took a deep breath and prepared to talk with Royce's parents.

"Chief Doherty, can you please tell us why the state police got us out of bed in the middle of the night and brought us here?" Mr. Edwards started. "It's not good. Just tell us."

"Mr. and Mrs. Edwards, earlier tonight there was a house fire."

"A fire!?" Mrs. Edwards exploded. "The damn fire department. What's happened to Royce!"

Trying to soften the blow, Chief Doherty decided to give more information about the incident. "Ma'am, during the course of the fire Firefighter Edwards and Firefighter Quinn were directing the initial attack and executing a search and rescue for a child."

"What happened?" she screamed.

Skipping the set-up, Jim moved to the gut punch. "Firefighter Royce Edwards was killed in the line of duty."

Collapsing with a wail, Mrs. Edwards was saved from falling to the floor by her husband.

As the two were crying, Chief Doherty helped guide them to a small sofa.

The chief sat in a chair opposite the small sofa, not saying a word. He was waiting for the initial wave to pass, hoping that he could provide some support to the grief-stricken parents. Chief Doherty had delivered this kind of news many times over the years, but he never hung around after the survivors were told. He didn't know what to do.

After a few minutes Mr. Edwards gained enough control to ask, "Was anyone else killed?"

"No."

"Royce was the only one—" Mrs. Edwards sobbed—"hurt?"

Mr. Edwards, holding his wife asked, "What about the other firefighter you mentioned?"

His wife's face was buried in her husband's chest, quietly sobbing.

"Firefighter Quinn was injured and is being treated."

"How come he's not dead?" a small voice came from the face buried in Mr. Edward's chest followed by soft sobs.

At a loss for what to say, Chief Doherty sat silently for a few minutes watching the parents filled with grief, openly weeping over their loss. When he realized that they just needed some time together, sharing their grief, he quietly left the room.

He went to Steve's room and quietly entered; Ted was asleep in the chair. Steve was asleep in the bed. *Robby and Larry must be getting some coffee or something*, he thought. He stayed for a few minutes just staring at the two and then quietly left.

About an hour later Chief Doherty was heading to meet Steve's mother.

When she was brought in the trooper couldn't dump her fast enough. Steve's mother had been acidically haranguing him since he knocked on the door, starting with how rude it was to send the police to her house in the middle of the night. "The neighbors must be thinking terrible things," she said, while secretly hoping that they saw the police knocking on her door. "If this is so important why didn't they send someone in charge?" she grumbled. The ride was mixed with indirect attacks aimed at the state police in general and directly at the trooper driving. She never seemed to stop talking.

She was escorted to another meditation room by the ER admissions clerk, Nancy. The clerk had dealt with many upset people, both patients and parents. This person would be remembered as one of the worst. She did not ask who was hurt, what happened or why she was here. She only complained about being dragged to the hospital in the middle of the night, apparently against her will. And when would she see someone in authority, since the people she had dealt with so far were peons and messengers, none of them worthy of her time.

Nancy opened the door for the woman, directing her into the room. Relief washing over her as she left her in the meditation room.

Alone in the small room, she could hear people crying from the room next door.

Moments later the door flew open and a man came in.

"Ma'am, I'm Chief Doherty," he began.

She glanced at him long enough to recognize that he was in a uniform, and asked with acid in her voice, "Why am I here?" She knew it was one of her two kids in an accident.

Trying to get eye contact, the chief asked, "Are you Mrs. Quinn?"

"No. Mrs. Quinn was my married name. My name is Ms. Steiner."

"Sorry Ms. Steiner, you are Steve Quinn's mother?"

"Was he in an accident? Is he dead?"

"No ma'am. He is not dead. He was hurt and is being taken care of."

Starting to put the information in perspective she began to form the scene in her mind. "Was he driving when the accident happened?" She assumed that Steve was in a car accident.

The chief was caught off-guard by her question. It was not "Is he OK?" or "Was there anyone else in the car?" Just "Was he driving?" Stunned by the apparent lack of emotion, "No" was the only thing he could say.

"Then was there another kid driving?" she asked.

"No, no. I'm sorry, you're not here because of a car accident."

She looked at him, raising an eyebrow.

Trying to get control over the situation Chief Doherty went into a formal statement. "Ma'am, earlier this morning there was dwelling fire. While in the execution of their duties Firefighter Steve Quinn and Firefighter Royce Edwards were involved in an explosion. The explosion resulted in the injury of Firefighter Quinn and the death of Firefighter Edwards."

"What was he doing in a burning house?" she asked.

"He was on the first engine on scene. They entered the house to rescue a child."

"Why was he inside?" she continued. "He shouldn't have been in a burning building. That's dangerous."

"Mrs. Steiner your son was on the initial attack crew," the chief was explaining.

"Why was he in a burning house?"

"Ma'am your son was injured in the line of duty."

"What do you mean? He's not a firefighter!"

Stunned by her comment, he continued, "Ma'am, your son has been in the fire department for almost two years."

"But I thought he just directed traffic and helped around the fire house. No one ever told me he went into burning buildings!"

"Ma'am, these young men are highly trained firefighters." He was getting frustrated that Steve's mother had no idea that he was a firefighter.

"If you trained him so well, why did he get hurt?"

That comment seared into him. "They were trying to rescue a small child."

"Was Steve the only one hurt?"

"No ma'am, another firefighter was killed in the line of duty."

She only thought, *I'm glad my son's not dead.* Looking briefly around the room she began to think about the situation. With her son being injured in a fire, she thought, *I will be the center of attention. Talking about my son that survived.* Then with a slight frown her thoughts shifted. *I wonder if people will be more interested in the dead instead of the survivor?* The thought that she would not be the center of attention infuriated her. She was already starting to dislike the other boy's parents.

Overcome with frustration and emotion, Chief Doherty was on the verge of losing control. "Excuse me" barely escaped his lips as he dashed out of the room, down the hall and into a small office where he broke down into tears.

Over the rest of the morning several nurses came in to check on the three parents. They offered coffee and water trying to comfort them.

The responses of Royce's parents were at complete opposites. His father just sat in the chair staring, barely speaking a single word since they arrived. Most of his communication was done with nods and shakes of his head, emphasized by grunts. His mother was all over the map. She started by accusing the doctor of making a mistake and that her son was not dead. Then she moved to, "You must be confused; my son can't be dead. It must be someone else." She retaliated against her pain and loss by verbally attacking anyone who spoke to her. When she found out that anyone had anything to do with her son, it got worse. At one point during the early morning, the ER doc had given her a mild sedative to calm her down, hoping it would make the night easier for everyone.

She had always been against Royce being in the fire department, feeling it was not good for him. She thought that the people in the fire department were a bad influence, staying out all night, coming home smelling like smoke and oil. He was better than being a firefighter and her son was better than those people in the fire department. The worst attack was on Chief Doherty, and the event that triggered the sedative was when she accused the entire fire department of killing her son. "If he had been with a better team, he would still be alive."

Royce's father just sat quietly. Every once and a while it would appear that he was listening to someone talking, but his eyes were vacant.

Steve's mother demanded attention from anyone who came into the room, asking, "What's happening, when can I leave, why won't they let me see my son?" Every time someone offered her a drink, she demanded something else. She tried to overwhelm the situation and at one point started to boss the nurses around.

No one ever came into Mrs. Steiner's room twice to offer assistance and within the first couple of hours everyone in the hospital began to consciously avoid her.

During the hours in between meeting their parents Jim had wandered through the hospital. He had gone into the room where Steve was, quietly sleeping in the bed, Ted asleep in the chair, waiting for Steve to wake up.

I never signed up for this, he was thinking. Being in the department was supposed to be fun. Get to be a hero. Being chief was the pinnacle of his firefighting career. But now he was considering his choices. He was feeling sorry for himself. *No one was supposed to die under my watch – at least no firefighters. One dead. One injured.* Jim was fighting feelings that he had never encountered before. Feelings that he had never considered before.

Quietly slipping out of the room he was walking past the nurse's station when the duty nurse interrupted his thoughts. "Chief. The medical examiner called up. They're ready for you in the morgue."

The chief had never been to the morgue before. Being in the fire department for over forty years, he never had a reason to go there. It scared the hell out of him. Tonight, he had to face two personal horrors: going into the morgue and seeing one of his firefighter's dead. He envisioned the body coming off the table and ask why he had let them die. He found an empty room and cried for the second time.

Putting it off as long as possible, Chief Doherty came back into the room Ms. Steiner was in, his eyes puffy from crying. Steve's mother, lost in her own thought, did not seem to notice.

Taking a deep breath, Jim interrupted her thoughts. "Ms. Steiner. Ms. Steiner. Steve is still sleeping." He paused for a moment, not sure if she was listening or not. "I'll be back in a little while to take you to see him."

"Why can't I see him?" she demanded.

"The doctors are still with him," he lied, wanting Steve to sleep for as long as possible.

"How come, how bad is he?" she asked, thinking that the worse it was, the more she would be needed.

"He will be fine. Right now, he is sedated and under observation. The doctors want to wait until he wakes up before anyone comes to see him." Without another word Chief Doherty dismissed her with a slow blink of the eyes and left the room. Ms. Steiner was left standing alone in the room, silently fuming that she was not the center of attention.

With a deep breath he prepared to take the Edward's to the morgue so they could see their son's body. He was nervous and upset.

Moving down the hall to the room the Edward's were waiting Chief Doherty took them to see their sons' body.

The chief understood Royce's parent's behavior and reaction, but Steve's mother was unexpected. He didn't know how to handle her reactions. He couldn't tell if she gave a shit or not about her son being hurt. He had dealt with all kinds of people over the years in the fire department, but her reactions made no sense. He was wrestling with emotions he had never felt and trying to deal with this woman was becoming unbearable.

As he was walking the two through the back corridors of the hospital, he had tried to prepare Royce's parents for what he thought they would see. What they would feel. As they walked, he was talking to the parents to prepare them. "He has been cleaned up but he's not ready for the funeral." The chief was preparing himself more. "When you release Royce, he will be taken to McAlaster's Funeral Home. They're good, they took care of my grandfather last year and did a real fine job," he began to ramble. Regaining focus on the situation he continued, "The county will take care of all of the arrangements. If you have a church that you go to, we can coordinate with them for the funeral." As they came to the morgue he paused. "Over the next few days there will be a lot to discuss and plan. The county and fire department will be here to help you."

As the three entered the cool room the medical examiner was waiting for them. "I'm so sorry for your loss Mr. and Mrs. Edwards." Walking them over to the table with a body covered by a sheet, he continued, "It is difficult to see anyone close in this condition. When it is your child it is even more difficult." The medical examiner delicately pulled the sheet off of Royce's face. "Take all the time you want."

Seeing her son's face appear from under the sterile white sheet confirmed what all of these people had been telling them. Her son was dead. Royce's mother just gasped, put her hands over her face and ran out of the room. The burst of sobs could be heard echoing down the sterile hallway. His father simply said, "Thank you" and quietly left with his eyes focused on the floor.

Chief Doherty watched the Edwards' exit and then turned back to the body of Royce lying on the table. He could not imagine Royce sleeping on the bed. The gash above his right eye did not belong on his face.

After a few minutes lost in his own thoughts he mumbled a "Thank you" to the medical examiner as he left the room. Chief Doherty made his way to the hospital room Steve was in, intentionally avoiding his mother.

Chapter 17

Steve slowly opened his eyes trying to figure out where he was. Looking around, he saw the white ceiling, dull colored paint on the walls, steel rails around the bed covered with white linen, and plastic tubes coming out of his left arm. Recognizing the room, he realized he was in a hospital.

Sitting up to get a better look around, he immediately fell back, wincing with pain, radiating from his left side. With his eyes closed, he put his right hand over his left ribs, feeling the bandages taped to his chest.

"Finally done with your beauty sleep?" a familiar voice asked.

A smile crept onto his face. "At least I have beauty, you big ugly beast."

"In your fantasy world. How ya feeing?"

"OK" he shrugged. "Side hurts. Where am I?"

"Fallston."

"I thought wounded firefighters went to Shock-a-Rama?"

"Only for smoke inhalation. They have the hyperbaric chamber."

"What did the doc say?"

"Cracked and bruised ribs, bruised shoulder. You took a big hit yesterday."

"How's Royce?"

Ted sat silent in the chair. He had known that the question would come. Hoping that he would be able to answer the question, he was still unprepared.

"Is he in another room?" Steve found the button on the hospital bed and moved himself to a sitting position.

"What do you remember from the fire?"

"He's dead, isn't he?"

"Yeah."

Tears started to form in Steve's eyes. "I knew when I got him out." Using the sheet, he wiped the tears. "I was just hoping I was wrong."

"Do you remember what happened?"

"Yeah. We went inside because of the girl. After we hit the room the first time, I went to search while Royce kept hitting hot spots." He paused. "I found the kid. At least I thought I did. Turned out to be a doll."

Ted, eager to ask a thousand questions, quietly walked to the side of the bed.

"Then the blast hit. After I came to, I found Royce and got the hell out."

Ted, considering his next words, pressed the nurses call button to let them know Steve was awake.

"What did I miss?"

In a monotone voice Ted said, "When you got to the hospital, the ER doc declared Royce."

"Fuck!" Steve looked out the window, not bothering to hide the tear flowing down his cheek. With a loud sniff he asked, "Did you tell his family?"

"Yeah. Troopers woke them up about five o'clock and brought them here."

"I knew he was dead. When I saw Royce, I barfed. You and Darcy were there. I remember waking up in the ambo once. Then woke up here."

Ted silently nodded.

"Everyone else OK?"

"Yeah. Well, no one else is hurt. We're all pretty messed up over you and Royce," Ted continued. "Royce's mom is really upset. The doc gave her a sedative. She was yelling at everyone."

"She was never a fan of him joining the fire department."

"Oh, that reminds me. Your mom's here also."

Steve turned to look intently at Ted. He closed his eyes and let his head fall into the pillow, letting out a small sigh.

"She's in the waiting area."

"That was a bad move," Steve replied with his eyes still closed. "Whose grand idea was that?"

"Not mine. And I bet whoever brought her in is regretting it," he said with a shudder.

"I want to get out of here!"

"You have to hang out for a while. More doctor crap."

The door opened and in came Chief Butler. It was a relief to see him walking into the room. He had been at the nurses' station when Ted pushed the button to call the nurse.

"If you're here does that mean I'm suspended again?" Steve said with a sarcastic smile, attempting to push the pain into the dungeon of his mind.

"Not this time, you get a pass," the chief responded.

"Guess I have to take some time off anyway."

"Doc's on his way up. You just need to sit tight until we get the OK," Larry instructed.

"How are Royce's parents?"

"Pretty messed up by it," Larry answered. "Oh yeah, your mom has been haranguing everyone to come and see you. Chief Doherty has been trying to hold her back, but she won't be put off much longer."

"Great. Give me a while before you cut her loose."

"What should I tell her?"

A doctor walked into the room holding a clipboard in his hand.

"Make something up. Blame it on the docs," Ted suggested. "I know I'm not going to be here."

"What's our fault now?" he asked, coming up behind Ted with a smile.

"Wants to hold his mom off for a while."

"Easy. Doctors' orders. No visitors until we finish checking him out." He smiled. "I heard about her already. Everyone downstairs keeps avoiding some woman yelling about her firefighter son."

"Thanks Doc. I'll deliver the message," Larry answered. "Come on Ted, let's go and deal with the mother." As the two of them left, Ted formed his fingers into the shape of a gun, placed his index finger into his mouth and dropped his thumb, snapping his head back as he walked out the door.

Steve smiled at his joke.

"OK Steve, let's see how you're doing," the doc said cheerily. "I'm Doctor Jackman, the emergency room doctor."

"I'm OK."

"Glad you're feeling OK, but let's take a look anyway." The doc quickly checked Steve over. Shining a light in eyes and looking in his ears and nose. He moved to the chest. Steve winced as he touched the bruising on his ribs. Then he moved to the ankle. "You looked pretty rough earlier and I want to make sure I found everything."

"How banged up am I?"

"This is what we have. Cracked and bruised, contusions, abrasions. Twisted ankle. Not broken – we x-rayed it last night while you were sedated. Both will heal. Ribs are a bitch because there's nothing we can do but give painkillers. Ankle is wrapped. Crutches for a week and take it easy."

"Sure Doc."

"You're not going to listen anyway, but while you're in the hospital, be good," the doc said with a smile. "Now the tough one is your hearing. We will need to do some tests over the next few days to see if you get all of your hearing back."

"I couldn't hear anything last night."

"Yep. The noise from the blast shocked your ears. They're recovering and you're getting hearing back. We just don't know how much."

"Anything else?"

"Not much. You're an EMT, so you know the drill."

"Usually I'm not the patient though."

"What do you want? Codeine, Percocet, or just normal Tylenol?"

"Doesn't matter. Pain's not that bad, as long as no one tries to hug me."

"All right that's it for me."

Steve started to get up, relieved that he would be able to get out of there.

"Slow down cowboy. I'm done with you, but I'm just the ER doc. There's still a line of other doctors who want to do some more tests. You'll be spending one more night here."

"I need to get out of here."

"You'll be out of here soon enough. Now I'm going to send in your mother, then the chief and the other guys waiting to see you."

"Guess I have to face her soon enough."

"The nurse is going to take you for some hearing tests, and some follow up from last night."

Chief Doherty quietly slipped into the room and up to the other side of the bed, nodding at Steve. "How's it going?"

"I'm OK Chief," Steve began. "Just want to get out of here."

"I copy that. First you need to get checked out."

As the doc left the room Steve just stared out the window trying to let what happened sink in. He still did not believe that Royce was dead.

"Steve, the next few weeks are going to be hard. I want you to know that the entire department will be here to help you."

Steve sat quietly in bed, lost in his thoughts.

"Royce's parents have been here. They saw him. It was hard for them," Jim was explaining.

"They always hated the fire department. Hated Royce being with the firefighters. They weren't too fond of me either," Steve said.

"Why?"

"Don't know. Guess they thought I was a bad influence. Drank too much beer. That kind of stuff."

"Steve, later you'll need to talk to the fire marshal about what happened."

Steve swallowed hard as a tear ran down his cheek.

"No one's blaming you. We just need to document what happened."

The door flew open as a large orderly came in with a wheelchair. "Come on buddy, it's time for a hearing test. I'm your chauffer."

Steve was grateful that the orderly had momentarily diverted him from having this conversation. He flipped off the covers and started to fumble with the bed rails.

"Let me get that." With a practiced motion the orderly lowered the bed rail out of the way and began helping Steve out of bed.

Steve started to move to the edge while he wrestled with the hospital gown, trying not to let his butt flap out.

"You must be pretty special. I've been assigned to wait with you. Usually it's a dump and run."

Once Steve was situated in the wheelchair the orderly spun him around to back him out of the door.

"Chief," Steve asked. "Did they ever find the little girl?"

"We'll talk later."

Steve spent the next few hours having multiple hearing tests done, then was brought back to the room by his chauffer.

As he was coming down the hallway a couple of the nurses were whispering behind the counter. Finally, one of them simply said, "Hey, your mom's waiting in your room."

"Shit," Steve groaned. "Any chance of going back for hearing tests?"

"Word's out in the hospital. How bad can it be?" the orderly asked. "Just let her know you're OK and get on with it."

"You have no idea."

"Well, deal with her and you'll be a hero in the hospital."

"Done with being a hero. Just want to get the hell out of here."

"Stand tall, here we go," and with that the orderly rolled him into the room.

Steve took a long deep breath as he braced himself.

Chapter 18

Being pulled backwards through the door Steve heard his mother's ear piercing screeching, "Oh my god! Are you Ok? They came and woke me up in the middle of the night and told me to come to the hospital."

As Steve's wheelchair spun around to face her, he realized that she wasn't even looking at him. She was busy looking out the door for an audience to see her reaction.

"Of course, I told them I had to get dressed and that I would drive myself. But they refused to let me drive. I didn't even have time to put on makeup and do my hair," she huffed.

"Mom. I'm fine. Just a little bruised."

"That chief man said you were in a burning house. I can't remember his name. What were you doing inside a burning house?" she almost yelled.

"I'm a firefighter. It's what we do."

"I thought you stood around and directed cars. No one ever told me you were going into real fires!"

"Yes, I did. You just didn't bother listening to me." Steve Sighed.

"Well I'm going to have a talk with that chief of yours and set him straight. My son should not be going into burning buildings." She headed for the door.

"Mom, stop!"

She froze halfway to the door and turned to look at him.

"Well, someone needs to listen to me about my son!"

"There is enough going on, and you giving the department a hard time right now is not the best idea." Steve sighed.

"You got hurt. What else can be more important?"

"There is no audience for you. Everyone is focused on bigger issues. Royce died last night."

"Oh yeah, while I was waiting, I overheard some of the hospital people talking about the police getting someone else because someone died," she interjected. "Was it him that got you hurt?"

"Just shut up!" Steve's breathing was staggered as he tried to keep from crying.

Steve and his mother never really fought. In fact, they were seldom together. Since his parents had divorced Steve had occupied himself with the fire department. It was his safe refuge, away from the world. There he could disappear, be something else. He could hide from the world, away from his bitter mother.

"Steve, what's got into you?"

"You come storming in here giving everyone a raft of shit without knowing what the hell is going on," he unloaded. "Did you even bother to say, 'Sorry for your loss' to Royce's parents?"

She glanced at the floor. "I didn't think it was important."

"We went into the building to rescue a little girl. Did you bother to hear that when they were telling you what happened?"

"Um..."

"You don't give a shit about anyone else but yourself. Can you tell me what's wrong with me?"

"Ever since you father abandoned us, I have tried to do the best I can to give you a good life."

"He has nothing to do with this." His tone moved from the son to a professional dealing with a hysterical woman. "So far, this is what I heard you say." Holding up in first finger for emphasis, "The police came and woke you up. It was inconvenient for you." The second finger went up. "The chief told you that I was injured, and Royce was dead. All you did was complain because no one was paying attention to YOU." The third finger shot up. "When you were pretending to have hysterics as I came into the room, all you could do was look into the hallway to see who would see your 'perfect' reaction to you injured son."

"That's not fair, I came here to see if you were OK."

"When did you find out it was me and not your daughter or one of your friends?"

"Um, I'm not sure. Of course, the police officer must have told me when he knocked on the door. That must have been when I knew."

"I think you didn't bother asking. The hospital is small, and the nurses talk."

She quickly tried to change the subject. "The doctors said that you'll be fine, but we should get another opinion. I'm not sure this hospital is as good as the ones in the city. Maybe we should send you to Johns Hopkins!" she started.

"What's hurt?"

"You were in an accident. That's all they told me."

"Do you even know what happened?"

"Something about a fire. It was all very confusing."

"Confused or self-absorbed?" he stared at her with a tear running down his cheek. "You don't understand. You have no idea what the fuck is going on. What happened?"

"Steve, I'm sorry. I'm here for you."

"You're here for yourself." Steve was defeated. "Just go back home. I'll be there in a few days."

"But who will take care of you?"

"I will. Like I always have."

"Fine! If you don't need me then I'll just go."

"Mom, I just need some time to get my head around things."

"And you think it'll be easier if I'm not here?"

"Yeah. Then I can focus on what I need to. You can go and do what you want. I'll be fine."

"You were always the independent one," she began to acquiesce.

Steve sat quietly in the bed staring blankly at some point in space.

Beginning to feel as though she was not needed, she began to try to find a purpose. "What about the hospital forms and insurance stuff? I'm sure they need me to sign something."

"I don't think so. The fire department is taking care of everything."

"But don't I have to sign something?" She began to protest. "You're still my son."

In a flash Steve seized the opportunity. "You're probably right. Why don't you check with the nurse at the station?"

"Yeah, I can go and do that. I'm sure that there will be papers to sign." Her face lit up with excitement. "Then I'll go home. There might be reporters calling for an interview."

"Yeah. That a great idea. I'll talk to you later and let you know what's going on."

"When do you think you'll come home?"

"The docs are going to keep me here for two or three more days." He knew that it was a lie. He figured if she thought he was at the hospital she would leave him alone.

"OK. Do you want me to stop back by later on?" she meekly asked. "I can bring by some of your clothes."

"Yeah, if you want too."

"Well, I'm going to let you get some rest. I'll try to stop by later and check on you."

A malicious smile crept across her face. "The state police have to drive me home. Just imagine what the neighbors will think." With that she swept out of the room.

About thirty seconds after his mom left, Robby and Ted came into the room.

"Man, I'm glad to see you guys!"

"Yeah. Wanted to get in sooner, but your mom was in here," Robby replied.

With a weak smile Ted said "We hid down the hall for a few minutes to avoid her. She's like my crazy aunt. How ya doing."

"Bruised, cracked ribs, twisted ankle. I'll live."

"Not what I meant." Ted was serious.

"Oh."

"You know. Right?" Robby asked.

"Yeah," Steve sighed. "I remember what he looked like last night. I talked to Ted and Larry about it."

The three were silent for a few moments, lost in their own thoughts.

"Is he really dead?" Steve broke the silence.

"Yeah." Robby answered. "I talked to Darcy. She said he never felt a thing."

"Have you been down to see him?"

"No," Robby said while Ted shook his head silently.

"Not sure I want to see him," Ted mumbled.

The three sat quietly for a few moments.

"If I see his body then he will really be dead."

"We're not supposed to die," Robby started.

"I always thought we were invincible," Steve added

"We're supposed to be," Ted said.

"What happened in there?" Robby asked.

"It was wicked. The fire was rolling. We could feel the heat. The smoke stratified in the hallway."

The three of them began to relive last night. Their bodies remembering the high.

"That was the fire that we always wanted to fight," Steve started. The others were gently nodding.

"We weren't going to go in. When the woman was yelling that her baby was in the house, that changed."

Ted glanced at Robby.

"I was searching and thought I found the girl. Sitting on a chair under a blanket. When I checked, it was a doll." Steve smiled. "Scared the shit out of me. I thought I had found the body." After a few seconds of silence, he added, "I always thought that would be my trigger."

The "trigger" is an event feared by firefighters and first responders. This is the one thing they see that will push them over the edge. It is the thing that their minds cannot process. They melt down. They lose themselves in the dark place in their minds. No one knows what the trigger is. They speculate, they imagine, but they do not know. Some think it is dead children. Some think it is horrific deaths. Some think it is mass causalities.

Sitting around the fire house you sometimes talk about what will push you over the edge – and more importantly, what you will do when you see it. More often than not what triggers someone is completely unexpected. Maybe it's because when you imagine what your trigger will be, you prepare yourself for that very event.

"I was happy it turned out to be a doll." Steve sighed. "Did you find the body of the girl?"

"Yeah," Robby snorted with disgust.

Steve looked at Robby and then to Ted with a questioning glance. "What?"

"We found the girl," Ted started

"We didn't," Robby growled

"After the fire was out—" Ted paused to get control, "Larry went to tell the mother that we were searching the house."

"Stupid bitch shouldn't be allowed to have kids," Robby spat.

"Why? Steve asked.

"The girl wasn't in the house. She was at the grandmother's, two blocks away," Ted blurted out.

Shocked, Steve exclaimed, "She told us the kid was in the house!"

"When the smoke detectors woke her up, she panicked," Ted said.

"The only reason we went in was the kid," Steve stuttered in amazement.

"Yep," Robby sneered.

"Son of a bitch," Steve was mumbling. "Royce fucking died because the stupid bitch couldn't remember where the kid was."

Robby stood and began walking around the hospital room. Hiding his face as tears began to flow. With a stuttering sob he added, "We should have let the house burn to the ground."

The three silently sat lost in their own thoughts.

"Now what?" Ted asked to himself.

"Right now," Larry's voice interrupted their moment with authority, "there are a few things that we need to do."

The three had not noticed him entering the room. His direct commands focused the lost crew.

"First Steve has to see some more doctors today. You got one more night in the hospital for observation. Before you get out of here the fire marshal will talk with you." Turning to Ted and Robby, he added, "He'll want to talk to you two also. And the three of you are scheduled to see a psychiatrist."

"Why us?" Ted and Robby objected.

"We figured it was the right thing to do. You have appointments on Monday," he said, pointing to Ted and Robby.

"What about me? Do I get a pass on school?" Steve asked with a chuckle.

"No. You'll see the psychiatrist today. Get checked out by the attending and then you should be released."

"Great. I just want to get the hell out of here."

"Oh, here is a portable scanner. They're sounding the tones for Royce today at noon." Larry tossed the scanner on the foot of the bed.

The three firefighters just stared at it.

"I'm heading out boys. I'll check in on y'all later."

"OK Chief," they responded.

"Oh, at some point, you two"—he pointed to Ted and Robby—"need to go home and get some rest too." With that, he swept out of the room.

Chapter 19

The three firefighters sat in the room, making small talk, watching the clock tick time away.

At exactly 12:00 hours the scanner that Chief Butler left interrupted the trio.

The tone's screaming from the scanner focused their attention on the handheld device. "Beep boop, beep boob, dweedle dweedle dweedle. Box 808, Company 8, Joppa-Magnolia. Harford County Dispatch, last call, Firefighter Royce Edwards." The dispatcher's voice was shaking.

There was five seconds of silence.

"There is no response from Firefight Edwards."

Another pause. The three of them had tears streaming down their faces.

Driving towards his home Chief Butler pulled to the side of Mountain Road and cried.

"It is with deep sorrow that we report that, at 01:57, Firefighter Edwards completed his last shift and was called home to watch over his family and fellow firefighters for all eternity. The citizens of Harford County thank him for his service." The radio went silent for a few seconds.

"We strike the bell to bring the firefighters home. Today we ring the bell to call Royce Edwards home from his final call." Then over the radio the sound of a bell striking three times was heard.

The three openly wept.

The dispatcher laid her head on the desk and cried.

At fire stations across Harford and surrounding counties engines and ambulances blasted their air horns in eulogy.

Firefighter Andy Williams opened a bottle of whiskey and started drinking. He did not stop.

Firefighter Lawrence Taylor, sitting at his kitchen table, took the retirement paperwork he had been considering for seven months and signed them. In ninety days, he would no longer fight fire.

Firefighter Paul Johnston, listening to the broadcast in his kitchen, placed the barrel of a .357 revolver in his mouth and killed himself.

The patrol officers of the Harford County Sheriff's Office sounded their sirens in unison to bid farewell to their fallen brother.

Paramedic Dennis Adams was sitting in his kitchen listening to the tones when his wife asked him why they were sounding bells. In an uncontrollable rage he struck her across the face with the back of his hand, then continued to beat her until she was unconscious.

Todd Randal, 13-year-old son of Lieutenant Jeff Randal, swore to himself that he would be a firefighter so no one else would die.

The last tones echoing in their minds, the three cried, the reality of Royce's death setting in. The tears broke down the self-imposed walls, allowing the waves of conflicting emotions to flood their minds, if only for a few minutes.

As the wave of emotions subsided, the three quelled the tears and sobs at the loss of their friend and partner.

After about fifteen minutes the silence broke. "Did anyone tell the mother that Royce died?" Steve asked.

"What?" Robby asked.

"The mother. Does she know that someone died because she was stupid?" Steve asked, looking away.

"Don't know. Larry was the only one to talk with her," Ted answered.

"If she's not bright enough to remember her kid, she's probably not smart enough to understand," Robby said.

With a loud sniff Steve asked, "If there was no child inside, we wouldn't have gone in."

"That was the plan when we pulled in," Ted said. "Royce already decided to do an exterior attack. Knock it down, ventilate, then go in. That all changed when someone said there was a child inside."

"That's why you went in?" Robby asked.

"Yep," Ted said. "Royce was telling me that he was hitting it from the driveway when the guy came over and told us the kid was inside. Royce heard him."

Each of the crew ran through their minds trying to remember exactly where they were, what they were doing and how they reacted when they found out.

"I wonder if they found out what exploded?" Robby asked to no one in particular.

They were each thinking about the call. About the rush from the fire. About Royce being dead. Guilt beginning to build among the competing emotions.

"It was a good fire," Steve began. "When we were going down the hallway the smoke hung. You could see the thermal layer."

"Nothing had vented the smoke yet," Robby said.

"I see how someone can sleep though a fire," Steve continued. "It was silent in the house. All I heard was our breathing and the smoke detector. Going down the hall we stood up in the smoke. You don't get to do that very often. It was cool as the world disappeared. Couldn't even see Royce in front of me through the smoke."

"The only time I've done that is in training, in the smoke house," Ted said.

The rush was slowly building from the memory of the fire. The thoughts of facing the flames. Memories of other calls.

With a fix slowly building from the memory, Steve said, "The kid was an excuse."

Robby and Ted quietly agreed with the statement made out loud.

"We wanted to go in the house from the time we left the station."

"I know," Ted said.

"When we came around the corner Royce decided on an exterior attack."

"Why?"

Steve shrugged. "Hot, not vented. Textbook exterior attack until the building is vented, heat and smoke released. It would still have been a good fire, even from the outside."

"When the woman was screaming, I knew you would go in," Ted said.

"It was wicked. I still would go in again," Steve concluded.

The three sat silently in each other's company mourning their fallen brother.

The door swung opened. "Come on Steve," the cheerful voice called breaking the silence. "Time to go."

Recognizing the orderly pushing the wheelchair Steve asked, "Where to now?"

"Getting you out of the room to see new faces."

With a loud sniff, he asked, "That the shrink?"

"Yep. He's waiting for you in his office."

"Well let's get it over with."

"Hey," Ted interrupted, "I'm gonna blow out of here. Go see my home and catch some sleep."

"Me too," Robby added.

Moving from the bed to the wheelchair Steve asked no one in particular, "Can one of you guys send my jump bag from the station? I want out of the hospital gown."

"Sure. We'll put it on an ambo or bring it when we come back."

They each high fived as Steve rolled past them and out of the room propelled by the smiling orderly.

Silently rolling down the hall, into the elevator and out on a different floor, he didn't bother paying attention to the buttons being pushed or where he was going. He didn't really care.

The orderly rolled him into an office waiting room and locked the wheels. "Doc will be here in a few to grab you. When he's done have him give me a holler and I'll come and getch'ya."

Absently nodding as the orderly left, Steve sat alone waiting for the doctor.

Chapter 20

After a few minutes he started seeing where he was. Unlocking the brakes of the wheelchair, he began exploring the small waiting room.

Propelling himself, he navigated around the coffee table and quickly scanned the magazines. He was looking for something to concentrate on to keep from thinking about Royce's death. Not finding anything of interest he pushed hard against the wheels and tilted back, bringing the wheelchair up on two wheels. With the two front wheels hovering in the air, he intently focused on the physical action of balancing. Clearing his mind and forgetting momentarily the events that brought him here.

"Can you keep all four wheels on the floor please?"

Surprised by the unexpected voice, the wheels quickly dropped to the floor.

"You must be Steve," the man said, extending his had to shake Steve's.

"Yeah."

"Well, come on into the office so we can talk." Halfway toward the door leading out of the waiting room he stopped and turned. "I would offer to help, but you seem to be able to manage."

He silently rolled into the doctor's office. Steve looked around. He had never been in a shrink's office before. The high school counselor's office was the closest thing. This association did not give him a hopeful feeling. There was a seating area like a living room with a couch and a couple of armchairs, with a desk off to the side.

"I'm Doctor Jameson."

Steve nodded.

"Try to relax. I know this is going to be difficult for you," he was reassuring. "All we're going to do is talk. Do you know why you are here?" Dr. Jameson flipped through a medical file the entire time he was talking, never making any eye contact.

"Guess they want to make sure I'm not going to freak out."

"Who's they?"

"The fire department."

"Um hmm." Still not looking up. "Anyone specifically from the fire department?"

"I don't know. Everyone's just trying to do the best they can."

Looking up from his paperwork and making eye contact for the first time, "What are they trying to do, Steve?"

Confused, Steve asked, "What's who trying to do?" watching the doctor ruffle the paperwork in his hand.

"The people in the fire department. What are they trying to do to you?"

"Trying to do to me? They're not trying to do anything to me."

"Are you angry at the firefighters and paramedics who brought you in last night?"

"Why would I be?"

"Often times, survivors are angry."

"Angry? I'm glad they were there."

"Was there anyone else hurt in the accident?"

"Yeah."

"I see. How badly were they hurt?"

"He's dead!"

"That's very tragic. Did you know him?"

Lost in his own thought Steve simply mumbled, "Um'hm."

Great, Doctor Jameson thought. *Just another kid in a drunk driving accident whose parents paid for a good lawyer. Play crazy, be depressed, go into treatment for a few days. I'm here wasting my Saturday for this dribble.* He felt better when he told himself, *At least I'll get paid well for testifying. Must be pretty well off if I got pulled in on the weekend.* Trying to end the conversation quickly he asked, "Have you spoken to your parents since the accident?"

"Mom stopped by earlier today."

"Father?"

Steve responded with a shake of the head.

"He didn't come in with your mother?'

"Divorced."

"OK, what did your mother tell you to do?"

Confused, Steve thought for a few seconds. "She didn't tell me to do anything."

"Did she talk to you about the accident?"

"She didn't even know about it until she got here. The troopers didn't tell her why she was being brought here. The chief told her about the accident."

"Um'hm. How did she take the news?"

Shrugging, Steve said, "Too self-absorbed to worry about me. She was pissy and annoying everyone. I told her to go home and I would catch up with her when I got out of here. I think the hospital was glad to see her leave."

"Do you think you can handle the situation better than your mother?"

"I dunno."

"Was it your idea to talk to a counselor?"

"Nope."

"Whose idea was it?"

"No idea. Just know that the chief told me that I would be released after talking with you."

"I see. Who is 'the chief' that you mentioned?"

"Chief Butler, with the fire department."

"Is he a family friend?"

"Yeah, I know him."

Shifting the direction of the questions, Doctor Jameson made a leap. "Let's talk about the accident. We're you driving?"

"No."

"Was the other boy driving, the one who died?"

"His name is Royce, and no, Robby was driving."

"You and Royce were riding with Robby?"

"Of course."

"Did you have a lot to drink last night?"

Confused, Steve was now starting to pay attention to the questions. "What are you talking about?"

"How old are you Steve?"

"Seventeen. Why?"

"I'm just trying to understand everything that happed last night. Sometimes it's hard to talk about or you may not remember. When someone close dies we have many emotions and feelings that we need to sort through." He was trying to decide if the boy remembered what happened last night. Thinking to himself, *Bla bla bla. Drunk, accident, friend died. Sad. Rehab.* Same crap as always with these rich kids.

Steve started focusing on the conversation. "You have no idea why I'm sitting in here, do you?"

"Well, your parents followed the suggestion of the fire chief to have you talk to me about the accident."

Steve was now laser focused on the conversation. "Bullshit." He had instantly switched from a seventeen-year-old to a professional firefighter taking command of an incident.

"Beg your pardon?"

"That's bullshit. You're making this crap up as you go along."

This got the doctor's attention. "Why do you think that?" He was beginning to get defensive at the attack.

"I though they told you. Isn't it written in the file?"

"No, just your medical records. Looks like you were in an accident. Is that what happened?"

With a sigh Steve began, "Not like what you're thinking."

"Do you think you know what I'm thinking?"

"Well let me guess. You think my high school buddies and I were drinking or doing drugs and got into an accident." Steve's steady gaze drilling into the doctor. He was pissed.

Clearing his throat Doctor Jameson replied, "Well that's usually why I get called in on Saturday mornings." The boy staring at him made him uneasy. It is very unusual for a seventeen-year-old to stare the psychiatrist down. He was not used to being challenged.

"You're also thinking that my parents hired an attorney who told them to have me see a shrink, tell him I am depressed, want to kill myself, get committed for three days over at Shepard Pratt, and then I have a set defense showing remorse and guilt. At seventeen I get off as a juvenile and my record gets sealed when I turn eighteen."

Doctor Jameson's face turned red with embarrassment at the accuracy of this boy's statement.

"Last night Royce died in a fire."

"He was your friend?"

The anger seething Steve replied with an icy tone, "Yes."

"Tell me about it." The doctor was trying to recover control of the session. "At least what you can remember."

"Did you hear about the fire last night in Joppatown?"

"No."

"Jesus this is a waste of time."

"It's going be harder if you don't cooperate."

"Why are *you* here?"

"To talk with you."

"No, why did they call *YOU*?"

"I'm the on-call psychiatrist," he defended. "I got a call that there was an evaluation."

"Nobody told you anything else?"

"Not really, when I got to the hospital the chart was in the on-call box, I grabbed it and came up here." The doctor shifted uncomfortably in his chair.

"You didn't bother to ask anyone? The attending? The duty nurse?"

Shifting uncomfortably in his chair he answered, "Um, no. I like to see the patients without preconceived ideas."

"Now you want me to tell you why you're here?"

"Please."

"So, let me get this straight. You show up to see a patient, don't bother asking anyone what's going on. Walk into the room, see a kid sitting in the office, and you decide why he's here and what you are going to do?"

"I don't think that's entirely accurate."

"What did I miss? Oh yeah, someone told you I was in an accident."

Clearing his throat Dr. Jameson responded, "As I previously said, I like to get the information directly and not have other people provide a diagnosis or treatment." Intentionally switching to a very formal register, he hoped that this would intimidate he patient.

Ever so small, the rush began to seep into Steve's body. The slight surge took the edge off. Gave him the push he needed to get his anger under control. "Then let me tell you why I'm here. Last night there was a house fire. Royce died in the fire. I was hurt."

"I had no idea." The doc started taking notes, his interest now piqued. This was not the normal teen drunk driving eval. "Had you been doing drugs last night?"

Closing his eyes and tilting his head back in frustration he mentally prepared to talk about the horrible night. Ignoring the questions from the doctor.

The doctor was trying to guess ahead of the story. He felt that. "Take your time Steve." He tossed a box of tissues to him.

Catching the box of tissues, Steve was silent as he tried to keep from crying.

The doctor trying to jump ahead was too impatient to wait for the boy to continue. "Tell me how you ended up in the fire." He would come back to the drinking and drugs later.

Pulled back by the question. "What?"

Doctor Jameson was frustrated and looked confused, wrinkling his brow as he tried to get to the meat. "Was it your house or was it your friends that was on fire?"

"Neither."

"Was there someone else with you?"

"Yeah, Robby and Ted."

Looking at his notes, "Robby was driving?"

"Of course. He always drives."

"So how did you boys end up at the fire?" The doctor was pleased with himself as he determined that this young man must have guilt about his friend dying while they were partying.

Steve was getting frustrated. He decided that the doctor was an idiot. With a measured inhalation he held his breath for a moment. Slowly exhaling through his mouth, trying to get control of his feelings, Steve looked at the shrink and with emotionless eyes. He began telling him what happened. "Last night around 12:45 a.m., Company 8, Engine 8-12 was dispatched to a dwelling fire on Charmouth Court." His voice cracked as he tried to fight back breaking into tears as he was recounting the whole thing out loud.

Doctor Jameson was trying to understand what Steve was talking about.

Getting control of himself, Steve continued, "Upon arrival, it was a working fire." Shifting to third person, Steve moved from talking about himself to an unknown person in a report. "Firefighter Edwards and Quinn entered the building executing a primary attack and then a search and rescue of a little girl."

The doctor sat silently listening. Confused about what he was hearing. It sounded like a fantasy. *Is this kid delusional? That would be great*, he silently thought.

"During the search of the room there was an explosion." Tears began to stream down his face as he was talking.

The doctor was confused. "You're Quinn and Edwards is your friend?" he clarified. "Why did you go into the burning house?"

Steve shook his head, trying to clear the emotions and control himself. "It's what we do." He realized that this quack was completely lost.

"I'm sorry, I didn't hear you." He heard just fine, but he wanted Steve to say it again. *Are these kids into some kind of arson thing?* he wondered.

"We are the fire department. Royce and I went into the house to search for the girl."

"What do you mean?"

"We are members of Joppa-Magnolia Fire Company, and last night we were the crew assigned to Engine 8-12."

"What? How can you be a firefighter? You said you're seventeen."

This was a normal question from someone who did not know about the fire department. Most of the people living in the territory never gave it any thought. The fire engine and ambo just show up when they need it. "The fire companies that service Harford County are volunteer. They have been this way since the area was settled."

Doctor Jameson was beginning to get uneasy at his lack of knowledge. "Shouldn't a fire department use trained personnel?"

"Every firefighter if fully trained before they are allowed to ride the equipment."

"Is this like a scouting group?"

"No. This is a fully functioning fire department. We have the same training as the City and County Paid departments." This was a question often asked. "You can join at sixteen with your parent's permission."

Doctor Jameson was completely off balance and confused. "I had no idea." Sitting in front of him was a seventeen-year-old boy who was working as a firefighter and he watched his partner get killed during a house fire. "Can you tell me what happened again?" He could not hide the surprised and confused expression on his face.

Recognizing the emotion on the doctor's face, he asked, "How much do you want to know?" Steve knew that the civilian doctor would never understand anything technical.

"Tell me about last night." The doctor started to gain control of his surprise at discovering that the firefighter was a high school student, and was there when his partner died. *This situation must be overwhelming for this boy,* he thought.

Realizing the doctor was finally understanding, Steve began to relax. "We got the call around one. When we go there it was rolling."

"What? What's rolling?"

"It was on fire. Flames were visible." The memory of the scene caused a small rush as he remembered the thrill of last night.

The doctor was enthralled with the story. It's the dark side that everyone possesses. Wanting to know about the tragedy, driving past an accident. Slowing to look out of the window, wanting to see the dead body, injuries and mangled cars.

"We were going to fight it from the exterior. But that changed when the mother started yelling." Steve sat silently reflecting, staring at a spot on the carpet.

"Why?" the doctor prodded.

"A woman was in the neighbor's yard. She was screaming that her child was inside the burning house. That's when we switched to an interior attack." A surge crept into his body. A junkie getting just a small fix.

"You went in the house?" He was in awe. "To try to save the little girl?" The doctor was getting a small rush, like going very fast over dips in the road. Your stomach falling as you crest the hill and quickly speed to the bottom.

"Yeah. We went down the hall and into the bedroom that was on fire. That where she said the child's room was. After we knocked down the fire, I started to search the room. Then there was an explosion. It knocked me on my ass. I don't know how long I was out, but I got up and found Royce. Got him out of the building and then passed out."

Still reeling with the thought that this child was a firefighter Doctor Jameson tried to push further. "Did you find the child?"

"No. Well, I thought I did, but it was a doll."

Trying to grab onto something tangible the doctor asked, "Why did you think a doll was a real child?"

"The room is hot, steamy and dark. Everything is wet that's not burning. The doll was life size and sitting in a chair. It was covered with a blanket. I thought the little girl was hiding until I looked at it."

"Looked at it?"

"Yeah, I had six to twelve inches of visibility. Got to pull it right up and into your face to see."

"You couldn't tell by the feel?" Doctor Jameson was asking more from his own morbid curiosity than needing the information.

"Thick, padded leather gloves turn-out gear, SCOT pack. With all that stuff on you can't really feel that much."

"But if you thought it was the child and you had to bring it that close to look at it, what did you expect to see?" The thought of having a dead girl's face six inches from his face sent a shudder through him thinking about how he would react.

"A dead child, maybe burned."

"That's a terrifying thought to have to experience that."

"I guess. Not the first dead body I've seen."

Thinking that he would have to come back and explore Steve's experiences with dead bodies he tried to stay on the immediate topic. "Are you upset you didn't find the child?"

"No."

"It doesn't bother you that you didn't save the child?"

"No. If I didn't find her dead, then there's still a chance she was hiding somewhere else. Maybe alive."

"Why would she hide."

"Fires are scary things. Buzzing smoke detectors, visible flames, heat. To add to that firefighters are vewy, vewy scawwry monsters in the middle of the night. Kids hide when they're scared."

"Tell me about Royce. How old was he?"

"We're in school together."

"High school." He was beginning to regain control. He was thinking about how badly he had misjudged the situation.

Steve stared at the spot on the floor, nodding yes.

The doctor was beginning to understand the situation. Not only did he have one firefighter dead, his partner injured. The survivor would need help, suffering from survivor's remorse, guilt and loss. But to make is worse, this was a boy who should be wondering what movie he would see. Where he would go on a date. This was something that could be the most exciting case of his professional career. "How does the loss of you partner make you feel?"

"I don't know."

"Well, are you mad that he's gone? Sad?"

Steve shrugged.

"Are you angry that you couldn't save him?"

With a wrinkled brow, Steve asked, "Huh?"

"Are you angry that you couldn't save him?"

"Why would I be angry?"

Clearing his throat, "I'm just trying to find out how you're feeling?" He had read some articles on Post Traumatic Stress Disorder. They were researching it among Vietnam Vets and soldiers mostly, but there had been some talk about people in traumatic situations experiencing it. The doc was experiencing his own adrenaline high. Treating a non-soldier with PTSD could be the pinnacle of his career.

"I'm not feeling anything right now."

An antisocial person, maybe a sociopath. The doctor was getting excited about what this patient was. "What do you mean?"

"I don't know what to think. I'm trying to get my head around everything."

"And how do you do that?"

"Don't know."

"What do you think you should do?"

"I don't know. What I want to do is get out of here."

"Is this conversation making you uncomfortable?"

"Not really. Should it?"

"Then why do you want to 'get out of here'?" the doctor asked, making quote signs with his fingers in the air.

"Get out of the hospital," Steve clarified. "I want to get out of the hospital."

"Does the hospital make you uncomfortable?"

"Um, Doc, look around. Dull green walls. White sterile environment. Quieter than a library. This is someplace you send someone to die. Not get better." Steve smiled at the private joke. This was often said around the fire department and the crews always joked about: "If I ever get hurt, dump me in a field so I can get fresh air and heal. If its terminal, give me a fifth and a .45." No one wants to just linger around waiting to die.

"Does this place make you depressed?"

Steve began to focus on the question that the doctor was asking him and realized that this was the same basic crap questions that you ask a patient who might be suicidal. His medical training began coming back, taking control. The surge was coming back. "Not really."

"Is it because your partner died."

Shrugging his shoulders Steve asked, "Should I be?" Fidgeting, he flipped up the footrest of his wheelchair.

"It's not uncommon," he began. "Being depressed because a friend died is very normal."

"No."

"If you're not depressed, then are you angry at yourself?"

"Am I supposed to be angry?" he flipped the footrest down.

"It's very normal in this situation."

"What situation?"

"The one you're in?"

"What's normal about the situation?"

"What do you mean?"

"What is the 'normal' situation that I'm in that I'm supposed to be angry about?"

"What situation do you think?"

"I think you are confused." He flipped the footrest up. He was getting irritated.

"We're not here to talk about me."

"I wasn't sure if you were talking about me."

"Why would I be talking about anyone else?"

"You keep asking me how I feel. You didn't even know what happened." Steve sucked in air, trying to hold back a wave of emotions. "And you don't seem to be listening to what I say."

"Why do you think that?"

"Every time I answer a question it's like you think my answers are wrong."

"I see." None of his patients had ever challenged him before.

"What do you see?"

139

"I see a confused boy trying to deal with emotions that are overwhelming."

"What emotions should I be dealing with?"

"That's what we're trying to find out Steve." The doctor was trying to connect with this young man.

"What is there to find out?"

"How you're feeling, so we can deal with those emotions."

"I'm feeling like it's the morning after I have been hurt in a fire and my partner is dead."

"What does that feel like?"

"At the moment it feels like nothing."

"What do you mean by 'Nothing'?"

"I woke up a few hours ago. Between the doctors, my mother, and the tests I haven't had much time to think about anything."

His mother, this is something I need to focus on. "Tell me about your mother?"

"Why?"

Caught off-guard, the doc stumbled. "Well, you mentioned her earlier?"

"You asked me if my parents came to the hospital." Steve corrected. "What she thinks ain't important."

"Are you worried that you disappointed her?"

"Why would I disappoint her?

"Well, that you feel that you have disappointed her?"

"Why would I be a disappointment?"

"No, no. I'm not suggesting that you are a disappointment, only that you feel like you have disappointed her."

Thinking for a moment on what the doctor said he replied, "Why does it matter?"

"Well, often if you feel that you have disappointed your parents, it affects how you feel about yourself."

"Why would she be disappointed?"

"It's not that she is disappointed, but that you think she is."

"Why would I think she is disappointed?"

"I don't know. You tell me."

Steve sat in silence thinking about what the doc was saying.

After a few seconds the doctor prodded again. "Do you think she is disappointed?"

"I don't think she thinks anything. She has no idea what I do with the fire department."

"Does that make you angry?"

"Nah, she has her own problems."

"What do you mean?"

"About what?"

"About your mother's problems."

"Oh. She's trying to get her life back together after the divorce."

"Do you think you have to help her?"

"No. I think she's doing fine. I just try not to worry her."

"What about your dad?"

"What about him?"

"Where is he? Do you see him?"

"Every once and while."

"How does the divorce make you feel?"

"What's this got to do with Royce?"

"It's about you. How does the divorce make you feel?"

"I don't really consider it."

"You don't feel bad about your parents' divorce?"

"No. Why should I?"

"It didn't affect you?"

"Not really."

"You don't feel abandoned? Guilty about the divorce?"

"No. Should I?"

"Often time's children of divorce take it very personally," Doctor Jameson started to explain. "It sounds like you haven't really dealt with this change yet."

"What's there to deal with? I'm not the one who was married."

"You were, are a part of the relationship. It is important to understand your feelings and come to terms with them."

"Who says I haven't?"

"Well, since you can't really tell me about your feelings and emotions, I can only surmise that you haven't dealt with them." He was smug as he assaulted this boy's feelings. "Tell me, did you ever talk with anyone about your parents' divorce?"

"There wasn't much to talk about."

"I see."

Steve watched as the doctor wrote down a bunch of stuff on his pad.

"I think you have a lot of unresolved issues, your injuries, and your parents' divorce. Your friend's death."

Steve realized that this was going nowhere. Steve's experience in dealing with people made him understand that this Doctor Jamison had a one-track direction and would never change his mind. He would just try to get those around him to agree. Quickly adjusting, he pulled his training from the bowels of his mind. Removing himself mentally from the situation he changed the direction of his conversation. "Why?"

"It's normal for people to feel a certain way when people die. You're not confronting your emotions and that can be bad for you."

"How do you know I'm not dealing with my emotions? So far all you have been doing is asking questions that you should have known the answer to before we spoke."

This took the doctor off-guard. "What do you mean?"

"You show up. Jump into this session with me, making some bullshit assumptions about some high school kid in a drunk driving accident."

"Well, that is typically why I'm called in on weekends."

"Tell me something Doc, have you ever counseled a firefighter?"

"I don't believe so."

"So, what's your specialty?"

"Family and Child Psychology."

"So, you show up, not because of your experience, but because on paper I'm seventeen."

"I'm here to help you understand your emotions."

"What emotions?"

"Well, when you are dealing with issues there are emotions that are confusing and unexpected." The doc took a deep breath. "There are also emotions that you need to feel to go through the healing process."

"And if I don't feel these emotions, I'm broken?"

"Well, we're out of time today." The doctor was trying to understand what this boy was experiencing. "I think you still have a lot of unresolved emotions to deal with. I want to see you a few times a week for a while."

"Why?"

"I think I can help you understand and reconcile what you are feeling, but to do that we need to talk and work through your feelings." Without waiting for an answer Doctor Jameson quickly left through the door.

Steve sat in the wheelchair thinking about what the doctor had told him. *I'm supposed to have these emotions and guilt about everything. I don't have any feelings about what happened right now. What the fuck did that mean?* he wondered to himself.

Lost in his thoughts he didn't realize that the doc had called the orderly to take him back to the room.

"Let's get you back to your room partner," the orderly said as he came up behind Steve, catching him off-guard.

Lost in his own thoughts the next thing Steve realized was that they were pulling up next to his hospital bed. After climbing into the bed Steve was exhausted from the events and the constant stream of people coming and going. He lay in the bed with his arm over his eyes just trying to get his head around everything.

Throughout the rest of the day a few people stopped by, mostly nurses and a few ambo crews from other stations stopping by to see how he was doing.

After a fairly bland hospital meal Steve just lay in bed watching TV, trying not to think about Royce being dead and about what the doctor had been saying.

He never realized that he drifted off to sleep.

Chapter 21

Steve woke and sat up in bed coming fully awake in an instant, unsure of what had rocketed him from sleep. *Must have given me something to knock me out*, he thought, remembering he was still in the hospital. The pain in his ribs drove the point home. Falling back into the bed he took things more slowly. Fiddling with the side bar he managed to drop it and spin his legs over the edge, still in the hospital gown with his butt hanging out. "Crap, I hope someone left my clothes somewhere, so I don't have to go up and down the halls with my ass hanging out," he said out loud to no one in particular.

Standing on his good foot he slowly put weight on the injured foot wrapped in a brown Ace bandage. His swollen ankle hurt like hell, but he managed to hobble across the hospital room. Opening the closet with a small wish, he found his duffel bag set neatly inside. He let out a sigh of relief knowing there was a change of clothes in the bag. He would at least be able to put on clothes and begin to feel normal again. He wondered what crew ran it up and when they snuck into his room.

Getting dressed he felt pain in his left side and shoulder. With no mirrors in the room all he could do was try to look. What he saw was a large ugly bruise that took up his entire shoulder and upper arm spreading partway down his chest. It was getting purple and dark. Thinking about how he would take a drill bit and put a small hole in his fingernail when it got smashed, he wondered for a moment if it would do any good to cut the bruise and drain some of the blood trapped between the skin. *Nah, docs would have done that if they thought it would do any good*, he reasoned.

The memory of yesterday was beginning to come back. Wishing it was all a bad dream, remembering that his friend and partner was dead. The people coming to visit him. The shrink who was supposed to help him making it worse, creating more confusion and doubt.

Sliding quietly out of the hospital room he limped toward the nurse's station. He knew that he could have just rung the nurses' call button, but he wanted to do something. He wanted to get out of the room.

As he approached the nurses' station a middle-aged woman looked up from her paperwork and simply said, "You're not supposed to be out of bed."

"I'm tired of being trapped in the room and wanted to get a change of scenery. Any idea when I can get out of here?"

Standing she said, "First, if you need someone, there's call button. Please use it. I can't have you wondering around the halls." Moving around the desk she walked to his side and continued, "Second, let's get you back to your room. Your chief is waiting for you to wake up." She gently guided Steve back down the hallway by his right elbow. "As soon as I get you back into bed, I'll call them, and they should be right up."

"When can I get out of here?"

"I'm sure the doctor will be stopping by to check on you. He can tell you." Directing him to the bed with a slight push the nurse instructed, "Now, back in bed." As she walked out of the hospital room, she looked back over her shoulder and shot at him, "I want a quiet shift and don't need to spend it doing paperwork on a patient falling."

Alone, he was thinking about what happened the night before while he waited for the chief to show up. Remembering the fire, memory becoming sharper. The fire. The blast. Breathing the air from the SCOT pack. Flames, steam hanging in the air. The relief as he realized the air was sending life into his body. Finding Royce unconscious. Pulling him out. The stairs. Busting out of the burning house. Funny what he remembered.

The door swung open and Chief Butler burst through it. "How ya doing today?"

A smile appeared on Steve's face. The thought of someone coming to visit made him happy. Something to get his mind off everything. To forget. Before he could respond he saw the second person entering the room. He recognized him instantly. "How come the fire marshal's here?"

"This is the official visit Steve," the fire marshal responded. "Just need to ask a few questions."

Richard Thorton was one of the state fire marshals and covered Joppa-Magnolia territory. When Rich showed up at a fire scene everyone on the crew was interested in what he found. It was a game they all competed in: who could figure out what the fire marshal would find. Rich was great. He would always walk through the burnt-out building then take the time to ask the crew what they thought. He would then explain in detail what he saw, what the fire told him. From accelerants, flame patterns, heat signatures and the way the fire reacted as the crew put it out.

"Was the fire arson?" Steve asked.

"Doesn't appear to be," Rich responded.

"Steve," Chief Butler interjected. "When someone dies in any fire the marshal has to do a formal investigation."

"Usually we want to get to the witnesses ASAP, but since I know you and knew where you were going to be for a few days, I decided to wait. Give you a chance to get your head on," Rich said. "I've been through the scene and concluded the physical investigation. Need to get the last witness statement as to what happened and make sure I can close out the investigation."

"Sure. What do you want to know?"

Grabbing the chair and pulling it over to the bed Rich said, "Tell me what happened." Sitting down, he flipped open the black leather portfolio stamped with the Maltese Cross on the cover that he always carried.

"Well, there was an explosion in the fire," Steve began.

Chief Butler quietly sat in the second visitor chair watching the two.

"Go back farther Steve. Tell me about the entire shift."

"What, from the start?"

"Yes."

"OK, why?"

"I want to understand everything that happened. Starting at the beginning of the shift helps me get a complete picture. Going from the start of the shift will help you remember. This isn't an interrogation, it's just a conversation."

"We started the shift around three thirty."

"Where did you come from?"

"School."

"Straight from school?"

"Swung by my house to grab my gear. Then headed over to the station for the shift."

"Anything unusual at school?"

"Not that I can think of. Is it important?"

"Don't think so, just trying to get the conversation moving," Rich reassured. "Tell me about the shift."

"It was pretty normal. We checked over the engine and got our gear ready for the night," Steve said.

"Find anything out of the ordinary with the engine?" Rich asked.

"Not really. Royce's air bottle was low."

"What did he do?"

"Refilled the bottle at the Pie Truck and put it back in service."

"Ok. After the inspection?"

"Watched TV. After a while we got hungry and headed over to Stewarts to grab some dinner."

"Any reason you went there?"

"Foods good and free. How come?"

"Just getting you to remember all of the details." Rich smiled. "It's a memory trick. When you concentrate on remembering things that happened before the incident, your mind relaxes and you start to remember stuff that you aren't thinking of now."

Nodding his head with understanding Steve started describing the shift. "Ordered food. Waitress wanted to know about an accident that happened earlier in the week. Ate our burgers. We got our first call while we were finishing up eating."

"What d'ya catch?"

"10-50-PI on I-95."

"Any good?" Rich's easy way of talking to the firefighters made him one of them. They were always willing to talk openly with someone in the brotherhood, and Rich could talk trash.

"It was OK. Put a patient in a KED. Didn't need to cut him out or anything." Steve drifted momentarily at the memory of the call. "Ambo took him away and then we headed back to the station."

"What did you do at the station?"

"Not much. Shot some pool, watched TV. Just hung out until we hit the rack."

"Anything else happen? Anybody stop by?"

"Larry was there at the beginning of the shift." Steve nodded toward the chief who was silently listening. "Oh yeah. 8-92 stopped by and dropped off the KED we used earlier."

"Darcy Morgan was on duty, right?"

"Yeah. Her and John Sanders."

"Do the ambos normally bring the gear back to the station?"

"Not really. Every once in a while, they do, but normally they bring it back to Station One, or the officers will bring it back."

"Why did she bring it?"

Shrugging, Steve replied, "The ER doc took it off and it was ready before they left, so she brought it back to the station."

"Any idea why?"

Steve was wondering about the fire marshal's questions. It was more like he was trying get more information than just on the call. "Darcy likes us because we treat her like an equal and not some girl on the fire engine. Royce and I surprised her on her birthday. I think we were the only ones."

"It was her birthday?" Rich sounded surprised.

"Sure. She was working a graveyard shift at the hospital. We ran up and surprised her."

"Whose idea was it to surprise her?"

"What are you asking?" Steve began to smirk. This was the kind of question that the guys in high school asked when they were hot for some girl. It wasn't the first time someone was asking questions about Darcy. Steve was keenly aware, since in the past several people treated her like shit because she was a female firefighter.

Embarrassed he responded, "Nothing, I'm just trying to get you thinking to remember the fire call."

"Darcy's our big sister. She is the one who keeps Royce and I out of trouble."

"I see," Rich said. Trying to change the subject he asked, "What time did you go to bed?"

"Around eleven, eleven thirty."

"Nothing else until the house fire?"

"Yeah. We all woke up when the red phone rang."

"Who was on the phone?"

"Ted answered. It was Dispatch telling us about the house fire."

"What were the crew positions?"

"Robby was driving, Ted officer, Royce and I were in the jump seats."

"Who was where?"

"I was in the right jump seat and Royce was in the left."

"How was the ride?"

"We were pumped. Knew it would be a worker," Steve said distantly. "Road was wide open. It was weird. Didn't see another car all the way there. When we got there the house was rolling."

"Were there flames visible from the outside?" Rich asked.

"We could see them through the window. It hadn't vented. When we got there Royce told me to pull the one fifty. Wanted to knock it down from the outside. Blow out the window, vent and then go in and hit the hot spots."

"But you did an interior attack?"

"Yeah."

"Why?"

"The mother was screaming that her daughter was still inside."

"So, what did you do?"

"Now it was a search and rescue. We went into the house."

"What was the situation when you approached the house?" Rich asked. He knew that Steve was a pro. He knew exactly what he was asking.

"When we got the front door, it was open about six inches. We saw flames from outside in the window before we went up to the door. There was no sign of backdraft, so we went in."

"How was the fire?" he asked. The thought of entering a burning building even caused the tenured fire marshal to have an adrenaline rush.

"It was incredible. The heat, smoke." Steve was remembering being in the fire. The heat on his face, the reflection of the flames in his mask. The rush was coming back.

"Ok. What happened inside?"

"After entering we went upstairs and then headed down the hall. Smoke layer about three or four feet off the ground. Stratified. It was thick." Steve smiled at the memory of bobbing in and out of the smoke layer. "You could see the thermal line. Went straight to the end of the hall to the bedroom that the girl was supposed to be in."

"Did you pass anything?"

"Bedroom on the right. Door closed. Bathroom on the left, door open. Master bedroom on the left past the bathroom."

"Did you check any of those rooms?"

"No. We were focused on the fire. Went straight to the room that the girl was supposed to be in. Went right in and went to work."

"Was there a backdraft when you entered?" Chief Butler asked.

Rich threw his hand up at the chief without ever looking away from Steve, signaling him to stop talking.

Steve had forgotten that the chief was still in the room. "No. Royce checked the door. It was latched so he turned the knob and opened it. Door opened into the room. After Royce opened the door, we made entry. He hit the room from the doorway. Knocked the fire down. That's when I split off and started searching the room."

"Describe the search."

"After we hit the room it went black from smoke and steam. Through the door I broke off and went to the right." Steve's eyes were distant as he was re-living the fire.

"What did you find?"

"Made it about five or six feet up the first wall, came across a desk and a chair. Then I found what I thought was the girl. Almost shit my pants."

Rich was watching Steve's face intently as he was recounting the events. He was looking for signs that Steve was making up the story rather than remembering.

"Turned out to be a life-sized doll, partially burnt and soaking wet from the attack."

"That's pretty intense," Rich said. "What happened next?"

"Just after that was the blast." Steve looked at Rich for the first time since he started talking. "It was weird. Everything got quiet. I could feel the difference." Taking a deep breath, he continued. "It was like all the air was sucked out of the room. Like a vacuum. The flames stopped moving, like they were frozen in time. Then the blast."

The three men sat in silence for about twenty seconds before Steve continued.

"I was knocked on my ass. I don't know how long I was out. Must not have been too long, since when I came to I still had air in the SCOT. I found the wall and started moving back to where I left Royce."

"How did you know the direction?" Rich asked.

"Firefighting 101: room search always go to the right. Always keep going to the right."

Both Rich and Larry smiled and nodded.

"When I shook it off, I found the wall and started to go to the left. I found the door and the hose. I followed the hose to the right. I would eventually find the nozzle, Royce or both." Steve took a breath. "Found the nozzle. I opened the hose and whipped it around. Knocked down the room. Then started to sweep for Royce."

"You found him in the room?" Rich asked.

"Yeah, he was a few feet away. Face down. I rolled him over and started to check him out. That's when I figured he was hurt bad."

"Why's that?" Chief Butler couldn't help himself.

"Started checking him from head to foot looking for the big injuries. That's when if found half his face mask missing." Steve broke into a series of uncontrollable sobs.

Chief Butler covered his mouth, trying to hold back his own sobs. Rich just calmly waited for Steve to get control.

"I flipped him on my shoulder." Smiling at his own pun, he said, "Fireman's Carry down the hall, down the stairs. Came out and fell. That's when Fred and the new guy took him."

Rich sat for a moment franticly scribbling some notes on his pad. "Thanks Steve. That is consistent with the other information I got."

"Do you know when you hurt your ankle?" the chief asked.

"Yeah. When I came out of the front door, I missed the step." Steve's voice choked as he asked, "Inspector Thornton, do you know what caused the explosion that killed Royce?" His eyes pleaded for answers.

"Fire originated from an electrical outlet. The house had aluminum wiring on copper outlets. That's consistent with the other houses of the area. Builders used the aluminum to reduce costs."

"What about the explosion?"

"Still trying to finalize. The room was filled with paint and solvents. There was acetone, mineral spirits, and cans of spray paint in the room," Rich said. "We may not figure out exactly what caused the explosion, but it doesn't appear to be arson or foul play. It was just an accident of circumstances."

"Everyone else OK?" Steve started. "What about the girl?"

"What do you know?" Chief Butler asked.

"Ted and Robby told me that the girl wasn't in the house."

"The girl that was supposed to be in the house was actually spending the night with her grandmother. Her room smelled because of the paint, so she spent the night," Inspector Thornton told him.

"And her mother didn't remember?" Steve added.

"She panicked," Chief Butler said.

"It happens. She was tired, worked all day painting her seven-year-old daughters' room. Her mother only lives about two blocks away over on Acadia. The grandmother came over to see the granddaughter's room. The girl complained that the room smelled, and Grandma offered to let her spend the night," Rich explained.

"And mom didn't remember?" Steve spat.

"She was tired, it was late. She fell asleep around nine or nine thirty. Was out until the smoke detector woke her up." Rich continued, "She's lucky she had a detector. If it hadn't woken her up, she would have died."

"Instead, Royce dies because the bitch couldn't remember where her kid is." Steve sniffed, fighting back tears.

"Steve." Rich looked directly at him as he began to talk. "It's no one's fault. We choose to fight fire. We are the best last hope for those that call us."

Steve was looking at the fire marshal. Hoping for answers.

"Sometimes people die."

Steve looked away toward a spot on the floor.

Rich moved to put his face in Steve's line of sight, not letting him look away from his intense stare. "Sometimes firefighters die. There is nothing that we can do to change that. When it's your time it's your time. No one can change that."

"If we hadn't gone in Royce would still be alive."

"If you hadn't gone in you wouldn't be firefighters. You would be civilian's staring at the neighbor's house burning down. Royce would have died in a car accident, hit by shrapnel from the explosion. Hell, he could have fallen out of the bunk and broken his neck. His time was up and there is nothing anyone could have done to stop it."

"It was Royce's time," Chief Butler added.

"We always say that. If we had done one thing different, he would be alive."

SCOTT OFFERMANN

"Yeah, but someone else may be dead," Rich said. "While you're recovering check out something called the 'Butterfly Theory'."

Steve was silently reflecting on what the two older men had said. After a few moments he simply asked, "What's next?"

"Well, from the investigation side we're about done. I need to write up an official report and then I'm done," Rich said.

"What about the explosion?" Steve asked.

"Nothing. Truthfully, it's not worth spending the time or money on the analysis," Rich said.

"We keep moving forward. From here we get ready for the funeral," Chief Butler said. "It's going to turn into a circus with all of the damn politicians and media." Making a grimace he continued, "My damn phone hasn't stopped ringing. The answering machine filled up twice."

"What do you mean it's not worth spending time to find out why Royce died?" Steve asked.

"Truth about the world, Steve," Rich started. "We know why he died. We know to ninety percent certainty what caused it. We concluded that the fire was not arson and not done with malicious intent." Rich paused for a moment.

Chief Butler moved from the chair and was staring out the window with his back toward the room.

Steve just stared with a look of innocence on his face.

"I'm working six other active cases and still have to investigate three or four fires a week. Our office is thin and underfunded. We need to decide what the priorities are. Where we spend our time and where we spend our money. Royce's death does not warrant our continuing." His eyes became shiny as they filled with tears.

Steve had watched people die, made life and death decisions, and told a family that their father or child was dead. This was alien to him. A business decision. A decision based only on financial impact. He could deal with someone dying, but the idea of not doing something because of time and money was something he had never considered before. "You're not going to find out because you don't have the time and money?"

"Sometimes you have to make the hard choices," Chief Butler responded with his back still towards Steve.

"He was a firefighter. Doesn't that count for something?"

"We don't necessarily find every answer. We investigate until we reach a conclusion," Rich answered. "We've got enough information to validate that it wasn't criminal. We know why the fire started. We know how to prevent future fires. Case is closed as far as the state fire marshal is concerned."

"It sucks. We wouldn't have been in the fire if that lady remembered where her kid was," Steve said.

"Why did you go in?" the chief asked.

"Rescue the child."

"Why did you go in?" the chief repeated more sternly.

"It was a working fire. Rolling. It was awesome inside," Steve answered.

"So, if no one was inside you would not have gone in?" the chief asked.

Steve nodded.

"But you wanted to?"

Slowly Steve answered, "Yeah. I wanted to go in the second I saw the flames. Shit, we all did."

Chief Butler, with a distant look in his eyes, said, "When I got there, before the explosion, I wanted to go in too. I was envious that the kids got to go play."

"Steve, you can't change what happened, and from what I've put together you and Royce followed every procedure to the letter. His death is an accident," Rich said.

"One we have to revisit I think," Chief Butler said. "The procedures are to keep you safe. The unwritten rule of 'If there is someone inside it's OK to go in' needs to be looked at."

Steve was staring into space, lost in his own thoughts.

Before any more conversation could take place, the door swung open, letting the doctor from yesterday into the room. Recognizing that he had interrupted a conversation he simply said, "Don't let me stop the party boys."

Coming back to the present Steve responded first. "Hey Doc."

The fire marshal and chief responded with a nod towards the doc.

"How ya doing today?" the doc asked Steve.

"OK. Same as yesterday I guess."

"Well good news is no reason for me to keep you hostage here. Wanna get outta here?"

"Hell yeah!"

"OK. Instructions." Looking into Steve's eyes, making sure he was paying attention, the doc continued, holding his index finger up on his right hand and counting off the orders. "Crutches two weeks."

Steve nodded.

Flipping his middle finger into the air with the number two. "Ribs: take it easy and let the cracks and bruises heal." Now the ring finger flashed into the air. "When you're feeling up to it, you're released. No need to follow up with me or another doc."

Steve started to get out of bed, excited to be set free.

The doc moved back in front of his face and flipped up his pinky. "If it hurts, DON'T DO IT! The nurse has a script for painkillers. Use it when you need it. Don't get hooked on it 'cause I'm not refilling the script."

"That it?" Steve asked.

"Yeah." The doc smiled at his excitement. "I already signed all the papers. Figured you wouldn't wait for me after I told you. Just swing by the nurse's station – she has all of the paperwork for you."

"Thanks for everything Doc," Chief Butler said, shaking his hand.

"Oh yeah Steve, one more thing," the doc added.

Looking at the doc with his forehead wrinkled in a question Steve waited for the next order.

"You will be seeing Doctor Jameson three times a week for the next few weeks," he instructed. "He has an office in Joppatown where he will see you."

Steve rolled his eyes in disgust.

"Appointments have already been made." The doc sternly countered his rolling eyes. "The nurse has all the discharge papers, the appointments and the prescriptions. We bent the rules so you don't need to go to the discharge desk in the lobby."

"He'll go," Chief Butler assured the doc.

"We're done."

"Let's get out of here." Steve began to get out of bed.

"OK, let me go check with the nurse," Chief Butler volunteered.

"Steve, we've lost firefighters before. It's going to be hard over the next few days and weeks. A lot of crap is going to be thrown at you. Make sure you don't crawl into a dark hole. Talk to someone. If not the doc than someone else," Rich counseled.

"Don't worry about me, I'll be fine."

"Take care of yourself and get better," Rich said. "I'll see you around. If you need anything, give my office a call."

"Thanks." He sat quietly reflecting as the fire marshal left.

The door burst open a few minutes later with Chief Butler dragging a wheelchair, "OK, we're all clear. Let's get you out of here and back to your home."

"No, back to the station," Steve said.

"You sure you don't want to go home and rest? Check in with your mom?"

"No," Steve said as he grabbed the duffel bag. "My car's at the station."

"We can have a couple of the boys bring it to your house."

"No. I want to go to the station."

"Alright. Let me bring my truck up and we'll get out of here."

Chapter 22

The two rode back to the station in silence, neither knowing what to say.

When they arrived, the station appeared deserted. No cars in the parking and all the bay doors closed.

"Want me to drop you near your car?" Larry asked.

Shaking his head, Steve said, "I want to go in."

Parking his pickup truck in front of the fuel pump at the entrance, Larry said, "OK. Let me get the crutches out of the back." Sliding the gear shifter into park, he opened the door and quickly moved to the back to retrieve the crutches.

Steve did not wait for Larry. He opened the door and swung his injured foot out of the truck, stood on his good foot and began to hop towards the door.

"Slow down," Larry said as he caught up with Steve. "Don't push yourself, there's no hurry. Let your foot get better for a few days." Handing him the crutches he reached into his back pocket and pulled his wallet out, activating the entry lock without bothering to take the card out, pulling the door open, letting Steve walk into the dark station.

Pausing just inside the door, Steve rested his weight on the crutches, looking into the dark station.

"I need to check a few things in the office," Larry said as he moved around the frozen man and disappeared into the office area.

The clicking of the door brought Steve out of his deep thought. Using his crutches, he walked to the door Larry disappeared through and flipped on the eight light switches, turning on all of the lights in the fire station. The fluorescent fixtures flickered to life, flooding the bay with the cold white light.

He let out a small sob as he saw 8-12 in the light, the realization of everything that had happened hitting him again.

The engine was covered with ash and soot from its last fire call. The one that killed Royce. The first thought that entered his mind was, *This engine needs a bath.* Fighting a wave of emotions, he stared at the dirty engine realizing that no one has touched it since it got back.

A feeling of loneliness engulfed him. He wondered if the engine was abandoned because of Royce's death, would he be abandoned by the others also. he would be shunned by the others just as they had shunned the engine. Would they think Royce died because of him? The tears stung his cheeks.

After a few moments he regained control from the onslaught of emotions and used the sleeve of his shirt to wipe his eyes and nose. He did not know what to do next, so he just started walking around the engine. Moving to the back he glanced up and noticed that the hose had been re-laid, ready for the next call.

Noticing the gear rack that held everyone's turn-out gear, he moved along the rows of gear, smelling the imbedded smoke and sweat. He felt the rush building. Re-living the many calls that he and Royce had been on. He was fighting between feeling the rush and the loss of his friend.

Coming to his locker he found his helmet, coat and boots where they had always hung since he joined the department. His turn-out pants were missing. He wondered where they were.

After surveying the station for a few more minutes Steve began to make his way back to the office. It was time to leave for a while. He needed to get away from the station and clear his head. Get control of his emotions. Lock them in the dungeon.

"Hey, Chief," he hollered as he managed to get himself through the doorway fighting with the crutches. He was OK walking around with the crutches, but he had no idea how to manage them when he needed to use his hands. "I'm gonna get out of here for a while."

Sticking his head out of the office he said, "'K. You gonna be OK driving home?"

"Yeah. I still got one foot."

"Alright, I'll check in with you later."

"Don't bother. Just going home, grab a shower and some down time. I'll probably come back this evening and hang out."

"If you don't come back tonight, I'll call you. We still need to discuss your doctors' appointments and stuff."

Steve raised an eyebrow and tilted his head with a question.

"The appointments with the shrink are set up, but I need to check with his office. I'll call you later with all of the information."

"What about school?"

"That's not a problem. We can make arrangements for you to miss school."

"That's gonna be the weird part."

"How so?"

"What do I say to the other kids in school?" he began. "Most of them don't even know that Royce and I were in the fire department. How will I deal with their questions?"

"I guess just one question at a time," the chief coached.

Steve nodded as he backed out of the doorway, making his way to his car.

After the door to the lounge closed Chief Butler quickly made his way to the window in the bunk room, watching Steve get into his car and leave.

He wasn't sure how to deal with the young man. Hell, he didn't know how to deal with himself. He wondered if making Steve feel better would do the same for him?

Moving back into the office area he picked up the phone and made a call. "Hey, it's Larry. Steve just went home. Where are we at with everything?"

The voice on the other end asked, "How's he doing?"

"Can't really tell. Don't know if he is tired, depressed, guilty, or just pissed off."

"Well hopefully he'll come out of it. It's no one's fault that these things happen," Chief Doherty said.

"They've never happened to us."

"Keep an eye on him."

"Yeah, I'm going to have a trooper run by his house, make sure he made it home. What's going on with Royce?"

"Jesus, it's a damn circus. You can't believe the bullshit I have to deal with."

"Why?"

"So far, on Sunday morning, I have had calls from the County Superintendent, the mayors of Bell Air and Aberdeen, the fire chief in

Baltimore County, Baltimore City, Anne Arundel County and every fire department in Harford County."

"Bad news travels fast."

"Shit I've even had calls from other states, and New York City wants to send bagpipes."

"Jesus Christ. What the hell for?"

"The funeral. Everyone wants to be a part of it," Chief Doherty answered.

"Wow. That's great that all of the departments are supporting us. No one wants to lose a man."

"No, that's not the reason. It's politics. They want to be in the news, supporting the firefighters. Some are to show support." Jim sighed. "It's all just bullshit."

"I don't understand."

"Everyone wants to be a part of the parade of grief. They want to send engines and men to be seen at the funeral. The politicians want to have their name splattered all over to show their 'constituents' that they support the fire department." He sighed. "The worst part is that they all want to be one ahead of the other. Want to be first in line. Want to sit in the front of the service."

"Sounds like a colossal mess."

"Everyone is pressuring me to 'Take care of them'. It's becoming a dog and pony show rather than a funeral."

"So where are we at? We're gonna have to talk with Royce's parents and the others."

"Yeah. Funeral is taken care of – McAlaster's mortuary donated everything. Services will be at Mountain Christian Church. The body will be interned at Mountain View Cemetery."

"You got that planned quick."

"Not me. It's Jack McAlaster, the owner of the funeral home. I worked with him when I had to bury my Grandad last year. He really knows his shit. He has everything put together. He even warned me that the politics would be out of control."

"Guess that's good for us."

"Yeah. He is sending over a package with all of the details." With a sarcastic laugh Jim continued, "He called it the 'staging of the services'."

"What's that mean?"

"It is the plan and layout of the service. From the time we bring the body into the services to the time it's put in the ground. He told me that it would include who was needed to escort the casket, when there would be opportunities for honor guard, bagpipes, twenty-one-gun salute, the works."

"That's good. Do we just fill in names?"

"That and let people know where they will be sitting, when they will pass the casket, the route that the engines will travel to the cemetery."

"So, what's left for us to do?"

"We have to put in the names, the politicians, the order of the fire engines and who will speak during the ceremony."

"Looks like McAlaster's took care of the hard stuff. The rest sounds easy."

"Don't kid yourself. Whatever we decide it's going to piss off someone. And I'm going to be the target of the anger."

"This is why I never wanted to be the chief." Larry laughed. "Can't handle the politics."

"Well, this is as shitty as it gets." Jim sighed.

"We'll get through this," Larry replied. "Just think: the worst that will happen is we'll get fired from a volunteer job."

"Humph. Makes me wonder while I continue to put up with all this shit" Jim confessed. "Keep me posted."

Chapter 23

Steve was driving his Duster through the quiet streets of the small community, easing his way towards his home.

Hope mom's gone out somewhere, he was thinking to himself. *Don't really want to deal with the crap.*

Pulling into the apartments on Harborside Drive he knew he would have to walk up to the third floor.

Grabbing his bag and hooking it over his shoulder he placed the crutches under his arms. Glancing around, he took note that his mother's car wasn't in the parking lot. Not having to deal with her was a relief.

They had moved into this apartment about five months ago. After his dad moved out, they sold the house. The only reason that they rented this apartment was so that he could finish high school. His mother reminded him constantly of this fact. Constantly haranguing him that she would rather be in the city, where the action was.

Truth be told, no one ever asked him. He just came home one day, and his mother told him that they were moving. Gave him the address and a set of keys to the new apartment and told him to move the stuff in the house. They had fifteen days to get out.

When he first looked at the two-bedroom apartment on the third floor he had only one question. "Where's the third bedroom?" His mom asked what they needed another bedroom for. "My sister, your daughter," he had replied with astonishment.

Her only response was, "She is at college and won't be visiting often. Besides, with the crappy amount of money your father is giving me, I can't afford anything else."

That question launched a three-hour husband/your father bashing session.

Gingerly working his way up the empty stairs, he managed to make it to the apartment door without hurting his foot too badly.

Relieved that he was at the top, he leaned against the door for balance and fumbled with his keys, trying to arrange the one that unlocked the door.

The door flew open. He grabbed the frame and stepped on his injured foot, wincing with pain, to keep from falling over. Managing to keep from falling on his face, he realized that his mother was standing in the doorway holding it open.

"You didn't call," she whined. "I would have come and picked you up."

"I'm good mom. Chief brought me back to the station. He was waiting for me to finish an interview."

"There was an interview!?" his mom shrieked. "I wasn't there. When will it be on TV?"

"Not that kind of interview. I had to talk to the fire marshal."

"Well, he should have called me to come and get you from the hospital."

"No. I just wanted to get out of there."

"OK. You're home now," she started. "Some TV station called and wanted to talk to you. I think they wanted an interview." She was becoming excited. "I offered to talk to them, but they really wanted to talk to you. I have their number so I can give them a call for you!"

"Stop. I don't want to talk to anyone. I just want to get a shower and a few hours of rack time."

"Well, when you get up, I can call them."

"Where's your car at Mom? I didn't see it in the parking space." He tried to change the subject and get her off of talking to the TV station.

"Oh. I let one of my friends borrow it because hers is in the shop."

"How were you going to pick me up if you didn't have a car?"

"Doesn't matter because you're home. What do you need?"

"Nothing. I'm going to take a shower." With that he headed to his room to drop his bag and grab some clothes. Over his shoulder he threw back, "You need to stop trying to help everyone."

Heading from his room to the bathroom he heard his mother on the phone talking with god knew who. "I don't know. I'll probably call after he wakes up."

He paused in the hallway for a moment to listen. "I will be on the news. Everyone will see me." With that he ducked into the bathroom for a shower.

Sitting down on the toilet he began to unwrap his injured ankle, carefully rolling the elastic bandage as he unwound it from his leg. Then he removed a roll of gauze that was also wrapped around the leg. *Someone took the time to protect my delicate skin*, he chuckled to himself. *Guess they were worried that the elastic bandage would chafe me.*

He then removed the plaster splint from around his foot. This was a temporary splint from the ER. Soak it in water and then place it on the area you want splinted and it forms to whatever shape and position is needed. Let it dry and it becomes hard.

Looking at his ankle in detail he saw the dark purple coloring of the bruise with tinges of yellow appearing around the edges. The ankle itself was swollen about half the size of a softball. It was swollen enough that he could not see the Lateral Malleolus.

In a flash he made the connection. *Guess I'm not going to ride the engine for a while.* The thought brought on a moment of fear as he realized that he would not be able to get the rush that he constantly craved. *Hope I don't miss any good ones in the next few weeks.*

Sliding off his pants and shirt he let out a sharp hiss as he was reminded of the injury to his ribs. Standing in front of the mirror he looked over the rest of his injuries.

Falling into the routine of his training he disconnected himself from his body and viewed the image in the mirror as an unidentified victim who was now his patient. He began to assess the situation with cold precision. Head to toe.

Hair was dirty and messed up. It was apparent that he had been physically active from the sweat and grease of unwashed hair. There was a line around his head. Above the line there was little debris. Below the line there was dirt and particles tangled. This person was wearing a hat that protected the top of his head.

Face appeared to be mostly free from injury. Along the sides of the face the skin was red. First and second degree burns from exposure to the steam. Eyes were bloodshot and puffy from irritation and crying. There was a smear of blood along the hairline. It looked like someone tried to clean the blood off the face but didn't quite get it all. There were no injuries to the face. The blood was not his. Overall, the face was clean, like someone washed it with a cloth. They stopped at the edge of the face and neck. The line of dirt was visible if you took the time to look. Like the girls whose makeup ends at the edge of the jaw, without blending it into the neck. His neck was also red with burns.

His eyes stopped at the large bandage covering the left side. He reached for the bandage and began to slowly pull, testing how hard it would be to remove. After peeling the first corner slowly off, he realized that it was not stuck to any injury. He ripped the bandage off. A slight hiss escaped from the sharp pain of ripping tape off. "Thank you for not inheriting a full chest of hair."

Carefully raising his left arm above his head, he examined the injury. It was a deep purple bruise slightly forward of his left side. It was about six inches wide and ten inches tall. This bruise was also starting to show signs of yellowing. There was little to no swelling of the area. Carefully probing the area with his right hand, he was feeling for any signs of breaking.

He found the damaged ribs as the pain shot through his body.

Looking over the rest of the person in the mirror he saw a few minor bruises on the legs. Nothing worth mentioning or taking notice of.

Now that he had surveyed the patient and was satisfied with his assessment, he changed his focus from assessing a patient to looking at himself. Overall, his injuries could be much, much worse.

This thought hit him hard. It could be as bad as Royce. He could be dead. He struggled for a few moments to keep from breaking down. He regained control.

Now he started getting angry. *We were not supposed to die! We shouldn't even get hurt.* He was thinking, *What the fuck happened?*

Clearing his mind, he reached over and turned on the shower. *Time to knock the stink off*, he thought. *I bet I smelled like shit in the hospital.*

Stepping under the hot water the shower began washing the dirt, sweat and smoke smells off his battered body, the hot water flowing over his muscles, toned by high school swimming and the physical exertion of firefighting.

He washed with soap and shampoo three times, using the water to wash away the memory and emotions. Like a victim of assault trying to wash the attack away. Washing the darkness of the previous days off his body. His shower ended as the hot water turned cold.

Stepping out of the shower he pulled on clean shorts, looked at the bandages for his ankle and decided that he wouldn't bother with splinting it until later.

He quietly snuck out of the bathroom, trying not to let his mother hear him, and quickly hobbled down the hall to his bedroom.

Closing the door, he turned off the light to get some sleep. Out of habit he reached across his desk and turned on his Plectron Scanner and crawled into his own bed.

Drifting off to sleep he was re-living the excitement of the fire in his mind. The high slowly filling his body, satisfying his craving.

With the feel of the high he drifted off to sleep.

Tones exploding from the Plectron, the darkness interrupted. "Beeb boop, beep boop, boooop. Box 804, Company 8, Medical assist...." He tuned the rest of the call out. He wasn't interested in the ambo call.

Rolling out of bed, he moved to a sitting position with his feet on the floor. The sharp stab of pain in his ribs jolted him. When his foot hit the floor the flash of pain reminded him to move carefully.

Looking around he realized that he had been sleeping for about two hours. Being awake, he decided to get up and get moving.

After getting dressed and wrapping his ankle, not bothering with the splint, he moved out of his room looking for something to eat.

Coming out of his room he was expecting to see his mother somewhere. He was getting ready to deal with her and get it over with.

Walking through the living room and circling around to the kitchen, his mother was nowhere to be found. Relieved at not having to deal with her, he started rummaging through the fridge.

After grabbing some food and tossing the dishes in the dishwasher, Steve decided that he was restless and didn't want to sit around doing nothing. He decided to head over to the station and check out what was going on.

Changing into his jeans and t-shirt he grabbed his keys and started to head out the door. As he opened the door his mother was standing with a shopping bag, fumbling with her keys.

"You're up," she said. "I figured you would sleep for the rest of the day."

"Nah. Woke up and decided to head over to the fire station to catch up with the guys." He noticed that the bag was from one of the high-end stores at the mall. "Went shopping?"

"Yeah. I ran out to grab an outfit," she smiled. "If I'm going to do interviews, I decided that I needed a new outfit."

"What interviews?"

"Well with you getting hurt in a fire, I figured that the TV station would want to interview me for the 'mother's view'. Good idea, don't you think?"

"Not sure anyone is interested," he sighed. "Haven't even seen a newspaper today. Don't know if the fire was mentioned."

"Oh, I never thought to get one," she dismissed.

"I'll be back later on."

"Do you want me to go with you? They might be at the station for an interview."

"No. I'm sure that the chief chased them off."

"OK. You 'comin home for dinner?"

"Don't know. I'll let you know what's going on." This meant that he would leave a message on the answering machine.

"OK. I'm not going to be home anyway."

He was used to this kind of response. Always wondering why the hell she offered to do something when she was not going to be around anyway. He had stopped being frustrated at this years ago and just let it go. Making his way past her he headed for the stairs, crutches in left hand, right hand on the railing as he hopped on one foot the entire three flights.

Reaching the bottom, he headed over to his car, not bothering to use a crutch under each arm. Pulling the door open he shoved the crutches in the back seat. He clambered in and fired up the engine. The throaty roar of the V-8 acting as a repellent for all things unwanted. He quickly left the complex, escaping his narcissistic mother and headed to the fire station.

Chapter 24

Steve crested the hill pulling into Station Two, quickly surveying the scene. About eight cars were parked at the bottom of the hill across the tarmac and a group of people were tossing a football. Deciding he didn't feel like disrupting the game – or, more importantly, walking with his crutches in front of everyone – he pulled his car up to the fuel pump, knowing that no one would give him a hard time since he was on the injured list.

The men in the parking lot recognized the car and rushed over to see what was going on. This is what they were spending Sunday afternoon waiting for: the chance to see someone who had been at the fire. For those who were there, someone who was at the fire before they were. Slowly gathering throughout the day, each one secretly hoping that the crew would stop by the station and they could hear firsthand about the call. Steve's arrival was the motherlode. They were each secretly envious that they did not get to go into the fire. The next best thing was to hear from someone who was there.

The open bay doors seemed to highlight Engine 8-12 sitting in the first bay, silently waiting to go out to the next call. He wondered if anyone had bothered washing it yet.

As Steve was lost in thought, staring at the engine, the driver's door opened, and a face appeared. "Hey, good to see you Steve."

Steve, still focused on the engine, did not hear what the person had said. He only had a slight recognition of someone talking in the background. Tearing his eyes off the engine, he tried to focus on what was going on. Who was talking to him? The emotions he was feeling flooded through him. Unable to get a grasp on any single feeling he pushed them down into his mind.

"Heard you got banged up on your last call," the man at the driver's door said, trying to help him out of the car. "Glad to see you're up and moving around."

"I'll live. Just a few bumps and bruises," he said, recognizing Pat as he swung his bandaged foot out of the car.

"You got crutches?" Pat asked trying to help Steve get out of the car.

"Back seat," he answered with a flip of his head.

The others started with a wave and a "Hey." The game had come to a stop as the group surrounded their injured brother.

Steve had started to walk leaning on the hood as he limped on his injured foot.

"Hey, wait for the sticks," Pat said. "No one here is in any kind of a hurry."

At the front of the car Steve sat against the grill, knowing that everyone wanted to pepper him with questions about what happened. He didn't know if he was ready to have the questions thrown at him, but he realized that sooner or later he would need to tell the others.

Gary had come over and sat on the hood next to him. It was a position he had taken often over the time he and Steve hung out together. He missed the big call. In fact, he hadn't caught a call in about six weeks. He wanted a rush. He was suffering from withdrawal. Any rush, even something as simple as listening to his injured brother's new stories, was welcome.

Addiction to the rush was not physical, but it is worse than being hooked on drugs or alcohol. Because it isn't physical you can never get it out of your system. You are addicted for life.

Pat was standing on the crutches in front of Steve, trying to balance with both feet off the ground. "Sucks what happened."

"Hey, give the guy a few minutes to get his bearings," Gary intercepted.

"It's OK. We can talk about it," Steve said.

"I can't believe that Royce is really dead," Fred said.

Others nodded in agreement with a quick "yeah" and "it sucks." There were a few firefighters that had been at the scene, after Royce and Steve had been taken to the hospital.

Those who were not at the fire were secretly jealous. The few who had shown up late at the scene wished they had been there earlier. The crave of the rush drove the desire to relive the fire, even vicariously through the stories. They had an opportunity to hear it from the one person who had lived through it. Just the excitement of talking about the fire gave them a rush.

All day they had been talking about Royce dying, but the reality of a dead firefighter had not set in. Everyone knew most members of the department, but most of them did not know each other well. To most of this group Royce was an acquaintance.

Standing, Steve reached for the crutches, just as Pat was swinging back and forth. Taking them, he started to work his way into the station. The rest of them either walked ahead or followed along as he made his way past Engine 8-12 towards the pool table sitting behind it.

"What happened at the fire?" John, a new member with only about four or five months with the department, asked.

Taking a moment, he separated himself emotionally, imagining that he was not the firefighter from the story, imagining that the story he was telling was about someone else. Protecting himself from the emotions he sat on the tailboard of the engine. "When we got to the house it was rolling," Steve began. "Saw the flaming through the bedroom window. Drapes were on fire. Could see the glow. We grabbed the one fifty and went inside."

The group eagerly waited for him to continue.

Staring at an imaginary spot, Steve paused while he was running over in his mind everything that he and Royce had done. What they could have done differently. Anything at all to tell him why Royce was dead. Why had he survived? What had they done wrong? What could he have done to save him? Steve was fighting with himself to get control of his emotions.

Will, one of the older firefighters, seeing Steve fighting for control, offered some senior advice. "It sucks that we lost Royce." The crowd nodded in agreement. "We all know the risks of what we do and we each accept those risks."

"When it's your time, it's your time," Fred offered.

"No one forces us to go into fires. We do it to save lives and protect the property of those who can't," Will continued. "I'm sure over the next few weeks we will be putting together a training on the call. We'll be getting more details along the way."

"Let's give Steve some space," Pat commanded.

"No, it's all right. Need to talk about it sometime," Steve offered. "When we got the call, we were stoked. Dispatch called us before the tones. Riding over, both Royce and I knew in our bones it was a worker. When we arrived, it was 'rollin."

"But you did an interior attack?" Dave asked.

"Yeah, but that wasn't the plan. When we go there Royce was going to surround and drown. Knock the fire down and then go inside and clean up."

"Why did you go in?" Andy questioned.

"When we got there, as we were pulling the one fifty, some screaming woman told us her daughter was still in the house."

"Wow, you got to do a search and rescue?" Sean, one of the new members, asked in awe.

With a slow nod Steve continued. "That changed everything. From the outside it looked like a single room was engulfed. We decided that we would go inside and attack." The rush was consuming Steve.

The others were starting to feel the excitement, adrenaline trickling into their bodies. Imagining themselves being in Steve's position.

"We went into the house. It was one of the split levels. Up the stairs." Steve paused for a second, re-living the memory. His sadness over losing his partner was suppressed with the memory of the rush. He wanted the fix again. "When we got to the top the smoke had stratified. Three feet above the floor." He held his hand out, showing the height of the thermal. "We stood up in the smoke to see what it was like."

"Cool. Most of the time the building vents," Gary interjected. "What happened next?"

"We moved down the hall to the last room."

"Didn't you search the other rooms first?" Pat asked.

"Nah. We knew the house. The mother told us that the room at the end was where the kid was. With the condition, we decided to go straight to that room to see if we could find her."

"When did the other crews show up?" Dave wanted to know.

"Don't know," Steve said, shaking his head.

"Just as Royce and Steve were going into the house, 8-52 showed up," Ted answered. He had come up the driveway a few minutes ago and was unnoticed by most of the small crowd gathered around the back of the engine.

The crowd nodded and greeted him.

Steve and Ted locked eyes as he continued. "The Ladder rolled in and I had them set up in front of the drive so they could vent the roof."

"Did you worry about a backdraft?" John wanted to know.

Steve continued, "Some. House hadn't vented, didn't see any signs. Once we got inside, the door to the bedroom was closed. We went fast in case of a flashover. Royce got the nozzle ready, pushed the door open. Royce blasted the room with a fog. After the initial attack, we moved into the room." His body involuntarily reacted as he relived the fire, a surge easing its way into his body. His addiction satiated.

"Wow, was it engulfed?" Sean said trying to sound more experienced.

"About halfway. Once we hit the room, it blacked out from the steam and smoke." He could almost feel the moist steam crawling across his exposed skin. He could remember the feel of the steam burning his skin.

"After Royce hit the room, I split off and started the search." He was getting into the groove of telling the story.

"What were the other crews doing?" Will asked.

Steve looked at Ted, "Don't know. I was kinda focused on the interior."

"8-52 showed up just as they were going into the house. I sent the ladder crew to the roof to vent. 8-14 arrived just after. They picked up the hydrant. The crew went over to 8-52 to take over the aerial attack. Because Jack and Jason were on the roof cutting in with the K-12 when it happened," Ted began.

Steve focused on Ted, waiting for him to continue. The rush was creeping into his body. This was the first time he was going to hear what happened from someone else.

"Larry showed up at the same time 8-14 brought the supply line and Robby was getting it set up on 8-12." Ted paused, taking a deep breath. "I was standing out with the other lieutenants in the middle of the cul-de-sac when the explosion happened. We dropped to the dirt like we were under attack."

Now it was Ted's turn to feel the returning rush.

"Jeez, that would have scared the crap out of me," Will commented, trying to show the younger firefighters it is OK to be scared and nervous.

"Honestly, I was frozen. After the blast I didn't know what to do," Ted admitted. "Larry started to bark orders at everyone. He verified that everyone around was OK, then he sent Mark to the back to check on the crew. Wanted to know who was inside. If Robby had any flow."

"Shit, sounds like a cluster fuck!" Pat commented.

"We didn't know what to do. When Larry started giving orders, we all fell in and started to get our heads together," Ted admitted. "We started to pick it up. Fred and Jeff grabbed the 100 footer to attack from the outside. Mel and Kirk were with Bill to finish setting the ladder and start the deluge gun." Sweat was breaking out on his brow as he was re-living the event.

"What happened to the guys on the roof?" Greg asked, knowing that they were ok.

"Don't know what happened in the back, but after a few, they came back to the front. 8-92 was there."

"Were they OK?" a voice from behind asked.

"They were walking. Darcy was checking them out on the back step of 8-12. They were getting the hundred footer ready when Steve and Royce busted out of the house."

Ted and Steve, who had been looking at each other, suddenly had to turn their faces away, fighting the onslaught of tears that welled within. Ted walked quickly to the soda machine, popping in a couple of quarters. The memory that they each had of the very next moments brought these two to the edge of losing control.

The group was mesmerized by the story. Each imagining themselves at the fire scene.

Taking a deep breath Steve continued his part. "After the initial attack, I was searching and found what felt like a child's body."

Gasps of excitement erupted from the crowd.

"I found someone hiding on a chair under a blanket. When I dragged it off the chair and pulled the body close to my face so I could see."

"Was it burnt up?" Jay questioned.

"It was a doll."

Sighs and groans came from the surrounding men. Steve wasn't sure if it was relief because it was a doll or if it was disappointment that it wasn't a child.

"That's when the blast hit. Everything got quiet." Steve's eyes were distant, and his mind took him back inside the burning house. "It looked like everything froze. I could see the flames frozen in midair. There was no noise. I remember complete silence. Then 'Boom!'"

"Did it knock you over?" Dave wanted to know.

"I don't remember. I woke up lying on my back. I knew I wasn't out long, still had air in my pack."

"Is that when you found Royce?"

"No. It was black-out conditions. I found the wall and started going back to the door."

"If it was black-out, how did you know what way to go?" Sean, the new firefighter asked.

"You go left," Pat answered. "Weren't you paying attention in basic training?"

Ignoring the question, Steve continued, "I couldn't hear anything. The blast took out my hearing."

"You're not deaf now are you?" Gary was concerned.

"What?" Steve asked bringing a hand to his ear, causing chuckling from his audience. "No. Temporary. Might have some loss when I get older."

"That sucks," Pat countered.

Shrugging, Steve continued, "I followed the wall back and found the hose. Followed hose to nozzle and knocked down the room. That's when I found Royce."

"Was he dead?" several people asked at once

"Probably, but I couldn't tell, I know his face mask was busted up. Couldn't tell if he was breathing. That's when I decided to get him out."

All of the men surrounding the two were imagining themselves in the fire, dousing the inferno caused by the explosion. Rescuing the fallen firefighter in the dark steam-filled room. Mightily carrying his unconscious body through the raging fire, flames lapping at them as the rafters fell, barely missing them. Busting out of the house, door exploding off the hinges, flying down the steps from a single solid kick, landing mangled from the force. Victoriously coming down the steps and gently placing Royce onto the stretcher as he moaned and started to regain consciousness.

Steve became silent as Ted continued, "That's when Steve came out of the door. By the time he got down the steps, Fred and Kirk grabbed Royce. Darcy ran up the drive. It was all a blur. Everyone running toward them." He took a drink of his soda, pausing to get control once again.

"Did you hurt your ankle getting Royce out?' Gary asked.

"Nope," Steve stated. "I twisted in on the last step. When they were pulling Royce off, I hit the step wrong and twisted my ankle."

The crowd was silent as they were thinking about the fire, Royce dying, what they would have done.

"That's when we tossed them both in 8-92 and sent them to the hospital."

"What happened after that?" Gary prodded.

"We knocked down the fire and cleaned up," Ted finished.

"What ever happened to the kid that was inside?" Will wanted to know.

Another voice came from around the engine. "After the fire was out, I went to tell the mother that we were looking for the body. That's when she told me the kid was never in the house," Chief Butler said.

Ted nodded at Larry in agreement.

"What do you mean she wasn't in the house?" someone from the back asked.

They were painting. Room smelled so she went to her grandmother's house to spend the night," Larry explained. "In the panic of the fire the mom thought she was in the house."

"Shit, I can't believe that the mother didn't know where her kid was!" Andy exclaimed.

"Chief was so pissed off; he told the crews to gut the house 'checking for hot spots'," Ted emphasized by making quotation marks with his fingers.

"We finished up. Fire marshal did his investigation, and we packed it in," Chief Butler finished.

With the conclusion of the story the group of firefighters were mulling around, not sure what to do next.

"Alright, enough of the war stories for today," Chief Butler began. "Let's get this place in order. Someone pull the engines out and let's get these girls cleaned up."

Will and Andy looked at each other and with a nod of the head indicated what engine they would pull out. The others started to scramble around the station, collecting the buckets and soap used to wash down the engines.

In short order the entire group was busily washing, buffing and polishing the engines. Someone turned on a radio. Music blasted in the air as water was sprayed, sponges thrown at each other that resulted in a massive water fight while they washed the engines. The tension of the fire, the death of their comrade momentarily blocked by the fun of the afternoon.

The brief interlude from the sad reality provided Steve and Ted the opportunity to laugh with the other members of the fire station. Fear of being ostracized, fear that they would blame him for Royce's death was forgotten. The washing of the fire engines provided more than just the opportunity to hang out, it provided the opportunity to wash away the pain.

While everyone was working on the engine's, Larry gave Steve the painkillers the doc had prescribed.

As the engines were dried with the chammies and returned into the firehouse, those hanging around started to wander off, going home to have Sunday dinner with their families and get ready for the week. Everyone there was a volunteer and worked another full-time job somewhere else.

Ted said his goodbyes as he headed off to grab dinner with his parents. "Steve. Hey, you doin' OK?"

"Yeah, I'm OK. How you doin'?" he asked.

"Still messed up by it all. Not sure what to do."

"You going to school tomorrow?"

"Sure, what else is there to do?" Steve asked.

"You gonna be OK?"

"No idea. Don't know what's gonna happen at school," Steve replied. "If they go into some kind of memorial crap, I'll cut out."

"OK. I'll be around tomorrow if you need anything."

"Great. I'll probably come to the station after school."

"The only thing I got going is meeting with the counselor."

"I've got an appointment too. Larry's going to call me with the info."

"Same one you saw in the hospital?"

"Yeah."

"Never did ask, how was it?"

"Bullshit."

"What happened?"

"He thought I was drinking and driving. Killed Royce in a crash."

"He didn't know that he died in a fire?"

"Nope. He didn't bother reading the chart. He just guessed that since he was called in on a weekend that I was some rich kid whose parents were bailing him out."

"Great. Think it's the same guy I'm going to see?"

"Probably. He was on-call, so they just let him see the whole crew."

"Is that gonna help?"

"We'll see."

"Well good luck tomorrow. Let me know how it turns out."

"You got it," Steve smiled. "If I don't see you here, I'll see you, hear."

"Catch you on the flip side," Ted replied.

Chapter 25

The next day Steve pulled into the high school. It was early and the lot was empty. The school was a closed campus and once on school ground, students were not allowed to leave. He knew that there were blind spots in the parking lot where the school administration couldn't see a car leaving. Locating a parking space that he could get to without being seen, he pulled through so he wouldn't need to back out. He figured that if the day was shitty, he would cut out.

With no one else around he took advantage of the solitude to prepare for the onslaught at school. The countless questions from ignorant classmates. "What happened?" "How did he die?" "Was it gross?"

He had already decided that when asked about his injuries he would tell them, "I twisted my ankle coming down some steps while I was carrying a heavy load." It wasn't a lie, and the non-excitement would stop further questions. Most of his classmates didn't even know he was in the fire department. Some of his closer friends knew, but he wasn't sure if they remembered. He didn't hide it from them, it just never came up in conversation. He wasn't even sure that anyone knew that he and Royce knew each other. They moved in different circles in school.

By the time he made it to his locker the students had started to arrive en masse. It took longer to get through the busy halls. Not wanting to talk to anyone, he tried to disappear in the halls as he stopped by his locker to toss in unneeded books.

"Wow, what happened to you?" the girl two lockers over asked.

"Twisted my ankle."

"That sucks. Later."

With a nod of the head, he flipped the locker shut and spun around to merge into the flow of other students making their way to homeroom. Pleased that the first encounter was over, he headed off to his homeroom. Arriving at the classroom about five minutes before the bell he slid into his seat to wait. Usually, he hung around talking and would come into the room just before the bell sounded. But having to navigate with a bum ankle and crutches, he decided to just go sit in class.

The teacher sitting behind the desk looked up from the papers she was working on and smiled. "Looks like you had an exciting weekend?" Ms. Fillmore said.

"Looks worse than it is. Just a bad sprain."

Reaching into a desk drawer, she pulled out a pad of paper and scribbled on it. "I was on crutches last summer. They are a pain to get around on." She stood and walked over to where he was sitting and handed him a slip of paper. "Here is a hall pass. Don't worry about being on time. If someone gives you a hard time just hand them the pass." She smiled.

"Thanks," Steve mumbled as more of the students wandered in. He appreciated that she didn't ask how it happened.

The bell rang and a few straggling students skidded through the door. Ms. Fillmore looked around the class to take roll while the speaker on the wall screamed to life. "Good morning students. Please rise for the Pledge of Allegiance."

The students obediently stood next to their desk and recited the pledge in a Monday morning monotone. "Thank you to the Junior Varsity Cheer Squad for leading the pledge this morning," the speaker said as the students plopped back into their seats.

Braced for the next announcement, Steve was ready for some huge declaration to the entire school telling them of Royce's death and his injuries. Closing his eyes, listening to the next announcement, he heard, "The baseball team...."

Eyes flying open he looked around the room to make sure he was sitting in homeroom. No announcement. He didn't know what to feel or think. The only other time a student had died – in a car crash – that was the first announcement of the day. Between the over-emotional weeping in the halls all day and the ones associated with the car crash hiding from everyone, the school was a mess. Today, nothing.

A swirl of emotion was rising inside. Relief, neglect, and anger quietly growing. *They didn't even let anyone know he is dead*, he thought.

The announcements ended with no mention of Royce dying. As Steve was stewing over the lack of announcement, he realized that the school probably did not know. Who would have told them?

The bell rang and everyone else jumped up and started loudly moving to the first class of the day, their lives unaffected by the events of the weekend.

Steve stood, grabbing his crutches, and began making his way through the day.

Spending the day trying to concentrate on school, floating between surges of emotions, he managed to go unnoticed. His friends and some of the students he was acquainted with asked him why he was on crutches. No one even talked about the house fire.

Meeting up with the regular group at lunch, Steve made small talk about his crutches and twisted ankle. Steve stuck with his rehearsed script about the injury. He wasn't ready to talk to the other high school students about it yet.

There was small talk about what the others did over the weekend, homework due and high school trauma drama.

Steve knew that the world he walked in was very different from other high schoolers. He was finally realizing just how much. He never thought much about the people who died. The people in accidents. Didn't give much concern over houses burning down. He focused on doing his job. Interacting with these people for minutes out of their life. Sometimes a firefighter would have an unexpected impact on the patient. He realized that in the past two years of firefighting he had seen more death and trauma than most people will see in their entire life.

Once, about three weeks after a call, the mother of a child brought him to the station house to thank the firefighters for "rescuing" him. He was messing around in his house and got his head stuck in the metal railing of the stairs. The mother was experiencing full-on panic.

The boy was just crying, trying to pull his head out.

When they arrived, she was yelling, "You got it in there, just pull it out!"

All they had to do was get one person on each banister and pull, bending the rails slightly. His head slid right out.

Most people never even notice the fire department unless they need it. In this community very few people had any idea that the fire department was voluntary, until after they needed them. Just like wandering through the high school unnoticed, firefighters and paramedics were seldom noticed.

It was really cool for the kid to come by the station. It made the crew feel wanted when they were not needed.

"Steve." Greg was bumping him with his elbow.

"What?"

"Where did you go?"

"Sorry, zoned out for a few." Steve was trying to regain his focus. "What d'ya say?"

"Ken's folks are going to be out of town over the weekend." Greg was smiling. "We're getting' together for a small party. His brothers said he'll get us some beer for the weekend."

Steve made a mental note about the party. Chances are there would be a call or two out of it. More importantly, if there was one party, there would be others. Stupid high schoolers would compete over who had the biggest and best party. "Cool. Depending on what's up I'll stop by."

The alcohol didn't really excite him. Being in the fire department he was already able to drink freely. Not only did he look old enough to drink, most of the firefighters believed that if you could run into a burning building you could have a drink.

The rest of the day he went through the motions of being a student, with no interest or enthusiasm. He blended easily with the other students. Several of the classes he tried to concentrate on the subject and lectures, trying to get his brain from running in circles. It didn't work. He kept thinking about the fire. Royce dying. The rush. Students who didn't know or care.

The final bell rang, and Steve was free. What a crap day. No one mentioned Royce. The fire. Anything! *Shit*, he thought. *No one gives a fuck that Royce died.* This thought darkened his mood. Mulling over the mixed emotions, he headed home.

Going up to the apartment he tossed his bag on the floor as he walked in. His arms aching from using crutches all day, he decided to try to walk without them.

His foot was tender, but if he went slow, he could get weight on it and walk around.

Limping around, feeling a little better about getting back to normal, he noticed the red flashing light on the answering machine. Pushing the button, he waited to see who called.

"Steve, this is Chief Butler. You have an appointment with Dr Jameson Tuesday at 10:00 a.m. Call me to let me know you got the message. OK, bye."

He pulled out his wallet and removed a card. This had all the phone numbers he needed for the station. Finding Chief Butler's work phone number, he picked up the phone and dialed.

"Hello," the chief's voice came through the phone.

"Hey Chief, it's Steve."

Hey Steve, how's it going?"

"I got your message," he sighed.

"You will be there." It was a statement.

"Yeah, I'll be there. I think it's a waste of time, but I'll be there."

"OK. The office is in the building across from the library."

"Yeah, I know the one," Steve confirmed. "Hey, what about getting out of school? I don't want my mother writing a note. She may insist on coming with me."

"I'll take care of it. In fact, I'll call right after I hang up with you." The sound of the chief flipping through a phone book could be heard. "I'll call Roger Bancroft and get it straightened out."

"Hey, Larry."

"Yeah."

"They never said anything about Royce dying over the weekend."

There was silence from the other end of the receiver.

"Chief."

"No one ever told the school!" Larry exclaimed. "Shit, I hope they didn't call Royce's parents telling them he was delinquent."

"That would suck."

"I got to make some calls. You gonna come up to the station tonight?"

"Nah. I'm gonna hang at home and rest my foot."

"Ok. Call if you need anything."

"Thanks Chief." He didn't wait for a response as he placed the receiver into the cradle.

He hobbled to the living room, passing the TV and turning it on and grabbing the cable box remote as he made his way to the couch. Placing his injured ankle on the coffee table he flipped channels until he found the Captain Chesapeake show. Some cartoons and *Gilligan's Island* would clear his head.

He spent the rest of the evening flipping through his homework and surfing TV, grabbing food out of the fridge and eating in front of the TV.

He went to bed earlier than normal. He was tired from walking around on crutches and the emotional fatigue.

His mom was asleep when he left for school. She normally had some kind of meeting every night of the week. Book Club, Social Groups, going to the movies with one of her friends. She was seldom home in the evening. With her daughter living at college and her son spending the evenings at the fire station, she naturally found something else to fill her time.

Chapter 26

The next morning Steve left his house and headed to school. He parked his car in the same spot as the day before and made his way into the school. *Guess I need to swing by the office and make sure that Chief took care of my excuse*, he thought.

Walking into the school office, he wasn't sure who he needed to talk to. He saw a line of four students and joined them. He was waiting behind another student turning in a note from her parents explaining her absence from the day before. Lost in thought, he had never been to the office for an absence. He or one of his parents called in so he didn't have to stand in line.

"Mr. Quinn," a voice from behind him called.

Turning on his crutches, he saw a woman calling from a doorway that separated the administrative offices from the reception desks. It was a barricade to keep the unruly crowd of students away from the principal and vice principals. She was the gatekeeper. To be taken into this area was bad for a student.

"I'm glad you're here. Mr. Bancroft sent me out to find you." She smiled. "Please come with me," she instructed. Mr. Bancroft was the school's principal. You never went to his office unless there was something serious going on. Steve recognized the principal's secretary but couldn't remember her name. She never went into the jungle to hunt students down. He wondered why she was looking for him.

"Don't worry, you're not in any trouble." She turned and disappeared into the doorway.

Steve followed her. She was sitting down at her desk by the time he caught up. Pointing to an open door she said, "He's waiting for you."

He had never been in the principal's office before. It had a large wooden desk and the walls on either side were built-in bookcases filled with books and a few awards and trophies.

"Steve, we've never had the opportunity to meet before, and that's usually a good thing in high school," Mr. Bancroft. "Grab a seat."

Sitting down Steve looked at the man across the desk and asked, "Why am I being called in to your office?"

With a smile he replied, "Relax. Chief Butler called me yesterday and briefed me."

"I guess it's OK to split for the doctor's appointment?"

"Of course. In fact, anything you need, swing by, let one of the girls know and we'll take care of it. And as a side note, stop parking in the far corner of the lot. If you need to leave come by the office, don't sneak off. Too much paperwork for the staff if you sneak off."

Confused, Steve didn't understand why the principal was being so easy to deal with "Why?" Steve asked.

"Larry briefed me about everything yesterday. I know about Royce and the fire."

"Did anyone call his parents yesterday when he didn't come in?"

"No. I got to it first thing. Told them that when Royce was reported absent to notify me and do nothing else."

"How come?" Steve questioned. "I though you didn't talk to the chief until last night?"

"That is when I got the 'official' notification."

Steve was confused.

Seeing his confused look Mr. Bancroft explained. "I heard the tones on Saturday." He paused to take in a deep breath.

"You heard the tones?"

"Yeah. When I'm not babysitting you kids, I'm an Assistant chief with Bel Air."

"You're a volunteer too?"

"Yep, have been for about twenty years," he said with a distant look in his eyes.

Steve smiled, knowing that there was someone in the school that had at least some kind of clue what he was dealing with made him feel better.

"Look, if you want to talk, if you want to cut out, just come by and I'll take care of it," he offered. "Today we are going to announce Royce's death to the students. I had the chance to call most of his teachers yesterday and brief them."

"What did you tell them?"

"Died in an accident," he responded. "I did not tell them he died in a fire and I did not tell them that you were injured in the same accident. I figured that it's your story to tell. If you want."

Steve felt a wave of relief. He wasn't sure why he was relived. He was also disappointed that no one would know how Royce died. They wouldn't know he was hurt also. Pushing his conflicting emotions to the dungeon of his mind he decided that he would worry about it later.

"We set up to have a couple of extra counselors here at the school for the rest of the week. We'll offer that students can come and talk if they feel the need," he paused. "If any of the counselors connects the dots and want to talk to you, let me know and I'll stop it. I don't want them screwing everything up with their delusions of being a shrink."

Steve smiled at that comment. Most of the students thought the counselors were useless. Seemed that the principal had similar thoughts.

"Get out of here and go to class. Swing by the office and check out when it's time for you to leave." He stood and started walking around the desk. "See my assistant and she'll give you a super pass to get around for the next week."

Steve stood and nodded. "Thanks Chief." The title identified Principle Bancroft as one of the brotherhood and not the disciplinarian of the school. It made Steve feel better. More in control. It was a relationship that provided order in his confusing world. It made him feel better that the principal was no longer an adversary.

With a stern look Chief Bancroft said, "Don't abuse the pass, and don't let your friends know that you have it. I'll never hear the end of it with them all whining to get one."

"Yes sir. Thank you." He stopped by Principal Bancroft's secretary's desk and picked up the pass. Reading her name off the plaque on the desk he said, "Thanks Mrs. Denison."

Smiling she watched him swing out of the office and into the high school crowd.

The announcement came over the loudspeaker about Royce's death during home room. No one in the classroom reacted. Steve overheard the girl three seats in front lean over and whisper to her friend, "Did we know him?"

She shrugged her shoulders.

Later in the day Steve went into the bathroom and overheard a couple of guys talking about going to the counselors and telling them they were friends and upset. They were going to convince the counselors to let them leave school. It pissed him off that they were using his partner's death to hook school.

He was sitting in World History at nine twenty-five, trying to listen to the teacher drone on about World War One, when he decided it was time to head to the shrink's office. Quietly gathering his books, he stood and grabbed his crutches.

"Can I help you Mr. Quinn?" Mr. Mullins asked.

"No thanks I can manage," he said starting to make his way to the door. Mr. Mullins had always been an asshole. None of the kids liked taking his class.

"I don't believe I gave you permission to move around."

"I have to leave for a doctor's appointment."

"You don't have my permission to leave the room."

Getting pissed off at the teacher, Steve replied, "I wasn't aware I had to have your permission."

"You can just take your seat."

"I don't think so." Steve gave an icy glare at him. He wasn't in any mood to take crap from the asshole.

Startled at the student's response, he was at a loss for words.

Steve began digging in his pocket for the note signed by the principal giving him free rein at the school. "I just assumed the office would have told you that I was leaving."

"The office did not tell me."

Handing him the note Steve glared at him and said, "Guess Principal Bancroft didn't think you needed to know."

Staring at the note, Mr. Mullins was stunned. He had known that the principal could write these notes, but he had never actually seen one. In fact, he couldn't remember the last time he even heard about one being written.

Steve took the note back without waiting for Mr. Mullins to hand it to him, put it in his pocket and turned to head out the door.

"How do I know that's legitimate?"

"I guess you can call the office and ask if you're worried about it," Steve said as he left the room. *Dickhead*, he thought. He didn't deserve any respect and it felt good to dis him in front of the whole class.

He stopped by the office and told the admission clerk that he was leaving for a doctor's appointment. Checking the list, she saw his name on the list of students who could leave during the day. Smiling she said, "See you after your appointment."

Steve smiled and nodded at her. He had no idea if he was going to come back or not, but he would deal with that later.

Chapter 27

Steve found Doctor Jameson's office on the third floor of the medical building. Walking in he recalled the few fire calls he had been to in the building. Twice he was on an ambo assist, taking patients from doctor's offices to the hospital. The other time was for a fire call. It turned out that the fire alarm malfunctioned. The memories gave him a small rush, easing into his body as he relived the excitement in his mind.

After checking in with the receptionist he sat in the waiting room, wondering what the session was going to be like. There was a woman sitting in the waiting room, aimlessly reading a magazine. Looking at her sitting there he quickly created a picture in his mind of the woman waiting for her child, a daughter about twelve years old. He could picture her behind the door with the doctor talking about her mother and father. Probably divorcing. The girl was taking advantage of the situation, getting more toys for herself as she manipulated the guilty parents.

A door opened and Doctor Jameson peered around. "Hey Steve, come on in."

The office looked like someone's living room. There was a couch with a couple of large armchairs with a coffee table in the center. It was similar to the set-up at the hospital, except to one side was a play area with toys for small kids, an easel with a large pad of paper, crayons and markers. There was also a big box of dolls and a bookshelf full of board games.

Doctor Jameson sat in a large armchair with notepad in his lap. "Have a seat," he said sweeping his arm around.

Thinking about the arrangement, Steve sat in the armchair opposite the doctor, knowing he would expect him to sit on a couch, like a child in front of his parents.

Glancing up Dr. Jameson blinked twice as he realized that Steve was sitting in the chair. He placed his hand on the arm rests and picked up his body slightly turning to face the chair. Slightly annoyed, he thought, *People don't sit in that chair until after a few visits*. After getting himself adjusted he asked, "Have you ever seen a therapist before Steve?"

"Only when I saw you in the hospital. Doctor Jameson." He decided that every time the doc would say his name, he would use the doc's. Eventually he might make the connection.

"You seem very comfortable."

"Is that a problem?"

"No Steve. It's just usually someone's first time seeing a therapist they are very nervous."

"Why should someone be nervous Doctor Jameson?"

"Oh, they shouldn't. It's that in new situations it's normal for people to be nervous."

Silence hung in the air for a few seconds. Steve knew the doc was waiting for him to start talking. Most people don't like silence and they start talking. Steve had learned to just be quiet and let people talk. Soon they would tell you what you wanted to know.

"How are you doing today Steve?"

"I'm doing OK Doctor Jameson," Steve replied. Steve sat and stared at the doctor with soft innocent eyes, arms on each arm rest with hands hanging over the end. He didn't want to reveal any emotions through his eyes or body language. He was nervous and he didn't really trust the doc, but he didn't want to let him know.

Flipping between two pages of his notes the doc paused. "Why don't we continue where we left off Steve?" Doctor Jameson had been eagerly waiting for this appointment. The seventeen-year-old survivor of a horrific accident was an exciting change from his typical clients.

Steve just sat there, thinking that this dick hadn't even reviewed his notes before the appointment. "Where did we leave off Doctor Jameson?" He remembered exactly where they had left off. He just wanted the doctor to do his job.

"We were talking about the accident that killed your partner and your unresolved feelings over the loss of your friend."

"I don't remember any 'unresolved feelings.' When I last saw you, Royce had died less than twenty-four hours before. I was out of it most of the day on Saturday dealing with the hospital and doctors. I hadn't had much time to spend thinking about it."

"Let's start by going over what happened. Now that you've had some time to think about it maybe you'll remember something else." This young man was very good at avoiding the questions. He would have to take a harder approach to get to him to admit his feelings.

"What do you want to know?"

"Tell me about your friend who died."

Taking a deep breath and slightly slumping he tried to show defeat and start talking about the issues. "We were in a fire. There was an explosion. When we got out Royce was dead."

Doctor Jameson shifted in his chair. "Help me understand about the fire department. What types of things do you do there?"

"Everything a paid firefighter does. We train, maintain the equipment and respond to fire calls."

Stopping for a moment he asked, "Isn't the fire department from the county?"

"Nope. Harford County is covered by volunteer fire departments. When you call 911, it's volunteers who respond."

"There are no professional firefighters?"

"I didn't say that. Every firefighter is a trained professional. Most of them have more training than the paid firefighters."

"But they are volunteer? How do they make money?"

"They work."

"What kind of jobs?"

"Everything. Auto mechanics, factory workers, prison guards, lawyers, engineers, even school principals."

"I didn't know that there were only volunteers."

"Most people don't. Until after a call. Then they realize it."

"To make sure I understand, you and Royce were responding to a fire call when he was killed?"

"We were on duty when the call came in."

"Can you explain what that means?"

"Every Friday we volunteer to cover the shift."

"Why?"

"To make a quicker response to a call."

"So, you were on duty?"

With a shrug Steve replied, "We were standing by at the station, waiting for a call."

"Were other people with you?"

"Yeah. Robby and Ted were on duty also."

"Is this normal for you?"

"Yeah. We are the regular Friday night crew."

"Do you normally have a fire?"

"No. This is the first working fire we've seen in about six months."

"So, you weren't expecting a fire call?"

"We were hoping for a call. Wanted to turn wheels."

"And you got the fire call for a house fire. Do you get a lot of house fires?" This was more curiosity. Doctor Jameson's was wondering about houses burning down.

"We get a few house fires. Most of the time we get there and its out or was just some smoke. Getting a working house fire is rare."

"Tell me about being in the fire."

"It was rolling when we got there. Could see the flames as we pulled in." His eyes were distant with the memory.

"Is this the first time you were in a 'working fire'?"

"No, been in a few. But this was the best. Working dwelling fire. Could see the flames."

"Why was it the best?" Doctor Jameson was trying to understand why a high school student would be going into a burning building. Hopefully from there he could get him to acknowledge his guilt and other feelings.

"The house was rolling. We could see the fire from the window."

"And you went in, tried to save a little girl?"

"Yes. We were going to do an exterior attack, but the woman told us her daughter was inside."

"What's an 'exterior attack'?"

We would throw water on the house from the driveway. Busting out the glass window with water pressure from the hose."

"I assume it's safer to do an exterior attack."

"Yeah. You don't need to go in, but it leaves more damage to the dwelling." Pausing, Steve said, "Surround and drown."

"So, the woman told you that there was a child in the house, so you went into the burning house to save her?"

"Pretty much."

"And Royce died in the fire?"

"There was an explosion."

"And the explosion killed him?"

"He was hit in the face with shrapnel from the explosion."

"That sounds horrible. How do you feel about your friend's death?"

"Feel? I'm sorry that Royce is dead. I wish there was something that could have been done to save him."

"You said you're sorry that he is dead. Why are you sorry? Do you think it's your fault?"

"Why would I think it's my fault?"

"I am asking if you feel it's your fault."

"Why should I?" Steve was wondering if he should have done something different. Breathing calmly, he maintained control, struggling not to get defensive. Was this man accusing him of killing Royce? Or at least believing that he was responsible for his death?

Writing down some notes Doctor Jameson did not even look up when he replied. "People have many different emotions when someone close to them dies. We are trying to explore those emotions. To help you deal with them."

Wrinkling his brow, Steve was concerned. He didn't feel any emotions about Royce dying. He was wondering, *Am I fucked up? Should I be feeling something different?*

"Do you feel guilty that you lived?"

"No. Should I be feeling guilty?"

Finally looking up from his notes Doctor Jameson asked, "What are you feeling?"

"Not feeling much of anything."

"What do you mean?"

"Look, I'm sorry he's dead. It sucks, but I have spent the last few days going over it in my head. Given a chance to do it again, I wouldn't do anything differently."

Doctor Jameson was not expecting the lack of emotion. He quickly changed the topic to see if he could break through in a different way. "You also mentioned that your parents were divorced." Doctor Jameson shifted the questions, hoping to get him talking about emotions. "How did that make you feel?" He was beginning to worry that there was no emotion over his friend's death, wondering if he had any emotional connections. Secretly hoping he was a sociopath or at least antisocial.

"Not much different. I was glad that I didn't have to listen to them arguing all the time."

"How has it changed your life Steve?"

"What do you mean Doctor Jameson?"

"What is different? Did you move? Do you see your mother or father more or less? That sort of stuff."

"Yeah, we moved."

"Tell me about it."

"Not much to tell. Parents sold the house and we moved into an apartment with my mom so I could finish high school."

"Did you grow up in the house?"

"Nah. Only lived in that house for three years."

"Tell me about you room in the house."

"Um, it was a room."

"Anything special about it?"

"Not really. What's this got do with anything?"

Ignoring the question, the doctor continued to probe at the young man. "Tell me about your new room."

"Um, it's a room."

"Do you like it better or worse than your room at the house?"

Shrugging his shoulders, he replied, "Same as the room at the house."

"Did you decorate it? Hang any posters?"

"Nah. I'm not into that stuff."

"Did you do anything to make it your room?"

"Dumped my stuff. Should I have decorated or something?"

He felt a concern that this young man did nothing to make his room his. "Most of the time kids your age decorate their rooms. You said that you've been in the house for about a year and a half. Where did you live before that?"

"We moved from the Midwest."

"Was that hard leaving your friends when you moved?"

"I guess."

"Was it hard to make new friends here?"

"Nah. It took a few weeks, but I have a good group of friends at school and at the fire station."

"You said school and the fire station. Are they separate?"

"What do you mean?"

"The way you identified with school and the fire department individually. Do you have friends that are in the fire department and at school too?"

"No. The kids at school don't have anything to do with the fire department."

"Was Royce in school with you too?"

"Yeah. But we run in different circles." Steve drew in a breath. "Ran."

"What do you mean?"

"He hangs with the shop group; I hang with the nerds."

"But you hang out at the fire station. How do you balance that?"

"There's not much to balance. When I'm with the kids from school we do high school stuff."

"What kind of 'high school stuff' do you do?" Doctor Jameson asked, making quotation marks in the air with his fingers.

What a dick, Steve thought. "What's this got to do with Royce?"

"It's about you Steve. I'm just trying to understand you so that I can help you."

"Understand what?"

"How you're feeling about your friend's death, parents' divorce, things like that," he clarified. "I'm trying to get a feel on how you socialize. What you associate with. What you like. It's not about anything specific, just trying to get to know you better." He was digging for the one event, the one situation that impacted his life.

Steve wrinkled his brow. He wasn't sure he liked someone poking into his life like this.

The doctor was getting frustrated. Usually the kids open up immediately about parents, school, how unfair life is. This boy was not. Switching tactics, he asked, "What do you want to talk about?"

"Don't really want to talk about anything."

"Steve, it's not good to bottle your feelings up. Hide from them."

"Do you think I'm bottling up my feelings?"

"Well let's find out. Are you angry that he's dead?"

"No."

"Do you feel guilty that he died?"

"No. Do you think I should feel guilty?" Steve asked with acid in his voice. "What?"

"Do you think I should feel guilty? Do you think I should have saved him?"

"Do you think you could have?"

"If I could have, he would be alive."

"I see. Would you have done anything different if you had known that he was going to die?"

"Sure, if we had known there was no one inside we wouldn't have gone in. If that stupid bitch had known where her kid was, Royce would still be alive."

Thinking for a moment, he started to grab onto a thought. "So, do you think it was the woman's fault that Royce died?"

"When we got to the house, we were going to do an exterior attack. Then there was a woman standing out front yelling about her kid being inside. That's when we decided to go in."

"You went into the house on fire because someone told you there was a child inside?"

Steve nodded his head.

"You called her a 'stupid bitch'. Are you angry at her?" It was the first significant emotion he could identify.

"Yes."

"Why?"

"If she remembered where her kid was, we wouldn't have entered," Steve explained. "It was supposed to be a surround and drown." His brow wrinkled with anger as he spat, "How the hell can a parent forget where their child is?"

Doctors tend to answer simple questions quickly and move on. "Being a parent is difficult," Doctor Jameson immediately interjected, trying to get him to understand how hard raising children is. "Sometimes parents make mistakes." He was thinking that this may relate to his parent's divorce.

"A mistake is forgetting a toy. Not completely forgetting where your kid is."

"Do your parents know where you are all of the time?"

"I'm not seven."

"So, you blame the mother for Royce's death?"

"No. Not his death." Pausing for a moment he continued, "I blame her for being stupid."

"You don't blame her for Royce dying, so why do you blame her for being stupid?"

"He died trying to save someone, even if there was no one to save, he died trying," Steve explained. Mumbling, he continued, "We wanted to go in. Wanted to dance with the devil." A sly smile crept across his face as he remembered the fire. The smoke hanging in the air. The heat of the fire. The rush of a rescue. Adrenaline building, coursing through his body. Bringing the fix he craved. Focusing his mind. "It was an excuse to go in. We jumped."

"You decided to go into the house after she said that the child was inside."

"We decided that it was the excuse to go in."

"You decided to go into the house. No one told you to go into the fire."

Steve nodded his head, remembering the feeling of being in the fire. "Didn't matter if they did. We decided that we had a good reason to go in."

"So, did you make the decision to go in or did Royce?"

"The whole crew did. I know Ted and Robby wanted to go in."

"Why do you say that?"

"That they wanted to go in? They told me."

"Why would they want to go in?"

The high was coursing through his body. "To fight the fire. For the rush."

"Is it exciting going into a fire?"

"Oh yeah. There is nothing else like it."

"So, Royce decided to go into the house with you."

"Yep. We both decided to go in. He had the nozzle. He was the first through the door."

"I'm curious. Most people, when they lose someone close to them are severely impacted. They have many feelings about the loss. I am concerned that you are aware of the loss, but not having any emotional reaction to his death."

"Death is not something new to us. We face death every day. Car accidents heart attacks. Not only do you see people injured and dying on a regular basis, we know what we signed up for. Know that we can get hurt or killed at any time." Steve paused. "We talk about it often. We talk about others dying. We talk about us dying."

"Tell me more?"

"About what?"

"You and your friends talking about death." Doctor Jameson was trying to decide if his patient was suicidal.

"Not much more to tell. We have all talked about what we want done if we're hurt or crippled. We talk about going into a fire and not coming back out."

"That's some pretty heavy stuff for teenagers. Why do you talk about dying?"

"We're not your normal teenagers. We watch people die from heart attacks, car crashes. Scrape bodies off the highway. Why wouldn't we talk about people dying and not our own death?"

"I see. It's just not normal for people to sit around talking about death and dying." He looked at his clipboard and continued, "Our time's about up for today. If you need anything or feel like talking, the receptionist will give you all of the information."

"That's it?"

"For today. We have more appointments set up." He was writing on the clipboard and without looking up he said, "Can you use the door by the play area to leave? The receptionist will see you there."

Steve left the doctor sitting in his chair writing down some notes. Finding the receptionist, he grabbed the small packet of information. On top was a list of the scheduled appointments. With a thank you he left, thinking he would look over the rest of the information later.

Steve was mentally exhausted after the session. Rather than feeling better the doc had made him wonder about his mental stability. Was he messed up?

Rather than heading back to school, he decided to blow off the day and went to Jericho Bridge. He liked hanging out there because there was no one around and he could just clear his head and think.

He went to school the following day and just kept on plodding through one day at a time. Over the rest of the week, no one was talking about Royce's death. The high school students were not interested in the news. No one cared about his crutches, it was old news. He just faded into the crowd. He didn't bother going to the station either. What was the point? Until his ankle got better, he couldn't ride the engine and he didn't feel like re-living the event over and over with each person walking in. It was a tough week. His time was filled with being a high school student. Homework. After school cartoons.

The week was interrupted by the two more visits to Dr. Jameson. Each time he left he was in a darker mood than when he started. Every day the doctor kept telling him that he did not have the right feelings. He was not upset enough. He should have acted differently when his parents divorced. He should have thought that it was is fault.

Steve determined that the doctor was an armchair idiot, only reading the journals that he liked and tries to apply it to every patient he sees.

The worst of it was that he was craving a fix.

Chapter 28

On Friday night Steve went to the fire station to see what was up.

The bay doors were open as he came to the top of the hill. Scanning the lot, he saw Robby and Larry's trucks, along with a couple of other cars. He parked with the others and walked across the parking lot, leaving his crutches in the back seat. He had decided that one week was long enough to use the sticks. His ankle was better, and he wasn't limping at all.

As he walked into the lounge, he said, "What's up?"

"Hey. See you lost the sticks," Pat quipped.

Robby stuck his head out of the office still sitting on the rolling chair. "Hey. Wondering when you would come back."

Coming around the corner of the office he gave Robby a high five as he spotted Larry sitting at the desk with a pile of paper in front of him.

"Glad you stopped by," Larry started. "I was gonna have to go and hunt you down tomorrow if you didn't show up."

"My timing is good. What's up?"

"Robby, shut the door."

Robby got up, closing the door, "Take the chair, I've been sitting for a while. Need to stand."

Sitting down Steve started poking around the papers on the desk.

"We're working on Royce's funeral," Larry explained. "Wanted to coordinate with you."

"Why?"

"Because you're a part of everything. Look, we need people to deliver the eulogy and were hoping that you would be able to say something."

"What about Ted and Robby?"

"I'm not gonna get in front of everyone and talk!" Robby interjected.

"Chief Doherty and Darcy are going to say something and then myself. I was hoping that you could also say something."

"I guess so. What should I say?"

"It's up to you," Chief Butler explained. "Here's what's going on. We will go up to the funeral home and get Royce's body. Using 8-12 we'll take it over to Mountain View Christian Church. The plan is when 8-12 pulls up, 8-14 and 8-11 will be there lining the walk. The other firefighters will be standing at attention. You, Ted and Robby will be on the engine. when you get there three other firefights will help unload Royce and take him into the church. There will be a one-hour service. I'll speak, Darcy, you, Chief Doherty and Royce's brother will deliver the official eulogies. The priest will ask if anyone else wants to say something.

"Sounds simple" Steve said.

"You don't know the half of it" Robby corrected. "You should hear the phone calls he keeps getting."

"Everyone is trying to get in the fucking spotlight." Larry grumbled. "Between every officer in the department, plus every officer from every other fire company calling me so they can have a part in the funeral."

"Why do they keep calling you?" Steve asked.

"They all have my number from me teaching firefighting classes over the years. They think I can pull some strings and get them in."

"Other than the eulogy what else is there?"

"There are bible readings, prayers and hymns that people can do." Larry sighed. "That's what everyone is jockeying for."

"What 'cha gonna do?" Robby asked.

"Jim and I decided that only members of Joppa-Magnolia will take part in the services. At least that stops the other departments from harassing me. Anyway, after that we will move the casket back to 8-12 and drive up to Bell Air Memorial Gardens where we will bury Royce."

"When?"

"Tuesday."

"A little over a week to bury him."

"Yeah, it takes some time to put this stuff together. This actually went really quick." Larry was swiveling in the chair back and forth. He continued,

"Thanks to Chief Doherty it got together quick. He didn't take any shit from the politicians."

"Yeah, I was up at his office on Thursday while he was making calls," Robby said. "He was not taking shit from anyone!" he chuckled. "At one point he was talking to the governor. I heard him say, "With all due respect governor, I don't give a shit about politics. I ain't running for any office.""

"Yeah sounds like Jim," Larry added.

"I'm glad he's dealing with the politicians." Larry commented. "I couldn't keep civil with those types."

"How are Royce's parents?" Steve asked. "Anyone talk to them?"

"Both Jim and I have talked to them several times. Both are pretty messed up," Larry said. "How 'bout you Steve? Haven't seen you around this past week."

"I'm OK. Decided to take some time off. Can't ride the engine 'cause of the ankle. Figured hanging around the station would just make me feel more useless."

"How's it going with the counselor?" Larry asked.

"Honestly, he's a dick head," Steve stated. "How the hell did you find him? I don't think he has ever dealt with anyone but some kid whose parents are divorcing."

"Didn't. The ER doc recommended him." Larry sighed. "We didn't know any better, so we called him. I honestly thought it would help. How did it go with you Robby?"

"OK. You're right, he's a dick," Robby agreed. "I just told him what he wanted to hear."

"What d'ya mean?" Chief Butler asked.

"Every time he asked me if I felt bad, I would just say 'yes' and make some shit up." Robby laughed. "I'm sure he thought that I was a well-adjusted person going through grief."

"Do I have to go back? It's a waste of time," Steve asked. "Every time I speak with him, I feel like I'm some kind of mental case."

"The way the doc's talked figured it would do you good to get you talking 'bout stuff." Larry commented.

"It's a waste. Do I have to go back?"

"Nah. If you don't think it's doing any good then I'm not going to force you."

Steve nodded with a little smile, relieved that he didn't have to go back.

"How's your ankle? See you dumped the sticks."

"It's good. Doesn't hurt so much anymore, little tender but that's it," Steve explained.

"What about the ribs?" Robby asked.

"They're fine. Don't hurt at all."

"When you gonna be ready to ride?" Robby asked.

"Don't know. Chief, when can I come back?"

"Whenever you're ready," the chief explained. "There's no formal process. When you're ready, grab your gear."

"Cool." Steve figured he would hang out over the weekend and see if he could grab a call. He needed a fix.

"Back to the funeral," Chief Butler continued. "After the eulogies, the priest will do his thing. Then we'll take the casket to the hearse, 8-12 will follow behind. She'll be dressed out in black. The three of you will be in the jump seats. The other pallbearer's will be on the back step. Over to the gravesite and into the ground."

"Sounds simple," Robby said.

"Hopefully it will be," Chief Butler sighed. "There's a bunch of logistics that can go wrong."

"Well, guess I have to write some kind of eulogy."

"Thanks Steve," the chief started. "I know it's gonna be hard, but honestly there ain't anyone else in the department who can get up and talk in front of a crowd. Hell, I'm scared shitless!"

"What about Darcy?"

"She volunteered. Called Jim and me a couple of days ago and just told us she was speaking at the funeral."

"Guess she really wanted to give a eulogy," Robby commented.

"She always stands up for herself. No bullshit from her. Alright, you two get out of here. I need to do some paperwork."

"Yes sir!" Robby answered. "What are you up to tonight?"

"Just going to hang at the station."

Moving from the office to the breakroom Robby just said, "Sounds like a plan."

The two of them settled into the lounge and wasted the night. No one was asking about the fire call.

Chapter 29

Engine 8-12 rumbled up to the front of the church, parking at the walkway leading to the entrance. The three remaining crew members exited the engine that they had spent the previous day prepping. Washed and waxed to a high shine, across the front was a black cloth that ended wrapped on the side view mirrors. Black tape was placed over the Joppa-Magnolia emblems. The final touch was that the seat that Royce rode in was draped in black as well. His helmet was sitting on top of a neatly folded new turn-out coat on the jump seat.

The crew looked around. There were over 400 uniformed firefighters and police officers and over fifty pieces of equipment. They came from all over Maryland, Pennsylvania, Washington DC, Virginia, Delaware, Ohio, New Jersey and New York. As the crew stepped off the engine the entire crowd of firefighters and police officers turned to the engine and saluted in unison.

Scanning the crowd, the crew could see many with tears on their faces. They did not look at each other, knowing that they were each barely holding it together. It was going to be an emotional day for all of them. Chief Doherty and Chief Butler were standing at the top of the sidewalk just behind 8-12 at full attention.

The crew returned the salute each facing in a different direction, acknowledging the gathered brothers. Standing at salute for a few seconds, the entire crowd snapping their hands to their sides.

With a nod to the crew of 8-12, Larry started to organize the mass of people into some semblance of order. With about forty-five minutes before the service Larry gave commands to the crowd using a loudspeaker he had borrowed from one of the visiting engines. "Can I have everyone's attention.

We will open the church doors in about fifteen minutes. We need to get staged for the services." Pausing, he pulled a handkerchief from his pocket and wiped his nose. "There is only room for about 200 in the church. The first two rows on both sides are reserved for the family, friends, and Company 8 personnel. The family and friends will go in first, then be followed by the crew participating in the funeral and then the officers of Company 8." Pausing for a moment, he let the information settle.

As orders and logistics were given the entire gathering focused intently on the assigned duties, momentarily forgetting why they were gathered.

"Next will be the commanding officers of the state fire departments, police and visiting state officers followed by the politicians and dignitaries. After that we will allow the members of Harford County fire departments into the church. When the church fills, we will stop allowing anyone else to enter."

The members of the crowd looked around trying to figure out where they would stand, judging if they would be able to get into the church.

Chief Butler continued, "For those who will be goin' in the church, line up to the left and right on the sidewalk." He pointed to the sidewalk along the entrance drive where 8-12 was parked. "We'll signal you to come in after the others are seated. For those not going in the church I need two lines, one on either side of the sidewalk leading in." He signaled to the sidewalk leading from the drive to the church entrance. "The rest will stand in parade order in the drive, in front of the church. We have installed speakers outside so that everyone can hear the service. There will be a break after the service so that everyone can file past the casket and show our respect."

The crowd murmured as he continued, "There's a lot of people here today. Please keep moving past the casket. When you go up, pause, salute and keep moving. After the service, the casket will be brought out and loaded. We will then proceed to Bell Air Memorial Gardens for the internment. After 8-12 pulls up followed by the family, all of the fire and police equipment will follow. If anyone drove their personal car, you will follow the equipment."

The crowd started to move and undulate in seemingly random movements. The firemen were silent as they moved about, assuming their places.

Larry fired off one last announcement. "Oh, the media will be staged at various locations, directly behind 8-12, to get shots of people coming in and out and inside. If they are setting up where they block the precession, please have them shift the location. But be polite about it. They are not trying to get in the way."

That comment caused a murmur through the crowd. Everyone gathering outside had had run-ins with the news crews, getting in the way at fire calls and rescues. Trying to get them to tell confidential information about victims and accidents. They were always a pain in the ass during a call.

While Larry was giving instructions to the crowd, Jim had gone inside to check on the arrangements. Four firefighters from Company 8 were stationed just inside the doors to usher the attendees. The casket was closed and sitting in front of the church altar. Flowers surrounding the entire area. White lilies. A picture of Royce in his uniform placed on an easel to the left. This was his picture from the Fire Academy. The entire event was orchestrated for maximum effect.

After seeing everything set up and having a quick word with the pastor officiating the service, Jim headed back to Engine 8-12.

The five men were waiting impatiently at the back of the engine and the mass of firefighters were casually standing in their designated areas looking for an unidentified sign signaling them to begin the procession.

A large black limousine pulled up behind Engine 8-12, leaving about thirty feet between the two vehicles. The driver emerged and opened the door closest to the church. A hand extended from the open door and a woman dressed elegantly in black emerged, quickly followed by a well-dressed man. From the other side a younger man emerged. Royce's family had arrived.

Chief Doherty and Butler met them at the car. With a brief greeting the two men escorted them into the church.

As the firemen lining the sidewalk realized that this was the family of the fallen fireman, they snapped to attention in unpracticed unison and saluted the family.

The family disappeared into the church. The firemen finished the salute, remaining at attention for the next wave of people to enter.

During the procession, Darcy, Gary, and Pat joined the others. They had been selected to be the pallbearers, each standing stiffly in dress uniforms trying to fight their emotions and their fears of what was coming. Mixed with the excitement of carrying the coffin of their fallen comrade with the sorrow of the loss, each struggled with the conflicting emotions.

When the door closed, the six began to walk. Slowly they formed into a secretly pre-arranged order: Robby at the front on the left, Ted front and to the right. Directly behind Ted was Steve, Darcy was behind Robby, Gary behind Steve and Pat behind Darcy.

As the crew slowly made their way up the sidewalk, the firemen saluted. Several of them openly wept as the crew of 8-12 passed. The display was so moving to those watching, no one else made their way to the church for several minutes, allowing the effect of the display to hang in the air. After a few minutes, more of Royce's family members were entering the church, unsure as they walked down the line of firefighters standing at attention.

As people entered the church the ushers quickly spoke with them and escorted them to the appropriate positions. On the right side of the church was Royce's family. Directly behind, various politicians from the county and state were seated. The left-hand pews were filled with the members of Company 8. In the first-row Chief Butler sat in the aisle, then Darcy and then Steve. These would be the ones delivering the eulogy at the service. Robby was next to Steve, then Pat and Gary.

In the second pew Chief Doherty sat at the aisle with other officers from the department next to him. The third row across both sides held the officers from every company in the county. Row four held the firefighters from Company 8 who could attend. Filling the next three rows on both sides of the church was an assortment of visiting company officers and politicians. The remaining seats were filled with firefighters from everywhere.

As the firefighters filled the church, the organ groaned to life, belting out Chopin's funeral march. One of the firefighters ushering closed the door as the final person entered and signaled to the minister. With a slight nod, he rose and moved to the pulpit.

Pausing to get the attention of the attendees the minister began the service. "Thank you all for joining us today. I am Pastor Bishop. It is with sadness in our hearts that we are gathered to say farewell to Firefighter Royce James Edwards. The loss of a loved colleague and a friend is always hard. When that loved one is taken in their youth the sorrow is multiplied. Today we are gathering to honor his memory and to join together, sharing in our sadness at the loss of our son, brother, and friend."

"I did not have the privilege of knowing Firefighter Edwards personally. I have only known him through talking with his family and fellow firemen over the past few days. What I have come to know is that he was a beloved son and a member of Joppa-Magnolia Fire Company and will be greatly missed."

"I learned that Royce decided to become a firefighter when he was a child. He insisted on joining even against his parents' advice. It was his persistence and conviction that finally convinced them to allow him to join. It was this passion that drove him to become a better and better firefighter. He wanted to save all those that called. He wanted to make a difference in the world. Concern for his fellow man drove Royce to excel as a firefighter."

"Today we speak of sacrifice. It is the sacrifice given by Royce that causes us to grieve. We grieve because we no longer have the pleasure and joy of being with Royce. In John 15:13 Jesus tells us 'Greater love hath no man than this, that a man lay down his life for his friends.' Jesus was speaking to his disciples about the sacrifice he was about to make for them. Jesus knew what would happen to him and he willingly accepted his destiny."

"It is with this in mind that we turn our thoughts to Royce and his sacrifice. Royce made the sacrifice not for a friend, but for a stranger. It was these strangers that Royce dedicated himself to protecting and saving."

"I'm not the best person to stand in front of all of you talking about the man we are honoring; I'm going to let those who knew him best talk about him. As we remember Royce's life, let's also remember his dedication to protecting those who needed his help." Pastor Bishop nodded at the men sitting in the front row as he walked from the podium. "Now Chief Larry Butler would like to say a few words."

Chief Butler rose and made his way to the podium. The blood emptied from his face as he walked for what felt like a mile. He had been dreading giving the eulogy for days. He had taught firefighting classes for the past ten years and had never had any issue speaking in front of people. But today, he was doing everything possible to keep from shaking in front of the crowd. Larry came to the podium, took a deep breath as he looked across the crowd and began. "I have been in the fire department for twenty-three years and this is the first time I have had to send an active fireman home." He rifled through some papers.

"I have not been blessed with children of my own. Each one of the young men that come into the fire department are my children, my wards. It is up to me to look after them. Help them make good decisions and bridge the gap from youth to manhood."

"I remember Royce when he joined. He came into the fire station one afternoon and asked about joining. After a few minutes I asked him why he wanted to join, and he told me that a few years ago his house had a small kitchen fire. That's when he found out about the fire department. He told me once that the fire scarred him. His parents made him go outside and he didn't know what to do. When the fire engine showed up, they saved his house. After his house caught fire, he decided that he was going to be a fireman. He was one of the best and brightest of the recruits. He loved riding the engine and was a natural at fighting fire."

"He kept asking me to let him take firefighting courses. Courses that were supposed to be above his level. He would beg me to take the courses. The only way I could get him to leave me alone was to sign the waivers for the advanced courses. He wanted to get as much training as possible."

"I remember when the four of them came together on 8-12. It was by coincidence that they took a call together. Something about them clicked. The four young men on the engine that night were the best. Together there was nothing that they couldn't handle. During the year and a half of working together they each found their strength. Each one complemented the others."

"The night that 8-12 got called to the dwelling fire, Royce did not hesitate to react. When the engine arrived at the scene the mother was yelling that her daughter was in the house. In the burning room. Without regard for their safety, into the house they ran to action. Not worrying about themselves they attempted to save the trapped child." He let out three sobs at the thought of one of his team dying.

"This is why we honor and celebrate our fallen brother." After a brief pause, he continued. "We have been trained to provide comfort to those in need and crisis. To provide strength to those in desperate situations. We are not used to comforting after the fire is out and the engine is parked back in the bay. We must now look to each other to provide comfort at the loss of Firefighter Royce Edwards."

"I'm not supposed to bury the kids, they are supposed to bury me." Fighting back a sob he continued, "There's nothing I can say that will ease the pain of loss endured by his family and friends. All we can do is honor Royce's memory as we share in our grief."

He gathered the papers and turned to leave the pulpit, stopped, and leaned back to the small mic and said, "Thank you."

Coming back to the pulpit Pastor Bishop paused to shake Larry's hand, then took his place behind the podium. Adjusting the mic, he continued. "Thank you, Chief Butler. Now Captain Samuel Weimer will share a reading with us.

Captain Weimer came to the podium and began, "A reading from Psalms 91, Verse 11 and 12. For he will give his angels charge concerning you, To guard you in all your ways. They will bear you up in their hands, That you do not strike your foot against a stone."

When he was done he quietly picked up the paper and left the podium without looking at the crowd, eyes fixed on the ground.

Pastor Bishop had taken his place back in front of the audience he continued, "Thank you for those words Captain Weimer. Now Paramedic Darcy Morgan will say a few words." Nodding to Darcy he moved back to the side of the altar.

Sliding past Larry, Darcy gently touched his shoulder as she passed.

Taking her place at the pulpit she placed the papers she was carrying, spreading them out. A brief pause as she swallowed hard. She began. "I'm not used to speaking in front of crowds." A weak smile appeared, causing a quiet chuckle from the people sitting in the church.

The break in the silence gave Darcy a prod to continue with her eulogy. "I met Royce about a year and a half ago. While this is a short time, it feels as if I have known him forever. He was special from the day I met him. I came to think of him as a younger brother. But more than a brother, he has always been a hero. I was the first female firefighter in the department. It was always a struggle to have the other firemen to recognize that I was a firefighter. There were even a few who would not get on an engine with me. Royce never had any issue riding with me. In fact, he always defended me, even to the more senior members. He..." She paused as a tear ran down her face. "When I would walk into a crowded squad room, Royce was always the first to wave me over and make room for me to sit. On my last birthday, Royce and Steve showed up at the hospital where I was on graveyard shift at the ICU. They snuck into the hospital with a huge bouquet of flowers for me." Smiling with the memory she continued, "It made me feel so special to have someone, two someone's bring me flowers." She shot a quick smile at Steve as three uncontrollable sobs escaped, and the tears began to flow freely. "His kindness was not only to me. Royce also spent a great deal of time with the new recruits. He would always take the time to work with them to make them better firefighters, better people.

"Now he's gone. He will not be at the station hanging around waiting to catch a call. He won't be there to say happy birthday." With a sniff she wiped the tears from her face. "I always thought of him as my own guardian angel." Getting control, she finished, "Royce was always looking out for others. Looking out for me. I could always count on him when I needed a brother or a friend. His heart was too big to be kept here on earth. I think that his heart was so big and the need to help too strong. God called him to take his rightful place in heaven, looking out for others as a guardian angel. He was called home not as punishment, but as a reward. He will take his place with the greatest of angels to guard over others. I will miss him, but I will always know that he is watching over me, watching over us, from above." She left the podium quickly.

As Darcy rushed to her seat, trying to keep her emotions under control, Steve slid past Larry and stood in the aisle. As Darcy approached, he reached out to squeeze her shoulder, giving her some support – and giving himself some strength to stand in front of the crowd and speak.

Reaching out she grabbed him in a firm hug, burying her face in his shoulder. He could feel her sobs and the wetness from her tears. After a few seconds, she took a deep breath and released Steve. Without looking, she slid into the pew, sitting close to Larry for support.

Pastor Bishop once again took his place at the podium. "Thank you, Paramedic Morgan. Now Captain Brian Creamer will share reading from the New Testament."

Without looking up Captain Creamer began "A reading from Second Corinthians. Blessed be the God and Father of our Lord Jesus Christ, the Father of mercies and God of all comfort, who comforts us in all our tribulation, that we may be able to comfort those who are in any trouble, with the comfort with which we ourselves are comforted by God.'

"Thank you. Next we will hear from Firefighter Steve Quinn." Pastor Bishop said.

Steve headed to the pulpit. He was still not sure what was going to come out. He had spent several days writing and rewriting the eulogy. Now he had no idea what he would say.

Standing at the pulpit he adjusted the mic. "I came here today with a speech prepared. I spent the past several days working on it. As I revised it and rewrote it, I thought it was going to be perfect. I wanted it to recognize and honor my partner and my friend. I'm standing up here today looking out at Royce's parents and family. I look across the sea of faces. The faces of my fellow firefighters, my comrades, my brothers and sisters, and I realize all of the carefully thought out words on these papers are meaningless." He waved the handful of papers for the crowd to see.

"As I reflect on why we are here I realize that we could be here having the funeral of a seven-year-old little girl, but we are not. We are here having the funeral of one of the firefighters that was trying to save her."

"One of our own has died. He died in the line of duty. He died trying to perform a rescue. Trying to rescue a little girl who was inside the burning house. He knew that the chances of the rescue of the child were slim. Deciding that any chance was better than no chance. He also knew that we were doing more than just trying to rescue the child. We were rescuing the mother. Giving her a glimmer of hope of saving her child. Giving her the ability to say, 'They did everything possible.' Just knowing that the firemen tried would give the mother the strength to carry on. Without hesitation, he led the interior attack." Pausing he swallowed his emotions and kept control.

"We train. We practice. We prepare. We preplan. Our minds are filled with creating scenarios of disaster, destruction and injury. We discuss past calls and learn from them. The good and the bad. We talk with doctors, fire marshals, senior firefighters to discuss what we can do better. We dedicate our time to preparing to help others."

"When the tones sound, we know that responding to the call can mean the difference between life and death for the victim. The way we act, respond, extricate, fight and treat them have a lasting impact on those patients. What we often forget is that our actions also have an impact on the victims' families. Our actions not only save the victims but help the victims' families.

"We do these things without regard to ourselves. We sacrifice our families in helping others. We put ourselves in danger. We go into places others won't. We stay calm, we take action, we lead in situations that send others screaming or into a catatonic state. Ultimately, we all know that there is a possibility that any one of us will be called for the ultimate sacrifice."

"Over the past days, I believe that everyone has asked themselves, 'If I were called to make the same sacrifice, would I?' Each one asking, 'Would I go into the inferno to save a stranger?'

"All of us firefighters and paramedics have made the decision to be ready for the sacrifice. We train and prepare to be at our best when those we are serving are at their worst."

"We may never be called to the challenge. Hopefully we never will. To be called means that someone needs to be saved."

"Royce is one of the best." With a slight pause, Steve corrected himself. "Was one of the best. Not only did he make the patients and victims feel safer, he also made the other firefighters feel safer.

"We are saddened because our brother is no longer here. We will miss him in our daily activity. We won't see him on the engine at calls. He won't be there to give support. We also share the sadness with his family. He won't see his parents retire. He won't see his nephew and nieces be born and grow. He won't have a family of his own."

"For those of you who don't know, I was with Royce the night he died. He was doing something that he loved. He knew the risk. He knew what was at stake that night. He was happy to take on the challenge to try to save a life."

"That night Royce displayed honor and heroism. We gather here today to pay our respect to our fallen brother, our fallen son. We also gather to honor the hero. We gather to celebrate Royce's life. We gather to share our grief."

"The sadness and sorrow of the loss is real. It will fade with time, but it will never be extinguished. This is one ember that no firefighter can extinguish. We will always hold a place in our hearts for Firefighter Royce Edwards. We will honor his sacrifice every time we climb on a piece of equipment. Every time we give aid to those in need. Every time we answer the tones. Every time a piece of equipment rolls down the road, a part of Royce's spirit will be guiding it."

"When I joined, and completed basic training, I was given a Saint Florian Medallion." Pulling a chain from around his neck Steve extracted the Saint Florian Medallion that he always wore and removed it, holding in both hands for the audience to see. "Now that I think about today, perhaps Darcy is more right than she thinks. Royce has moved onto the ranks of the guardian angels. As we head toward the next fire call, I will be sending a silent prayer to the Angel Royce Edwards, our newest guardian angel." Steve quietly exited the pulpit and took his seat. Not looking at anyone, forcing control of his emotions.

As Steve sat down Pastor Bishop returned to the podium. "Thank you, Firefighter Steve Quinn." Pausing for a moment to clear his throat, he said, "Now we will hear from Chief James Doherty."

Moving to the podium Chief Doherty addressed the congregation. "I want to thank all of you for coming today. Supporting Firefighter Edwards' family, honoring his memory. I'm not going to say too much more than what the others have. He was indeed a valuable member of the company. I am sure I speak for those who are not here, those being the countless people he has helped during his tenure as a firefighter. Without Firefighter Edwards countless people would have very different lives. Many would not have lived."

"He was meticulous in performing his duties, from preparing and maintaining the equipment to actions on a fire scene. He held himself to the highest standards of professionalism in the performance of his duties. He insisted on those around him adhering to the same standards that he set for himself."

"He was also highly conscious of teaching the new firefighters. He would spend countless hours working with the new recruits, preparing them for what they would encounter. When I asked him one day why he drilled the newbies as much as he did, his answer was very simple. He told me, 'One day they may have to rescue me or my family. I want them to be ready'." Jim paused. "It struck me that his response was so practical and so selfless, I wanted all of the firefighters to have the same attitude. It is this attitude and focus to duty that we will remember."

"We have been honored to work with Firefighter Edwards. He was taken from us in his prime. We will miss him. Thank you." After the short eulogy he quickly returned to his seat.

"Thank you, Chief Doherty," Pastor Bishop said. "Now we will have the final words from his older brother, Walter Edwards."

Walter rose from the pew and made his way to the pulpit.

"Our family wishes to thank you all for showing your respect and joining in grief with our family. It is a sad day when parents must bury their children."

"It is true that when Royce wanted to join the fire department my mother and father were worried. How could a high school student be a firefighter?"

"Well, he convinced them. They put up with him getting up in the middle of the night. Jumping up from the dinner table and running out to a call.

Coming home smelling like smoke." With a small smile, he continued. "I frankly got a little tired of him telling all the firefighting stories."

"What we have come to realize is that in the fire department he found his calling. He found another family. It was something that he loved." Walter looked at his parents. "It is comforting to know that even though he was taken from us early, we know that he was respected and had found himself. That he had found a group to belong to."

"Thank you." Walter quickly left the pulpit and returned to his seat.

Pastor Bishop retuned to the pulpit. "If there is anyone else who would like to say a few words, please feel free." Scanning the faces in the crowed he hoped no one would volunteer. "In a few moments, we will be moving to the burial site. By way of closing, please rise and join me in the prayer located on the back of the service bulletin."

The congregation rose and recited in unison the prayer that was known by most of the gathering. The firefighters outside followed along with the prayer as well.

When I am called to duty, God
Wherever flames may rage
Give me strength to save a life
Whatever be its age.

Let me embrace a little child
Before it is too late
Or save an older person from
The horror of that fate.

Enable me to be alert
And hear the weakest shout, and quickly and efficiently
To put the fire out.

I want to fill my calling
To give the best in me,
To guard my friend and neighbor
And protect their property.

And, if, according to your will,
While on duty I must answer death's call;
Bless with your protecting hand
My family, one and all.

As the prayer ended Steve, Ted, Robby, Gary and Pat rose from the front bench. Walter rose on the opposite side. The six men slowly made their way to the casket. Each taking their place, they wheeled it slowly down the aisle.

As they began to move, every firefighter saluted. Civilians placed their hands over their hearts. A soloist sang Ave Maria as the casket made the long journey to the waiting engine.

As the casket was carried down the sidewalk all the firefighters were at attention. As the casket was placed into the hearse, the six pallbearers stepped back and saluted, the crowd of firefighters completed the salute in unison.

Royce's parents and brother climbed into the waiting limousine for the ride to the cemetery.

The five firefighters all climbed onto Engine 8-12. Gary, Darcy and Pat pulled on their turn-out coats and helmets, then climbed onto the back step where they would ride to the cemetery. Steve took his place in the passenger side jump seat while Ted climbed into the cab. Robby climbed in and the engine rumbled to life.

When the crew climbed onto 8-12 the other firefighters in attendance fell out and moved to the equipment brought to escort the body. As the equipment started the drivers began moving them into position to follow the family's car.

Chapter 30

Robby pulled the engine to the drive entrance, the hearse directly behind them then the limo, followed by several other cars with family members. The other equipment was starting to pull into line. As he was waiting at the entrance he looked over at Ted and said, "Let 'em know we're coming."

Ted reached up and grabbed the air horn, letting out a loud blast. The other equipment followed the cue and sounded their horns in unison. After about five seconds the horns stopped and the procession pulled onto the road, making its way to the cemetery.

Along the way, police and fire equipment had blocked off intersections. The crews were standing at attention as the funeral procession passed. Each Engine crew provided their own display of respect for the passing procession. Every member was standing at attention in full salute, emergency lights slowly rotating as the body of their fallen comrade passed. Several of the crews had their turn-out gear placed at their feet, coats folded neatly with helmets placed on top. One engine crew was seen kneeling in prayer behind their gear, one set of folded gear set in front of the others representing the missing man.

As Engine 8-12 approached the cemetery, two, one-hundred-foot aerial ladders were extended and crossed with an American flag hanging under the arch.

Robby parked 8-12 close to where the graveside service would take place, the hearse and family limo pulling in behind. There they sat and waited for the others to arrive and get situated for the service.

Chiefs Doherty and Butler arrived, parking the truck behind the limo.

As they were getting out other equipment parked behind the chief's truck. Moving to the officer of the first piece of equipment Larry gave instructions to move the men to the area on the left and right side of the grave. Once the men were in place, the family would be seated, and the casket would be brought to the grave. The few chairs would be reserved for the family and a few dignitaries. He left it to the first officer to pass the information to the remaining crews.

As the waves of firefighters migrated toward the spot that they would be standing during the ceremony the crew of 8-12 gathered at the rear step to get themselves organized. Royce's brother Walter had joined them, waiting to take the coffin to the gravesite.

With everyone settling into their respective places, the two chiefs escorted Mr. and Mrs. Edwards to the grave. The four stoically took their seats, waiting for the next ceremony to begin.

The wait was not long. From somewhere came the sound of bagpipes playing. The coffin was carried slowly to the grave, then set into the special rack that would lower it into the ground. The small group quietly moved to the seats that had been reserved.

As the bagpipes stopped playing, Pastor Bishop began speaking. "Thank you all for joining us in committing Firefighter Royce Edwards into his eternal resting place. We gather to honor the life and memory of our fallen brother and of a beloved family member."

Raising his arm to indicate that those sitting should stand, Pastor Bishop continued, "Let us pray."

"God our Father in heaven comfort and strengthen us as we honor our fallen comrade Royce James Edwards who has made the ultimate sacrifice, giving his life to protect others in the line of duty. We now bestow unto you the soul of our beloved son, our brother. We pray that he is at peace in you. May you take him into God's eternal light. Amen."

From somewhere a voice spoke, "In the fire department the bell has been used to call firefighters to duty. The sound of the bell signified a call to action, placing the firefighter's life in jeopardy for the sake of his fellow man. When the call was complete, the bell sounded three times, signifying the end."

"Our brother Royce James Edwards has completed his task, his duties complete. The bell now rings in honor of his service, of his sacrifice and in tribute to his life."

From the distance a bell slowly rang three times, paused, and then rang three more times. Another pause, and then it rang three more times.

As the last bell strike was fading the casket started to lower into the grave. The bagpipes began playing again.

As the casket reached the bottom of the grave, the straps were retracted. Mr. and Mrs. Edwards came forward and each took a handful of dirt. Just as they were about to toss it into the grave a trumpet began playing Taps.

After Royce's parents had laid the dirt on top of the coffin, his brother repeated the same process, followed by the rest of the pallbearers.

When the last one had walked away from the grave. The trumpet stopped. The Edwards family walked back to the waiting limo and left.

Chief Doherty yelled, "Company dismissed," signifying the end of the service. By the time the first piece of equipment made it to the entrance, both ladder trucks had been lowered and were gone.

After the service, Company 8 had a reception at the fire hall in Station One. It was a catered event, with several local restaurants donating food and drink.

The gathering continued into the early morning hours. Throughout the night all of the officers made toasts to Royce and the other firefighters. As the alcohol crept into the firefighters' bodies, they became bolder in the toasts, each one trying to outdo the other in their accolades. Old men exchanged stories with the younger members. Trying to impress them with the old days. Talking about how things had changed. Fighting fires without air packs. How they would go into buildings to fight fire, holding their breath as long as they could. Trying to get fresh air off the fire nozzle. The newfangled training and equipment that they never needed.

When the ambulance was a scoop and swoop activity. Very little first aid given. No Cardiopulmonary Resuscitation. When CPR became the norm the ease of using the old Cadillac ambo. With the low ceiling, you could put your back against the roof while you did chest compressions. Never worrying about diseases like hepatitis and AIDS. Never wearing gloves or using facemasks. Just washing the patients' blood off after the call.

The gathering broke into groups, each re-living past calls. Recalling past firefighters. Telling stories about one another.

It went on until early the next morning.

Engine 8-12 left about two thirty in the morning driven back by one of the other lieutenants. The crew, drunk, having helped themselves to the free-flowing beer and liquor throughout the night, quietly rode back to Station Two.

When the engine had been put back in its bay the three found their bunks and quickly collapsed from the combination of the intense day and the excess of booze.

Chapter 31

The next morning, they were moving slowly, nursing hangovers. Without speaking the crew began to rise, starting with coffee. The gurgling of the coffee maker broke the silence and filled the squad room with a rich smell. Each of them grabbing a cup of the hot liquid trying to shake the cobwebs out of their heads. Knowing that burying their friend would take priority over everything else they had planned; they each dodged their mundane responsibilities.

Needing some time to recover from the funeral Steve decided to blow off school for the rest of the week. Robby and Ted had taken some time off their paid jobs. Taking the time to recover.

"I'm glad that's behind us," Ted said, breaking the silence.

"What are we supposed to do now?" Robby asked no one.

"Guess we just keep going," Ted answered.

"Keep going like nothing happened?" Steve asked.

"Do we have a choice?" Robby questioned.

"Funeral's over, but we still need to live with this every day. Every call," Steve said.

"I hope everyone will finally leave us alone," Ted said.

"No shit," Robby replied. "I am so tired of people who I have never talked to before asking how I'm doing or if there's anything they can do."

"That doesn't bother me half as much as people who like to say 'I know how you feel'," Steve said. "Last time I checked none of them had lost their partner in a fire."

The comments and concern had started by being kind and caring. After the first few dozen comments they became insincere, condescending and an insult. It was like you had to be in mourning and in misery. Every one of those people wanted to be connected to the death somehow. They wanted to be connected to the deceased firefighter.

"Take your time so you can deal with your feelings," Robby said. "When someone says 'Deal with your feelings' I want to take a halligan tool to them."

"Got that right. How the hell do they know we're not dealing with them?" Steve began. "It's like we have to hang a fucking sign around our necks, so everyone can read about what we're doing, how we're feeling."

"I feel like the whole world is waiting for us to break down," Steve said. "They want to watch us crumble to make themselves feel better."

"They expect us to be victims of our feelings," Ted interjected. "They want to see us fall so they can seem stronger."

"I just want them to stop," Robby ended.

"What gets me more are the ones who try to tell you that they would have done something differently. 'No one would have died on my watch'," Ted said mockingly.

"Who says that?" Robby asked angrily.

"I get that from a few old timers."

"They say that to you?" Steve asked in disbelief.

"Not outright," Ted sighed. "But listening to the way they talk down, you know that's what they're thinking."

Robby replied. "That pisses me off. They have no idea what we did or why we did it."

"Wish they would just listen to us then leave us alone," Ted said.

"The shrink wasn't any better. Kept trying to tell me how I should feel," Steve said.

"What did he say?" Ted asked.

"He mostly said that I'm fucked up," Steve said, staring into space.

"I felt the same after talking with him," Robby added.

Steve looked at Robby. "Did he use the repressed feelings crap with you too?"

"Yeah," Robby replied in surprise. "Told me I wasn't dealing with Royce's death." He smirked. "Also wanted to talk about my parents and how I felt about them."

Steve agreed with a nod of his head. "He basically told me that what I was feeling was wrong. That I should be feeling guilty that he died, and I lived."

"I just played along with him to get the hell out," Ted said.

"What do you mean?" Robby asked.

"When my grandfather died, the mortuary gave my dad a bunch of pamphlets about dying and stuff. Before I went to the appointment, I read through them."

"Shit, that was smart," Steve said.

"What did they say?" Robby asked.

"The biggest one was on the stages of grief," Ted answered.

"What the hell is that?" Robby asked.

"They are supposed to be the feelings that you go through when someone dies."

"I remember reading about the stages of grief in one of my mom's textbooks. Thought it would help dealing with patients," Steve added.

"Stages?" Robby questioned. "What are they?"

Ted looked at Steve. "I think they are shock, denial, anger." He paused, deep in thought.

Steve continued, "Then it's bargaining, guilt, depression and acceptance."

"What the hell is that supposed to mean?" Robby asked.

"It's pretty basic. It's the 'Normal' feelings and process you go through when someone dies. When you first hear of the death of someone close, you are in shock and surprise that they are dead. Then the next phase is denial. You deny that they are dead. Then it's anger. You get mad because they are dead." Steve took a breath.

Ted jumped in, "Do you have to go through the steps?"

"That's the question," Steve responded. "I guess according to Doctor Jameson if you don't you are 'repressing your emotions,' then you're messed up."

"What's the rest?" Robby asked.

"On to bargaining. You bargain to have them alive. Then you feel guilty about the death, depression because the person is gone then finally acceptance of the situation," Steve finished.

"Is that why the doc thinks you're a mess?" Ted asked. "'cause you didn't go through the steps?"

"Probably. Now that I think about it we don't fit the pattern. We can't go through the steps." Steve thought. "And we sure as hell can't go through them in order."

"What do you know about the steps?" Ted asked.

"Not much. I forgot about that death and dying stuff. I read textbooks and a few articles thinking that it would help me when we tell family someone is dead. Truth is, doesn't do us much good on the engine. We don't get much past shock and maybe denial," Steve said.

"So, what about us?"

With a small chuckle, Steve started, "We don't fit the mold."

"Why?"

"Think about it. We're not in shock or denial. As far as bargaining, we are not trying to switch places or change things," Steve said. "Shit, we're glad to be alive and I for one don't feel guilty about being alive."

"It was Royce's time," Ted said. "I don't want him dead, but we all made the choice."

"We knew that it could happen to any of us," Robby added.

"Yep. We've all talked about it. Dying. Hell, we have living wills on file telling the department what to do with us if we're hurt, when to pull the plug," Steve said.

"Yeah, we did that about six months ago," Robby remembered. "I had forgotten about that."

"They don't mean anything for Royce or me, but for you it holds legal authority."

"Why not for you?"

"I'm still a minor. No matter what I write down it's still my parents' decision until I turn eighteen."

"Good thing it's written down, they'll never show up," Robby laughed. "Shit, you'll turn eighteen while you're in a coma."

Laughing, Steve shot his hand up for a high five from Robby.

"Hell, the only way your mother came to the hospital is because the state police came and got her," Ted added as he broke into laughter.

"She's in her own world. At least she leaves me alone."

"You think she would be more involved," Ted commented.

"Well, she's not very interested in what I do, and to be honest I don't tell her much about what's going on," Steve said.

"My dad knows everything since he's in the department too," Robby said.

"You can't hide crap from your dad," Ted agreed.

"Most of the time Larry and your dad give me more parental supervision than my real parents," Steve commented.

"Is she freaking out now?" Ted asked.

"Naw. I'm not sure she even registered that I was on the same crew as the dead firefighter. All she kept going on about was interviews, being in the news, and what her friends and neighbors would think. I still don't think she knows that I run into burning buildings."

"Does it piss you off?" Robby asked.

"Not really. Since the divorce, she has been trying to figure out who she is. Not sure what I do registers most of the time. The only reason she is living here is so I can finish high school. I'm over it. It used to really bug me out that my family didn't fit the typical mold. I had a revelation about a year ago. What I realized is that it didn't make any difference. I could wallow in self-pity, feeling sorry for myself because I don't have the perfect family, or I could get over it and adjust. It was great that I hid in the fire department. My mom was glad I found a place and she stopped worrying about me, so she focused on herself. Frankly it's nice not having to worry about telling my mom where I'm at."

"Is that the revelation?" Ted asked.

"Nah," Steve answered. "The revelation is that it's her issues that she is dealing with, not mine. I could get all crazy trying to figure out what I was doing wrong, why she ignores me, what I did to cause it. Truth is I did nothing. I can't control how she thinks, acts or how she interacts with me. It's about her."

"I guess so. I just can't imagine what it would be like without having my parents all over me," Ted interjected.

With a shrug Steve shut down the conversation.

"Where does that leave us with all this stuff?" Robby asked again, trying to move away from an uncomfortable topic.

"Keep going," Ted said.

"It will be weird without him," Robby said. "It's gonna be tough having someone else on the crew."

"It's gonna suck not having Royce in the jump seat," Steve said.

"Shit, we'll have to break in a new crew member," Ted groaned.

"Don't know what you're whining about? I have to go into the burning building with them," Steve shot back with a smile.

"Hadn't thought about that. How you gonna handle that?"

"Just go back to firefighting 101."

Ted shook his head, trying to figure out what Steve was saying.

"By the book. Step by step," Steve said to clarify.

"Good luck with that," Robby laughed.

"That's the easy part," Steve began.

"How come?" Ted asked.

"You know I always thought that seeing some kid killed would be my breaking point," Steve said. "Been thinking: if the mom of that kid had the intelligence to know where she was, we wouldn't have gone in."

"As soon as she said the kid was inside, I knew you were going in," Ted said. "Shit, I wanted to go in."

"Yeah. But not to save the kid," Steve said

"What do you mean?" Robby asked.

"The kid was the excuse. The second we saw the house rolling, we wanted to go in." Steve's eyes were looking into space, remembering the call, the memory bringing a flow into his body.

"It was a good one," Ted reflected.

"It was fucking epic!" Robby said. "Even without Royce dying in the fire, we will be talking about it for years."

"Well, when I grabbed the doll and thought it was the kid, I realized that it didn't bother me to see a dead kid."

"What bothers you then?" Ted asked.

"Stupid people."

"That's why we're here, isn't it?" Ted asked. "To save the stupid people."

"Thinking back over the past calls I keep having the same question. 'Should we do it?'"

"I don't follow," Robby questioned. "You saying the rescue was a mistake?"

Shaking his head Steve explained, "Think about all of the idiots that we've helped over the years. The drunks, stupid kids, the stupid parents. All the stupid shit we have to see."

"Remember the family who killed their baby because they were heating the whole house with kerosene heaters?" Ted asked.

Robby responded, "Hell yeah." Pointing at Ted he continued, "You jumped in a state police cruiser to take the infant to the hospital instead of waiting for the ambo."

The rush flowing into their bodies.

Pointing at Steve, Ted added, "You bought a suspension for a week on that call."

"Yep. While I was checking the others and getting the worst on O2, the father poked me in the chest with his finger and said, 'Don't let my baby die,' like it was my fault," Steve said, anger creeping into his eyes.

"That's when you told him he killed the kid," Robby said.

"Can't stand stupid!" Steve began. "Stupid fuck! Killed his kid by being a cheap bastard, then he has to blame us for the kid dying." Looking at the others, he continued. "Why do we save the idiots? We train. We wait. When the world goes bad, they scream for help. We run to their rescue and they get mad at us."

The other two sat silently nodding in agreement.

"I don't expect to be worshiped, but a thank you would be nice," Steve said, pausing to refill his coffee.

"People are assholes!" Robby said.

"So, I've been asking myself, 'Should I save them?'" Steve pondered. "I know how. Shit, I'm good at saving the assholes, but do they deserve to be saved?"

The three were silent, each reflecting on what had been said aloud.

"What if the asshole kid we save today kills someone later?" Steve asked.

"Never thought about it," Ted replied.

"We don't worry about that," Robby said. "All we do is save everyone we can. Practice, triage, prioritize, save who you can. Move to the next."

"That's my point. We save people. Most of them are fine, but a good number of them are idiots," Steve explained. "They are in the situation because they did something stupid."

"I don't mind them being stupid," Ted said. "I hate it when they blame us for their stupidity."

"But it's the stupid people that keep putting others in danger," Steve said. "If they aren't around, then would other's get hurt?"

"Yeah, the drunk driver who kills the family and walks away."

"Parents who kill their kids because they can't be bothered to pay attention."

"Shit, just the civilians driving by accidents, almost running us over because they're more interested in looking at the wreck than driving," Steve said. "To get a glimpse of death. See something that is forbidden."

"What do you mean 'forbidden'?" Ted asked.

Fanning his face, in his best Southern lady's accent Steve said, "Why Mr. Ted. It's just not polite to discuss such things in civilized company." He finished by batting his eyes. "Everyone has a morbid curiosity about death. That's why they rubberneck at accidents. Secretly glancing over to get a glimpse of death."

"Remember when John ran the flare down that asshole's car?" Robby asked.

"The guy was so pissed he jumped out and threatened to beat the crap out of him," Steve added.

"Good thing Trooper Paul saw it go down and arrested the driver for attempted assault and failure to obey an official."

"We pretend to be brave. We laugh about being in danger," Steve started. "We fight our fear. We push ourselves further and further, chasing the rush." Pausing, he continued, "Are we just adrenaline junkies?" Steve asked.

"We're more than that. We help people. Preserve life and protect property, all that stuff," Ted said.

"What we do not many others can do," Robby said. "How many people have we seen just panic and freeze?"

"Hadn't thought about that, but you're right," Steve answered. "We're the ones that keep calm in a disaster. We are the ones that the public looks at to fix the accidents. But it's a cover for the real reason."

"The rush," they all said in unison.

"Yeah. If I didn't get the rush, I would be doing something else," Robby said.

"I just keep going back to 'should we?'" Steve said.

"I don't think we can decide if we should or shouldn't," Ted said. "We just keep doing what we do."

"If we didn't, who would?" Robby questioned.

"Maybe no one," Steve said. "That would thin the herd of idiots."

"Just forget about it Steve," Robby said. "You know you want to keep rescuing people. Running into buildings and cutting up cars. Shit, you're hooked on it just as much as we are."

"Yeah. But over the past few days I realize that it's not because I really care about helping anymore. It's because of the rush."

"Shhh. That's why we all do it. We just don't tell anyone," Ted chastised. "We don't talk about it."

This was new territory for all of them. They each knew about the rush, but they never discussed it openly before.

"That's our dirty little secret," Steve continued. "We pretend to do it for 'the good of mankind,' but that's bullshit. I think we do it because we are addicted to the rush."

Robby sat silently listening. Trying to focus on what was being said.

"When I was laid up with the ankle all I could think about was getting on the engine," Steve began, "catching the next call. Bigger than the one that killed Royce. I tried to imagine what would be better. More danger? More death? Maybe something only I could do, like a diving rescue."

"I've been wanting to catch another one too," Robby confessed.

"As I look back there are two things that are now echoing in my brain. I never considered the possibility of me or another firefighter dying and never giving a shit about who would have to die to get me the call. I didn't think about, or care about the sacrifice that needed to be made for me to get my bigger fix."

"I admit," Ted added. "I have been wanting a call too."

"I dream at night, but it's not about Royce or any one of us dying. It's about getting bigger and better calls. I wake excited. Relieved with the infusion of adrenaline. When I don't dream, I crave the fix. Like a junkie going through withdrawal."

"I get anxious when I think about going on a call. The longer between calls, the more anxious I get," Ted said.

"That's why I come to the station. To hang out and talk about calls. We talk about the last call we were on. We talk about the big ones. Is that me getting a fix in between calls?" Robby asked.

"I heard somewhere that serial killers return to the crime to relive it in their minds," Ted asked. "Do we do the same things?"

"Maybe we're no different," Steve said. "We've heard about the nurses who kill patients, parents who make their kids sick, maybe we are the vampires waiting for death and destruction to get our fix."

"Hey, you remember that one guy who didn't wash up after that car accident?" Robby asked.

"Who, the army medic?" Ted questioned.

"That freak!" Steve exclaimed. "I remember him. He creeped me out. I totally avoided him after that night. Would not get on an engine with him."

"What happened?" Ted asked.

"We were on a 10-50 on 95. It was a fatal. The guy was a medic, so he was working up the patient," Robby explained. "We got back to the station and he was just sitting on the couch, covered in blood from the victim."

"He was a freak!" Steve interjected.

"I told him to go into the bathroom and clean up," Robby continued. "He just sat there and said, 'It's OK' as he just stared at the blood on his hands."

"That's gross," Ted exclaimed.

"I swear, the way he was looking at the blood on his hands he had a hard on," Steve said.

"How long did he sit there?" Ted asked.

Steve said, "I told him he was a freak and left out of there."

Shaking his head Robby said, "Don't know, I left with Steve."

"What happened to the freak?" Ted asked.

"Don't know," Robby shrugged. "He just went away. I think after word got around, no one wanted to be on the engine with him."

"It's like the stories we hear 'bout firefighters starting fires so they can put them out."

"Maybe we're all messed up?" Ted questioned.

"I don't care how messed up we are," Robby said with a start. "I need a shower and some breakfast."

"That sounds like the best plan I have heard in a while," Ted echoed.

"I'll second that," Steve added.

That was the cue for each of them to gather their gear, dump out the rest of the coffee and get packed up to leave.

Chapter 32

Over the next couple of weeks things started to calm down and get back to normal.

Steve kept going to school and trudging through the classes, trying to pay attention. The teachers had been told by Principal Bancroft what had happened and to let him coast.

The station had gotten back to normal. After school Steve would swing by the station to see who was hanging out and wait to see if there was a call. They would sit around telling stories and talking about what was going on. No one talked about Royce or the fire.

It had been three weeks since Royce's funeral, and it was the first Friday he was pulling duty. No one had officially signed up for the jump seat left empty by Royce's death. Three or four firefighters hung around, waiting for a call. Around 10:30 Mel announced that he had decided to stay the night to make a full crew.

Ted, Robby and Steve dreaded getting the first call without Royce. It would mark the end of Royce. Someone would ride in his jump seat and in a few short months it would be like he had never been there. It was a change they were trying to avoid.

That night there was no call. Mel and Ted left when they woke up around 7:30. Robby and Steve hung around watching *Pee Wee's Playhouse*.

Around 9:00 in the morning the box on the wall exploded. "Beep boop, beep boop, dweedle, dweedle dweedle. Box 804, Company 8, Cardiac Arrest, 1427 D Court. Hanson Square. Time 09:03."

Without a word Robby and Steve shot to the engine bay, pulled on their turn-out gear and jumped onto the engine.

Robby started 8-12 up and pulled it onto the tarmac. The two waited for two other firefighters to show up.

Steve caught himself looking through the trees, expecting Royce to come running out of the tree line.

"Ambo 8-94 responding."

A car crested the hill and rolled across the asphalt to a stop. Phil jumped out of the driver's door and sprinted into the engine bay grabbing his gear. He waited anxiously at the front of the engine.

"8-94 responding 09:04."

It was an unwritten rule that everyone followed: first one in gets choice of position on the engine. The one and only exception is the officer's seat. This is always reserved for the senior member. There were a few of the members who would be an ass and pull rank on the younger members, tossing them off the engine for the good calls. Make them ride the back step or take the third or fourth jump seat that folds down.

There was a race going on. This increased the rush of the call. Who would get a full crew first? Station One and Station Two were about the same distance from the call, so whatever engine responded first would get to go to the call. The other engine would stand by at the station, the crew wishing they were on a call.

Waiting for the next car to speed up the hill of the fire station completing the crew, and imagining the officer clicking the mic key and excitedly announcing "Engine 8-12 responding," sending the message across the air. Everyone would hear that Station Two assembled the crew first. Station Two winning the unintended race. The crew members waiting at Station One would be disappointed, the surge quickly depleting, as they hear the announcement.

With the rush intensifying as the car crested the hill of Station Two, Phil reached for the mic just as the speaker came to life. "Engine 8-14 responding."

The crew sat on the tarmac for a moment, letting the adrenaline drain from their bodies. The surge quickly dwindling.

"Engine 8-14 responding, 09:07."

Phil rehung the mic in the clip and climbed down from the officer's seat. Never keying the mic.

Steve had jumped off the engine and walked around the back, standing behind the engine on the driver side so the driver could see him as he guided the backing engine into the bay where it would silently wait for the next call.

The car that crested the hill rolled to a stop, the driver recognizing that another engine had responded first by the way the crew moved slowly, lacking the enthusiasm from going on a call.

"8-94 on location."

Backing the engine into the bay, Robby quieted the engine, making it ready for the next call.

"8-94 on location, 09:10."

Pat came into the bay as Robby was climbing down from the driver's seat. With a "hey" and a nod of the head the two moved into the crew lounge, heading to the office. As they swung their heads around the office doorway, Steve came into the lounge after putting his turn-out gear on the rack, flopping onto the couch. They all knew that they had to wait until the call was done before they could leave the station.

"Looks like we missed that one," Phil said.

"8-14 on location."

"It was only an ambo assist," Pat responded. "Not really the most exciting call."

"8-14 on Location 09:19."

"They're all important," Phil responded.

"Any time we can turn wheels, it's worth it," Robby added.

"It's fun to roll down the road but honestly I'm not really interested in doing the medics' shit work," Pat said.

"What, you don't want to run back and forth getting equipment from the ambo?" Robby asked.

"Then stand there holding an IV bag like a lamp post?" Phil shot out.

"Then carry the 400-pound patient down a flight of stairs 'cause the ambo crew can't pick 'em up?" Steve called from the other room.

They each made excuses as to why they didn't want to go on the call, but each one knew they wanted to be on the engine. Lights flashing. Siren wailing. The horn blasting, pushing cars out of the way speeding to the call. Just thinking about taking a call made the high creep into each of them.

"Hey, you remember the time we had to take that really fat lady out of the second story window?" Pat asked.

"Yeah, she was too heavy to go down the stairs. It took six of us to pick her up," Phil added.

"That was before I joined," Steve commented.

"Wasn't on the call, but I heard it was brutal," Phil said.

"How do you move someone that big without saying something about it?" Pat asked.

Steve sat silently thinking to himself, *Why should we move a fat ass like that?*

"You just keep your mouth shut and hope you don't blow out your balls," Robby smirked.

"You take the good with the bad." Phil added.

"Well not much going on here," Steve said. "I'm going to cut out of here."

"You gonna wait till the call's over?" Phil asked.

"Sure," Steve shrugged. "Then I'm gonna take off for the rest of the day."

"You OK?" Robby asked.

"Yeah. Just not feeling it today."

"What d'ya gonna do?"

Steve shrugged.

"Wanna hang out?"

"Nah. Just gonna get some non-fire department time."

"Ambo 8-94 en route to Fallston General."

"You gonna come back tonight?"

"Might. Let's see what the day brings."

"8-94 en route 09:32."

"Well that wraps it up," Phil announced. "Now it's time for the honey-do list."

"Engine 8-14 in service, returning to station."

"Later guys. I'm outta here," Steve announced as he headed for the break room door.

"If I don't see you here, I'll see ya hear," Robby shot, hoping that the tired old saying would get Steve out of his brooding mood.

"I hear ya, see," he tossed back as he exited into the dark engine bay.

The three remaining men heard the door close.

"He seems depressed today," Pat commented.

"Yeah. He'll get out of his funk in a few weeks," Robby said hopefully.

"Does he blame himself for Royce?" Phil asked. He had been wanting to talk about the loss but never had the chance.

"No," Robby said with a shake of his head. "He's OK with what he did on the call. It's just one of those things." With a scowl on his face he continued, "Not sure what's going on. He seemed OK last night."

"Maybe he's just worried about someone getting hurt on a call," Pat said.

"Well, I'm heading home for a shower," Robby announced, signifying the end of the conversation.

"You guys gonna be around if there's another call today?" Pat asked.

"If it gets me out of Harry Homeowner shit, I'm in." Phil smiled.

"Yeah. Not doing much today," Robby replied still thinking about Steve's black mood.

The three left, leaving the station dark and deserted.

Chapter 33

Steve left the station and started driving with no destination in mind.

He was reeling with a wave of emotions. Fear, anger, excitement, boredom, and resentment rippled through him. All this combined with surges of adrenaline coursing through his body from remembering calls and the anticipation of the next big one. Wanting to feel the rush. Wanting not to need the rush.

He was trying to get a grip on how he was feeling. He wasn't nervous about going on a call, knowing that he could handle whatever was thrown at him. He was a little anxious about a new partner. He and Royce had it dialed. He worried about having a new partner contradicting him on a call.

He was also thinking about how torn up he was about the ambo assist. The surge of the call was wanted. His craving never decreasing. When they found out it was an ambo assist the level of the rush dropped, knowing that the call would not be very exciting. It was standard procedure to send the ambo and the engine to a cardiac arrest. This way whoever gets there first can start CPR. He was realizing that his anger was because it wasn't a "good" call.

It was also bothering him was that he was getting angry at the patient and the family, and he didn't even roll on the call. Imagining that they were probably too busy last night to take their father to the hospital when he had chest pains. This morning it didn't go away and instead of putting him in the family car and going to the hospital, they either waited until he coded or were too occupied to be bothered taking him to the hospital themselves. The ambo was the taxi.

Thinking over the past calls, re-living them in his head, he began to spot a pattern. He had always been the first to jump in and take the hard calls.

Extractions. Diving rescues. Hell, even body recoveries. He always told himself that he was doing it for the greater good. Helping patients, accident victims, the surviving families. He would even make extra effort to make the families believe that everything possible had been done. Taking the time to examine houses, making sure the family felt safe that all the fire was out. Doing CPR on patients that they knew would never be revived. Taking the time to talk to people in accidents, calming them. Joking with them. He always thought it made those he helped feel better about whatever the situation was.

Now he was realizing that it was never about the patient, the families or the survivors. It was all about himself. Everything he did was to push the rush harder, further, better than the last.

It was about getting a fix.

He was pumped when the call came in this morning. He didn't care it was only an assist. When 8-14 beat them out of the house, he got angry. It took him a while to put it together, but he soon figured out that the anger was because he didn't get to ride the engine. He didn't get to go to the scene. He didn't get to do CPR. He didn't get to...do anything. The fix was snatched away from him. Even if it was only an ambulance assist, he knew that somehow it would feed his addiction.

Was he a junkie living from fix to fix? Needing more and more. Increasing the surge in order to get a better and better high. The biggest, best rush came from the fire that killed Royce. Would he only get a bigger and better fix from another firefighter dying?

Was he a fucking freak?

The doctors kept saying his feelings weren't right. His emotions were wrong. He's not reacting right. He was screwed up. Was it true that his brain was wired wrong? Am I a monster? A freak?

What about the people I try to help? Most of them are assholes. Mad at the fire department for their cars being wrecked. Family members dying. Houses catching on fire. They yell at us. Blame us for the accidents. Sometimes curse at us.

He found himself driving up to Winters Run. Wandering through the twisting roads. Finding the dirt roads that surround the river, he wandered deep into the woods. He found a place by a quiet section of the river. Not a popular place for kids to swim. Peaceful and quiet.

Sitting by the side of the river, he just watched. The water was flowing, a few little fish were swimming near the shore. He could hear birds singing in the trees. A couple of squirrels were running around. It felt like he was the only human for miles around. He was enjoying the solitude, giving him the opportunity to think things through.

"Is it worth saving the assholes?" he asked out loud.

He realized that he had never questioned what or why he fights fire. Why he worked on the dying and injured from accidents. Why he jumped into the water to save the drowning, to recover the bodies. He knew that what he did, whether he saved someone or not, his actions gave strength to the survivors. Gave the living a way to say, "They did everything they could." It gave the survivors someone to blame for the results. Someone to shift their own failure onto.

Every once in a while, they'd run into someone who was a victim from a past call. They might recognize one of the firefighters or ambo attendants. Sometimes they'd say thanks. Most of the time they say something like, "My father didn't make it, but you guys did everything you could."

We never get to see the results after the fact. Scoop and swoop. Scrape 'em off the pavement. Throw them in the back of an ambo or into the helicopter and they're gone. We never hear from them again. We never get a follow-up. There is never a connection. The victims are just the focus during the call. The short-term reason that we get to run lights and sirens. Jump into the madness. Bring order. Calm. Command the situation.

The shadows were getting long as the sun dipped lower in the sky. Steve realized that it was going on four thirty in the afternoon.

It was time to get it together, still not knowing where he stood with all of the stuff going on in his head. This pissed him off because he never wanted to feel that he was the victim. Not in control. Dependent on someone else. Not being able to get his head wrapped around his feelings, his thoughts, made him nervous.

Time to head out. Park the feelings. Park the questions. Put them in the dungeon. Maybe I'll deal with them later. Maybe not at all.

Locked safely in the dungeon I won't have to worry about it. Won't have to deal with it.

He was heading back to his apartment, trying to decide what to do for the rest of the night, the scanner in his dash exploded.

"Beep booop, beep boop, dweedle dweedle, dweedle. Box 8-04, Company 8, 1050 P.I. Joppa Farm and Philadelphia Road. Time 16:57."

Without thinking, Steve's body reacted to the tones on the Plectron. His brain instantly stopped swirling the thoughts of the day through his mind. Instantly they were locked away. Blasting down Mountain Road, his car automatically turned right onto Pulaski Highway. Few cars were on the road, and he hit the light just right. He raced the Duster up to 65, flipping his head lights on. One mile and he would make a left onto Joppa Road. Then one half a mile on Joppa Road and a right turn onto Trimble Road. Then two tenths of a mile and he would be at the bottom of the hill to the fire station. He would be there in less than three minutes. Everything moved in slow motion as the adrenaline coursed through his body.

As he crested the hill 8-11 was pulled onto to the tarmac waiting for more crew members to arrive.

Gliding across the parking lot Steve recognized Ted's car. He also saw a car he seldom saw at the station: the bright new Chevy Blazer that belonged to Captain Brian Creamer.

Slamming the car into park he bolted across the parking lot and disappeared into the engine bay.

"Engine 8-11 responding."

Emerging seconds later carrying his turn-out gear, with no shoes on his feet, he leapt into the jump seat. Turning to look in the back window of the cab he recognized the crew.

The engine roared forward, gliding down the hill to the station as two more cars drove past them, responding to the call.

"Engine 8-11, responding 17:03."

The siren came to life as they reached the bottom of the hill.

The crew hated the siren on 8-11. This was the newest engine for the company. It had an electric siren rather than the air powered Federal siren. Everyone said it sounds like an ambulance or a police car. Not a real fire engine.

"Ambo 8-92 responding."

Steve was pulling on his turn-out pants, pulling the suspenders up. Ted was hanging onto his shoulder trying to steady him as the engine careened down Trimble Road. 8-11 had an open jump seat. There was no engine between the two sides.

Now settled in all the gear, Steve and Ted rode the engine with their heads above the cab of the engine.

"8-92 Responding, 17:05."

Ted leaned into Steve's ear and yelled, "You got this. Tell me what to do."

Nodding his head Steve realized that this was the first 10-50 that he had taken without Royce. It was the first time in the past year he remembered Ted riding jump seat. The world was spinning.

The engine crossed Interstate 40, passing the Roy Rogers and constricting to a two-lane road. In a short distance they would pass the train bridge. The road would become a single lane under the bridge. This was not the first accident on this road.

Everyone on the engine knew that there was a huge tree on the edge of the road. It was in the middle of a turn. Many drivers had accelerated out of the tunnel and met the tree head on.

Eagerly they peered ahead wanting to see what they were rolling up too. The high pulsing into their bodies.

The engine drove past the big tree; no cars were there. The bark was missing large chunks from years of cars hitting it.

As they approached the intersection, they spotted two cars crumpled together. The first car was a white sedan and it looked as though it had T-boned the second car, a blue two door, as it was turning left from Philadelphia Road onto Joppa Farm Road. A few people were mulling around the damaged cars.

"8-11 on location."

"Go and check the blue car. I'll check the white one."

Ted nodded.

As the engine was pulling up to the scene, Steve climbed off the engine and grabbed the medic box out of the first cabinet.

"8-11 on location 17:07."

Approaching the car, he saw a woman in the driver's seat, her head slowly wobbling back and forth. She was obviously dazed by the accident.

The front windshield was also broken on the passenger's side. He figured there was a passenger who probably wasn't wearing a seat belt.

Ted approached the other car. The door was closed but not latched. He didn't see anyone in the driver's seat.

Coming up to the driver's window Ted looked around and yelled, "Where's the Driver?"

A kid about eighteen or nineteen walked over and said, "It's my car."

"How are you feeling?"

"Not really great," the driver replied. "I think my car is trashed."

"Let's worry about you first, then we can look at the car." Ted signaled for him to sit down by the side of the road. "What's your name?"

"Jim."

"Do you remember what happened?"

"Not really. I was turning onto Joppa Farm, heading over to the town center. The car came out of nowhere and slammed into me."

"OK, let's take a look at you and check a few things out." Taking his penlight, Ted checked his eyes. Seeing that the pupils were equal and reactive, Ted quickly reviewed the young man's body, checking for any signs of injury and bleeding.

"Am I gonna be in trouble?"

"Don't worry about that right now," Ted tried to reassure him. "Let's make sure everyone is ok, then we can sort out what happened. Just relax and we'll get everything sorted out."

At the same time, Steve headed over to the white car. He saw two men standing at the driver's door frantically waving at him. Steve walked up to the driver's side of the white sedan and saw someone down on their knee talking to someone inside. As he approached, the men standing moved out of the way. Coming up behind the person in the door he asked, "What's going on?" as he quickly surveyed the scene. No steam or smoke from the hood. Tires were still inflated. The car seemed to be staying in one place. Not threatening to roll.

"She won't wake up!" the man kneeling by the driver's door almost yelled.

"Were you with her?"

"Un-uh. Saw the accident. That kid turned in front of her."

"OK, let me get in and take a look."

The man moved out of the way, relieved that someone else was dealing with her.

There was a woman sitting in the front not moving. Kneeling, he scanned the interior of the car. There was no passenger, but all sorts of debris was flung around the car.

The female in the driver's seat appeared unconscious. No visible bleeding. No seatbelt. Reaching in he took a moment to check for pulse and breathing. Feeling a pulse and seeing her chest rising and falling he moved his focus to the rest of the interior. He would start treating as soon as he had done a quick survey. The car was still in drive, so he reached across and grabbed the column shifter, sliding it into park. Then turned the ignition off, pulled the keys and tossed them in the center consul. Continuing to survey the car he looked to the passenger's seat. In it was a child seat. Facing forward. Belted in. His mind was racing as he added the pieces together. Car seat; broken windshield. There may have been a child in the seat that flew out when the cars crashed.

The woman in the car started to moan as Steve was leaning into the car. He pulled himself out to look at the woman. "I'm with the fire department, we're here to help you." He pulled his penlight and checked her pupils. *Equal and reactive*, he decided.

Brian came up behind Steve. "What d'ya need?" he asked, bending over to open the medic kit.

"Hand me a small cervical collar. Let's get it on before she wakes up too much."

Taking the collar, Steve quietly said, "There's a child seat in the front seat."

"What?" Brian asked. He hadn't looked inside the car.

The state police cruiser arrived.

"There's a baby seat in the front. Front windshield is cracked from an impact." With practiced easy he quickly slipped the back half of the brace around her neck. Then he secured the front piece and secured the Velcro. Standing up he said, "Keep an eye on her. I need to go check the rest of the car." The two men switched places as Steve slid past and walked around the back of the car.

Brian was a firefighter, but he had spent enough time on accident scenes to hold her head until the ambulance got there as Steve checked the rest of the car and came back.

"We'll put her in a KED. If you see someone, have them pull it from the engine and bring it over."

Steve opened the passenger's door and looked inside. The car seat was buckled into the car, and there were papers and trash on the floor. *Idiot parents*, he thought. *Can't even read the direction to put in a car seat.* He looked at the spiderwebbed window and knew something hit it from the inside. He just had to figure out what.

He heard the woman in the driver's seat starting to moan as he reached into the car to move the paper and debris, making sure there was no baby in the car. "Hey honey. I'm with the fire department. What's your name?" he asked as he was sorting through the garbage.

The woman mumbled something. A quick look between the two firefighters confirmed that neither could understand what she had said.

"She's starting to come around," Steve said. "Hey! Were you by yourself in the car?"

He didn't find anything in the front seat. Thankful he didn't find a tiny little body but he knew that he didn't find anything that could have broken the windshield either.

The woman was moaning. Mixed in with the moans she was trying to say something. Both men were straining to understand her.

As Steve moved to the back door of the car, he carefully surveyed the back seat, checking to see if it was safe. Looking for anything that might be dangerous. Anything he might not want to step on.

Climbing into the backseat, he was checking the passenger's side floor and under the seat. As he leaned in to get his hand under the seat, he spotted a small body behind the driver's seat. Instantly he knew he had found the cause of the broken window.

Sliding all the way into the car, he shouted, "Got a child." Bending his body into an unnatural position he reached down and tried to find a pulse. The child was lying face down with his head against the center drive train hump. He couldn't get to a good position to check for a carotid pulse. He jammed himself into a ball and spun inside the car, moving from the passenger's side to the driver's side, and then unfolded himself as he opened the rear driver's side door. He slid out of the car, kneeling on the ground with his body across the seat. Never taking his eyes off the lifeless body.

"8-92 on location."

From this position he could get better access to the child. From the scene he knew that the child was probably in the car seat. When the accident happened, he was thrown into the windshield and then bounced into the backseat. It always amazed Steve how stuff was thrown around in an accident.

Ted had finished up with the other driver and the state trooper was talking to him. He came over the car to see where he needed to be.

"8-92 on location, 17:12."

Steve was focusing on the child, thinking about what he needed to deal with. Head injury, neck injury, spinal injury, broken bones and maybe dislocations. Needed to find out if it still has a pulse. Steve froze. Staring at the small unmoving body, a thought flashed in his head. *Should I even bother? If it's alive it's going to face a lifetime of fucked up!* His senses shut down while he was inside the dark part of his mind.

A woman's voice broke his thought. "Seth."

Brian saw Ted approaching the car and asked, "Got this?" Brian slid back to let Ted sit next to the woman. "I need to go get the KED."

Ted nodded as Brian headed over to the engine. Kneeling down next to the woman he began checking her out. "What's the plan?" he asked Steve.

Ted's question pulled Steve back from his thoughts. He quickly looked around, catching up with what was happening. The driver was regaining consciousness. Picking his head up like a turtle Steve tried to peer through the windows of the car to see who was nearby.

Spotting the ambo crew arriving he instructed Ted, "Give me a half board."

Yelling across the scene Ted relayed the message to the ambulance crew.

Cindy was the medic on the ambo. She was stepping out of the ambulance as Ted yelled to her. She waved back acknowledging and disappeared into the side door of the ambulance.

Ralph, the ambulance driver, climbed out and quickly walked to the back of the ambo waiting to pull the stretcher out.

"When the ambo crew gets here, I'll pull the baby out and we'll put him on the backboard," Steve announced to whoever was listing.

Steve positioned himself to get the baby out of the car. He had to keep the head, neck and back as still as possible to prevent any more injuries. He could clasp him from the front and back to stabilize his neck and back. Then he would be able to move him out of the car and onto the board.

The ambo crew had brought the equipment to the car and got set up to help with the child. Ralph parked the stretcher and grabbed the half backboard, ready to help. Captain Creamer was waiting on the passenger side of the car in case the crew needed anything.

Cindy put her hand on Steve's shoulder and said, "Backboard is ready."

Getting the child ready to be moved, he unfolded the legs and straightened the best he could. Then he slid his right hand under the child, gently lifting the tiny body with his left until his right hand was wrapped around the tiny face. Pausing for a fraction of a second, he tried to feel for breathing, a pulse. Any sign of life. He then placed his left arm over the spine with his left hand on the back of his head. Checking his grip, he lifted the child off of the floor in one movement. Raising it above the seat he backed out of the car with the lifeless body extended out in front of him, the adrenaline giving him the strength to move the child.

Cindy moved around so she could grab the small legs dangling in space. When he was flipped over, she didn't want the legs flying around twisting the tiny body.

Fully standing with the child face down, Steve said, "Board."

Ralph took the half backboard and held it over the child.

Steve removed his left arm from the back of the baby and let Ralph lower the backboard in its place. He then put his left arm on top of the backboard, again sandwiching the baby.

Ralph positioned himself opposite Steve. His hands were over Steve's, making sure that there was a good grip on the baby and backboard when it was flipped over.

"To my right on three," Steve commanded.

The two locked eyes as he began to count. "One."

Ralph nodded slightly.

"Two."

Cindy shifted, getting into a better position to deal with the moving child.

"Three," and the three of them expertly flipped the backboard over.

Ralph and Cindy moved to the sides and grabbed it, allowing Steve to release the child. Moving the board and child two steps, they set it on the stretcher.

Cindy immediately began working the baby. "Got a pulse."

With an audible sigh the men standing around were relieved that the child was not dead.

Flicking her penlight into the child's eyes, she reported, "Left pupil is dilated and unresponsive. Let's get this one moving fast."

Captain Creamer headed over to the fire engine and grabbed the radio mic.

Cindy grabbed the blanket folded at the foot of the stretcher and rolled it into a tube. Then she wrapped it around the child's head before they quickly strapped it down.

The speakers on the fire engine came to life with their customary beeps. "Box 804, Company 8, 10-50 P.I. Joppa Farm and Philadelphia Road. Requesting second amb'lance. Time 17:17."

The ambo crew quickly whisked the baby into the back of the ambo and sped away, hoping they would get to the hospital with the child still alive.

The siren blasted the air as the ambulance was leaving the scene. "Amb'lance 8-92 en route to Franklin Square Hospital."

"Ambulance 8-96 responding."

"Amb'lance 8-92 en route to Franklin Square. Amb'lance 8-96 responding to 10-50 P.I. Time 17:19."

With the child gone, Steve turned his attention back to the woman. Ted had been monitoring her while the rest of the crew dealt with the baby.

"How's she doing?" Steve asked.

"No change. Looks like she's starting to come around." Ted Said. "Brian's get'in the KED."

As Steve was taking over, his mind was wandering. *Idiot mother didn't bother putting her kid in the car seat right and probably killed it. Wonder if I should even bother with her.*

With Brian bringing the KED, Steve and Ted quickly got the woman strapped in, ready for transport.

The second ambo arrived, and she was quickly moved out of the car and onto the stretcher. The crew whisked her into the back of the Ambulance.

"She never quite came to. Probably has a bad concussion," Ted said as they were packing up the scene.

"From the way she used the car seat, not sure she had any brains to scramble," Steve acidly replied.

The ambulance pulled out as the two were carrying the equipment back to the engine.

They cleaned up and got all the gear replaced on the engine. Then they just hung around talking with the trooper while they waited for the tow truck.

When the tow truck got the cars loaded, the engine returned to the station. The crew was quiet during the ride home.

When they got back to the station, Steve stowed his gear without saying a word and started to head to his car. "I'm outta here," he announced in passing. He jumped into his car and roared down the drive, disappearing onto Trimble Road.

Chapter 34

The ringing phone shook him from sleep. "Butler," he answered groggily.

"Hey Chief, it's Pat."

"What's up? Is there a call?

"No. It's Steve. You told us to call you if anything was going on."

Larry was now fully awake and intently listening. "Is he OK?"

"Don't know. He's sitting on the hill across from the station. Just sitting there."

"When did he get there?"

"Not sure. I thought we heard a car about fifteen minutes ago. No one came in so we looked out and saw his car. That's when I saw him up on the hill."

"OK, anything else?"

"Went to see if he was OK. Walked over. He told me he was just thinking. He had a bottle with him."

"How bad off is he?"

"He was OK when I talked to him a few minutes ago, but he is slamming it hard."

"Alright."

"What do you want me to do?"

"Nothing, I'll be there in a few minutes. Just make sure he doesn't drive off."

"Ten-four Chief. I'll make sure."

Pat hung up the phone and made his way into the pitch-black bunk room of the station. Standing to the side of the window he secretively watched Steve sitting on the hill, every few minutes taking a drink from the bottle he held.

Pat decided that if he moved to the car, he would stop him. He waited in the dark. He watched.

Ten minutes later Chief Butler's truck came up the drive, the lights cutting across the hill twenty feet from where Steve sat, drinking himself into oblivion.

Parking his truck at the far end of the lot, Larry walked across the asphalt and up the hill.

Steve stared into space as Larry approached him, seemingly oblivious to the chief's presence.

Larry sat next to him; the half-moon was eerily illuminating the station. The monolithic building looked abandoned in the night air. Larry had never looked at the station from here before.

"It's strange to look at the station from here," Steve said.

Larry just sat, completely surprised by the unexpected feelings, startled by Steve speaking.

"Sitting here, looking at the dark building, you're disconnected. Not a part of anything. Just present." Taking a swig, he continued. "I imagine it's like that for astronauts. Looking down onto earth from space, totally disconnected. Wanting to be on earth. Not seeing anything moving around. It's lonely."

Larry was listening intently to what he said.

"From here you are a gnat on the ass of life. Nothing. Disconnected. Non-essential," Steve was orating in a monotone voice. "Not connected with anything. Sitting here, I'm insignificant. Alone. Walk ten steps down the hill and across the parking lot and you become the hero. The envy of other men. The angel of hope. Just the association gives you a pass in society."

Taking a quick drink, he casually handed the bottle to Larry.

Taking the bottle from Steve, Larry started to take a quick sip from the unknown bottle. After a small taste, Larry again returned his lips to the bottle and drew a mouthful of the warming liquid. Letting it linger in his mouth, savoring the taste as the flavor engulfed him. After a few seconds he swallowed the smooth tasting liquid.

"Damn that's good. What is it?"

"Twenty-five-year-old Glenlivet."

"Wow."

"Dad's a scotch drinker. This was his pride and joy."

"Um, does he know you snagged it?"

"Nope."

"Never met your dad, but he'll probably be pissed."

"Fuck it. Why bother with the twelve-year-old stuff? If I'm going down, I'm doing it in style. Cheers Chief."

Hesitating for a second, Larry thought, *I'm drinking a two hundred-dollar bottle of scotch with a seventeen year old*. He was torn between stopping the boy from drinking and letting the man who watched his partner die get drunk. He took another drink from the bottle then said, "This would be better in a glass with an ice cube. Want to go back to my place?"

"No. Just gonna sit here for a while. Get a different perspective. I'm not going anywhere or going to do anything stupid. I'll crash in the bunk room or on the floor." He pulled another long drink from the bottle. Then asked, "Did one of the guys call you?"

"Yeah. Pat heard you pull in and saw you just sitting out here."

"How long you been doing this Chief?"

"Doing what?"

"Fighting fire."

"Haven't thought about it till the funeral. It'll be twenty-four years this summer. I joined the fire department when I was sixteen."

"Why?"

"Dad and granddad were firefighters. It was expected."

"You've lived here your whole life?"

"Yeah. I was born in the area. Granddad was a farmer. Lots of farms when I was a kid. Why did you join?"

"Ted."

"Ted?"

"Yeah. He was dating my older sister and was telling me 'bout the fire department. He made it sound cool. I figured that having this on a resume would help me with school or something."

Larry sat silently, letting Steve speak in his own time. He started to reflect on himself as well. He hadn't thought about how long or why he fought fire for a very long time.

Another draw on the bottle and Steve continued, "When I came and checked it out it was like I found a place to be. Someplace that I wasn't a child or a kid. I was an adult." The bottle passed between the two, each slowly sipping the liquid. The two of them sat in silence, letting the moonlight wash over the landscape.

"I'll never forget my first fire call where we had to put on the SCOT packs. My first real fire. It was Tuesday, May 18th, 1982. We were just sitting around the station. The older guys were talking shit. I was getting stoked up about going on a call. The tones sounded at 19:27. I can still hear the tones. 'Box 808, Company 8, building fire, 1002 Joppa Farm Rd, Joppa Cinema.' The red phone rang on the wall as Captain Creamer was walking by.

"'Company Eight' was all I heard. My heart began to race as I realized that I was on the duty rotation to take the jump seat. I was assigned to the crew, so no one could bump me. I was trying not to sprint to the turn-out rack. I was trying to be calm like the rest of the crew but inside I was electrified with energy. I remember being frustrated because everyone but me was moving so damn slow. I was alive with energy.

"'Smoke in the building, coming from an electrical panel.' the captain yelled as he pulled on his boots and coat, grabbing his helmet as he climbed into the cab of 8-12."

"When I finally got to my gear, I stepped into my boots, pulling the yellow pants up. I reached for the red suspenders hanging at each side and fumbled, missing, grabbing the right one the second time, then finally slinging them over my shoulders, my fly flapping open. They were brand new. First real call. They were bright yellow and bright red suspenders, still had the stretchy in the elastic. I heard the engine roar to life behind me. Pulling on my turn-out coat and placing my helmet on my head I sprinted to the jump seat. I remember the smell of the cotton duct coat. Everyone thought the pants and boots were presents from my parents for finishing basic training, but the truth is I bought them myself a few days before. They were more powerful than a pillowcase cape over my shoulders as a five-year-old. I was ready because my superhero uniform transformed me into some sort of superbeing able to withstand the fires of hell."

Larry was listening. He had a small smile as he remembered the feeling of the first call. His first helmet. His turn-out gear was a hand-me-down from his father, but the helmet was brand new bought for Larry.

"Climbing into the jump seat I began buckling the pants and turn-out coat in preparation for the raging fire we were going to find at the movie theater. It took all of my effort to stay focused and get ready. I turned on the air pack and heard the air pressurizing the regulator with a quick hiss, followed by the strike of the bell. I could smell the smoke of hundreds of fires when I was putting on the pack. I hung the face mask over the regulator and stood up."

After a pause he continued. "I was so excited and so nervous I kept checking and rechecking everything. Making sure I could pull air from the mask, making sure my gear was on right. I was jumping up and down in the jump seat. I couldn't sit still."

"I still feel that way..." Larry sighed. "...especially when there is a really good call."

"Ya know, I love the sound of the SCOT pack springing out of the clip. It's the starting gun for the working fire. That was the first time I got to stand on the engine fully geared up. The wind blowing in my face. The diesel engine growling down the road with the screaming siren. I held on so tight my hands hurt as we sped down the road. I remember watching Brian blowing the air horn, blasting it as we neared the intersection. I felt the blast of the air horn in my chest. The cars stopped and let the engine through as we blew the intersection. The fire engine parted the sea of cars."

Steve paused, taking the bottle back from Larry, and took a swig.

With a smile Larry just said, "I remember that call."

Steve continued, "I remember the whole thing. As we came down Trimble to Joppa Farm, I looked across the intersection. I saw the theater. People were standing in the parking lot milling around. People standing out front of the theater, waving at us. I felt like superman. I was scared shitless. That was my first real rush."

Larry took a drink. Quietly listening.

"I saw the captain reach for the mic in the cab and a few seconds later I hear the dispatcher over the PA speaker say, 'Engine 8-12 on location, investigating.'

"When we pulled up, I tried not to run past the captain and rest of the crew. I couldn't remember what I was supposed to do but I didn't care. I remember seeing you at the scene. I was in awe of you. Had never spent much time with you. For you to be on the scene meant it must be big. I remember you and the captain – so cool."

"Yeah. I was on a date, trying to get a movie in." Larry snickered. "She wasn't as impressed as you were. Never had another date."

"Watched you and the captain go into the theater. We just stood outside the building, waiting. I was so pumped up. Pat was busy scoping the crowd looking for people he knew and good-looking girls to hit on. Fred was at the pump panel spinning knobs and checking pressures. If you listened closely you could hear him ramping the pump up and down to a rhythm using the fire engine as an instrument to play out some tune in his head. I was the only one who didn't know what the hell to do."

They handed the bottle back and forth, taking swigs in turn.

"I thought I was so freaking cool until Pat asked me if I was OK. He said I looked like I was gonna puke. Told me to relax and breathe. I was overwhelmed. The excitement of being on a real fire call. The rush of the crowd staring at us. I thought it could never get any better than that moment."

"All I could think of was, *Why the hell does being a fireman always mess up my life?*" Larry said. "It's funny how two people see the same thing differently and both be right."

"That was the day I was hooked. It didn't matter that I had no idea what to do, no idea what was going on. I was one of the only four people in the world that could save the theater from certain disaster. That was the day I became a junkie."

"What are you talking about?" Larry asked quickly, concern in his face that there was more going on with Steve.

Seeing his expression, Steve gave a quick smile. He remembered that Larry did not even know what a bong was. "Don't worry Chief. I'm not into drugs. I was hooked on the rush."

A sly smile reached Larry's lips, relieved that he did not have to deal with some kind of drugs. He handed the bottle back to Steve. "What d'ya mean 'rush'?"

"You know, the adrenaline high you get from being on a call. The more spectacular, the more exciting, the bigger the rush. It was an urge at first, then it became an obsession to get the rush," Steve continued after swallowing. "I wanted to get more and more. A bigger fix. A stronger rush."

Larry sat for a moment reflecting on what Steve was saying. "I never thought of it that way. I guess I felt the same way. I still get excited on every call." Pausing for a moment he continued, "What d'ya call it? A 'rush'?"

"Yep. The rush."

"Why do you call it that?"

"It's the body's response. Your adrenal gland secretes adrenaline. Just like when you're scared or ride a rollercoaster. It rushes into your body." Steve paused. "It's fucking great."

"You gonna go to a paid department when you're old enough?"

"Nope. I knew I would never be a paid firefighter. Glasses," Steve added while pointing to his face.

"Yeah. Me too." Listening to Steve, Larry slowly made the transition from chief listening to a firefighter with a problem to two men talking about how they got to where they were in life.

"You were married right?" Steve asked Larry.

Larry nodded.

"Did the fire department kill it?" Steve asked.

"I would like to blame it all on the fire house, but I helped," Larry began. "I guess that's what started it. Spent too much time at the station. Not enough with her. She said that she wanted to be someone's priority and not someone to come and visit when nothing better is going on."

The two paused in conversation while they sipped the scotch.

"You couldn't help yourself, could you?" Always wanting to catch the call?"

"How so?"

"That's what your wife used to bitch about right? Always at the fire station. Always dropping everything to get a call."

"Yeah. It was a big part of it."

"Did you try to change?"

"Sure. At least I thought I did."

"I worry I'll end up like that too."

Someone came out of the station, walked to their car and pulled out. Never seeing the two on the hill.

"How are you dealing with all this Chief?"

"All what?"

"Royce dying. Damaged crew."

"Haven't given it much thought. Was busy with the funeral and all of the other stuff that went with it. I've been keeping tabs on you. Had a few of the guys keeping tabs on you. Chief Bancroft watching you in school."

"Have you ever lost anyone before?" Steve asked

"My parents. One of my friends died in a car crash a few years ago."

"What about one of us?"

"Firefighter?" Thinking for a second, he replied, "I've known a couple who died in the line of duty over the years. No one close."

"It sucks that Royce is dead," Steve said.

"You mad?" Larry asked.

"What do you mean?"

"I don't know. Want to make sure you OK. Not blaming yourself." Larry was uneasy. "Everyone's worried. The shrink from the hospital told us that you may do something stupid and to keep an eye on you. Look for changes in personality and behavior. I had the guys keep an eye on you. Make sure you didn't do anything stupid or crazy."

"Don't worry Chief. I'm OK. Royce's death just has me thinking at lot. And in case you haven't figured it out, that doc is a fucking quack." Steve took a healthy swallow. "The civilians are what pisses me off." The scotch was taking effect.

Larry reached for some more liquid. "What d'ya mean?"

"We go out in the middle of the night to car accidents, fires, injuries, people dying." Another swallow. "What the fuck for?"

"We help people. Save lives, protect property."

"I used to believe that too. But it's a lie."

Larry just listened.

Steve continued, "I used to believe all that crap too. Royce's death made me really think hard about it thought. What I figured out is that I don't really care if the patient lives or dies." Another swallow.

"I don't understand."

"I have been thinking 'bout why I ride the engine. I'm not altruistic." Pausing to take in a deep breath. "I ride the engine for the rush. The high that you can only get trying to save someone. Fighting a fire. Tearing a car apart with the jaws."

With a sigh Larry said, "Hadn't thought about that, but yeah I like the rush. Guess I always have."

Steve and Larry each took a drink, sitting in silence.

"I've been thinking about it for a while," Steve said. "Why we do what we do. It's about me."

"No, I don't believe that's why we do it."

"Then why do we do it?" Steve had started slurring his words slightly as the scotch began to kick in.

Thinking for a moment Larry finally said, "Shit I dunno." He took a swallow. "Help people, serve the community. It's what my dad told me I needed to do."

"Yeah. I get that, but it's not why we do it." Steve was feeling the effects of the alcohol and he was letting his well-structured defenses down. "I always made the same excuse for being a firefighter. Save lives, protect property. That's bullshit. All that shit is an excuse that's created by us wanting the rush. It's the rush. The high I get on the engine."

"It is good, but I still think I do it to help people."

"How fucked up am I Chief?"

"What are you talking about? I don't think you're fucked up. Right now, you're drunk. You're tired."

"Think about it. I don't ride the engine to help anyone but myself. To get the proverbial high every time I jump on the engine. I don't think I would do it if I didn't get the rush."

Larry silently thought for a few moments before answering. "About half the calls give me a rush. I just keep doing it and I don't know why."

"That's the first revelation I had. But what's worse is today on the call I looked at the baby and the only thing I thought about was how I should just let the kid die. It would be so much easier on the family, the mother."

"Not our choice."

"Then I thought about how the mother should be dead instead of the kid. She didn't even bother to put the kid in the car seat. Probably in too much of a hurry to be bothered."

"People never think about what could happen. They make mistakes."

"And they hurt and kill others around them because of it."

"The world is screwed up."

"And there I am in the middle of it, getting off on everyone else's stupidity. I don't fix it or make it go away, just get stoned from the rush."

"I think it's a plus."

"Yeah. But that don't make me any more or less fucked up. On top of that shit, I have everyone around me telling me that I'm not acting right."

"What d'ya mean?"

"People telling me that I should be sad, depressed, angry. Should feel guilty. I don't."

"We all have baggage we have to carry."

"It's not about the baggage I'm carrying."

"What's it about."

"It's about carrying the wrong baggage."

"What the hell are you talking about? "

"Look, we've seen some shit. People dying, burned, broken, bleeding. It's the stuff that makes horror movies. And we just push it aside and keep going." Taking a drink, Steve continued, "We take all the bad shit and bury it deep in our brains and lock it away. We never talk about it. We never think about it."

"Yeah. We just bury it and never let it get to us."

"So, we have that shit in our head and if that's not bad enough I now have to wonder why I'm putting myself through that. Knowing that I'll have dark shit to lock away. Now I have to wonder at every call 'Am I doing this for the victim or am I doing this for myself?'"

"Does it matter, if you continue to help people?"

"There's the missing piece Chief!"

"I don't follow?"

"Does it matter if I help people?" Steve was starting to get angry, the alcohol working through his body. "I keep wondering if they deserve to be helped. If we hadn't tried to help the little girl that the stupid mother forgot about, Royce would be sitting here with us now!"

"You don't know that."

"What about the shit head kid who wraps daddy's car around the pole and then blames us. The old lady who codes out and the family that tell us it's our fault for her dying. The parents who kill their kids, not putting them in seatbelts, not watching them, letting them wander off to get run over or drown, then telling us it's our fault for not saving them."

"People get scared. They just blame whoever they can."

"What about the mother today?"

"She made a mistake."

"Yep. They take no responsibility for what they do." Steve's eyes were getting heavy. "When thing they don't like happen, it's the firefighter's fault."

"Come on, you're drunk and tired. Let's get you into the station." Larry started to pull Steve up. "We can ponder the minds of civilians tomorrow."

"OK Chief."

Walking across the lot Larry asked, "You gonna be OK?"

"Big question." Steve paused. "I'm sad Royce's dead, but we all signed up for it. I'm mad that people in general are stupid and don't take responsibility. I'm mad that parents don't know where their kids are. I'm mad that parents don't put their kids in car seats. I'm mad 'cus I don't know if I SHOULD save them. I'm mad because I'm hooked on the rush."

Pat met the two at the door as they came in, grabbing Steve by the other arm, they led him to the bottom bunk and guided him while he flopped down. Pat grabbed a blanket and tossed it over him.

As they were walking out Steve continued. "OK? Who the hell knows? I have the shrink telling me that my brain is messed up 'cuz I don't feel right. I'll just take it a day at a time." As he was shifting around, he muttered "How the hell am I going to get a bigger rush?"

Moving into the lounge area Larry asked, "You gonna be here for the night?"

"Most of it. I have to pull out 'bout five."

"I don't think he's going anywhere tonight. I'll swing by in the morning to check on him."

The next morning Larry pulled into the station on his way to work. He was surprised that the lot was empty, having expected to see Steve's Duster parked where he had left it last night. *With as much scotch at Steve drank last night, I figured he would be out till noon*, Larry thought.

Parking at the entrance Larry walked into the station and into the bunk room. It was empty so he moved into the lounge then into the office. The station was empty. The silence was eerie. Something did not feel right. Looking around the office he saw what he was hoping not to find. Sitting in the center of the desk was a badge and the key card to let you into the building. He knew that this was Steve's badge and key card.

I've lost another firefighter, Larry thought. This one was harder because somewhere inside he was thinking that there should have been something he could have done to stop it. With tears building, he picked up the badge and access card and put them in his pocket. "I'll hang onto these for a while."

Chapter 35

Sitting at the table, Steve was drained from telling the story.

"In all the years we've been together you've never told me any of this," Debbie said.

Steve just stared as his glass of scotch, swirling the ice cubes around the glass.

"Why didn't you tell me?"

"I never thought it was important. It all happened before we met, a long time before we met." Tossing back his drink, he continued. "It was buried in the past. I wasn't supposed to come up ever again."

"I knew that you were a firefighter. You said something about a firefighter that you knew died, but you never said it was your partner," Debbie continued to pry. "You look like you're going to be sick."

The kids had wandered into the dining room, listening to their dad telling about his past. This was a story they had never heard before. They didn't realize that no one had heard the story before.

"I always thought that you being a firefighter was a joke or something," his son said.

His daughter was nodding. "I thought you were joking with us."

With a big smile, he replied, "No. It was real. Look, this will be hard for you to understand and wrap your head around, but I want to talk to you about it."

"OK. We're all ears," Debbie said, hoping that he would make sense, taking comfort that her teenage kids were jumping in.

"I tried to forget, but it never really worked." Crunching on the ice, he finished. "I tried to fight it. Tried to control it."

"Is it about Royce dying? Do you think it's your fault?"

"What?" Steve was vigorously shaking his head. "It's not Royce, it's the rush. The way I feel about people."

Debbie leaned back, trying to relax, "What are you talking about?"

"The rush. It scares the shit out of me 'cause I know I'm addicted."

"It's been thirty years! What are you scared of?"

"The addiction."

"What do you mean you're addicted?"

"I crave the rush. I want it. The wanting it is what scares me. Remember when I quit smoking and I used to say, 'A puff away from a pack a day'?"

"Sure. You quit cold turkey and you said that you constantly craved a cigarette."

"You used to smoke?" his daughter asked with wide eyes.

"Yeah, before I met your mother. When we got married, I decided to quit. For about two or three years I was always craving a cigarette. It took about ten years before the cravings went away."

"What else don't we know about you?" his son asked.

Smiling Steve answered, "A lot of things. More than you can imagine. Your mom too." With a wink at Debbie, he finished. "We have many, many secrets. Most of which we can't tell you about."

"Stop!" Debbie commanded. "You'll have them imagining all kinds of stuff."

"You're just messing with us," Chris shot at his dad.

With a sly smile Debbie continued. "Besides, you don't want your kids snooping around the secret room hidden in the basement."

With a look of shock Michelle said, "We don't have a basement."

Reaching across the table and condescendingly patted her daughter's hand. "OK dear. Just keep thinking that."

Looking between her mom and dad with wide eyes she said, "I can't tell if you're joking or not."

"We're messing with you," Steve said with a deadpan and stern face. "There is no secret entrance to the hidden basement in our closet. But that's not what we're talking about."

Debbie was relieved that he had begun to joke with his family. He was acting more like himself. Hopefully he would relax and talk about what is bothering him.

"You know that when your mom and I met we were in a gun fight."

Debbie rolled her eyes and shook her head.

Pointing accusingly at his wife Steve continued, "In fact, as I remember it, you shot at me first!"

"What were you doing in a gun fight?" Chris jumped in.

"As a matter of fact, I did take the first shot."

"Wait," Michelle interrupted. "You told that story before. It was water guns at Kings Dominion."

"A mere technicality," Steve smirked.

"Stop. You were talking about the rush. Let's get back to that," Debbie instructed. "You're trying to change the subject."

"I'm really good at doing that and hiding my feelings. I have had years of locking them up so I don't have to deal with them, but they don't go away. Thirty years later I still crave the rush." His eyes were distant. "I can remember the feeling as the adrenaline flooded my body." He closed his eyes, reveling in the memory."

"I don't get it."

"I'm scared of the rush."

"Why?"

"I want it."

"So? Is that a bad thing?"

"It's a scary thing."

"What do you mean? You're not making any sense?"

"It's about being sucked into something I escaped once."

"You're freaking me out. I don't understand what you're talking about."

Taking a breath, Steve tried to get himself under control. Debbie shifted impatiently waiting.

"It took me some time to put everything together. It was before we met. Being a firefighter was great, but I eventually realized that it was great for different reasons."

"Why did you start?" Chris asked.

"Sounded like a good thing to do. I thought it would be good for references for school, work, stuff like that." After a brief pause, he continued. "I loved riding the engine, running into buildings. Car accidents. After Royce died, everything changed."

"Like what?"

261

"Saying things changed is wrong. Nothing changed, I just woke up." He poured himself another scotch. "You know, I have been thinking about this moment for years. Been dreading it for years."

"Dreading what? I never seen you scared or worried like this before."

"Saying it out loud."

Debbie was surprised by that comment.

Seeing the look in her face Steve laughed. "I guess you didn't expect that."

"I don't know what to expect."

"After the fire department, I tried to move on. Tried to forget. It didn't work."

"What's that mean?"

"After a few years away from firefighting I figured that the craving would stop, but it never did. I fight it every day. I crave the rush. I want the feeling again."

"What are you talking about?" she insisted. "You're not making any sense."

"I've been trying to explain it to myself for years. Trying to have it make sense in my head before I say it out loud. What I've realized is that it's like being a drug addict. Until you say it out loud it doesn't exist." His breath shuddered as he inhaled.

"What drugs are you talking about? You don't do drugs?"

"What's being a firefighter got to do with drugs?" his son asked.

"Not the kind of drugs you're thinking 'bout," Steve clarified. Focusing on explaining it to his kids he began to regain control.

"Dad's talking about some kind of adrenaline rush," Debbie said.

"I am addicted." Pausing, deeply inhaling, Steve continued. "I'm addicted to the rush. I want it. I crave it."

"What do you mean you're addicted?" his daughter asked.

His son inserted, "How can you be addicted? And what does the fire department have to do with it?"

"Addictions are more than just sticking chemicals in your body. Sometimes addictions are actions or responses. You little people," he said waving his hand at his kids, "are addicted to smart phones. Others are addicted to gaming. Mom loves to exercise. If she doesn't make it to exercise it throws her off for the day."

"I'm not that bad. I just like to work out." She gave him a kick under the table.

"Yeah. I hear it's the endorphins or something." Steve smiled back. "It's like that." Eyes drifting between his family Steve was looking for a spark of understanding. "Mine is the adrenaline rush." His body involuntary shook as thirty-year-old memories flooded his mind. He felt the dungeon door of his brain starting to open. The rush starting to flow into him as memories were breaking free after spending three decades locked in the vault of his mind. Stronger than the last miniscule fix he got a few months ago. The fear of losing control began to overwhelm him. He struggled in his mind as he slammed the door to the dark places closed. Imagining the clanging of steel on steel echoing in his skull as the door slammed shut. The sounds of massive tumblers sliding into place as the door was relocked and secured. Safe for the moment, Steve regained control. The memories again safely locked away.

Debbie saw the change in his face, his body, and in his eyes most of all. He was unrecognizable. In almost twenty years of marriage she had never seen that look. Whatever he was battling was new to her. With a small smile she squeezed his hand.

Returning the squeeze, he continued. "The rush. It's what we called it. Never out loud. Only to ourselves. The adrenaline causes the rush. It's incredible."

"An adrenaline rush?" Chris asked. "We learned about that in biology. It's supposed to give you super strength or something. The Incredible Hulk stuff."

"Something like that," Steve answered. "It gives much more than that. From a scientific view it helps with the fight or flight reaction of animals. If you're scared, you run. If you need extra strength to survive it gives you that."

"Like when someone scares you?" Michelle questioned.

"Yes, that's one way."

"Ridding a rollercoaster," Chris added.

"Yes, like that too."

"Debbie asked, "How do you know all this stuff?"

"After I figured out what was going on, I studied up on adrenaline. Tried to understand. When you get scared, frightened, excited, your body produces it naturally. it helps you. Sometimes it's with the flight or fight. You can run fast, or a long way to save yourself. Sometimes it gives you strength to do things you wouldn't normally do."

"Lift cars?" Chris blurted out,

"Yeah. There are cases where someone has lifted a car to save someone like their wife or child."

"I don't get it. So far all you've said is you like getting scared or riding rollercoasters. Why is this so horrid?" Debbie said. "Tell me what your scared of."

"It's not riding the rollercoaster one time. It's never getting off that scares me."

"You lost me."'

"The feeling is addictive. Like any other addiction. It is all-consuming and overwhelming. Just like a junkie who will sell everything to get a fix, the rush is just like that."

"The rush will make you sell your things? What the hell are you talking about?" Debbie was confused. "You don't have to go and buy the stuff, do you?"

"Actually, you do, just not in any obvious way."

Debbie just stared at her husband, waiting for him to explain.

"You will give up everything, sacrifice everyone to get the rush."

She was trying to understand. "What do you mean 'bout giving up everything? Help me understand"

Seeing the unsatisfied look in her face, Steve quickly continued. "Do you remember a few years ago when I got so wrapped up in work, I didn't spend any time with you and the kids. When I was here, I was disconnected. Checking my email, not putting my phone down at dinner, constantly taking calls."

"Yea, I finally had it and yelled at you." Debbie smiled.

"That was easy. I was over focusing, trying to go above and beyond for the job. I never really got anything out of all the work."

"I got that. You thought you would get a better promotion if you worked hard. Is that any different than wanting to go on a fire call?"

"In the fire department it starts off small and simple. After you get a fix, you want more. You crave more. You wait for a fire call. You start hanging around the station more. You listen to the scanner more. When you hear the tones, the only thing you can think of is to run to the call. Get in on the action. Because the addiction. You push everything else away. You hang out at the station whenever you can. Forget about your wife, girlfriend, kids, whoever. If you're out, you'll leave the people you're with to get a call."

"Don't they understand?" Chris asked.

"I guess to start with, they understand. But quickly it turns bad, and you choose the fire over family. Pretty soon you're spending so much time waiting for a call you spend more time at the station than with your family. That's what leads to divorce."

"That's easy, just schedule the time you will take calls," Debbie said.

"That sounds easy, but it gets worse over time. When you can't catch a call, you go and hang out at the station. You become consumed with catching a call."

"So, you just hang out so you can be there for a fire call?" Chris asked.

"Yes and no. It's so you can talk to other firefighters. Swap stories. Talk about past calls, whether you were there or not."

"Why?" Michelle asked.

"To get a fix from memories. Just talking about calls can give you a small rush. Just enough to get a fix. It holds you for a while," Steve explained.

"So, you talk about past calls and stuff to remember the rush?" Debbie asked.

"Yeah."

Chris's eyes lit up. "Like serial killers that go back to where they killed someone?"

"Exactly like that," Steve said. "When you can't get a good fix, you go into withdrawals. You will do anything to get a fix. But turns out that just sitting around trying to remember the good calls is a bad thing. It doesn't fix anything just puts off the withdrawal for a little while."

"How do you have withdrawals?" Debbie asked.

"Just like any other drug, I guess. Caffeine, nicotine, heroin," Steve explained. "When I didn't get a fix, I used to get twitchy, anxious, just plain grumpy and bitchy." Pausing briefly to think, he continued. "I remember there were more fights. Tempers were quick."

"At the station?" Chris asked.

"No, when we were running around. When we would run into someone in the world, we were quick to get in their face. Not take any shit. There were a few fights. The shitty part is that after the fight, we would feel better. It wasn't the same thing, but any rush is better than nothing."

"I've never known you to fight," Debbie said. "Well, I have seen you lay into someone before verbally. Never seen you get into a fight."

"Most of the time it was posturing and puffing up our chests, but when you had two or three guys wanting to get into a fight, most of the time they walked away. "

"The withdrawal made you more aggressive?" Michelle asked.

"Yeah, I guess it did. But we also did some other stuff too. We used to go out at midnight and go graveyard hunting."

"What's that?" both kids asked at the same time.

"You go into a graveyard in the middle of the night and look for stuff on the headstones."

"What kind of stuff?" Debbie asked.

"You make it up. Oldest head stone. Oldest person. Youngest person. Most people in a family plot. Most decorated. Whatever you dream up at the time."

"Weren't you worried about ghosts?" Michelle asked.

"You hoped you saw a ghost." Steve smiled. "You hoped to get the crap scared out of you or scare someone else. That gave you a rush. It's a different kind of rush, but something is better than nothing."

"Does it happen to everyone?"

"Yeah, everyone gets the rush. If you go on more than a few calls, you're hooked," Steve continued.

"Was there a lot of divorce?" Debbie asked.

"Yeah. There was. I was younger and didn't pay too much attention at the time, but I know that most of the married guys fought about how much time they spent at the station."

"Did it ever work out?"

"I've known couples who were in the department and made it work. I guess 'cause they both wanted the rush. They understood it."

"That was long before we met," Debbie said. "It's not happening now?"

"Actually, when I think about it, it does happen. You know how you always get pissed when I have to jump up and take care of an 'emergency'?"

"You mean when something happens at work?"

"Yep. Or when a friend calls me with a crisis."

"But that's part of your job, and you like helping people."

"It is, but sometimes it's over the top."

"I thought it was part of your job to go out and take care of stuff."

"It looks good, but no. I don't necessarily need to go to the site. I just like the excitement. That's me chasing the rush."

"What do you mean?"

"You know how I am always 'pumped' after something happens. Can't sleep. Twitchy. I'm always wired?"

"Yeah. You drive me crazy."

"That's a side effect of the rush."

"But the stuff you do is nothing like fighting fire."

"You're right. Just the least little bit of a rush is a fantastic feeling." Steve looked intensely at her. "This is what I'm saying. I don't need to go, I want to. It doesn't matter what's going on. I jump up and run."

"You never told me any of this stuff before. Why not?"

"This isn't an instant revelation that just jumped into my head one day. I have been thinking about this on and off for the past thirty years. Trying to figure out why I tick."

"So, what did 'ya figured out?"

"How I feel. The fire department. Been thinking about it on and off for a long time. Once I figured out the feelings, I had to be able to explain it. I'm still not sure it makes sense to anyone but me. This is the first time I've talked about it. The first time I've said it out loud. It's like telling someone you're an alcoholic or a drug addict. You're scared that they will think you're a monster. Evil. They won't understated."

Debbie said, taking his hand. "You're not a monster. I guess I don't get it about the adrenaline, why it's such a big deal?"

"I'm addicted to the rush. Even for a small fix I'll drop everything and run. The best high in the world is fighting fire. I'm scared that I'll want the rush so bad, I'll leave everything to go back. I imagine it's like an alcoholic being in a bar."

"So, what do we do?"

"I'm not sure 'we' do anything. I think it's more about 'me' doing something."

"Like what?"

"Like not getting drawn into the rush. Not getting hooked."

"Not good enough." Debbie was stern. "You were alone when it all happened. Now you're not. I'm here. The kids are here. We are a family and we will stick together."

With a small smile Steve squeezed her hand. "I have to go back for the funeral."

"It's been thirty years; do you need to be there?"

"I want to," Steve said. "I think it's time I put all of this stuff to rest."

"OK. Guess we need to make some arrangements."

Let me make some calls and figure out what's going on." With a diabolical glance Steve asked, "You ready to meet a bunch of ghosts from my past?"

Chapter 36

Steve and Debbie were waiting at the hotel bar. They had grabbed a four-seat table and ordered a couple of drinks. It was empty, only a few business travelers scattered around. Robby had called and was bringing his wife to meet them for dinner. The funeral would be held tomorrow. Steve's mood was sullen. He wanted to see his old friends. Wanted closure to his past. He was scared that they would hate him. Reject him.

"How long's it been since you've seen him?" Knowing the answer, Debbie was trying to get him talking.

Being brought back from his thoughts he answered, "Thirty years, more or less."

"How will you know him?"

Before he could answer a voice from across the bar bellowed, "Steve?" A shiver crept up his spine as he imagined Robby being angry at him dropping off the face of the earth for the past thirty years. He hesitated, bracing himself for an onslaught. Looking up Steve spotted him walking towards the table. Standing as he came to the table, he said, "Damn it's good to see you." He hadn't expected the flood of feelings. Remembering the feelings of belonging, being a part of the group. From his earliest adult interactions, he had been a member of this specialized group of people. He was fighting fear of being rejected. Knowing that it was his choice to walk away, to disconnect and cut the group off, he had feared that they would reject him when – if – he returned. Uncertain of how Robby would react, knowing he deserved whatever anger was about to be unleashed, he braced himself for the attack.

Robby reached out to shake Steve's hand, firmly gripping it, and pulled him in for a hug.

Relief spread through Steve.

Releasing Steve, Robby looked at Debbie. "Hi, I'm Rob."

Putting her hand out Debbie said, "I'm very pleased to meet you."

Looking at the outstretched hand Rob smiled and stretched out his arms. "If you're married to that one, then you're part of the family. This family hugs." And he wrapped her in a comforting hug.

"Hi Steve, I'm Barbara, Rob's wife."

Steve gave Barbara a hug. "Good to meet you."

"Hi Barbara, I'm Debbie." Their eyes briefly locked, and the two women momentarily let each other know that they were concerned. The two women gave a quick hug, each knowing how much this reunion meant.

Steve waved to the server so they could get some drinks as they sat down.

"So, the prodigal son returns," Barbara jumped in before anyone else could start the conversation. "I have heard so much about you, I thought you didn't exist."

"Most of it is lies. Unless it good, then of course it's true."

"After you quit, I kept tabs on you for a while. I remember you moving to the Edmonton area, then I lost track," Rob started. "You just kind of disappeared."

The server picked that time to come by and check on drink orders, giving Steve a few moments to get his thoughts together.

As the waiter disappeared with the drink order Rob continued "What happened after that?".

"Well, my mom got a job in the city and wanted to move closer. That's how we ended up in Edmonton. Was there for about two years then moved to Baltimore County, bounced around for a while at different places."

"OK, tell me about you and Debbie."

"Not much to tell. We met in 1993, got married in '96." Steve Grabbed his wife's hand. "Got two kids, boy and a girl. Chris is a senior in high school and Michelle is a sophomore in high school."

"You always talked about jumping on a boat and heading off to the sunset," Rob remembered. "What ever happened to that?"

"Well, I was living on a sailboat when Debbie and I met. When we decided to get married, we cashed in the boat and moved to Arizona."

"Here are pictures of the kids." Debbie was flipping through pictures on her cell phone.

"They take after their mother." Rob snickered. "Good thing too."

"How 'bout you two?" Steve changed the subject.

"Been married about fifteen years now," Rob said. "What are you doing for work?"

"Work for a large property management company," Steve answered. "I know you're still with the city fire department."

"Yeah. Been with the city for twenty years now."

"Still jumping the engine?"

"Nah. Got my blue helmet and then about seven years ago moved off the engine to administration. Counting down the days till retirement, working Monday through Friday."

"A real live blue helmet," Steve teased. "How long you got?"

"Going to keep going for another five years or so," Rob replied.

"And off the engine for good?"

"Yeah, decided I didn't want to run into burning buildings as much anymore."

"Roger that, but why."

"Not to interrupt, but what's a blue helmet?" Debbie asked.

"Officer," Robby answered. "Yellow helmet is a firefighter. Blue is lieutenant, red is captain and white is chief."

"Always said we wanted to be a yellow helmet, so we didn't have to make decisions or do paperwork," Steve interjected.

"Yeah, nowadays I spend my time on administration and employee issues," Rob lamented. "No more running into the buildings the rats are running out of."

"Managing the people is the worst," Steve said. "There is more stupid crap you have to deal with, wondering why you have to have these childish conversations with what are supposed to be adults."

"No shit. I wonder if anyone ever told these prissy kids how to dress in the morning."

"Steve always says the only difference between his job and mine, is that I get to put the kids in time out," Debbie interjected.

"If I didn't have to deal with people at work, my job would be perfect," Steve said as he took a drink.

"That is no lie," Robby agreed, holding his glass up in a toast.

"I always wonder why people have to be such a pain in the backside," Barbara asked.

"It's everywhere," Debbie said. "We think the zombie apocalypse hasn't happened, but it's here. People today are mindless; their brains are infected and rotting away."

"Why did you move off the engine and into the office?" Steve asked Rob.

"Just got tired of it."

"Of what?" He was pushing to test his theory that dealing with people is more troublesome that getting the rush.

"The people." Pulling a drink, he continued. "There was no more joy. They treat us like shit. They blame us for their family dying. They make it our fault they do something stupid. I just got tired of trying to help people. They were so angry at the world."

"I know the feeling," Steve agreed.

"Yeah. I figured that's why you bailed," Rob said.

"That's part of it. But I didn't figure it out till later."

"You figured it out before me." Rob stated. "Was it Royce that pushed you over?"

"Yes and no." Steve waved to the waiter for another round, giving him a few seconds to collect his thoughts. This is the moment in time he had been dreading for the past thirty years. This is when everything he had been thinking about, trying to figure out, was coming to the first test. A test against someone who had been there with him. This was his friend, and he knew what was bullshit and what was real.

Both Barbara and Debbie were wound tight with fear, expectation, hope. They had both dealt with their husbands trying to come to grips with their inner emotions. Neither of the men letting too much go. Always holding the dragons in check, locked in their minds in the deepest dungeons. Knowing that they could never have the conversation that the two were having with each other, they hoped that this would set them free, but worried that it would break them down.

"Royce dying made me wake up. Cleared the fog. I had always told myself that I was fighting fire to help the victims," Steve continued. "What I realized is that I was fighting fire for me."

"Running into a burning building is a rush," Rob agreed.

"Yep. I was chasing the rush. Royce too." Steve took a drink. "That's why he died. For no other reason than to get a good high. No one forced us to go in. No one told us we had to. Shit, no one could have stopped us from going into the fire. We were crack heads. I can still remember it like it was yesterday."

"I remember that night. That fire is still the best house fire. The only one with an explosion," Rob commented. "We still talk about it. We use it as a case study for training." After a pause. "I never tell anyone I was there that night. I don't want the questions. I don't want the recruits staring at me, asking about the fire, Royce dying. I just don't want to talk about it. Scared the demons will break out."

Steve nodded as he continued, "First I realized that I was doing stupid shit because I wanted the rush. Bigger, badder, more epic."

With a smile Rob said, "Nothing has matched that day. That fire. Royce dying." He sighed. "I feel guilty saying it, but that was the best call of my career."

"Me too. I began wondering how the hell was I gonna get a better rush? There would be nothing that I could think of that would be better, bigger rush, than that day. That call. Shit, how many more people would have to die? How could I ever beat that day?"

Raising their glasses, the two toasted with a clink of the glass. "The rush," they both said in unison.

A man was sitting a few tables away, quietly listening. Unnoticed.

"We never would have been able to talk as openly about this back then," Rob said. "Shit, even today if we talked like this at the station, we would be sent for a psych eval."

"We were manly men, dressed in plaid and we would never admit to emotions, fears, demons. We were the invincible." Steve took a drink and continued. "I hate to admit it, but I needed to grow up to deal with this shit." With a look of shock, he added, "Oh my god! Are we OLD!?"

"I think we are," Rob said. "All the recruits look up to us old timers, wanting stories."

"Not sure I want to be a wise old bastard in a diaper that people trek to the desert to ask a single question." Steve paused. "Wanting to know about Royce dying. Us too scared to explain how we felt."

"I always wondered if it made me a bad person for getting such a kick out of my friend dying?" Rob asked. "I was scared to say it out loud. If some shrink heard me, I would be shipped off to the psych ward."

"It's that kind of thinking that fucks up everyone's brain. This may sound backwards but we should revel in the rush. Don't ever say that your feelings are wrong or bad," Steve explained.

"Remember we used to joke that we run into the buildings that the rats are running out of," Steve said. "Do you ever stop to think why?"

"No."

"We run in to get an adrenaline high. Everything else is just a bullshit excuse for chasing a high. The civilians don't think about any of this stuff; they just expect the magic to happen when you dial the magic 911."

"911 makes the fireman cum." Rob smiled at the juvenile joke.

With a smile Steve continued, "We don't care why. We don't care who. We only care about the rush. The nastier the better."

Rob asked, "You worried about going off the deep end? Always looking for better rush?"

"I was addicted to the rush. Everything I did in the fire department was to chase the rush. Hurst Tool, Rescue Diving, EMT. It was about me getting a fix. It didn't matter if we saved the patient or rescued the trapped motorist. It was OK that some of the people got to live a little longer when I helped, but I realized that was not why I did it." Squeezing his wife's hand, he continued. "It was always the rush. I knew I would never be a paid firefighter, eyeglasses. I kept picturing myself hanging out at the station, waiting for a call. Listening to the scanner, waiting for the tones. Always wanting a bigger rush. I didn't want to end up old, divorced, with no life but being a firehouse squirrel. One of the guys we made fun of."

"So, you quit?" Barbara asked.

"That's part of it. More important is that after the fire, Royce dying things changed." He paused, taking another drink. "I questioned if I should save someone."

"You had all of the rescue training for just about every situation. Of course you could save them," Rob stated. "Shit, you were the only one who actually liked school. You liked the training. You could figure stuff out in your head that no one else could."

"You missed it. Not **could** I save them, but **should** I save them? Did they deserve to be saved? The drunk kid who wrecks daddy's car. The parent who is too busy to put the kid in a car seat. The mother who can't remember where her kid is?"

"We don't question. We just react," Rob said.

Steve took another drink. "After Royce died, I started asking should we save them?"

Silently they tried to reconcile their feelings with Steve's admission. Realizing that they were all guilty of these thoughts.

"We run into places that others flee. We go into situations that cause others to crumble." Steve was gazing into space as he explained. "What we never, never ask ourselves is 'Should I save this person?'"

"We're not there to think," Rob said.

"That's my point. We run into burning buildings, car accidents, heart attacks. Blindly we do everything possible to help the nameless. What if one of those nameless that we save is Hitler, Jack the ripper, a serial killer."

"I thought you just saved everyone you could?" Debbie said quietly.

"We're supposed to. But what do you do when you're staring at the patient and stop to ask, 'Should I save them?' When you look at a patient, an accident scene, a house fire and ask yourself if the people deserve to be helped, it causes some pretty bad conflict." Steve took a drink. "Before, when I helped someone, I always thought that it would make the person's life better. Their family better. After Royce, I lost faith in humanity. I lost the faith that what I was doing was good."

"I see what you mean. Never thought about it that way before." Rob considered. "I guess, when I think about it, that's why I went to admin and got off the engine."

"It's like a priest not believing in God," Barbara said.

"Here is a scary thought. I got out when I was young, before I even started a career. You made a switch and got off the engine. You found a place that isolated you. How many are feeling the same and are stuck? Too far into the job to quit? Too close to retirement to make a change? Too scared to admit how they feel? Too messed up by everything to be truthful with themselves?"

After Rob thought about this for a moment he said, "When I think about the firefighters who leave, it's always because they retire, or they do something really stupid and get fired." Rob considered. "The ones that quit in the first few years, just can't handle the shit they see."

"Maybe we missed stuff. The firefighter who beats his wife and kids, the drunk," Steve continued. "I figured there are only four reasons for leaving active duty. Retired, Fallen, Disgraced and the Foundered."

"What does that mean?" Debbie asked.

"The retired are those who just can't fight fire anymore. Too old, too broken, but once a firefighter always a firefighter. The fallen are those who have died. Disgraced are those who are fired or quit before they get fired. They have disgraced the uniform. Disgraced the department."

"That makes sense," Barbara said. "But what are the – what did you call it – 'Foundered'?"

"The Foundered. Those are the ones who fall between the gaps. They're the ones who are broken. It's the ones who leave the job, walking away. Those who see the one thing that they can't handle. Get tired of the mass stupidity of the public. Those who just can't bring themselves to run into the burning building. They are broken, lost the faith." Pausing, the group was focused on their own thoughts. "Problem is with the Foundered who don't leave. They're stuck in the job being miserable."

"PTSD," a new voice announced.

Chapter 37

Looking up, the group saw Ted with a glass of bourbon in his hand.

"Didn't know you were going to make it," Rob said.

"Wasn't sure if I was going to," Ted replied. "Wasn't sure if I wanted to walk back into the shit show."

"I heard you went with the City. What happened?" Steve asked.

"Yeah. Moved from the engine to safety. Hurt my back and took a medical after about twelve years."

"Wife and kids?" Steve asked.

"Wife left me a few years ago. I still see the kids, but they're grown and have families of their own."

"That sucks. Sorry to hear about Rene" Rob said.

"What you said is right," Ted refocused the group as he waved his glass at Steve.

"What's that?"

"The fire department eats you up. Burns you out," Ted said with hatred in his eyes. "I've been here for a while just listening," Ted said. "Trying to decide if I was going to jump or not."

"Didn't even notice you sitting there," Steve said. "This is my wife Debbie. Debbie, this is Ted."

"The Ted who got you into the fire department?"

"The very same one," Ted replied with a bow. "Don't hold it against me, I was young and stupid."

"Then I am glad to meet you and very glad you decided to join this little party."

Rob jumped in. "This is my wife Barbara."

"Come and join us. We can squeeze more into this table," Barbara replied, waving at Rob to get another chair.

"You guys stay in touch?" Steve asked.

Looking at each other the two responded, "Nah."

"We never ran into each other in the city," Rob said.

"We saw each other at Joppa every once and a while, but I got fed up with the politics and turned in my key card," Ted explained. "Got fed up with the amount of time and pressure to be at the station. I thought I could fix my marriage by quitting, but it was too late."

"You still with Joppa?" Steve asked Rob.

"No. I quit too. About four or five years ago I checked into rejoining."

"Did you?" Ted asked, a little surprised.

"Nope. When I went to rejoin, a bunch of little punks who I taught firefighting told me I had to go through all the training again and be a probee. When I reminded them that I taught them how to drive the engine, they didn't care. Just wanted to make themselves feel important."

"That was stupid," Steve said.

"Yep. Told them to go fuck themselves. Haven't had any contact since."

"Stay in touch with anyone?" Steve asked.

"Darcy, Larry, Gary every once in a while. Don't think Ted and I have seen each other in, what, six or seven years?"

"Sounds about right. I took a medical retirement about seven years ago. Got tired of the bullshit. Hurt my back and took an early package. When I walked away, I tried to leave everything fire related."

"What you doin' now?"

"Not much. Got a place in Pennsylvania. Try to keep busy."

"You said PTSD," Rob reminded him.

"Yeah. Everything is blamed on Post Traumatic Stress Disorder," Ted said. "I tell everyone I hurt my back, but I'm out on PTSD."

"What d'ya mean?" Rob asked.

"After I hurt my back, I was out for a while. When I was recovering, I spent some time thinking." Ted took a drink as he sat down. "You're right 'bout the rush. I always wanted a bigger rush. The night Royce died was the top of the mountain for me. I kept trying to get a better high. Never found it again. I was always angry and never really knew why, but you pretty much nailed it. I was mad 'cause I couldn't get a fix. I was always angry, and it fucked up what life I had."

"I don't follow?" Steve probed.

"I was always angry at everyone, everything. The politics, the people, new policies – everything pissed me off. The bullshit with the changes happening every year. Shit, seat belts on the fire engine! I felt like we couldn't fight fire anymore. We just rode around on a big pretty truck and told people to stand back." With a snicker he continued, "Had to see a shrink after my on the job injury and I told 'em I was scared of going back into fires 'cause of my back. Little pukes were so excited to have a nut job on the couch they were happy to diagnose me with the PTSD." Ted paused, taking a swig of his drink. "You were talking about the rush. You're right. I was mad 'cause I didn't get the rush anymore. I wanted it but could never get it. Truth is, I just didn't want to be angry anymore. I burned out. What'd y'all call it, lost the faith?"

"Yeah. The thing inside that sparks someone into action. I just call it the Faith."

"Can't fight fire?" Debbie asked.

"Yeah. They changed the rules," Ted spat.

"You got that right," Rob added.

"What are you talking about?" Steve asked.

"Things have changed. It's not so much fun anymore," Rob said. "Can't stand up in the jump seat. Can't ride the tail board. Damn engine won't even move if you're not in your seat. There are seat belts in the jump seats."

"I loved standing in the jump seat with the sirens blaring. Watching the cars as we went by. Sleeping on the engine after a long call," Steve lamented.

"We can't do interior attacks without special permission. The department won't invest in the right equipment. Expects the firefighters to put out fires without ever putting themselves in danger," Ted explained. "It still pisses me off. I spent most of my time being angry, but what I realize is that I was angry because they took the rush away. Can't get the high without some excitement and danger. So, when I got hurt, I took early and got out."

"You pulled the 'PTSD' Card?" Rob asked.

"Yeah. No way to prove it. No way to get better."

"And more importantly, no one ever questions it. Everyone is so scared of 'IT' they won't even talk about what's going on," Steve said. "Everyone has PTSD."

Looking at Steve, Ted asked, "So what happened after you left the department?"

"Not much. I hopped a private meat wagon in the city for about two years while I tried to go to school."

"How did that go?" Rob asked, "I thought when you walked out you were done."

"Well, with my EMT I got a job that paid better than anything else I could find. Rode the graveyard shift. Didn't have to deal with anyone, no supervisors. It was quiet," Steve explained. "I was in school trying to get a degree and figure out what I wanted to do with the rest of my life. I figured college professors were smarter but every time one of the professors found out I used to be in the fire department, and had divorced parents, they wanted to analyze me. It felt like every time I turned around someone was telling me I was screwed up. So, I decided to study psychology. Ya know, 'Physician, heal thyself'."

"Is that how you got over it?"

"Hell no, it just made it worse. Whenever I talked to someone, researched an issue, everything kept coming back to one thing. Your brain is not wired right. You're broken. You're not normal. You're a victim."

"You are not a victim," Debbie jumped in. "In fact, you are the least victimized person I know."

"Yep. Because I choose not to be a victim."

"I don't understand?" Barbara said.

"Well, when I discussed my parents' divorce, I was told that it was OK to feel bad. OK to feel responsible. OK to feel abandoned."

"Yeah. People are supposed to deal with their feelings," Barbara said.

"They say that it's OK, but what they really meant was that if you don't feel this way, you're messed up. Since I didn't feel any of those things, I was tagged as a troubled person. When I discussed the fire department a few times, I was told it was OK to crumble into a lump. It was OK to not be responsible because of the guilt that I MUST have because of Royce's death. Shit, every time I wanted to talk about something, the teachers and counselors always told me how I should feel. They expected me to melt into a puddle of goo, sucking my thumb and whining."

Rob was nodding his head as Steve was talking.

"Didn't finish college then. After listening to everyone tell you that you're not right, I didn't bother going back to school."

"What about the ambo job?" Ted asked.

"I figured out that it was not the best place for me."

"What happened?" Debbie gently touched the back of his hand. "I never knew you worked on an ambulance."

"One day we were taking a stroke victim to hospice. He was totally thrashed. Thirty-five-year-old male. Cheyne-Stokes breathing. His brain was scrambled eggs."

"Thirty-five!" Barbara exclaimed. "Having a stroke. Wow."

"What's Cheney-Stokes?" Debbie asked.

"You breathe really fast, like hyperventilating. Then stop breathing. Then you start again," Ted explained. "Or not. Your brain can't control your breathing because of the damage."

Nodding, Steve continued. "We had the No-code papers. Everything in a little bow. Knew he was going to the hospice to be P.U.D."

"What's PUD?" Barbara asked.

"Park Until Dead", Ted explained. Both Rob and Steve were slowly nodding their heads in agreement.

"Halfway to the drop off he stopped breathing. After about two or three minutes I decided I didn't want to do the paperwork, so I reached over" – Steve emphasized as he lightly tapped the table with a closed fist – "gave him a precardial thump."

The group sat in silence sipping their drinks as Steve's confession sank in.

"That kick-started him. We dumped him at hospice. End of the shift, I handed in my uniform and quit. That was the last call I ever was on."

"Why was that so bad?" Barbara asked.

Ted answered, "No-code. You're not supposed to resuscitate. It's time for the patient to die."

Steve continued, "I often wonder how much longer the guy lived as scrambled eggs. How much it cost the family to keep him going. What the family felt while they watched him just keep going."

"That's a bitch," Rob said.

"Yeah. That's was when I realized I really don't like people in general. Let my certs expire. Haven't been certified in anything since."

"Nothing! Not even CPR?" Barbara asked.

"Nope. Have no desire to do first aid to anyone," Steve said. "I always say, if you fall out in front of me, I'm kicking you in the head on my way by because you made me step over you."

"Well at least you got out," Ted said. "I was stuck."

"What d'ya mean?" Rob asked.

"After a few years as a paid firefighter, I hated it. I hated the patients. I hated the department. I hated the crowd yelling at us on calls." Ted took a drink. "I moved to the safety officer position, so I didn't have to deal with the public. Thought it would be easier. Less bullshit."

"That sucks," Rob responded.

"It must have been hell, hating going to work every day," Debbie said.

"What's worse is that I loved fighting fire," Ted sighed. "I always wanted to do it. When it was real, I hated it. Now thinking about it, I hated it for the wrong reasons."

Steve asked, "Did you question everything in your life?"

After a pause Ted answered, "Yeah. When I think about it now, I did. I wondered if I married the right girl, I wondered if having kids was a mistake, I wondered if I bought the right house, lived in the right neighborhood."

"It felt like everything else was wrong, didn't it?" Steve asked.

"Yeah. Took it out on everyone around me."

"Did you talk to anyone about it?" Steve asked.

"Mandatory counseling after the accident. After I talked to them, I felt worse than ever. They had identified all of the unresolved feelings," Ted continued. "Apparently I was really fucked up. That's when the doc said I was suffering from PTSD and let me take a medical retirement."

"I never knew that," Rob said. "I heard that you got hurt on a call and threw out your back. Took a medical because of it. No one ever said that you went out on PTSD"

"The problem's not you," Steve began. "The problem is with the doctors. What I figured out is that all of my issues – all of my feelings, lack of feelings, debilitating mental issues – was caused by one thing and one thing only."

The others were listening intently while Steve took a drink and waved at the waitress, signing for another round.

"It's the fucking doctors. You know what PTSD really means?" He paused. "Pretty Tired of Stupid Dickheads."

The two men laughed as they nodded their heads. The two women looked confused, not wanting to interrupt but wanting to ask questions.

Seeing the women's confusion, Steve explained. "Every time I saw a counselor, they told me I didn't have the right feeling, or I wasn't acting the right way. The stupid dickheads could only tell you what you were supposed to think. Every time I said that I didn't feel a certain way, they jumped to PTSD and told me I was broken. I wasn't dealing with my 'feelings.' They couldn't handle anyone who thought differently."

"Goddam right!" Ted jumped in.

"Thought differently?" Barbara asked.

"When my parents divorced, they told me I should feel guilty. Should feel bad they were separating. Told me I should feel this way and that. When I told them that my parents divorcing didn't bother me, I was damaged goods. When I told them I was glad because they always fought and hated each other, they looked at me like I had two heads."

"You're right," Ted jumped in. "When I was talking to the shrinks, they kept telling me my feelings were wrong. They kept asking me if I felt all kinds of stupid shit. They kept telling me I wasn't dealing with my unresolved feelings."

"I used to get asked if I felt bad because someone died on a call, or if I felt guilty because I couldn't save them," Rob added. "Got so tired of people freaking out when I didn't think it was anyone's fault, I just stopped telling people."

"Yep. Every time we are put into those situations, we always walk away questioning ourselves, our actions, because the person who is supposed to be helping us tells us we are fucked up!"

"Hear, hear," Rob said toasting the group.

"Well, I figured out the cure to PTSD," Steve announced. "The cure for PTSD is DSTP."

"What the hell is DSTP?" Ted asked.

"Disregard Stupid Therapist Psychobabble. Every time they think they are helping it turns out that they are more fucked up than anyone else. I swear that ninety percent of the therapists are there to heal themselves. When they realize that they can't fix themselves, they have to make everyone else messed up, so they look sane."

"I don't follow." Barbara was confused.

"It's really simple," Rob cut in. "When something happens, the therapist expects someone to act a certain way. When someone dies, you're sad, in denial, all that death and dying stuff."

Barbara was nodding in understanding.

"When you sit and talk to someone who doesn't have the same emotions or the emotions that the shrink thinks they should have, they are broken."

"When the shrink can't figure out why you are thinking that way, they tell you you've got PTSD," Ted finished.

"They're too narrow minded to actually understand that there is not one mold. People react differently to the same situation," Steve added.

"When you're on a call, in the group of people there is always someone who is screaming, someone who is catatonic, someone who doesn't know what to do, just follows people around, and someone who wants to be in the action and gets in the way," Rob said.

"Everybody acts differently," Steve explained. "So, when we see something, we respond the way we were trained, from our experience and from our ability to maintain calm in an emergency. This moves into every part of our world and it makes first responders, military, police all think and react differently than what is expected. You know what would be great is if someone actually said, 'You don't need to feel bad that you lived'."

Ted asked, "So how does this help us?"

"First you, we, all of us need to understand that we are not broken, abnormal or damaged. The next is that we need to understand what we feel is OK, even if someone else doesn't understand."

"What d'ya mean?" Rob asked.

"When someone dies and it doesn't bother us, that's OK. When a soldier kills someone, that's OK. When a cop has to shoot a suspect, that's OK. When one of these things happen, that person is told 'You should feel guilty' when they don't. Why should they? Instead of telling them how come they're wrong, we should be asking 'Are you good with your choices?' and then deal with those people who aren't."

After pausing to take a drink Steve continued, "When the soldier kills a child and says, 'I'd do it again to save my life,' why is this wrong? When a survivor says, 'I'm glad it wasn't me who was killed,' why is this bad? When one of the crew dies and we say, 'Hell of a rush' why is this bad? When we say, 'I'm sorry he's dead but glad it wasn't me,' how is this bad? When no one forces us to fight fire and one of us dies and we don't break down in tears, why is this wrong?"

"Why do they get to decide what's wrong?" Rob responded.

Ted added "Most of them have never left an armchair or a library."

"That's my point. People who have no idea what we go through, what we see, what we have to do are deciding what's right and wrong. What's good and bad. Then they take it on themselves to tell us were messed up. Damaged goods."

"Yeah, I got that too," Ted said.

"We're only messed up by their standards and they're too self-centered to realize that. They create the issue, then tell everyone in the world that if they don't believe them, they're the problem. They are so focused on telling me what they think is wrong we never talk about all the shit I still have locked up in my brain. Most of the shit can stay there, but every once in a while, some of it seeps out and I have to face it."

"Like what?" Debbie asked.

"The taste of vomit. Feeling a dead body under water. The smell of blood so strong you can't smell anything else. The anger I feel as some asshole tells me it's my fault their kid, wife, girlfriend died," Steve said, anger in his eyes.

"And don't fucking tell me 'I know how you feel'," Ted interjected. "I hate it when someone who can't spell firefighter tries to tell me they know all about it."

"Hey, do you remember that time we were in the kitchen fire and you answered the damn phone Ted?" Steve asked.

"For real?" Barbara asked.

"Shit I forgot about that," Ted laughed. "Chief Butler yelled at me for thirty minutes."

"What happened?" Debbie asked.

Laughing Steve tried to explain, "We had just knocked down a small kitchen fire, some pot on the stove. We were both noticing that the phone on the wall had melted. The plastic was drooping down on the case. While we were looking at it, the damn thing rang." Pausing to wipe the tears away, the story was interrupted by the laughter.

Ted regained a small amount of control and continued. "We both jumped about ten feet in the air. Scared the shit out of us."

"Ok, but what was so funny?" Barbara interrupted.

Ted and Steve were both grabbing the edge of the table trying to get control of their laughter.

Steve continued, struggling to control his outburst. "Well superman over there decides to answer it."

Chuckling Rob said, "I haven't thought about that in years. We all had to go to a special training for that one."

"Why what was so bad?" Debbie asked.

Pointing at Ted Steve continued, "All I heard was 'Hello. Oh, is that who lives here, they can't come to the phone right now'." He lost control again and put his face in the crook of his arm on the table.

"After I said 'Hello', they asked to speak with someone, the wife, mom whatever. I didn't mean to say, 'Is that who lives here?' out loud. The lady on the phone got all freaked out and wanted to know what was going on."

Regaining control Steve continued. "Ted says 'I'm not sure but the chief probably has them in the front yard'."

"She got really freaked out and wanted to know who I was, what I was doing, so I told her I was Firefighter Essex and we were tending to a small kitchen fire."

"You left off the part where you asked if they wanted to leave a message with you," Steve finished.

"Outside some crazy woman comes screaming from a block or two away. Apparently, it was the lady's mother. Had no idea that the house was on fire. She was screaming about people being dead and stuff." Rob added, "It took Larry about fifteen minutes to calm her down."

"That was mean. You probably gave the poor woman a heart attack," Debbie said.

"Yeah but we laugh our asses off every time we think about it," Ted concluded.

"You guys have a weird sense of humor," Barbara scolded them.

"This is the point. This is exactly what we've been talking about," Steve countered.

Barbara became defensive. "What do you mean?"

"This is a stupid example but what we did we thought was funny as hell. Who cares if it upset the old lady? It was funny," Steve explained. "Your immediate reaction was 'that was mean.' You're probably right. I don't think I want to find out about a fire in my kids' house from the guy putting it out, but it doesn't make us broken, damaged or fucked up. We just learned not to let people's emotions, fears and pain get in our way. It doesn't bother us. Now we switch and go to a topic that no one wants to face, it goes from 'weird sense of humor' to 'damaged goods.' It never bothered me that I couldn't save someone. It never bothered me that the family was in tears as someone lay dead on the floor."

"When we scraped someone off the pavement it was just a job we did," Ted interjected.

"When Royce died, I think we were all glad it wasn't us laying on the stretcher," Rob concluded.

"I agree with you Rob. Truth is, what we got upset about was NOT getting the rush. When the call wasn't exciting or never happened. We were just a bunch of junkies. No one ever told us to get over it and live without the rush. I don't think any of the shrinks even knows about the rush," Steve said. "I'm not even sure that many people will admit to the rush."

"Somewhere I heard that soldiers are being counseled by other soldiers and they are having better results," Rob said.

"You think it's 'cause they have been there and made the same decisions?" Ted asked.

"One of the guys that worked with me was in a veteran group therapy. He told me that it was a shit load better than talking with a shrink. He got to hear how others dealt with the stuff. More important, no one said 'I know what you mean' unless they really went through the same shit."

"So, do you think we need some of that group therapy stuff?" Ted pondered.

"No, I think you and I are the Foundered. It's what we are. What we have to do is just accept how we feel. Understand that it's not wrong or bad. It's what makes us who we are."

"So that's it?" Debbie asked.

"We live with ourselves," Rob said.

"What does that mean?" Barbara asked.

"It means we need to stop being controlled by other people's ideas and perceptions. Our experiences make us who we are. They don't define us, they enhance us. They test us. Without the experience I would not be the same person, have the same beliefs, have the same opinions. I would believe different things."

"What d'ya mean experiences and beliefs?" Ted asked.

"Well when I was in the house with Royce. I was in the right place when the explosion happened. Maybe if I was one inch either way, I would have been dead too. Some people look at that as a miracle, others see it as luck. Some call it fate. If I was religious, I would have called it a miracle, say I was chosen by God for greatness." Steve paused in thought. "Crap, I just realized that I blew my opportunity to start a cult."

With a chuckle Rob added, "I can see that. What would you call it? The Cult of the Foundered Souls?"

"Not bad," Ted said. "I could get behind it."

"Maybe we are the start of a new following. 'The Order of the Foundered Souls.' Come and join us to find and rekindle your faith. Groveling not required, however genuflection at the presence of the founders is highly encouraged," Steve elaborated.

"Oh, oh can I pick the robes you boys get to wear?" Debbie joked. "I'm seeing various shades of purple to signify hierarchy."

"Can we make the new members chant and slam their foreheads with a board?" Rob continued.

Laughing Steve said, "Guess we need a shrub in there somewhere."

"Don't forget the sandal and the gourd," Ted finished.

"What the hell are you talking about?" Debbie laughed.

"Monty..." Ted started.

"Python!" both Rob and Steve shouted at once.

"I should have known it was some male adolescent reference." Debbie scolded. "I remember when you made the kids watch that 'Holy Grail' movie." Looking at Barbara she clarified "I actually have three children."

"Every time one of the movies came on, we would all hang out at the station and watch," Steve defended.

"Those were one of the few nights we didn't want a call. The whole damn station used to recite the lines to the movies," Ted laughed.

"Forget about the cult. What about you guys?" Barbara asked.

"Us? We're gonna be fine," Rob said. "Ya know I was really scared 'bout coming here. Meeting up with you guys."

"Me too," Steve agreed. "I was nervous about walking into the whole fire department thing for starters. More importantly, I was terrified that you guys would be pissed."

"Why?" Rob asked.

"'Cause I just disappeared. Walked out and left y'all hanging. Thought you'd be mad."

"Brother, you're family. We fight, we yell, but we are always family. You never have to worry about us abandoning you. And you didn't abandon us either," Rob said.

"Yeah. Like I said, I wasn't sure I was going to hang around," Ted said. "I sat at the table for about fifteen minutes before I jumped into the conversation. Figured if it started getting weird, I would just walk away."

"Well, we're all here, no weirdness, so let's just hang out."

The night went on with a string of old memories from the group. They wrapped up as the hotel bar closed and went off to their rooms to catch some sleep before the chief's funeral later that same day.

Chapter 38

The following day the group met in the hotel, heading to the funeral.

The simple service was held in a funeral home with about one hundred people in attendance. Scanning the crowd Steve didn't see anyone he knew. There were a lot of old faces in the crowd and a few younger ones. It had been too long and too many years etched into the faces for him to recognize anyone.

The service was boring and canned, with only the pastor speaking. At the end he asked if anyone would like to say anything.

Silence from the attendees. There were no family members left. Larry was the last. The lack of family, lack of close friends to stand and tell a litany of old stories about the man in the casket caused sorrow. The faces in the crowed, all firefighters and spouses, kept their eyes on the ground, making sure the priest at the podium did not call on them.

After a minute of silence, the priest came back to the podium and began, "If no one has anything to say about..."

He was interrupted by someone standing and making his way to the center.

Steve crawled across several people and headed to the podium. Not certain what he would say.

From the podium he started. "Thank you all for coming and showing your respect for Larry Butler. Most of the time when someone stands to deliver a eulogy they focus on the deceased, their story, trying to comfort the family for their loss. I'm not going to do that. Instead, I am going to talk about us. You and I. We are here today because of one binding idea. That is the Idea of the Fire Department. I use the word 'Idea' for a very specific reason. At some point I believe that most of us here have all engaged in the action of firefighting, or at least have been close to someone who has. I'm not talking about the actions; I am talking about the 'Idea.' It was an image we created as children, young men and women. Watching the big red truck blowing down the road with sirens wailing, the ambo cutting through traffic, racing to save some poor unfortunate victim. It is the transition, realization and sometimes recovery of moving from the idea to the reality. Throughout this process we have each encountered obstacles, challenges and decisions that we have struggled with. We have each struggled with the difference between the actions required against the idea we created in our minds. Today we take a few minutes to reflect on this.

"Thirty years ago, I stood at a podium much like this one. I looked into a gathering of firefighters, paramedics, first responders for a similar reason. We sounded the last tones for a fallen firefighter. That was a day of sorrow as we said goodbye to one of our brothers. Today we are here for a similar reason but with a different intent. Today we don't grieve for the loss of Larry Butler, we rejoice in his life. We rejoice because we had the unimaginable honor of knowing him. Larry Butler was my chief. He is still my chief. At different times throughout my life he was my mentor. He was my brother. He was my father. He gave me advice and guidance. He gave me strength when I needed it the most. He did this in ways that I try to copy in my life every day. He never hid his weaknesses. He exalted in them. He shared his failures. He shared his successes. It was through these actions that he took hundreds of boys and girls turning them into young adults and then into men and women. He guided them into being good husbands, good wives, good parents, and good people. Today we are all here to remember and to pay respect to Chief Butler. Whether it's here and now or somewhere else later, we will remember him. We will remember the calls. We will tell stories. We will remember Chief Butler catching us doing something and starting off with 'Boys, let me tell you a little story about...'. I remember that we always said, 'You ain't shit until you are one of Chief Butler's stories.'

"As time moves on, things change. Those things we always take for granted are suddenly gone. Today is one of those days that mark the changing of the world. Chief Butler has left us. He has already passed command to each one of us in that it is now our responsibility, our duty to continue mentoring, coaching, advising and supporting the people around us. Mostly we will honor our chief with our actions and with our lives. Chief Butler would tell you that he didn't have kids. But the truth is every one of us are Chief Butler's children. We are now given the privilege and the responsibility to carry on what Chief Butler taught us."

He silently walked back to his seat. The crowd was silent.

A deep baritone voice broke the silence with "Amazing Grace." For the first time in almost thirty years, Rob sang in public, marking the end of the service.

Chapter 39

As the crowd was leaving the service several people approached Steve, Rob and Ted.

A few people from their past came by and recognized them. The exchange of niceties was going on with miscellaneous "nice singing" and "lovely eulogy." A woman came dashing out of the crowd slamming into Steve with a huge hug. Steve was shocked as he politely tried to extract the woman from around him, a look of surprise as he looked at his wife.

"I thought you were gone forever!" the woman said. "I didn't think anyone would find you."

"Darcy!" Steve replied recognizing the woman. Stepping back to look at her he asked, "How are you? It's really good to see you."

"That was a fantastic eulogy you gave for Larry. You made me cry."

Debbie was watching the exchange, trying to figure out who the woman was.

Reaching over Steve gently grabbed Debbie's elbow and pulled her close, "This is my wife Debbie. Debbie, this is Darcy."

"Nice to meet you Darcy."

"Excuse me," the pastor interrupted. "Since Mr. Butler didn't have any relatives could I ask for you gentlemen to be his pallbearers?"

"Sure," Ted replied. "Give me two seconds and I'll grab a couple of more guys."

Glad to get rescued from an inquisition, Steve moved toward the casket with Rob to wait for others to help move Larry to the waiting hearse.

Debbie and Darcy talked while they moved the casket, joined shortly by Barbara.

After a short graveside service, Darcy had to leave but made Steve promise that he would get in touch so they could reconnect.

The group of five was heading back to the hotel when Steve said, "I want to go visit Royce."

After a brief silence, "I'm in," Rob announced.

"Me too," Ted said.

"Well, I think that this is something that the three of you should go do. How 'bout it Debbie, want to head to the hotel while the boys do their thing?"

"I think you're right. Drop us off at the hotel and you boys go and do what you need to."

Each of the three men were feeling an onrush of their own emotions as they drove to the cemetery. It was strange that they remembered exactly where Royce was buried. Walking in silence they found Royce's headstone.

The three men were silently standing at the gravesite, lost in their own thoughts.

Steve broke the silence, "I can feel the rush from that night. Does that make me a horrible person?"

"No. You just said it before me," Ted said. "My first thought wasn't about Royce; it was the fire."

"Remembering it still gives me chills," Rob said. "I always thought it would be weird coming here. Seeing Royce."

"Is this the first time you've come here?" Ted asked.

Rob answered with a nod of his head.

"I haven't been here since the day we buried Royce," Steve said.

"Well it's unanimous," Ted said. "None of us ever came here."

"I thought about it a few times, but never got around to it," Steve said. "I never saw much point in staring at a piece of stone with Royce's name carved into it."

"So why now?" Rob asked.

"With Larry's funeral, reconnecting with you two, feeling nostalgic I guess."

"We talked about some deep shit yesterday, but we never talked about Royce much," Rob said. "I don't know if it's good or bad?"

"Neither," Ted said. "It just is."

"Know what's really strange?" Steve asked. "I don't miss him."

"What d'ya mean?"

"Well, I mean I'm sad that he's not here, but I've been wondering if my life would be different if he hadn't died. I think about it and I'm not sure it would be."

"Would you have lost the faith in humanity if he lived?"

"Yes. It would have just taken me longer to see it. When I really dissect my life, Royce was just a small part of the process. I knew I was never going to be a paid firefighter. Eventually we would have drifted apart anyway."

"Ya know, after he died, you left, the world just kept spinning. Same shit, same stupid people. We just kept on moving, like nothing happened. New faces on the engine was the only thing that changed. I never really tried to make friends with the new guys. I never pulled another overnight shift. It just didn't feel right without our crew there. Not really because I was scared that someone would die again. It was more because I didn't really need them to be my friend," Rob said.

"Honestly, after the fire department I never really connected and had friends like you guys," Steve confessed. "Same as you I just never really bothered getting close to anyone. Just stayed to myself and did my thing."

"I felt like I was just walking through the world and not really being a part of it. When I looked at people, talked to people, I just kept thinking that they have no idea what makes me, me. What I went through. What I've seen. What I've done," Ted said.

"The guys that I work with in the fire department are pretty much the same. Young guys want to hang out, go to bars, hear war stories. The old guys just come to work and go home. Never thinking about work after quitting time. I just never bring work home," Rob said.

"When I was in the department, my wife and kids never understood what I did or why. When I tried to tell them about it, I spent more time feeling crappy because I felt like she thought I was some kind of freak," Ted said. "I would tell her about an accident and all she wanted to know about was if the person lived, was all right, if the family had been told, that kind of stuff. She would lose interest before I could even tell her what I wanted to tell her. So, I just stopped telling her."

"That wasn't my issue. My wife wanted to talk about and know everything. It's that I didn't want to say the dark stuff out loud," Steve said.

"The dungeon," Ted mumbled. "The shit in our dark place there for a god damn good reason. To hide from it so we don't have to deal with it."

"No. I think we have dealt with it," Steve said. "It's just how we deal with it. Everyone says it's bad to lock the stuff away, but if you think about it some of the stuff needs to stay there forever." Steve took a deep breath before he continued. "The way I wanted to beat the asshole to death that killed his girlfriend, wife or kid in a drunk driving accident. The parents who killed their kid because they were stupid."

Rob snickered. "That's the easy stuff. What about wanting to throat punch the shit head who says, 'I know just how you feel'."

"Being scared you're going to lose control and beat the crap out of your wife or kid because you're mad at something that they had nothing to do with," Ted added.

"Getting situations confused. Like when a car backfires and you think it's an explosion. When someone gets in your face and you remember when the asshole on the 10-50 took a swing at you," Steve said.

"We lock the stuff up, so we don't think about it," Rob said. "It's 'cause that stuff's from a different life, different time. Do we lock it up so we don't confuse it with this world?"

"I think that's a big part of it. We saw it, we faced it. We don't need it in our lives now. So we can bury it. Then there are the things we don't want to deal with. Saying out loud we cared more about getting a high than anything else," Steve said. "I used to wonder if I did or didn't do something that pushed the rush."

"Like what?"

"Well, cutting up a car when I didn't really need to. Taking some extra time before putting out a fire. Doing stuff to make a simple call more exciting. Getting a bigger rush."

"You know I kind of understand how people can go bad fast," Ted said.

"Don't follow you?"

"We get a rush out of running into burning buildings, rescuing people, stuff like that. I can see why serial killers keep on going. They chase the rush in their own way. Fucked up and wrong, but I kinda get it." Ted said.

"I figured that out too," Steve confessed. "I was worried that after the Royce fire I would just go deeper and deeper trying to get a better rush. Shit, just trying to match it would take a lifetime. I thought about doing adventure stuff to get a rush. Downhill skiing, Skydiving, base jumping, rollercoasters.

Tried a few before I got married, but nothing gave me the same rush. Nothing ever came close."

"Wonder why?" Ted asked.

"I can only guess that it's something like being attracted to women, men, whatever. It's who we're attracted to. I like one kind of woman; Rob likes a different kind. You like another kind. Some people find Asians hot, others European, still others, Africans. Some think the same sex is attractive. Nothing's right or wrong, just a preference. We prefer getting our rocks off on fire calls. Something else is OK, but it's not the same."

"At least we did," Ted said. "Now I want nothing to do with firefighting."

"You're pissed at firefighting?" Rob asked.

"Yeah. It destroyed everything," Ted sighed. "Wife, family, career. I always wanted to be a firefighter. Now I'm lost 'cause I don't know what I want to do."

"No, it didn't," Steve said. "Just like it didn't ruin my life or change me. What it did was give me experiences, challenges that made me use my brain. Made me deal with stuff, make decisions. We think the fire department, our jobs define us, but it doesn't. Our actions don't even define us. It is how we decide on what action to take that defines us."

"Thought about this a lot?" Rob asked.

"Only for the past thirty years or so," Steve smiled. "Look, I was angry too. But the reason wasn't because of 'firefighting.' It was because first and foremost we couldn't get the fix. Like a junkie who sells everything to buy drugs. When I finally accepted that the motivation was for the rush, I was able to get past it and think about other stuff."

"Shitty part is that you can't even buy a fix," Ted said.

"I gave up on the fix years ago," Rob added. "When I came off the engine I knew I'd give up the rush. Just didn't connect it with an adrenaline rush. I hadn't had a good call in years anyway, so it wasn't a big loss. It wasn't anger. I think it was surrender. I just accepted that I wasn't ever going to see a rush again. At least not like on an engine."

"You know, after the department I longed for the rush for years. I chased it for a few. Eventually I stopped craving a rush. I stopped looking for one. I think you just get over the addiction. Like stopping smoking," Steve paused. "Even today just a little rush is really good. I get all excited when there's a problem at work, when I gotta rescue my kid from some imaginary crisis. It scares me that I'll want more and more, and I know how to get it."

"It's not worth chasing anymore," Ted said.

"So, where does that leave us?" Rob asked.

"The Cult of the Foundered Souls," Steve joked. "We're standing here for the first time in thirty years, in front of our brother's grave. All we can talk about is the rush WE got when Royce died."

"That's fucked up," Rob said.

"We're damaged goods. Not wired right," Ted lamented.

"No. Foundered? YES. Damaged! NO. Fucked up? Absolutely not," Steve said. "The shrinks tell us what we think is wrong. They tell us what we feel is wrong. They tell us how we react is different, not normal. Well, I think how I feel is normal for me. Yes, I'm glad that I didn't die in the fire. And fuck anyone who thinks that's messed up. At least I have the balls to say it! I'm not going to cower in the corner sniveling with self-pity. And you know what! No one needs to tell me how I feel is OK because I know it's OK for me. I don't care if you don't feel the same way 'cause you ain't me. Haven't had the same experience, don't react the same way."

"You're right," Rob said. "Royce dying didn't change a thing. What I'm pissed off about that night..." Rob took a deep breath. "...is that I didn't get to go in the house."

"Roger that," Ted agreed. "That fire was incredible. Never saw anything like it again."

"Bla, bla and all the politically correct crap, I'm sorry Royce died. Sorry we lost a crew member. Wish he didn't. Maybe things would be different if he hadn't. But he did. And I'm glad I didn't die. Got to have a wife, kids. Looking forward to watching them grow and have families of their own," Steve said. "That sounds selfish and it is, but I don't care. It's what I feel. And ya know what? I'm OK with that."

Ted and Rob nodded their heads.

"Let's blow this taco stand," Ted said. "No reason to stand here looking at a rock."

"Yeah, let's get back to the hotel, hang out for the rest of the day and swap old stories, tell a few new ones," Rob said.

They spent the rest of the day hanging out at the hotel. A few people from their past wondered by and spent some time swapping stories with them.

As they closed the bar for the second night in a row, they promised to stay in touch but knew it would be erratic. The three men did agree that there were four rules that they live by.

- I do not feel guilty for what I have done
- I don't ask for permission to feel how I feel
- I don't ask forgiveness for those feelings
- I don't ask you to feel the same way

ABOUT THE AUTHOR

Scott Offermann is an author and public speaker. He moved to Maryland in his sophomore year of high school where he was a volunteer firefighter, emergency medical technician and sailing instructor. He found a profession in Facilities Management, is a subject matter expert on Critical Environments and Facilities Management including international business in 45 countries over several decades. He is currently living in Arizona with his wife, two kids and a very spoiled family dog.

NOTE FROM THE AUTHOR

Word-of-mouth is crucial for any author to succeed. If you enjoyed *Engine 8-12*, please leave a review online—anywhere you are able. Even if it's just a sentence or two. It would make all the difference and would be very much appreciated.

Thanks!
Scott

Thank you so much for reading one of our **Action/Adventure** novels.
If you enjoyed the experience, please check out our recommended
title for your next great read!

Three Degrees and Gone by J. Stewart Willis

"An exceptional story of the future that quietly sounds an
alarm about extremities of human behavior."
–KIRKUS REVIEWS

View other Black Rose Writing titles at
www.blackrosewriting.com/books and use promo code
PRINT to receive a **20% discount** when purchasing.

www.ingramcontent.com/pod-product-compliance
Lightning Source LLC
Chambersburg PA
CBHW011128100726
47898CB00009B/2895